I gave a little exclamation of surprise and the man who was standing there lifted his mask briefly and then let it drop. He had shown me enough. He was the man I had seen in the shop in St. Mark's and who had watched my window from the canal.

"At last we meet," he said.

"Who are you?" I asked.

He put his hands to his lips. "At the moment let me remain your mysterious admirer," he said.

He held my arm in a grip which was firm and which belied his ingratiating manner. I attempted to wrest myself free but his grip tightened and I knew I was in danger.

"You will take your hands from me," I commanded.

He brought his face close to mine. He smelt of delicate perfume—musk or sandalwood. There were several rings on his fingers and jewels in his cravat. "Is that an order?" he asked.

"It is," I replied.

"How charming!" he murmured. "But it is time for me to give the orders."

THE
LOVE CHILD

Philippa Carr

FAWCETT CREST • NEW YORK

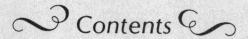

Contents

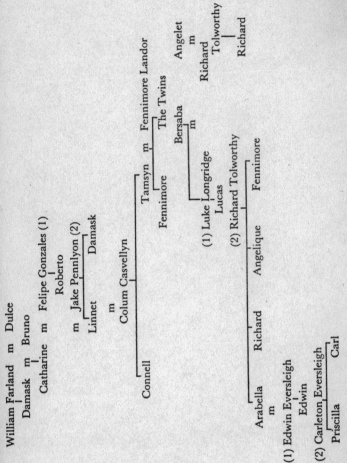

✒ The Plot ✑

I was first aware of mystery when my father, who had hitherto for the most part seemed unaware of my existence, suddenly decreed that Mistress Philpots, who had until this time been my governess, no longer possessed the required qualifications for the task, and must be replaced. I was astounded. I had never thought that my education would be of any great concern to him. Had it been my brother Carl, who was some four years younger than I, that would have been another matter. Carl was the centre of the household; he shared my father's name—Carl being short for Carleton since it would have been misleading to have identical names in one household—and he was being brought up to be exactly like my father which, summed up in my father's phraseology, was "making a man of him." Carl must be complete master of his horse; he must lead the hunt; he must excel at archery and gunnery as well as drive a good ball in pall-mall. If his Latin and Greek were a little weak and the Reverend

9

George Helling, whose task it was to instruct him, despaired of ever making a scholar of him, that was not of great importance. Carl must first and foremost be made into a man, which meant being as like our father as one human being could be to another. Thus when he made this announcement, my first reaction was not "What will Mistress Philpots say?" or "What will the new governess be like?" but amazement that his attention should have come to rest on me.

It was typical of my mother that she should demand: "And what is to become of Emily Philpots?"

"My dear Arabella," said my father, "your concern should be with your daughter's education, not with the welfare of a stupid old woman."

"Emily Philpots is by no means stupid, and I will not have my servants turned out because of a whim of yours."

They were like that together always. Sometimes it seemed that they hated each other, but that was not the case. When he was away she was anxiously waiting for his return, and when he came back the first one he would look for—even before Carl—was she; and if she were not there, he would be restive and uneasy until she was.

"I have not said she should be turned out," he insisted.

"Put to grass... like an old horse?" said my mother.

"I was always devoted to my horses and my affection does not end with their usefulness," retorted my father. "Let old Philpots retire and nod over the fire with Sally Nullens. She's happy enough, isn't she—as happy as she can be without an infant to drool over?"

"Sally makes herself useful and the children love her."

"I've no doubt Philpots can share the usefulness if not the love. In any case I have decided that Priscilla's education can be neglected no longer. She needs someone who can teach her more advanced subjects and be a companion to her, a woman of good education, poise and scholarship."

"And where shall this paragon be found?"

"She is found. Christabel Connalt will be arriving at the

end of the week. That will give you plenty of time to break the news to Emily Philpots."

He spoke with finality, and my mother, who was very wise and shrewd in a rather innocent way, realized that it was no use protesting. I could see that she had already decided that Emily Philpots *had* taught me all she had to teach and I must move into a higher sphere. Moreover my father had presented her with a *fait accompli* and she accepted it.

She questioned him about this Christabel Connalt. If she did not approve of her she would not accept her, she insisted. She hoped he had made that clear.

"She will naturally know she has to please the lady of the house," retorted my father. "She is a pleasant young woman. I heard of her through Letty Westering. She is well educated and comes from a vicarage. Now she needs to earn a livelihood. I thought this would be an opportunity to do her and ourselves a good turn at the same time."

There was a certain amount of argument and finally my mother agreed that Christabel Connalt should come, and set about the unwelcome task of tactfully telling Mistress Philpots that there was to be a new governess.

Emily Philpots reacted in the way my mother and I expected. She was, as Sally Nullens said, "Struck all of a heap." So she was not good enough anymore to teach Miss! Miss must have a scholar, must she? They would see what would come of that. She communed with Sally Nullens, who herself had a grievance because Master Carl had been taken out of her hands since, as my father put it, it was not good for a boy to be mollycoddled by a pack of women. Moreover my parents had added to her indignation by not producing more children—neither of them being of an age when it would be impossible to populate a nursery.

Emily declared that she would pack her bags and be gone, and then we would see, she added darkly. But when the first shock had worn off and she began to consider the difficulties of finding a new post at her age, and when my

11

mother pointed out that she would indeed be lost without her for there was no one, she was sure, who could do such fine feather stitching as Emily could, nor put a patch that was almost invisible on a garment, she allowed herself to be coaxed to stay; and with a certain amount of self-righteous sniffing and dark prophecies in Sally Nullens's room over the glowing fire with the kettle singing on the hob, she prepared herself for the new life and the coming of Christabel.

"Be kind to poor old Emily," said my mother. "It's a blow for her."

I was closer to my mother than I was to my father. I think she was very much aware of his indifference towards me and tried to make up for it. I loved her dearly, but it occurred to me that I had a stronger feeling for my father, which was very perverse of me in the circumstances. I admired him so much. He was the strong, dominating man; almost everyone was in awe of him—even Leigh Main who was something of the same sort himself and had always insisted, ever since I had known him, which was the whole of my life, that he was not afraid of anything on earth or in heaven or hell. That was a favourite saying of his. But even he was wary of my father.

He ruled our household—even my mother, and she was no weak woman. She stood up to him in a way which I knew secretly amused him. They seemed to enjoy sparring together. It did not make a peaceful household exactly, but that they found contentment in each other was obvious.

We were a complicated household, because of Edwin and Leigh. They were twenty-one years old on my fourteenth birthday, and they had been born within a few weeks of each other. Edwin was Lord Eversleigh and the son of my mother's first marriage. His father—*my* father's cousin—had been killed before he was born—murdered on the grounds of our home, which made him seem mysterious and romantic. Yet there was neither of these qualities about Edwin. He was merely my half brother—not quite as tall or as forceful as Leigh, overshadowed by

Leigh actually, but perhaps that was just in my eyes.

Leigh was no relation to us really, although he had been brought up in our house since he was a baby. He was the son of my mother's friend of many years standing, Lady Stevens, who had been Harriet Main, the actress. There was something rather shameful about Leigh's birth. My mother didn't speak of it and it was Harriet herself who told me.

"Leigh is my bastard," she told me once. "I had him when I really shouldn't, but I'm glad I did. I had to leave him to your mother to care for and of course she did that far better than I ever could."

I was not sure that she was right. Her son, Benjie, seemed to have a good time and I often thought what an exciting mother Harriet would be. I was very much attracted by her and she often invited me to her house as she was aware of my admiration, which was something she loved no matter whence it came. I could talk to her more easily than I could to any other grown-up person.

Edwin and Leigh were in the army. It was a family tradition. Edwin's two grandfathers had both been famous soldiers who had served the Royalist cause. His parents had met during the days of the King's exile. My mother often told me stories of the days before the Restoration and her life in the shabby old château of Congrève where she had lived while they were waiting for the King to come into his own.

She said that on my sixteenth birthday I should be given the family journals to read. Then I would understand a great deal. In the meantime it was not too soon for me to start my own journal. I was appalled at first. Then I started and the habit grew.

Well, that was our household—Edwin, Leigh, myself, seven years younger than they were, and Carl who was four years younger than I.

There were numerous servants. Among them our old nurse Sally Nullens, and Jasper, the head gardener, with his wife Ellen, who was the housekeeper. Jasper was an old Puritan who regretted the disbanding of the Common-

13

wealth and whose hero was Oliver Cromwell. His wife, Ellen, I had always thought, would have been quite jolly if she had dared to be. Then there was Chastity, their daughter, who had married one of the gardeners and still worked for us when she was not having children, which she did with annual regularity.

Up to that time life had been easy for people like us in Restoration England. I was too young to feel the immense gratification that had been the mood of the country with the return of the Monarchy. Mistress Philpots told me during one of my lessons that there had been such restriction of freedom that people had gone mad with joy when they were rid of their bonds. The country had thrown off an excess of religion and had become quite irreligious, with the result that there was too much levity everywhere. It was all very well to open the theatres, but Mistress Philpots believed that some of the plays which were performed were downright bawdy. Ladies behaved in the most shameful way and the fashion was set by the Court.

She was a Royalist and did not wish to criticize the King's way of life, but he did create scandal with his numerous mistresses, and that was not good for the country.

My father was often at Court. He was a friend of the King. They were both interested in architecture, and after the great fire there was a good deal to be done to rebuild the city. It used to be exciting when my father returned from Court with stories of what went on there. The King's illegitimate son, the Duke of Monmouth, was a great friend of my father's, who once said that it was a pity Old Rowley (the King's nickname, said to have been taken from an amorous goat) did not legitimatize him so that there would be an heir to the throne other than his humourless, morose brother who was a Catholic.

My father was, rather strangely for a man of his kind, a strong adherent of the Protestant Faith. He used to say that the Church of England had put religion in the place where it belonged. "Get the Catholics in and we'll be having the

Inquisition here and people walking in fear, just as they did in the days of Cromwell. The two extremes of the case. We want to steer a middle course."

He would grow very serious when he talked of the possibility of Charles's dying and his brother James taking his place. Whenever I heard him on the subject I was amazed at his fierceness.

My mother used to accompany him when he went to Court. When Carl was a baby she hated to leave the house but now she freely went. Sally Nullens said that my father was a man who needed a wife to watch over him, and I gathered that before his marriage there had been many women in his life.

That was our household at the time Christabel Connalt entered it.

It was a misty day at the end of October when she arrived. She was traveling by the new stage which would bring her to Dover, and from there my father was to meet her in the carriage. I thought that he was putting himself out a great deal for my education. A room had been made ready for her and the servants were all agog with curiosity to see her. I supposed their lives were fairly humdrum and her coming was quite an event, particularly as Emily Philpots had made such an issue of it and had uttered such prognostications of evil concerning the new governess that I believed half the servants thought she would turn out to be a witch.

Carl was practising his flageolet in his room and the mournful strains of "Barbary Allen" could be heard throughout the house. I went into the gardens because I felt the need to escape from the dirge as well as the overpowering atmosphere of the house. I strolled out as far as that spot where there had once been an arbour and where I had heard that my mother's first husband had been murdered. Flowers grew there now, but they were always red. My mother wanted other colours, but no matter what was planted there they always turned out red. I was sure old Jasper arranged it because he believed that

15

people should be punished and not allowed to forget the past just because it would be comfortable to do so. His wife said of him that he was so good that he saw evil in everything. I was not so sure of the goodness and was suspicious of such a display of virtue; but I reckoned that was true about seeing evil in everything. However, although I was sure my mother deceived herself into thinking that what had happened at that spot was forgotten, memory lingered on and the servants said it was haunted and Jasper's blood-red flowers continued to bloom.

As I was standing there I heard the carriage drive up. I waited, listening. I heard my father's voice as he shouted to the grooms. Then there was silence. They must have gone into the house.

I was pensive, suddenly overcome by the contemplation of change. It would be inevitable. Christabel Connalt would be very erudite, strict, no doubt, and determined to make a scholar of me. Emily Philpots had never achieved that. Looking back, I realized that she was rather ineffectual and with the cunning of children, Carl and I had known it, for before Carl went off to the rectory for tuition, she had taught him too. We had plagued poor Emily sorely. Carl had once put a spider on her skirt and then shrieked at her. He had then removed it with a show of gallantry for which I reprimanded him afterwards, telling him that the incident showed he had a deceitful nature. Carl had folded his palms together and looked heavenwards, and in a fair imitation of Jasper had declared he had done what he did for old Philpots' sake.

I had built up a picture of Christabel Connalt in my mind. Brought up in a vicarage, she would be religious of course, and more censorious of the customs and manners which prevailed in the country even, than Emily Philpots. She would be middle-aged, verging on elderly, with greying hair and steely eyes which missed nothing.

I shivered and was sure I should look back nostalgically on the weak rule of Emily Philpots.

She and Sally Nullens had talked continuously of the

newcomer. When I went into Sally's sitting room, which Carl called "Nullens's Parlour," I was aware of an atmosphere of growing tension and mystery. The two women would sit over the fire, heads close together, whispering. I knew that Sally Nullens was a firm believer in witchcraft, and whenever anyone died or developed a mysterious illness always looked round for the ill-wisher. Carl used to say that she regretted that the days of the witch finders were over.

"Can't you imagine old Sal going round examining the pretty maidens . . . just everywhere, for the marks of their lovers? They're succubi or is it incubi for girls?"

Carl might have been the despair of the Reverend George Helling where Greek and Latin were concerned but he was very knowledgeable about the facts of life. Even though he was not yet ten years old, he had an eye for the young serving girls and he liked to speculate on who was doing what with whom.

Sally Nullens said: "He's another like his father. Up to tricks before they're out of swaddling."

An exaggeration, of course, but it was true that Carl was progressing fast along the road to manhood—a fact which pleased my father and bore out Sally's words that Carl was another such as he had been.

My thoughts were running on, propelled by the contemplation of the change Christabel Connalt would bring.

"The master seemed glad to bring her in," I had heard Emily Philpots say to Sally when they were sitting together in Sally's room—Sally mending and Emily doing some fine feather stitching on one of my mother's petticoats.

As the remark was followed by a sniffing which I knew from the past meant an indication that there was something profound behind it, I had been guilty of listening. This was because it concerned my father, and about him I had this obsession to which I have already referred.

"And *who* is she, I should like to know?" went on Emily.

"Oh, he gave all that up. Mistress wouldn't stand for it."

"There's some as never gives up. And it wouldn't surprise me . . ."

"Walls," said Sally portentously, "they have ears. Doors too. Is anyone there?"

I went in and said I had brought my riding skirt which I had torn the day before and would Sally mend it please?

She cast a significant look at Emily and took the skirt.

"Nice and muddy too," she commented. "I'll give it a sponge. It's one body's work looking after you, Mistress Priscilla."

It was sad in a way. It made me want to comfort her. She was always stressing how useful she was and demanding to know how we should get along without her. Now Emily Philpots would be the same. I knew they were both preparing to dislike the newcomer.

I gazed at the roses, valiantly clinging to life although their season was over; and they reminded me of those two aging women.

I looked towards the house and saw it afresh. Eversleigh Court, the family home. It really belonged to Edwin, although my father managed the estate and everything would collapse without him. He was a proud man. I wondered whether he resented Edwin. Edwin had everything—the title and the estate, and it would have been so much more suitable if my father had had it because he was the one who had saved it during the Civil War by posing as a Cromwellian and fooling everyone, just that he might keep the estate in order. Edwin had not been born then. My mother called him the Restoration Baby. His birthday was January of the year 1660, so his arrival into the world was only a few months before the King's return.

It was a gracious old house and, as such houses always do, gained with the years. So many generations of Eversleighs had added to it; tragedies and comedies had been played out here; and Sally Nullens said that those who could find no rest came back to wander about their homes unseen, but their presence was known to the discerning . . . like Sally Nullens.

There were many houses like it in the country. It was the big house of the neighbourhood built in the days of Elizabeth with the traditional **E** type of plan in homage to Gloriana. East wing, west wing, and centre; hall that was as high as the house with vaulted ceiling and broad oak beams. Some of the rooms were elegantly panelled, but the hall was stone walled and hung with armoury to remind coming generations of the part Eversleighs had played in the country's history. Over the great fireplace was the painting of the family tree which had to be added to now and then and would no doubt in time spread across the great hall. I was there—not in the main branch, of course. Edwin was on that, and when he married his children would be there right in the centre. Leigh used to get angry because he wasn't on it. He could not understand in those days why he should be left out. I believe it had an effect on him and made him want to score over Edwin in every other way. I began to brood and came up with the idea that often what happened to us in childhood had its effect on the rest of our lives.

But I was only thinking lightly of these things as I stood by the haunted flowerbed, and I knew that I was putting off the moment when I should go and meet this woman who I knew instinctively was going to change my life.

Chastity came out to me, waddling slightly, for she was pregnant again.

"Mistress Priscilla, where be you then? They want you to meet the new governess. Your mother says to go to the drawing room at once."

"All right, Chastity," I said. "I'll come." I added: "You shouldn't run, you know. You ought to consider your condition."

"Oh, 'tis all so natural, mistress."

I calculated this would be her sixth and she was young yet. I reckoned she had time for at least another ten.

"You're like a queen bee, Chastity," I said reproachfully.

"What's that, mistress?"

I didn't explain. I thought how provoking fate was to

give Chastity one child every year while my parents had only Carl and myself (not counting Edwin who was my mother's alone). If they had had more, Sally Nullens wouldn't be sniffing out witches all the time and Emily Philpots would be considered good enough for the young ones. Moreover, I should have been pleased with some little brothers and sisters.

"Have you seen her, Chastity?" I asked.

"Not as you might say, mistress. She was took to the drawing room. My mother sent me to find you. Said Mistress was asking for you."

I went straight to the drawing room. She was there with my mother and father.

My mother said, "Ah, here is Priscilla. Come and meet Mistress Connalt, Priscilla."

Cristabel Connalt stood up and came towards me. She was tall, slim and very plainly dressed; but she was not without elegance, which I believed came naturally to her. She wore a cloak of a blue woolen material, which was caught at the throat with a buckle which might have been silver. I could see that the bodice beneath was of the same blue material; it was cut low but she wore a linen kerchief about her neck which added a touch of modesty to the bodice, which came to a deep point and was laced down the front with a silver-coloured cord. Her skirt, still of the same material, fell to the floor in folds. Attached to the cloak was a hood which had fallen back from her head, disclosing dark hair unfashionably unfrizzed and hanging in loose curls, which were tied back from her face.

But it was not her clothes which struck me—after all they were more or less what one would expect of a daughter of a parson whose stipend was so inadequate that his daughter must earn a living in this way. Neat not gaudy, I commented inwardly. And then I looked at her face. She was not beautiful, but there was distinction about her. She was by no means as old as I had expected her to be. I guessed she was in her mid-twenties—old to me, of course, but as some would say, in the prime of life. Her face was oval in shape, her skin smooth and with the texture of a flower petal; her eyebrows were dark and well defined; her nose was a trifle large; her eyes were large, too, with short, thick dark lashes; her mouth was mobile, by which I mean it betrayed her feelings, I was to discover, far more than her eyes ever did. They would be quite impassive; the eyelids would not flicker but something happened to the mouth which she could not restrain.

I was too taken aback to speak because she was not in the least what I had expected.

"Your pupil, Mistress Connalt," said my father. He was watching us with a certain twitching of his lips, which I had come to know meant an inner amusement which he was trying not to betray.

"I hope we shall work well together," she said.

"I hope so, too."

Her eyes were fixed on me. They betrayed nothing, but the lips moved a little. They tightened as though she did not exactly like what she saw. I told myself that I was allowing Sally Nullens and Emily Philpots to influence me.

"Mistress Connalt has been telling us something of her teaching programme," said my mother. "It sounds very interesting. I think, Priscilla, you should show her her room. Then you might let her see the schoolroom. Mistress Connalt says that what she wants is to get down to work as soon as possible."

"Would you like to see your room?" I asked.

She said she would, and I led her out of the room.

As we mounted the staircase, she said, "It's a beautiful house. What a mercy it was not destroyed during the war."

"My father worked hard to preserve it," I replied.

"Ah!" It was a quick intake of breath. She was walking behind me and I could feel her eyes on me, which made me feel uncomfortable, and I was glad when we had mounted the staircase and could walk side by side.

"I gather your home is a rectory," I said conversationally.

"Yes, it's in Westering. Do you know Westering?"

"I'm afraid not."

"It is in Sussex."

"I hope you don't find it bleak here. It is, they say in the southeast. We're near the coast, too. We get the full force of the prevailing wind which is east."

"It sounds like a geography lesson," she said, and her voice had laughter in it.

I was pleased and I felt happier after that. I showed her her room, which was next to the schoolroom and not very large. Emily Philpots had occupied it, but she had been moved to a room on the floor above, next to Sally Nullens. My mother had said that the governess should be next to the schoolroom. It was another grievance for poor old Emily.

"I hope it is comfortable," I said.

She turned to me and replied: "It's luxurious compared with the rectory." Her eyes went to the fire in the grate, which my mother had ordered should be lighted. "It was so cold in the rectory, I used to dread the winter."

I thought then: I believe I'm going to like her.

I left her to unpack and wash, telling her that in an hour's time I would come up and show her the schoolroom, where we could look at some of my books and I could explain to her what I had been doing. I would show her the house and gardens if she would care to see them.

She thanked me and she smiled at me rather shyly. "I think I am going to be very glad I came here," she said.

I went down to my parents. As was to be expected they were talking about the new governess.

"A very self-possessed woman," said my mother.

"She has a certain poise without doubt," replied my father.

My mother smiled at me. "Here's Priscilla. Well, my dear, what do you think of her?"

"It's too soon to say," I parried.

"Since when have you become so cautious?" My mother continued to smile at me. "I think she will be very good."

"She is clearly well brought up," added my father. "I think, Bella, she should join us for meals."

22

"Join us for meals! The governess!"

"Oh, come now, you can see she is different from old Philpots."

"Undoubtedly different," agreed my mother. "But to join us at table! What if there are guests?"

"She'll mingle, I don't doubt. She seems articulate enough."

"What when the boys come home?"

"Well . . . what?"

"Do you think . . ."

"I certainly think you cannot condemn a young woman of her breeding to lonely trays in her room. Obviously she can't be with the servants."

"It is always like that with governesses. How I should hate it!"

"What do you think, Priscilla?" said my father, and so astonishing me by asking my opinion for the first time in my life—I certainly never remembered its happening before—that I stammered and could find no ready reply. "Let her join us," he went on, "and we'll see how it works."

The servants would think it very strange that one who was only slightly higher in the social scale than they were should sit with the family at dinner. I knew that there would be a great deal of gossip in the Nullens-Philpots combine.

I couldn't help thinking that it was rather mysterious that my father should concern himself first with the state of my education and then the comfort of my governess.

So there was mystery. I should not have been myself if I did not wonder what it was all about. Christabel Connalt would bring change, I knew. I could feel it in the air.

For the next few days she was the centre of attention in the house. Sally Nullens and Emily Philpots discussed her endlessly and the rest of the servants only slightly less so. Naturally I spent more time with her than anyone and I felt I was gradually getting to know her. She was not easy to know; I changed my opinion of her from hour to hour. There were times when I thought her completely self-sufficient and at others I seemed to sense a certain vulnerability. It was that telltale mouth which would turn down at the corners when it expressed all sorts of emotions. There were times when I fancied she harboured some sort of resentment.

There was no doubt of her erudition and ability to teach. The Reverend William Connalt had determined to send her into the world equipped to earn a living. She had taken lessons with the sons of the local squire, and I fancied that she had made an attempt to keep up with them if not surpass them. There was something I quickly learned about Christabel; she wanted to be not only as good as everyone else but better. I presumed that came from being poor.

At first there was a certain amount of restraint between us, but I determined to break that down and I did succeed quite well—largely because she found me somewhat ignorant. It appeared that my father really had been right and that if I had been left any longer to the mercies of Emily Philpots I should have emerged into the world of adults as a somewhat ignorant young lady.

All that was going to be changed.

We studied Latin, Greek, French and arithmetic, at all of which I scarcely shone. At English literature I was not so bad. Visits to Aunt Harriet (as I called her, though she was not my real aunt) had made me interested in plays and I could quote passages of Shakespeare. Aunt Harriet, though long retired from the stage, was still fond of arranging little entertainments and we all had to become players when we were there. I enjoyed it and it had the effect of arousing my interest.

I noticed that during our English literature sessions Christabel was less pleased than during others. It was then that I realized she was happy only when she could show me how much cleverer she was than I. She did not have to stress that. She had come to teach me, hadn't she? Moreover she was about ten years older than I so she ought to have learned more.

It was very odd. When I made stupid errors, although

she would speak gravely, her mouth told me that she felt rather pleased; and when I shone—as I did with literature—although she would say, "That was excellent, Priscilla," her mouth would form itself into that tight line, so I knew she wasn't pleased.

I had always been greatly interested in people. I remembered the things they said which taught me something about them. My mother used to laugh at me, and Emily Philpots said: "If you could only remember the things that mattered, you'd be more credit to me." The longest rivers, the highest mountains, I simply could not care about them. But I was completely intrigued by the way people thought and what was going on in their minds.

That was why I quickly discovered that there was some resentment in Christabel; and if it had not seemed so absurd, I should have thought it was directed against me.

My father had said that Christabel should take one of the horses from the stables which suited her and ride with me. She was very pleased about this. She was a fair horsewoman and told me that she had been allowed to exercise the Westerings' horses.

We would often stop at an inn when we went riding together, and drink cider and eat cheese with clapbread, which was made entirely of oats, or eat crusty bread straight from the oven.

Sometimes we rode down to the sea and galloped along the shore. I discovered that if I suggested a race and let her beat me, she was overcome with a sort of secret joy.

I believed this was because she had had a very unhappy childhood and that she was vaguely envious of mine, which had been so comfortable and secure that I had never thought about it until now.

Carl had taken a fancy to her. He used to come in sometimes and share a lesson, which was strange, for when he went to the rectory, he had always reminded me of the schoolboy creeping like the snail unwillingly to school. He asked what her favourite tune was and tried to play it—with distressing results to all within earshot.

She did not seem to want to talk about herself at first,

but I set myself to lure her into confidences, and once she started to tell me she seemed as though she wanted to talk. It was rather like opening the floodgates.

Soon she had made me see that loveless household: the rectory which was always cold and damp, with the graveyard close by so that on looking out of her windows she could see tombstones, and when she was a child had been told by the washerwoman that at night the dead came out of their tombs and danced, and if anyone saw them, they themselves would be dead before the year was out.

"I used to lie in bed shivering," she said, "while I was overcome by the temptation to get out of bed and go to the window to see if they were dancing. I remember the cold boards and the wind that used to rattle the windows. I would stand there at the window terrified, freezing, yet unable to go back to bed."

"I should have done the same," I told her.

"You have no idea what my childhood was like. They thought they were so good, and they thought that to be good one had to be miserable. They thought there was some virtue in suffering."

"We have someone here like that. There is old Jasper, the gardener. He's a Puritan, you know. He was here during the war when my father was pretending to be a supporter of Cromwell."

"Tell me," she cried, and I told her all I knew. She sat listening, entranced, with her mouth curved and rather beautiful then—so different from when she had talked of that cold humourless rectory.

Sometimes I thought she hated her father and mother.

I said once: "I believe you are glad you have left home."

Her lips tightened. "It was never like a home . . . as this is. How lucky you are, Priscilla, to have been born here . . . to your mother."

I thought that was a strange thing to say, but she did say strange things sometimes.

I liked very much hearing about the rectory and the things they did there. How the rabbit stew was watered down to make it last longer until it tasted of nothing at all; how they had to thank God for it; how their underclothes were patched and darned until there was little of the original left; how they had to kneel for what seemed like hours in the cold drawing room for morning prayers which went on interminably; how she had to stitch garments for the poor who, she was sure, were better off than she was. Then there were the lessons in the drawing room—so cold in winter, so hot in summer. How she used to study all the time because it was the only way in which she could thank God for being so good to her.

How her mouth betrayed her bitterness! Poor, poor Christabel! I recognized at once that what was wrong with that rectory was not so much the poor quality of food or the scarcity of it, nor the knees sore from too much kneeling in prayer, nor the long hours of study—no, it was none of these things. It was the lovelessness of the home. That was what came over to me. Poor Christabel, she wanted so much to be loved.

I could understand well, because in a way I had felt the same about my father. My mother had lavished care on me and I did not forget that. And then there was Aunt Harriet. I was a special favourite of hers and she made no secret of it. I could not say I was not loved. Even my father was not unkind; he was just indifferent, shrugging me aside because I had failed to be the boy men of his kind always cared so much to have. I had developed an obsession about him. I yearned to win his approval, to attract his attention.

Human beings were very much alike, so I could understand Christabel's feelings.

Her mood changed when she talked of the Westerings. She made me see that Sussex village—after all there were such places all over England and our own community was very similar. There was the church with its draughty, cheerless rectory and graveyard of tottering tombstones imbued with an uncanny atmosphere through the folklore and legends attached to it; the small cottages, the big house dominating the village—the home of Sir Edward Wes-

27

tering and Lady Letty, a lady in her own right, being the daughter of an earl. Lady Letty cropped up rather frequently in Christabel's conversation. She was what Harriet would have called a character. I could picture her sailing into church at the head of the Westering family—Sir Edward walking a pace or two behind, followed by the Westering boys, who before they went away to be educated had taken lessons at the rectory with Christabel. I could imagine Christabel, in a blue serge dress shiny at the elbows, and her patched underwear, watching with those dark-rimmed eyes which betrayed nothing and that mouth which would be quirking with mixed emotions. I guessed she would be wishing with all her heart that she was a Westering and could walk into church with that important family and take her place in that special pew.

Now and then Lady Letty would glance her way. Christabel would drop a curtsy to denote appreciation of the notice of such an exalted being. Lady Letty would say: "Ah, the rector's girl. Christabel, is it?" For she would not be expected to remember the name of such an underling; and informed that it was, would give her a sharp look and a nod or even a smile, and pass on.

It was Lady Letty who had said that the rector's girl should be taught to ride and then she could exercise a horse from the Westering stables. "Good exercise for the horses," she had added. "In case," said Christabel, "I might think it was for my benefit."

The Westerings were the universal benefactors of the village. Blankets and geese for Christmas were distributed from the rectory by Mrs. Connalt with the help of Christabel. Lady Letty intimated that the rectory might also have its blanket and goose, but taken unostentatiously, of course. "We picked out the biggest goose," said Christabel with her wry smile, "and the largest of the blankets."

At Easter and Harvest Festival she would go to the Westering estate to select flowers and produce from the kitchen gardens, which the gardeners would then bring

28

over to the church. Lady Letty would often be there and would talk to her and ask her about her education. It was rather embarrassing, and she wondered why Lady Letty now and then asked her to the house, for when she was there, her ladyship's one thought seemed to be to get rid of her as quickly as possible.

I gathered that Lady Letty was something of an enigma. It appeared strange that she should interest herself in the life of the village because she was more often than not at Court. Sometimes there was entertaining at Westering Manor when the fashionable arrived from London. Once the King himself had come. That had been a very grand occasion.

I certainly enjoyed hearing about her life.

"It seemed as though it would go on and on and never change," she said. "I saw myself growing older and becoming exactly like Mrs. Connalt...dried up, shrivelled like a walking corpse who is really finished with life and somehow continues to make the motions of living. Joyless, seeing sin in pleasure...."

I thought how strange it was that she should refer to her mother as Mrs. Connalt—as though she rejected the close relationship between them.

I was beginning to understand her. She was attractive in appearance in an unusual way and more than normally clever; she had yearnings for a more interesting life and she felt frustrated. She hated being patronized by the Westerings; she was a lonely person because there was no one to love her, no one to whom she could explain her feelings.

I was glad that she could talk to me, yet I was sometimes aware of that strange resentment towards me which I sensed was often present, though she sought to hide it.

Two weeks after her arrival my parents went to our house near Whitehall to be present at several Court functions.

"It must be most exciting," said Christabel. "How I should like to go to Court."

"My mother doesn't really care for it," I answered. "She

only goes because my father likes her to."

"I daresay she feels she must be with him." Her lips tightened a little. "A man like that..."

I was puzzled. I thought she implied some criticism of my father, and I had known for some time that he had an effect on her. She was always uneasy in his presence. I wondered why since he had taken the trouble to bring her to the house, and if she was happier with us than she had been in her rectory home—and it was hard to imagine that she could be less so—then she owed that to him.

Our days slipped into a routine—lessons in the morning, riding or walking after the midday meal and then a return to study about five o'clock. It was dark then and we would sit in the candlelight and she would usually spend the time questioning me on the morning's study.

I asked her once if she were comfortable in our house and she demanded angrily: "Why should you think I am not? This is the most comfortable house."

"I am glad," I said.

"*You* were one of the lucky ones." She spoke resentfully, and although I could not see the tightening of her lips I knew it was so.

One afternoon we went riding, and on our return, as soon as we came through the gates and into the stables, I knew something had happened. I was aware of a bustle of activity before I saw the horses. I thought at first my parents were home. Then I realized that it was not they who had returned. I half guessed and excitement possessed me. I could scarcely wait to get out of the saddle and hurry into the house.

I heard their voices and called: "Leigh! Edwin! Where are you?"

Leigh was at the top of the stairs. He looked magnificent in uniform. He was so tall, with rather gaunt features and wonderful blue eyes which contrasted with his black hair, just like his mother's. These eyes lighted up when they saw me, and I felt a glow of excitement which coming upon Leigh unexpectedly always gave me.

He dashed down the stairs and picked me up in his arms, swinging me round and round. I called: "Stop it. Stop it." He did stop, and taking my face in his hands gave me a smacking kiss on the forehead.

"You've grown," he said. "Yes, you have, fair coz."

He always called me "fair coz." He had heard the term somewhere, and when I protested that we were not cousins and not even related, he retorted: "Well, we ought to be. I've seen you grow up from an ugly little brat to the lively little sprite you are today. You were like a little monkey when you were born. I really thought you were one and then you grew into a gazelle, my own fair coz."

Leigh talked like that, rather extravagantly. Everything was either wonderful or terrible. My father used to get impatient with him, but I rather liked it. The fact was that I liked everything about Leigh. He was the perfect big brother and I used to wish he were my real one. Not that I did not love Edwin. I did. Edwin was meek and never hurt anyone if he could help it. He was courteous to the servants. They were devoted to him naturally, but the women preferred Leigh, I knew.

Leigh was now aware of Christabel, her face slightly flushed from the exercise and her dark curls only very slightly ruffled under her hard riding hat.

I introduced them and he bowed gallantly. I was very much aware that Christabel was assessing him. I did not want to mention then that she was the governess, I would tell him that privately. I felt she resented having to work for us and would like to be mistaken for a guest . . . if only for a short while.

"We have been riding," I said. "When did you get here? Is Edwin with you? I thought I heard his voice."

"We came together. Edwin!" he shouted. "Where are you? Priscilla is asking for you."

Edwin appeared on the stairs looking very handsome— more so than Leigh really, though less tall, less robust. My mother had always feared for his health.

"Priscilla!" He came towards me. "How good it is to see

31

you. Where is our mother?" He had turned to Christabel.

"Mistress Connalt," I told him. And then to Christabel: "My brother. Lord Eversleigh."

Edwin bowed. His manners were always perfect.

I said: "They are at Court."

Edwin lifted his shoulders to register disappointment. "Perhaps they'll be back before you go. Can you stay awhile?"

"A week . . . perhaps longer."

"Three . . . four . . ." suggested Leigh.

"I'm so glad. I'll have your rooms made ready."

"Don't worry," put in Leigh, "Sally Nullens has already seen us and is running round in a flutter. She is so pleased to have her little darlings home."

"You know what nurses are, Mistress Connalt," said Edwin, "when their charges return to the fold."

He had realized that Christabel was uneasy and aloof and was trying to put her at ease. I knew that she was glad her status had not been revealed, although it would have to emerge eventually.

"I never had one so I can't say," she said.

"So you escaped that bondage," put in Leigh lightly.

"We were too poor," Christabel went on almost defiantly.

I felt uncomfortable and that I had to explain. "Christabel has come here to teach me. She lived in a rectory in Sussex."

"How is Carl getting on at the rectory?" asked Edwin. "And where is he, by the way?"

"Out in the summerhouse, most likely, playing his flageolet."

"Poor lad! He'll be frozen to death."

"At least we are spared the fearsome noises he can make," said Leigh.

"What were you proposing to do?" asked Edwin.

"We were going to wash and change and then it will be suppertime."

"We'll get out of our uniforms," said Leigh. He grinned from me to Christabel. "I know they make us look devastatingly handsome and you'll suffer a shock at the transformation, Mistress Connalt. Priscilla is used to us, so I don't have to prepare her."

I was glad he was trying to draw Christabel into the family circle. She reminded me of a child dipping her feet into water—wanting to plunge in and not daring to.

I studied them in their felt hats with the glorious plumes falling over the sides, their elaborate coats, their knee breeches, their shining boots, their swords at their sides.

"Quite handsome," I said, "though not devastatingly so, and we know it is only the uniform that makes them so, don't we, Christabel?"

She smiled and looked beautiful then. I could see that between them they had managed to charm away her resentment.

"Come on," I said, "we must wash and change ... all of us. The food will get cold and you know how they hate that."

"Orders!" said Leigh. "Odds fish, you're worse than our commanding officer. A sign we're home, eh, Edwin?"

Edwin said gently: "It's good to be here."

Christabel looked very pretty that evening. It might have been the candlelight which gave her that added lustre, or it might have been something else. My mother always said that candlelight was more flattering to a woman than any lotions or unguents. She wore a beautiful gown, too. The long pointed bodice was cut rather low, and worn without kerchief or collar showed her attractively sloping shoulders. One curl had been allowed to escape from those tied in the nape of her neck and hung over a shoulder. Her gown was of lavender silk and under it was a grey satin petticoat. I wondered at the time how she had come by such a dress in that cheese-paring rectory and I learned that it had come from Westering Manor. As she said, it was one of the "cast-offs for the needy," and when I saw it in daylight I would see that it had become too shabby for her ladyship's use.

I wore my blue silk, and although I had previously

thought it rather charming it seemed insignificant beside Christabel's.

Both Edwin and Leigh changed from their elaborate uniforms, but I thought they looked very fine—both of them—in their knee-length breeches and short jackets which were fashionably beribboned, Edwin's slightly more so than Leigh's, for Edwin followed the mode more slavishly than Leigh who I suspected was more than a little impatient with the laces and ribbons which had come into vogue as a kind of turnabout after the puritanical style of dress.

Carl was full of excitement because of the arrivals and we were a very merry party at the table. The servants were delighted as always to have the men home, and I knew how disappointed my mother would be to miss them.

They talked of their adventures. They had been serving in France, from which country they had recently come, but what I remembered from that night and what was really a prelude to the events which were about to begin was the talk of Titus Oates and the Popish Plot. It was like the overture before the curtain rises on the play. Being so much with Harriet had made me think that all the world was truly a stage and the men and women merely players.

"There's a feeling in England," said Leigh, "that wasn't there when we left."

"Change can come quickly," added Edwin, "and when you've been away and come back you are more aware of it than those who have had it gradually creep up on them."

"Change?" I cried. "What change?"

"The King is an old man," said Edwin. "He is past fifty."

"Fifty!" cried Carl. "It's ancient."

Everybody laughed.

"Only to infants, dear boy," said Leigh. "No, Old Rowley will live awhile yet. He *must*. A pity he hasn't a son."

"I was under the impression that he had several," said Christabel.

34

"Alas, born on the wrong side of the blanket."

"I'm sorry for the Queen," said Edwin. "Poor, gentle lady."

"To accuse her of being involved in a plot to kill the King is the utmost idiocy," added Leigh.

Carl leaned forward, forgetting his lamb pie—a favourite of his—in his excitement. Carl was old for his ten years. My father had always wanted him to grow up quickly and he had. He understood about the King and his mistresses and the right and wrong sides of blankets—a fact which Sally Nullens deplored. She would have liked to keep him in her nursery until he married.

"Was she?" he demanded. "Did she want to kill the King? Has she got a lover?"

"What a blasé old fellow this is!" cried Leigh. "My dear Carl, the Queen is the most virtuous lady in England—present company excepted." He bowed to us each in turn. "This Titus Oates will hang himself if he doesn't take care."

"In the meantime," said Christabel, "he has succeeded in hanging several others."

"If only it could be proved that the King had married Lucy Walter that would make Jimmy Monmouth the next to wear the crown."

"Is he suitable?" asked Christabel.

"I believe he is rather wild," I added.

"He is fond of feminine society, yes. Who isn't?" Leigh included us both in his smile. "None could be more devoted to your sex than the King himself. But Charles is wily, clever, shrewd and witty. He once said when he returned to England after that long exile that he was determined never to go wandering again, and I believe he meant that more than he ever meant anything in his life."

"The people love him," said Edwin. "He has that unmistakable Stuart charm. A good deal is forgiven to anyone who possesses that."

Leigh took my hand and kissed it. "Look what you forgive me, fair coz, for my unconquerable charm."

We were all laughing and it was difficult to treat any

subject seriously, and how could any of us have guessed that moment that the politics of the country could be of any importance in our lives?

Christabel sparkled that night. She looked quite beautiful in Lady Letty's cast-off gown; she was delighted to sit at our table and I was interested to see how between them Leigh and Edwin swept away that inner uncertainty or whatever it was that set the resentment smouldering. She was eager to show that she had a greater grasp of the country's history than I had and she turned the conversation back to current affairs.

"Perhaps the King will divorce his wife, marry again and get a son," she suggested.

"He never would," replied Leigh.

"Too lazy?" asked Christabel.

"Too kind," parried Edwin. "Have you ever been presented, Mistress Connalt?"

The bitter smile appeared momentarily. "In my position, Lord Eversleigh!"

"If you had," went on Edwin, "you would see at once what a tolerant man he is. Here we are talking of him thus. That would be dangerous in some reigns. If he could listen to us he would join in the discussion of his character and put us right even to his own disadvantage. Our assessment would be a source of amusement not irritation. He is too clever to see himself other than what he is. Is that not so, Leigh?"

Leigh said: "I am in wholehearted agreement on that. One day it will be realized how clever he is. It is a devious game he plays. We saw a little of that in France. The French King thinks he leads Charles by the nose. I would say that it might be the other way round. No, while Charles is our King, we shall get along. It is the succession which concerns the nation. That is why we deplore that with so many sons who according to convention should not have been born—and who are a perpetual drain on the exchequer—he cannot produce one who would be worth a little expense and give the answer to the burning question, Who next?"

"Let's hope that he lives on and on," I said. "Let's drink to the King."

"A health unto His Majesty!" cried Leigh, and we all lifted our glasses.

Carl was getting a little sleepy at this stage and trying desperately to stay awake. My mother had protested about his being allowed to drink as much wine as he liked, but my father said he must learn to take his liquor. Carl was learning.

Christabel drank sparingly, as I did, and the soft colour in her cheeks and the shine in her eyes was not due to the grape. She was different from the girl she had been so far. I realized that she was enjoying this with a sort of feverish excitement and I was sorry, for such occasions as this were not unusual in our household. We always had celebrations when my parents returned from Court or I or Carl had been away on a visit. How dreary her life must have been in that gloomy rectory!

She was far more knowledgeable about affairs than I was and she seemed anxious that both men should have no doubt of this.

"It's really a religious conflict," she said. "Political conflict almost always is. It is not so much a question of Monmouth's legitimacy as shall we allow a Catholic to ascend the throne."

"That's exactly the case," said Edwin, smiling at her. "James is a Catholic—no doubt of that."

"I have heard it whispered," said Leigh, bending forward and speaking in a whisper, "that His Majesty toys with that Faith . . . but let it not go beyond these walls."

I glanced at Carl who was nodding over his platter. Leigh was inclined to be reckless.

Edwin said quickly: "It is only a conjecture. The King would never wish to displease his subjects."

"What is he going to do?" I asked. "Legitimatize Monmouth or let his Catholic brother come to the throne?"

"I hope . . . most fervently . . . that it will be Monmouth," said Leigh, "for there will be a revolution if we ever have a Catholic King on the throne. The people will not have it.

They remember the fires of Smithfield."

"There has been religious persecution on both sides," said Christabel.

"But the people will never forget Smithfield, the influence of Spain and the threat of the Inquisition. They'll remember Bloody Mary as long as there is a king or a queen to reign over us. That is why it is imperative for Old Rowley to go on living for another twenty years." Leigh lifted his glass. "Once more, a health unto His Majesty."

After that we talked of the man Titus Oates who had caused a stir throughout the country by discovering, as he said, the Popish Plot.

Edwin told us that he had taken Holy Orders and had had a small living which had been presented to him by the Duke of Norfolk until he was involved in some legal trouble and had had to retire, after which he became a chaplain in the navy.

"He is a man who lives by his wits, I'm sure," Leigh went on, "and this discovery of the Popish Plot is meant to work to his advantage in some way."

"The country was ready to listen," said Christabel, "because the people have always been afraid that Protestantism might be in danger and, of course, with the Duke of York heir to the throne, and its being known where his sympathies lie, it is easy to arouse people's anger."

"Exactly," said Edwin, smiling at her with admiration I thought both for her intelligence and good looks. "The plot is supposed to be that there is a scheme among Catholics to massacre the Protestants as they did in France on St. Bartholomew's Eve, to murder the King and set his brother James on the throne. Oates has succeeded in arousing the wrath of the people. It's a dangerous situation."

"And not a grain of truth in it, I'll swear," added Leigh.

"Yes, it's nonsense," agreed Edwin.

"Dangerous nonsense," said Leigh. "But look what it has brought Oates—a pension of nine hundred pounds a year

38

and apartments in Whitehall where he carries out his investigations."

"How can it be allowed?" I cried.

"It is the wish of the people," answered Leigh, "so cleverly has he worked up feeling against the Catholics. I heard a disturbing piece of news and I was horrified to discover that it was true. A friend of ours, Sir Jocelyn Frinton, head of a Catholic family, was taken from his house, accused of complicity and executed."

"Horrifying!" cried Edwin. "It brings it home to you when it is someone you know."

"Was he involved in a plot?" asked Christabel.

"Ah, Mistress Connalt," replied Leigh, "was there a plot?"

"Surely your friend must have done something?"

"Oh, yes," said Leigh bitterly, "what he did was think differently from Titus Oates."

"It is a puzzle to me," put in Edwin, "and always has been why people who follow the Christian Faith in one way should become so incensed against those who follow the same faith by a slightly different road."

We were silent for a while and then Leigh said: "Enough of this gloomy subject. Tell us what you have been doing."

There was very little to tell, and the next day, said Leigh, we must all go riding down to the sea. We could go to the Old Boar's Head where they produced the best cider in the world.

Christabel reminded me that we had our lessons in the morning.

"Lessons!" cried Leigh. "I assure you we will endeavour to make the day most instructive for your pupil."

Everyone laughed. We were all in a very merry mood that night.

The next day we did ride out to the Old Boar's Head. We drank cider, which was a little heady and made us laugh immoderately over the smallest amusement. We galloped along the shore. Edwin kept very close to

Christabel because he sensed at once that she was less sure on horseback than the rest of us, having had less practice and only being able to ride when Lady Letty's horses were to be exercised.

The next day Leigh suggested we ride in another direction, and once again Christabel's objections to joining us were overruled. I could see, though, that she was very happy that they should be.

She grew prettier as the days passed, and the reason was that both Edwin and Leigh appeared to have forgotten she was, as she rather bitterly called herself, "only the governess," and behaved as though she were a guest and intimate friend at that. They both paid her a great deal of attention. They were affectionate to me as they always had been but it was Christabel whom they tried to please. Her eyes sparkled within that fringe of thick lashes; there was colour in her cheeks and her mouth had ceased to quirk and quiver and had become fuller and softer. The change in her was obvious to me.

I was uneasy, asking myself: Is she falling in love? With Edwin? With Leigh? I felt apprehensive. Leigh fell in and out of love with ease, and I wondered whether Christabel knew this. Edwin was different, more serious. But then he was Lord Eversleigh, with an important name, rich estates and a family tradition. I had heard my parents discuss his marriage, and I knew he would be urged to make what would be called a suitable match, which would mean someone of similarly aristocratic birth and a supply of worldly goods. There were two contenders already in sight for the honour of marrying Edwin. One was Jane Merridew, daughter of the Earl of Milchester, and the other, Caroline Egham, daughter of Sir Charles Egham. There had been mild overtures between the families and I knew that this was in the air. Edwin knew both girls and liked them well enough. My mother had thought that Edwin—always so mild—would do what was expected of him. He always had, so why change now?

Christabel was good-looking and clever. Personally she

was every bit as presentable as Jane Merridew or Caroline Egham, but she came from an impecunious rectory and I knew she would not be acceptable as the future Lady Eversleigh.

This vague apprehension clouded the happiness of those days, and then suddenly something so stupendous happened that I forgot about it.

It was about five o'clock, and a week since the return of Leigh and Edwin. It would have been dark, but there was a gibbous moon in the sky and it gave a shifting light as the dark clouds, whipped by the strong southwesterly wind, scudded across the sky.

It had been a pleasant day. We had gone riding through the woods where some of the oaks and hornbeams still carried wisps of foliage. Soon they would be quite bare, their branches making intricate patterns against the sky. We rode past brown fields where a faint line of green showed that the wheat had started to push through the earth. Winter was coming on. It would soon be Christmas. Most of the flowers were gone, though here and there was a spray of gorse. Leigh pointed it out with glee and quoted the old saying that the time to kiss a maid was when the gorse was out, and that was the whole year round. We saw just a few flowers—dead nettles, shepherd's purse and woundwort—pathetically determined to stay till the very last moment. There was something mournful about the occasional song of a bird. A blackbird tried a few notes and then was silent, as though disappointed with what he had done. And as we rode through the woods I heard the woodpecker. It was almost as though he were laughing in a mocking kind of way.

Yes, I thought, there is a warning in the air today. Winter is coming—a hard winter, perhaps, because there are so many berries, which are said to be nature's preservation for her children.

The woodpecker's laughter rang out again. Yes, there was a warning in the air that morning.

When we alighted at an inn I saw Edwin help Christabel

41

to dismount, and I thought he held her hand rather longer than was necessary. Edwin looked elated, yet serious; Christabel was radiant.

Oh, yes, I could see trouble ahead.

When we went back through the woods I deliberately lost them. It was a sort of game we played and so far they had always caught up with me. This time they didn't, so I came home alone. They had not returned when I reached the stables. I didn't want to go into the house. I wanted to think of what was happening and speculate on the outcome. And that was how I came to be in the garden at that hour of dusk.

I was thinking that my parents would be back sometime soon, for their visits to Court were not of long duration. I know my mother hated to be away from home for too long. Christmas would soon be with us and there would be preparations to be made. We usually had a houseful for the twelve days of Christmas. I wondered who would be our guests this year. If Edwin and Leigh were home, as they no doubt would be since they had returned from abroad, I was sure we would be entertaining the Merridews and the Eghams.

Christmas was a time to look forward to. We would go into the woods and bring in the holly and the ivy. We would decorate the hall; the carol singers and mummers would come; there would be hot punch and great joints of roasting meat; there would be gifts for each other— wonderful surprises and a few disappointments; there would be dancing, games and hide-and-seek all over the house. Christabel would be with us . . . and Edwin and Leigh.

I wished my mother were home and yet in one way I was glad that she was not. I feared that if she were here, matters would come to a head. Perhaps Christabel would be sent away. Where? Back to that cheerless rectory? She had made me see it so clearly; I had shivered when she had talked of it and actually felt the goose pimples on my arms. I had tasted the tasteless stews; I had felt the soreness of knees which had touched the floor so often in prayer. I had

42

really become deeply involved with Christabel. And now I feared she might be hurt again.

As I walked in the gardens, thinking of all this, my steps took me to the haunted flowerbed. A gloomy place—but only because of its associations. It was really beautiful. A few late roses were blooming still, desperately holding on to life, which the frosts and cold winds of winter would soon be snatching from them. Beyond the rosebushes was a shrubbery, and it occurred to me that it was this which preserved the legend of the flowerbed's being haunted. It looked eerie in the shifting moonlight, and one could imagine ghosts lurking there, hidden from sight by the short, stubby firs.

I stood there among the red rose trees, looking back at the house, and thought of Edwin's father being murdered on this spot. I did not know the details, of course, but I should learn them in due course when I was allowed to read the journals. That would be in two years' time when I was sixteen.

And then as I stood there I was aware of a sound in the shubbery, a rustle of leaves, a crackle of a branch. It could have been a rabbit strayed some distance from his burrow; yet somehow I knew it was not so. I could feel my heart thumping against my side. There was something in the shrubbery.

My first thoughts were that it was true the place was haunted. There *was* something here, and because I had thoughtlessly strayed out and come to this spot after dark, I was being made aware of it.

My first impulse was to turn and run back to the house, but my curiosity was greater than my fear and I remained still, staring at the shrubbery, my ears strained to catch every sound.

Silence.... The darkness of the trees was hiding...what? The clouds had now almost completely obscured the face of the moon. I had a sudden fear that supernatural powers were at work. There would be utter darkness and mysterious hands would reach out to draw me into the shrubbery.

There it was again—that cautious movement. I felt that someone was watching me.

I called out: "Who is there?"

There was no answer.

"I know you're there," I shouted. "Come out. If you don't I will bring out the dogs."

I thought of our dogs—Castor and Pollux—two red setters who loved everybody and only barked and pretended to be fierce when they were playing with bones.

Then a voice said: "I *must* speak to Lord Eversleigh."

I felt a great relief. It was a man after all, not a ghost.

"Who are you?" I asked.

"Please ask Lord Eversleigh to come here. He is in residence, I know."

"If you want to see him why do you not come to the house?" I asked.

"Are you his sister... Priscilla?"

This was clearly someone who knew the family and there was something pleasant about his voice.

"I am Priscilla Eversleigh," I answered. "Who are you? Come out and show yourself."

"This is dangerous," he said. "Please talk in a low voice, and please, *please* bring Lord Eversleigh to me."

I approached the shrubbery. Perhaps he was a robber; perhaps he was a murderer; perhaps he was a ghost; but I was always reckless and never thought of the clever thing to do until I had done that which was foolish.

I heard his voice then urgent and insistent. "Yes, please come into the shelter of the trees. It will be safer."

I stepped into the path among the trees and he came to meet me. He was wearing a cloak and a black felt hat over the kind of short periwig which most men had started to wear when the King's brother set the fashion. The moon had escaped from the clouds which had shielded it and shone on the shrubbery.

"I am Jocelyn Frinton," he said.

In such moments I suppose one should feel something intense, some premonition. I did feel an excitement which made me tremble, but that was because I remembered I had heard the name before and I realized that the events of which we had talked over dinner had moved nearer and that, remote in the country though I was, I was now being drawn into intrigue.

"I've heard of you," I said.

"They murdered my father. They are after me. Please... Eversleigh is here, I know. He'll help. I know he will. Go and tell him. Remember... only tell Eversleigh... or perhaps Leigh Main if he is there, too. Tell him. Either one of them. But tell no one else. It's dangerous... a matter of life and death. If they get me..."

"I understand," I told him. "You'll be safe here until the morning. No one comes here. They think it is haunted. My brother should be back by now. I'll tell him at once."

He smiled and I noticed how handsome he was. In fact I thought I had never seen anyone so handsome, and I felt a great desire to help him.

I went back to the house to find that the others had returned.

"Where did you get to?" demanded Leigh. "Why, what's the matter? You look as if you have seen a ghost."

I said: "Come inside. I want to talk to you. It's very important. I've seen... something."

Leigh put his arm about me affectionately. "I knew it was a ghost," he said.

"More dangerous than that," I whispered.

We went to the schoolroom—Edwin, Leigh, Christabel and I. As soon as the door was shut I blurted out: "Jocelyn Frinton is in the shrubbery."

"What!" cried Leigh.

"He's dead," said Edwin.

"No. It's the son of that one. He's being hunted. I went down there when I came in and I heard someone there. I shouted for him to come out and I threatened him with the dogs. Then he spoke to me and told me that he must see you, Edwin... or Leigh... because he wants you to help him. They murdered his father, he said, and they would do the same to him if they caught him."

"God help us!" cried Leigh. "It is this monster, Titus Oates."

"What are we going to do?" asked Christabel.

"We've got to help him of course," replied Leigh.

"How?" asked Edwin.

"Give him food for one thing and find him a hiding place for another."

"You can't keep him hidden long in the shrubbery," I pointed out.

"No," replied Edwin, "but this madness is going to be over sooner or later. Oates is beginning to show up in his true colours. People will turn against him in time, I'm sure of it."

"It could be a year...two years," said Christabel.

"Nevertheless," said Leigh, who had always been the man of action, "the first thing to do is to get him to a place of safety."

"There is the secret compartment in the library where my father hid our treasures during the war and saved them from the Roundheads," I said.

Edwin was thoughtful. "If he were discovered that would bring the family into it."

"My father hates the Papists," I said.

"There you have it," replied Edwin. "The country is being divided. That is what happens when there is an affair like this. Before Oates reared his ugly head people did not greatly care how others worshiped. It is because of this anxiety about the succession and rumours about the King's brother's religion..."

"I know, I know," interrupted Leigh impatiently, "but in the meantime we have to do something about Jocelyn Frinton. If he is caught it will be the end of him. Where can we put him?"

"We shall have to be careful," I cautioned. "We have a fanatic in Jasper. He would soon discover him if he remained in the shrubbery and there is no doubt what his reaction would be. He thinks Catholics are agents of the devil and talks often of the Whore of Babylon. He is a bigoted old man and a dangerous one."

"Then it can't be the garden and it can't be the house," said Leigh.

"I know a place!" I cried. "It would do for a while anyway. Your father was there, Edwin, when he came to England during the Commonwealth. I remember my mother's showing it to me. She came with your father. It was just before he was murdered."

"All right. All right," said Leigh. "Where is this place?"

"It's White Cliff Cave on a lonely part of the shore. Few people ever go there. It would be a good hiding place."

"It's the best suggestion so far," said Leigh approvingly. "Now we have to get to work quickly."

He was silent suddenly, putting his finger to his lips. He was clearly listening. Then he went quietly to the door and opened it suddenly. Carl almost fell into the room.

He grinned at us. "There's a beef pie in the larder," he said. "I'll get a great hunk of that for him. And some ale, too. I'll take it from the back and they won't know it's gone."

We were all astounded and realized how careless we had been. It might have been one of the servants—perhaps Jasper—instead of Carl.

Leigh gave him an affectionate push.

"Do you know what happens to people who listen at doors?" he asked.

"Yes," retorted Carl, "they come in and join in the fun."

It was not difficult to get Jocelyn Frinton to the cave. Leigh and Edwin rode off with him that night after the household was asleep. If it was discovered that they had been out, the servants would shrug their shoulders and would believe that they had been in pursuit of those adventures which were characteristic of men in a lax society. Jasper would shake his head and prophesy hell fire, but no one else would take much notice.

Carl had been useful prowling round the kitchen; he was known to have a voracious appetite and if he were caught making off with food no one would have been very surprised. Christabel and I gathered up some blankets which they had taken with them.

A seriousness had settled on us all, for we knew—even Carl—that this was an adventure which could result in death.

It was midnight when Edwin and Leigh returned, for it was about three miles to White Cliff Cave. Christabel and I were waiting up and had been watching from my bedroom window. We had prevailed on Carl to go to bed, promising him that when Edwin and Leigh came up, we would let him know if he were still awake.

"Of course I'll be awake," he said; but I had looked in on him at about eleven o'clock and he was fast asleep.

He was very excited about the adventure and could be useful, but I would rather he had not been concerned in it.

"My father, who is quite tolerant about some matters, is fiercely against Catholics," I told Christabel. "He dislikes the Duke of York. More than that he feels it would be a disaster if he ever came to the throne. He says the people won't allow it and there'll be a revolution. He is all for putting Monmouth up as the heir."

"What would he have done if he had found Jocelyn Frinton in the grounds?"

"I don't know. He knew his father and he must have been aware that they were a Catholic family. But a little while ago no one thought very much about that. It is only since Titus Oates came along with his Popish Plot that people started to worry. I know that if there was a conflict my father would be on the side of Monmouth rather than that of the King's brother. But that's politics. I know religion comes into it, but my father is not a religious man."

"No," said Christabel, "that seems to be clear at any rate."

"I don't know whether he would give him up, but I don't think he would help him or want us to. What Edwin does is his own affair because Edwin is a man and my father is not his father. What my mother would think I don't know. She would be alarmed because we might be putting ourselves in danger. But there's Carl, you see. My father dotes on Carl and Carl has insisted on becoming involved."

"He enjoys it. It's a wonderful adventure to him and I notice that he likes to be in everything."

"I should imagine my father must have been just like that when he was young."

"You could be sure of that." There was a touch of asperity in her voice, reminding me of the Christabel I had known before the coming of Edwin and Leigh, which had worked such a subtle change in her.

"Listen," I said, "they've come back, I think."

I was right. We stood tense at the window, and in a short time we saw Leigh and Edwin come into the house. We waylaid them and they came into my bedroom.

"All is well," whispered Leigh. "A very good spot. Full marks, Priscilla, for thinking of it."

I glowed with pleasure.

"He has food for tomorrow and he'll be all right provided no one decides to picnic there."

"Picnic in November in that bleak spot!"

"Bleak's the word," said Edwin. "But the blankets will keep him warm."

"How long can he stay there?" asked Christabel.

"Not indefinitely, of course," replied Edwin. "We'll have to try and think of something before the winter gets really cold."

"He'd freeze," I said.

"Priscilla is worried about Carl's being involved," Christabel told them.

"Yes, so am I," said Edwin.

"He's a good fellow," added Leigh. "It would be his extra exuberance which might give it away."

"I'll speak to him in the morning," said Edwin. "Where is he now? In bed, I suppose."

"Fast asleep. He wanted to stay awake to see how it went but I told him he should go to bed as normal. He did and was soon asleep."

"We ought to try to get Frinton away somewhere

before your father returns," said Edwin to me.

I agreed with that.

Leigh said: "Well, it is late. We mustn't stop chattering here. Who knows, we might be spied on. I don't think anyone saw us, but we must all understand that this is no game and it's no use treating it as such. It's deadly serious. It could mean death for that young man and serious trouble for us. So . . . take care. Act as normal. We've done all we can for tonight. He's safe temporarily. Tomorrow we'll get some more food to him. We'll ride out as usual . . . but we must take care."

They tiptoed quietly out of my room and went to their own. I could not sleep. I doubted whether any of them would. Leigh was right when he said we were involved in a serious matter. I kept thinking of that young man. There was something noble about him, something which had made me want to help him more than anything else.

My thoughts stayed with him in White Cliff Cave.

We all rode out together the following morning. I had told them in the kitchens that we were going into the woods and wished to take food with us as we did not want to go to the inn. This was reasonable enough but not something we could do every day. I supervised the packing of a basket and was a little shaken when Ellen said: "You've got enough food there to feed a regiment."

"There'll be three hungry men to provide for," I reminded her, "for when it comes to eating Carl can do as well as any grown man. One gets an appetite riding you know, Ellen."

Sally Nullens, who was there because Carl was going with us and she still thought of him as her charge, said: "He's eating too much of that pastry. More good red meat is what he wants."

She was going over the provisions with a sharp eye and I felt uneasy. I was afraid of Sally Nullens—and Emily Philpots, too. She was more sullen than ever because Christabel was being treated as a member of the family—something which she had never achieved. "After all I did for those children!" was her continual plaint; and I knew she spied on Christabel, longing to catch her out in some misdemeanour, and was, in any case, critical of everything she did. It might be a joke in normal times but we could not afford such spying now.

However, we got away all right, and I was wondering whether it would be wiser to warn Carl to be careful or to let it alone. He was heart and soul in the adventure, but it was true that he might be overzealous.

I shall never forget that late November day with the mist hanging in the air and the gulls shrieking overhead and the strong smell of seaweed in the air. We dismounted and managed to tether our horses to a rock and went down towards the cave, our footsteps loud on the shingle.

I imagined Jocelyn cowering in the cave, wondering who was coming.

Leigh went to the mouth of the cave. "All's well," he cried.

Jocelyn came out then and I saw him more clearly than I had the previous night. He was tall and slender with very fair skin, faintly freckled, and light blue eyes. He had very white teeth and was indeed handsome. His breeches were light brown velvet and of the fashionable Spanish cut, and his leather buskins were of the same colour. His coat, also of velvet, came to his knees. It was rumpled from the night spent lying in the cave, but he was clearly a very fashionable gentleman who had obviously ridden off in a hurry before he had been able to attire himself for a journey.

Leigh said: "Come out into the open. We're a party of picnickers. We shall hear anyone approach and in any case we can see for a long way. If necessary you can go back into the cave, but it won't be necessary."

We settled down and I opened the hamper.

"I don't know how to thank you all," said Jocelyn. "Thank God I remembered your place, Eversleigh. I guessed you would help."

"Of course," said Edwin. "You were right to come. It was luck that Priscilla happened to be in the garden."

Jocelyn turned to me, smiling. "I'm afraid I scared you."

"I thought you were a ghost," I admitted. "In any case I always wanted to see a ghost. I'm glad I was the one and not our old gardener."

"You had come all the way from your home?" Leigh asked.

"Not from the country. From London. It was to the Piccadilly house that they came for me. There is something almost obscene about Oates and his men."

"I know it well," replied Edwin.

"Where is this going to end?" asked Jocelyn. "I cannot understand why he is not seen as the villain he is."

"It is terrible to realize how easily people can be roused to violence," said Edwin sadly. "One observes it often. Individually they would never be capable of such actions as they will take when they become a mob."

"I am sure that philosophizing can at times be a useful occupation," Leigh put in, "but this is the time for practical suggestions. Now, Frinton, this place is all right as a temporary haven, but we have to think of something better. You can't stay here. You could be discovered."

"I'll come out and guard you," cried Carl. "I'll bring the dogs with me. I'll teach them to fight anyone who tries to get into the cave."

"There is one thing I want you to do, Carl," said Leigh.

"What is it? What is it? You only have to say."

"It's quite simple," replied Leigh. "You just obey orders."

"Aye, aye, sir," said Carl. "You're a sort of captain, Leigh. We have to do what you say. Does Edwin have to, too? Will you, Edwin? Perhaps you wouldn't like to, being a lord and all that."

"We are here to help Jocelyn escape," said Edwin. "That's all we have to think about."

"It's all I *am* thinking about," retorted Carl.

"Carl," I reminded him, "it will be necessary to say nothing of this to anyone . . . *anyone*, remember!"

"Of course I remember. It's a great secret. Nobody must know."

I looked at Leigh. "We've got to think of something quickly. I wonder if Jocelyn could come to the house as a traveller who has lost his way."

"We would be expected to put him on the right road immediately," put in Christabel.

"I wonder if he could come as someone to work in the house."

"As what?" asked Leigh. "A gardener? Can you garden, Frinton?"

"As my tutor!" cried Carl. "They're always saying that I don't learn anything with the Reverend Helling."

"That's a reflection on you, dear brother," I retorted, "not on the Reverend Helling. If we want a scholar in the family we shall have to get a new brother...not a new tutor. I think it's dangerous for Jocelyn to come to the house. How could he possibly do that? My father and mother must have met you somewhere."

"Yes," said Jocelyn, "I have met them."

Leigh, who had been rather thoughtful, sat there with a smile on his face. Something was brewing in his mind, I could see. I knew him so well that I realized he wanted to think about it before telling the rest of us and however I urged him he would say nothing until he had decided to.

Edwin was saying: "Well, that's no good."

"At least," said Leigh, "you are safe here for the time being."

We made all sorts of plans as we sat there on the beach but Leigh still said nothing of what I believed was brewing in his mind.

We would get a change of clothes for Jocelyn—something which would be more suitable for travelling if he had to go off in a hurry. One of us would come every day with food until we made up our minds what we were going to do. There must be no more picnics, as they would arouse suspicion. Emily Philpots would already be saying that we must be mad to think of such a thing at this time of the year, and Sally might even get someone to follow us to make sure that Carl kept his leather jerkin on.

No. We should come singly, or perhaps two of us

together. We should have to be very wary.

We all looked to Leigh. He was the natural leader. He was more bold and ruthless than Edwin. Edwin was always too much afraid of hurting people's feelings. It made him act overcautiously.

Leigh had always joked about being the elder of the two. He was, by a few weeks.

I think I admired Leigh more than anyone I knew, and I was gratified whenever he showed a special feeling for me.

We reached the house at about five o'clock. It was already dark and we went in as quietly as we could. Like a company of conspirators.

Ellen looked at the empty basket.

"So you finished off every crumb?" she said.

"It was the finest mutton pie you ever made, Ellen," said Carl.

"Then it was wasted on you," she retorted. "It wasn't mutton, it was pigeon."

A small thing, but it was an indication of how careful we must be.

Sally Nullens was fussing round Carl.

"And I hope you didn't hang about on the beach, Master Carl. If that wind gets down in your chest..."

"Oh, we didn't go on the beach."

"So you didn't go on the beach, then?"

"Only just to look at it as we went along the way."

"And you didn't sit on the shingle? Then what's this seaweed stain on your jacket, eh?"

Carl was embarrassed. "Well, perhaps we did sit a little bit."

He was looking at me appealingly.

I said: "You're always dreaming, Carl. Of course we were on the beach for a while."

Then there was old Jasper.

"Someone's been trampling on those new trees I put in. Well nigh broke them saplings in halves. Godless lot."

I was thankful that Jocelyn was safely away from the house.

I went up to my room and I didn't have to wait there long before there was a tap on the door. Leigh came in.

He grinned at me. "I shouldn't come into a lady's bedroom, should I? Oh, but this is only my little sister, so all would be forgiven, even by old Philpots, I reckon."

"Don't be foolish," I said. "What do you want?"

He was serious immediately. "I thought I'd talk it over with you first."

The waves of inexplicable anger which his reference to me as his little sister had aroused were swept away because I was his chosen confidante.

"After all," he said, "you know her better than any of us really . . . even better than I do."

"Who?"

"Harriet. My mother."

"Harriet! But where does she come into this?"

"I thought she might help us. She's the only one I can think of who would snap her fingers at the risk. And we are taking a great risk, Priscilla. What we have done could bring trouble on the whole of the family."

"What else could we have done?" I thought of Jocelyn Frinton, so handsome he had been, and his warm looks had been rather specially for me. I would have risked a great deal for him. But I saw what Leigh meant. We had to think of the family.

"I've been turning it over in my mind but I didn't want to say anything until I had talked it over with you. I thought of going over to Harriet and asking her if she would help. If she will, this is what I plan. Jocelyn calls on her. He will be an actor whom she knew in London . . . or somewhere. He will be John . . . Fellows . . . or something like that. We'll keep the initials. That is always wise. She does have a lot of odd people calling on her from time to time and no one would take very much notice of a new one. Nor would they think it strange that he turned up like that. She could keep him there for a while. She might make him act a bit in one of those plays she is always arranging. He would be more safely hidden in the open as it were than in some cave where he has to be fed from our end.

Besides, it would be desperately uncomfortable for him if the weather turned cold. Now what do you think of this?"

"Oh, Leigh, I think it's a wonderful idea."

"Do you think she would agree?"

"I'm sure she would. She loves intrigue and she hates intolerance. I am sure Titus Oates is just the sort of person she would dislike most."

"I'm glad you agree. What I propose is this. I ride over to see my mother. I shall have to be gone a week. It takes two days at least to get there . . . and two days back. You can be sure that I shall not stay longer than necessary. In the meantime the rest of you must keep Frinton hidden and get food to him somehow. You'll have to be careful. I shouldn't like him to be around when your parents return. I think your father might well smell a rat."

"It's a wonderful idea. I am sure Harriet will help. When will you leave?"

"Today. There's no time to lose. I really do want to get him out of the cave. I think I shall leave immediately. You can explain to the others."

"I don't think I shall let Carl into the secret," I said. "He means well but he could betray something unwittingly."

"Good idea!" He put his hands on my shoulders and kissed me. "I knew I could rely on my little sister."

"Oh, yes, and, Leigh, there is one thing more."

"What's that?"

"I am neither particularly little, nor am I your little sister."

He grinned at me. "I'll make a note of that," he said.

Within an hour he was on his way to Eyot Abbas, his mother's country home in Sussex, and we were all praying that Harriet might be at home and not, as she so much enjoyed doing, be on a visit to London. Harriet was not exactly a countrywoman; she liked the pleasures of Court, fine clothes, masculine admiration and above all the theatre; and as her doting husband, Sir Gregory Stevens, who, before he had inherited his title and estates, had been tutor to Leigh and Edwin (and it was at Eversleigh Court where he and Harriet had first met), always did exactly as she asked, there was a strong possibility that she would not be at home. If that were so, Leigh would have to go to London to see her, which would mean another week's delay at least.

Several days passed. We arranged that one of us took food to Jocelyn each day and did our best to keep his spirits up. He was embarrassingly grateful—especially to me—and he said that he regarded me as his saviour. I pointed out to him that Leigh was the one who was in charge of everything. We were all longing for him to come back.

There were constant alarms during those days. Carl was caught sneaking out of the kitchen with a large piece of cold bacon. Ellen said the boy had become a thief and anyone would think he was starved. The bacon was taken from him and I could see that henceforth Ellen's sharp eyes would watch the victuals.

Leigh had been away a week. December had come and it was going to be a hard winter, they said. Sally Nullens could feel it in her bones, and *they* never lied, she added ominously. We had had no snow yet but the rain fell incessantly. Jasper said that there was more of it to come—cloudfuls of it. It wouldn't surprise him if we were in for another flood. The world was wicked enough for God to want to drown it.

"He'd tell you," I said ironically, "and in good time so that you could prepare your ark to save the righteous. There wouldn't be many. You would be the only one to qualify, Jasper."

He looked at me under his shaggy eyebrows. He believed I would be one of the first destined for hell fire. The Lord did not like a woman's saucy tongue, he told me; and Ellen was always disturbed when—as she said—I came back "pat" with an answer for him. But at that time she was worrying about the disappearance of the remains of a tansy pudding to which she had been looking forward.

"They'll feel the vengeance of the Lord," said Jasper. "The whole boiling of them! I reckon Master Titus Oates be bringing a few of them to their just desserts."

In the ordinary way I should have challenged that. But I realized we were getting onto dangerous ground.

I was thinking of that scene in the kitchen as I rode over to White Cliff Cave. The rain, prophesied by Sally Nullens's bones, had started to fall. Sally was full of old lore. "I saw the cat washing his face and ears extra well," she had said, "and bless me if he didn't lie on his brain.

"'When the cat lies on his brain/That do be a sign of rain!' And my bones are telling me a story today. Mark my words it'll be raining cats *and* dogs before the day's out."

Emily Philpots said there was thunder about, too, because she always felt down in the dumps with thunder, and Jasper murmured: "Armageddon, that's what it'll be . . . and not before it's due."

"You going off riding again, Mistress Priscilla." That was Sally, reminding me that she had once been my nurse.

"It's good exercise, Sally."

"I reckon you'd do better staying in today."

I wished they wouldn't watch me so closely. Was it my fancy or did they watch me more intently than they had? Had Ellen mentioned the denuded larder to Jasper? If *he* were on the trail we should be betrayed.

So I rode out uneasily with the basket of food attached to my saddle and I wondered how long it would be before Leigh returned. We missed him. We needed his leadership when we were engaged in a dangerous exercise, as this undoubtedly was.

I came out to the lonely stretch of beach. To my relief there was no one in sight. I tied up the horse where he could take shelter under an overhanging rock.

I went into the cave. For a moment I could not see Jocelyn. The lantern we had taken to him was alight. Then I saw him. He was lying down fast asleep. He looked so young and handsome, like a Greek hero. He was even more handsome without his periwig, which now lay on the shingle beside him. His cropped fair hair curled about his head and he looked quite defenceless. I trembled for him.

What if someone had strayed into the cave and found him asleep!

I hesitated to awaken him for fear of startling him, so I tiptoed to the mouth of the cave and there I called his name softly. He sat up and smiled at me. Then he sprang to his feet.

"It's Priscilla. I was dreaming of you. I dreamed you came in and looked at me."

"I did. I was afraid because your lantern was alight and I thought someone might see it."

"Is there anyone about?"

"No one."

"I haven't seen anyone here since you brought me to the place."

"There might be people in the summer. But you will be well away by then. I've brought you a partridge and a piece of sucking pig."

"It sounds delicious."

"I think you could come out into the open. I'll keep watch. There's no one about for miles. It's stopped raining now but it'll start again soon, I'm sure. Come, let's make the most of the fresh air while we can."

I laid out the food. I had brought some ale, too, which he drank eagerly.

He smiled at me and said: "Do you know, last night I was thinking that I was glad this happened. It brought me to you."

"You have had to pay rather a high price for the introduction," I said.

He took my hand then and kissed it. "It has been the most important thing in my life," he said.

"You're alone too much," I replied. "It makes you think these things. I have hopes that Leigh will have some solution when he comes back."

"We shall meet again when this is over . . . you and I. I am sure of that."

"Oh, I expect so. Edwin says that opinion is turning against Titus Oates and when it does that will be the end of all this. We shall go back to normal again. Our families will meet now and then. I daresay my mother will invite you to stay with us."

"I shall make every effort to bring that about. I have met you in extraordinary circumstances. I should like to do so . . . in a ballroom, say. Do you often go to Court?"

"Not yet. I daresay I shall some time. They think I'm rather too young at the moment."

"You don't seem to be to me."

"Do I not? How old do I seem?"

"Seventeen. It's the best of all ages. I know because I was seventeen two years ago."

I was delighted to be told I looked older than my years. People of my age always are, I suppose. One is always eager to throw off one's youth when one has it and it is only when it is beyond recall that one wants it back.

"Perhaps," he went on, "seventeen was the age I wanted you to be."

"Why should my age be any concern of yours?"

"Because I wanted you to be nearer to me."

"Listen," I said, "I can hear something."

We were silent, straining our ears. Yes, there were voices from some way off being carried to us on the southwesterly wind.

"Let's get inside the cave," I said. "Collect everything and take it in. We don't know who this can be."

Hastily we gathered up the remains of the picnic. We went into the cave and listened. Jocelyn had become rather tense; so had I. I was imagining Jasper's face. I could hear him as he betrayed us. "They be up to something. Food gone from the pantry, so my wife tells me. They're hiding something . . . they're hiding someone. It's someone who's been up to sin, you can be sure of that. There's something more sinful than usual in the air."

Jasper could always be sure of sin. It was there all round him and he was the only one he knew who had not been contaminated by it.

The voices were undoubtedly coming nearer; I looked

at Jocelyn and felt sick with anxiety.

If Leigh were here . . .

But Leigh was not here and I could not think what he would tell us to do but remain quietly where we were.

In the distance I heard the crunch of boots on shingle. It was followed by the bark of a dog . . . more than one dog.

We were seated side by side on the hard rock floor of the cave and suddenly Jocelyn reached for my hand. He kissed it and went on holding it.

I whispered: "It's someone coming along the beach. They're coming this way."

"With dogs," he said.

"Jocelyn, do you think . . ."

He nodded. "We have been betrayed. Oh, Priscilla, this will be the end . . . for me . . . for us . . ."

"It might be people out for a stroll."

Out for a stroll! I thought. On a winter's day with heavy clouds louring! Out for a stroll on the beach with dogs! The nearest house was a mile away. Leigh had mentioned that when he had said what a good hiding place it was.

I whispered: "Come farther into the cave." We crept into the recess and took everything there was with us.

The rock overhung and we could crawl in even farther if we were on our hands and knees. We did so and lay down, very close, trying to hide ourselves. Jocelyn put his arms about me and we lay as one in that small space under the overhanging rock.

I could hear our hearts beating. The footsteps were coming nearer. The dogs kept barking.

Jocelyn's face was very close to mine, his lips against my cheek.

"You shouldn't be here," he whispered. "You shouldn't be in this . . ."

"Hush," I warned.

"Bruno! Bruno!" It was a man's voice. "What have you got, eh?"

The dogs barked. They were close now.

I felt sick with fear for Jocelyn. I believed in that

moment that I was never going to be happy again. They would drag him away. They would kill him as they had killed his father.

Nearer, nearer they came. They were very close now.

Jocelyn said: "I must say it. It's my last chance. I love you."

I put my hand over his mouth.

There was a shadow in the mouth of the cave. It was one of the dogs. He had entered it and he came immediately to us.

I heard someone call: "Bruno!"

The dog stood over us.

I thought of our dogs at home and I said very quietly: "Good Bruno."

He barked and then turned and ran out of the cave.

I heard someone laugh. "Bosun. Come here, Bosun. You too, Bruno."

We lay still, Jocelyn's arms still about me. We neither of us dared move, and then I realized that no one was following the dog into the cave. I could hear their voices farther away now. They had passed on.

"They've gone," I whispered. "They weren't looking for us. They were out for a stroll after all."

I began to laugh. Then I stopped suddenly. "It may be a trick. Oh, no . . . why should it be? They could have caught us so easily if they had been looking for us."

I crawled out from under the recess and stood up. Jocelyn was beside me.

"I'm going out to look," I said.

"I'll go."

"No. If they are looking for you they wouldn't take much notice of me. They'd be looking for a man."

I went out into the open. I could see two men with the dogs walking along the beach. One of them picked up a pebble and threw it from him. The dogs chased after it to retrieve it.

The scare was over, but something had happened.

Jocelyn took my hand and kissed it.

"Now you understand," he said.

I had turned away to look at the sea, grey with white frills on the edge of the waves and the wind carrying the spray far up onto the beach.

I said: "I understand how dangerous it is here. Leigh will come back soon."

"I shall have to go away then."

"It may be to Aunt Harriet's."

"You visit her often?"

"Oh, yes. I am a favourite of hers."

"I shouldn't want to go if it meant not seeing you."

"You must go where you will be safe."

He kissed me suddenly. "It has been a great adventure," he said.

"It is not over yet," I warned.

"Let's sit down close and talk."

We sat on the shingle and he said: "I wish you were older."

"What if I were?"

"We could marry."

"They would say I am too young."

"People marry young. When all this is over I shall ask your parents for your hand. May I?"

"Could I stop you?"

"No, I don't suppose you could. But I should want your consent, shouldn't I?"

"I know some people who have been married without their consent."

"You never would be. You would find some way out of an undesirable alliance, I am sure. Oh, Priscilla, I believe you have some feeling for me."

"Yes, I have."

"And it doesn't displease you that I talk like this. You seem content to listen."

"At the moment I can't think of much else but your lucky escape."

"Those people with the dogs..." He shivered.

"I was terribly frightened, Jocelyn, weren't you?"

He was silent for a while, then he said: "I thought they had come to take me, yes. I thought it was the end. When

63

they took my father and in a short time had murdered him—they called it execution, I call it murder—something happened to me. It was almost as though I felt there was no sense in working against fate. As I lay there with you in my arms, I thought: This is the end. But before I die I shall have known Priscilla and it was all this which brought me to her. You see, it is a sort of acceptance of fate."

"You are philosophical."

"Perhaps. If I am to die then die I must, but if fate is kind to me and preserves me from this, then I can think of my future and I want you to share it with me, Priscilla."

"You scarcely know me."

"In circumstances like this acquaintance ripens very quickly into friendship and friendship into love. You have risked a great deal for me."

"So have the others."

"But I prize what you have done most. Whatever happens I have had those moments with you in the cave when you lay close to me and your heart beat with fear... for me. I shall remember that moment forever and I should not have had it but for the fear which went with it. Most things that are worth having have to be paid for."

"You are indeed a philosopher."

"Events make us what we are. I know that I shall love you until I die. Priscilla, when this is over..."

I felt in an exalted mood. Too much had happened in such a short time. That fearful experience and then a proposal of marriage. And I was fourteen years old! I was regarded as a child in my home—Edwin's little sister. And that was how Leigh thought of me, too. Little sister! That had rankled coming from him.

"Priscilla..." Jocelyn was saying, "will you remember this... forever? Shall we plight our troth here on this desolate beach?"

I smiled at him. He was so handsome and melancholy in a way—a young man to whom brutal life had been revealed and it had made him accept it instead of rebelling against it. I admired him, and when he kissed me I was aware of an excitement which I had never felt before.

It was so comforting to be loved. Moreover, *he* did not regard me as a child, I thought to myself, and it was as though I were talking to Leigh.

"Jocelyn," I replied, "I think I love you, too. I know that if they really had been looking for you and had taken you, I should have been more unhappy than I have ever been before."

"It's love, my dearest Priscilla," he said, "and it will grow and grow and wrap itself about us for the rest of our lives."

So we kissed and plighted our troth, as they say. He gave me the ring he was wearing on his little finger. It was gold with a stone of lapis lazuli. It was big and would only stay on my middle finger and even then was in danger of slipping off.

It was hard to leave him then, but I knew that I must if I were going to get back before dark.

He was reluctant to let me go but I reminded him that we must be more careful than ever now.

"Do not have the lantern lighted when you sleep," I warned. "It could guide people to you. Oh, do be careful, Jocelyn."

"I will," he assured me. "I have the future to think of now."

Leigh came back that evening.

We were all overcome with joy at the sight of him and the news was good.

He told us about it as we sat over supper in the winter parlour after the servants had all gone away. Even so he spoke in whispers and warned us to do the same, and every now and then went to the door to make sure that no one was near.

"Harriet says she will have him," he told us. "He is to be John Frisby whose mother acted with her, and whom she knew as a child actor himself when she played in London. He can stay there for as long as he likes. She'll brief him when he arrives and make sure that if any other actors come visiting her, he will be warned about them. She's

65

excited. She was excited right from the beginning of the prospect. She said she was getting a little tired of being in the country, but now it would be as good as a play. I'm going off now to see him. I shall have to get a horse for him somewhere. In fact I have one at a horse dealer's... Shoulden way. I can collect it tonight and take it down to him. I want him on his way."

"Do we need food?" asked Christabel. "They are getting a little suspicious in the kitchen."

"No," said Leigh. "He'll have money and he can feed himself during the journey. Soon after he'll be with Harriet. All he wants is the horse and directions how to get there. I think our part of the plot is almost over."

I told him about the people and the dogs and how terrified we had been—but I did not mention our conversation and its results.

"Yes," said Edwin. "I guessed it would be tricky there for more than a night or two. It will be a relief when he is with Harriet."

We were all rather subdued, and as soon as supper was over Leigh went out again. I overheard one of the servants say: "Master Leigh's no sooner in than out."

"He's got his lady to see to. She's been without while he's been with his mother."

"If it's her I think it is she wouldn't have been without altogether... only without Master Leigh."

There followed giggles which annoyed me. But I had to curb my irritation. I wanted to say: It is not a mistress he is visiting tonight. But how foolish that would be. Leigh's reputation had served us well during this affair, but at the same time I felt irritated that he had it—and more so because I was well aware that he deserved it.

I was watching at my window for his return. It must have been an hour or so after midnight when he came in. I had to know what had happened. I slipped on a cloak over my nightdress, put on slippers and ran down to the hall. He came in quietly. The moon—now waning—gave a little light through the tall, narrow windows.

"Leigh!"

"So it's you."

"I had to know."

"All's well," he said. "I got the horse and he's now on his way. If he's careful there shouldn't be any mishaps. He's assumed his new identity—onetime child actor, John Frisby, on his way to see his old friend, Lady Stevens, who played with him in the past. Once he's in Harriet's charge all will be well."

"Thank God," I said fervently.

I had put up my hand to hold my cloak about me, and Leigh said: "You have a new ring. I haven't seen that before. It looks like a signet ring and it's too big for your hand."

I hesitated, then I said: "Jocelyn gave it to me after ... after the scare."

"Jocelyn! May I see it?"

I took it off and showed it to him.

"It's a signet. That's the Frintons' crest. You can't wear that."

"Why not? I want to." I snatched it from him. "He gave it to me."

"Then he must be mad, the careless fool! What if it were discovered with you! Don't you understand? People would want to know how you came by it. And what would your answer be then, eh? Tell me that?"

"I should say it was given to me."

"When? How? By whom? That's what you'd be asked and what would you say? By Jocelyn Frinton when we helped him to escape! Give it to me."

"Certainly not. It's mine."

"I only have to be away for a short while and people start acting senselessly. He had no right to give it to you."

"He has every right to do what he likes with his own property."

"Not when it means implicating you who have helped him. Give it to me. I'll return it to him and let him know what I think of him."

"I shall keep it," I retorted. "Don't be afraid. I do see the point. I won't wear it."

"It looks ridiculous on your finger anyway and everyone would notice it."

"I'll put it away."

"In a hiding place, please. How foolish of him! What did he want to give you a gift for! And such a one! He must have been mad. Both of you must have been mad."

I was silent. Perhaps it could be called a moment of madness. We had both been overwrought. I was sure Jocelyn would not have spoken as he had if those men with their dogs had not come along and brought such fear with them.

I gripped the ring tightly in my hands.

"Well, be careful," he said. "There's too much gossip and prying in a houseful of servants."

"I'll be careful, Leigh. I really will be. I'm glad you made me see it. I'll hide it right away. You know I would do anything...anything for his safety."

"He's a pleasant young fellow, I agree. I wonder what Harriet will make of him." He smiled, thinking of his fascinating mother.

"Time you were in bed," he said. "Heave a sigh of relief. Our dangerous adventure is over."

But of course it wasn't. It was only just beginning.

‑‑‑‑‑‑‑‑‑‑‑ Island Lovers ‑‑‑‑‑‑‑‑‑‑‑

We were all immensely relieved at Jocelyn's departure, for my mother had written that she and my father were preparing to return and we were certain that one of them at least would have discovered that something unusual was taking place.

Carl had been warned to be careful of what he said, but in any case the adventure was over as far as he was concerned and his entire attention was now focused on a new falcon he had acquired and which one of the gamekeepers was helping him to train. Carl's conversation consisted of nothing but this bird.

Leigh showed us a letter he had received from Harriet.

All was well at Eyot Abbas, she wrote. She had had to postpone the visit to town which she and Gregory had been contemplating. Benjie was in good spirits. He had taken quite a fancy to a visitor they had staying with them—a man with whom she had acted years ago. He was quite young, having taken child's parts naturally, and he had never really made the grade as an adult actor, poor fellow. But he was quite amusing and it was fun to have him. He fitted quite well into the household and she was not sure how long he could stay with them. She was happy to have him, for Leigh knew how much she liked visitors when they were in the country. Gregory had had a slight cold and was saying when were some of you coming to see us? ...

Leigh patted the letter, well pleased. "You can trust her to enter the spirit of the thing."

Christabel came to my room that night. She looked excited and quite beautiful.

"I wanted to talk to you, Priscilla," she said. "I'm sorry to come at this time but I wanted to be sure of our being alone. Do you mind?"

"Of course not," I said. "Come in."

She sat down. "I noticed the ring you were wearing," she told me. "What happened to it?"

"Leigh made me hide it away." I did not tell her that when I wore bodices with high necks I wore it on a chain hidden from sight.

She raised her eyebrows and a secret smile played about those mobile lips. She said: "Jocelyn gave it to you, didn't he?" I nodded.

"I believe he's in love with you."

"Why do you say that?"

"It was rather obvious, and then that day when you came back after the scare with the dogs, I guessed he had said something."

"I know it must sound ridiculous, but he has asked me to marry him if ..."

She nodded, understanding. "It's very romantic," she said. "I understand because ..."

It was my turn to study her. She burst out: "Nothing like this has ever happened to me before. I have always been wondering how I could ever have gone back to the rectory and now ... now I shall be here. I shall be one of you."

"What do you mean? You *are* one of us now. We all look

upon you as a friend . . . especially after this which we have all done together."

"It's strange but this matter . . . being in danger . . . conspiring together . . . it's done something to us all."

"To you, Christabel?"

"Yes, to me . . . and Edwin."

"You mean you love each other."

"I love him."

"Then he loves you, too. Oh, why didn't I see it? It's so obvious."

"As obvious as you and Jocelyn."

"Oh, Christabel, you look so happy."

"I *am* happy. It means so much to me. It is not only Edwin . . . loving him . . . knowing he loves me. It's other things besides. Well, perhaps I shouldn't think of them but if you had been brought up as I had . . ."

"I know what you mean. It's all going to be changed. It's going to be different for you. You can't help thinking of that as well as being with Edwin. Has he spoken to you then? Has he asked you to marry him?"

"He has shown me in a hundred ways that he loves me. He has told me so, yes."

I thought: Edwin is not the sort to take these matters lightly. He is not like Leigh. If Edwin were in love it would be serious. I had never heard the servants giggling together about *his* way of life.

"I am so happy for you," I said. "You will be a sort of sister. Now you won't have to think of leaving here. Oh, Christabel, I'm so glad you came."

"It was the turning point in my life." She laughed, quite joyously. She was quite different from the woman who had come to us not so long ago. It was as though the facade which she had built up to mask her feelings was evaporating. "And to think how frightened I was when I came here," she went on. "I remember sitting downstairs and facing your parents . . ." A shadow crept across her face. "Do you think your parents will accept this?"

I was not sure. I remembered the talk of the Merridew and Egham girls. I wondered what their reaction would be. My parents' attitude towards Christabel had made me speculate at first. My father had seemed anxious that she should settle in and had been considerate towards her, showing a little more interest than I should have thought was warranted. My mother would always be considerate to anyone who came into the household, but I fancy she regarded her with some suspicion, and I could see she often wondered why my father had brought her to us.

No, I was not at all sure what their reaction would be, but I had no wish to alarm Christabel out of her happiness, which it gave me great pleasure to contemplate.

So I said: "I am sure they will want Edwin to be happy, and Edwin is now of age."

She seemed satisfied with that and sat talking for about half an hour of this dangerous mission of ours, and we laughed over our alarms and congratulated ourselves on doing rather well.

After she had gone I felt the euphoria die out of me.

I wondered what would be the outcome for us both—Christabel with Edwin who might have to face opposition, and myself who loved a fugitive who was at this moment hiding behind an assumed name.

My parents had returned to the house and as was usual on such occasions there was to be a celebration to welcome them back. Consequently the house was full of the smells of savoury pies and roasting meats. Ellen was bustling around, full of importance. Chastity came in to help and all was activity.

We were all in the hall to greet them—myself, Carl, Edwin, Leigh and Christabel, who hovered in the background.

My mother embraced me warmly. My father scarcely looked at me but he studied Carl carefully. We were all a little anxious about Carl, although we had warned him to be careful. He could so easily betray what we had done, although he would try not to. His thoughts were now full of the falcon, though, and there was a new interest because Pollux was going to have puppies. I felt the old resentment rising. My father looked so distinguished, so different from all other men; I was so proud of him. Whenever I saw him after an absence I noticed these things about him even more than usual, and I longed for one look of approval or even of interest. It never came. He was aware of me to some extent, of course. He knew he had a daughter; he remembered my name, but I guessed he was not sure of my age—whereas he knew everything concerning Carl.

His first remark was: "I believe the boy's grown a few inches."

"One and a half," said Carl. "It's by the cupboard, truly."

He was referring to the schoolroom cupboard where his height had been measured throughout his life. There were others there too—those of Edwin and my own father, for both of them had been brought up at Eversleigh. Carl's ambition was to top his father. I sometimes thought my father wanted him to do that too. I felt hurt that girls should be considered of such small account because of their sex and I was almost glad that I had been involved in something of which I believed he would not have approved.

"That's good. You'll be almost as tall as I am one day," said my father.

"I'm going to be taller," boasted Carl. It was the sort of attitude which pleased my father. He gave my brother an affectionate push.

My mother slipped her arm through mine. She always seemed as if she wanted to make up for my father's neglect of me, but I really should have preferred it if she had pretended not to notice.

There was a certain normality about the house now that they had returned and I realized how difficult it would have been to have hidden Jocelyn if they had been at home. I had been wearing the ring round my neck that day, and for the evening I put on a dress which exposed my arms and neck, so I took it off and put it carefully away in a drawer behind some linen.

I met my mother on the way down and she started to tell me about the new hairstyles they were using at Court.

"They're wearing loose curls on the forehead. It's all curls. I don't think the forehead ones would suit you, but I like the style with the hair caught up with a ribbon to hang at the side of the face. These curls are called heartbreakers. They are supposed to be alluring." She had turned to me and touched my light brown hair, which was fine but abundant and certainly not inclined to be curly.

"Oh," she went on, "what's that mark on your skin? I see. It's that chain of yours. It's left quite a mark. It's been pressing on your skin. I didn't notice you were wearing the chain today."

"I . . . I . . . er I was," I said. I hoped I was not flushing as I feared I might be.

"But I didn't see it, darling."

"Oh, I was wearing it . . . for a time."

It was only a small matter, but it was an indication of how careful one had to be. She might begin to wonder and realize that I had been wearing the chain *under* my bodice. Now why should a girl want to wear a gold chain so that it did not show!

Over the meal my father talked a great deal about what was going on at Court. Monmouth seemed certain that he would get his father to legitimatize him.

"The best thing possible," commented my father. "It'll put York's nose out of joint and that's the best place for that to be."

Edwin asked: "Have you spoken to the King about it?"

"I? My dear fellow, Charles would not listen to me or anyone. I'd be told—with the utmost good humour of course—to mind my own business. And, who knows, in a short time there might be a cooling of royal favour. No, Charles knows what he is going to do and nobody's going to persuade him. He's insisting at the moment that he was never married to Lucy Walter and that Monmouth is therefore a bastard."

"In that case," said Leigh, "our next King must be James."

"There will be some who will not accept that because it means Popery."

"What's happening to Titus Oates?"

"He's still in Whitehall. There have been certain voices raised against him. He's not the most popular man in the country."

"Do you think that if he falls out of favour all this persecution of Catholics will stop?" I asked.

My father turned to look at me and I was deeply conscious of his cool, appraising gaze. I felt bitter. I wished he could have looked at me with interest just once.

He shrugged his shoulders. "Charles is not interested really. He's the most tolerant man alive. He loathes all the fuss."

"Then why doesn't he *do* something about it?" I cried impatiently.

"Too lazy," said Leigh. "But he did save the Queen. Oates would have had the axe for her if he could have arranged it."

"He's a beast!" I cried.

My mother said: "It will pass. These things always do."

"Yes," I retorted passionately, "but in the meantime people are being hunted and executed. It's cruel."

"Some say that the King is secretly Catholic," put in Christabel.

There was silence at the table for a few moments, then my father said: "He would never openly admit to it. He's too shrewd . . . too clever. He knows the people won't have it and he is determined to please the people. But the next King must be a firm Protestant. It will have to be Monmouth."

"But the Duke of York will never accept that," said my mother. "And I don't think it's wise to speak of these things of which we know nothing. There is a long letter from

Harriet. She is staying in the country for a while. She has a rather amusing young man staying with her . . . an actor."

My father said: "Harriet has always got amusing young men staying with her and they are invariably actors." He spoke coldly. He did not like Harriet and she did not like him. He was one of the few men who had not been fascinated by her. "When are you young fellows returning to duty?" he went on.

"Awaiting orders," answered Leigh. "It can't be long now."

"You'll have to tell us what you've been doing while we've been away," said my mother.

There was an awkward silence and my father laughed.

"It sounds, Bella," he said, "as though they have been up to some tricks."

We all laughed, rather falsely, I think. I heard myself saying: "We rode quite a bit. We even had a picnic once . . ."

"Good weather for it," commented my father.

"It was a rather special sort of picnic," cried Carl.

Four pairs of eyes were fixed on him warningly. He lowered his head. "Not really a special one," he muttered. "Just an ordinary sort of picnic."

"Very ordinary," said my mother, "in November!"

I thought again how fortunate we had been to have got Jocelyn to Harriet's before they returned.

Servants in a house such as ours are like spies. They know what we are doing at any moment. They are conversant with our daily habits and if we should step out of line they are immediately aware of it. I was passing Sally Nullens's room when I overheard her talking to Emily Philpots, and as I realized what they were talking about I shamelessly stopped to listen.

"Of all the impudence! Who does she think she is? Mark my words, didn't I say as soon as she entered these doors that I knew her sort? Adventuress. That's what she is." That was Emily Philpots.

Then Sally Nullens: "It can't be true she's got her claws

in my Lord Edwin. Not my Lord Edwin! A dear little chap he was—different from that Leigh. Now if it had been him . . ."

"I know what she's after. She fancies herself as Lady Eversleigh. If she ever became that I'd go in sorrow to my grave. I would, I'm telling you, Sally, I really would."

"It don't seem right if the reason she was brought here was . . ."

"Well, what would you say? It's not like him to take such notice of Priscilla's education. She was never of much account to him."

"That's true enough. I remember his disappointment the day she was born. It was a boy he wanted, and when Carl came along . . . proud as a dog with a couple of tails, he was. Now he brings *her* in. Why was he so interested in *her?* Do you really think. . . ."

"I do, Sally, I do indeed."

"What will he say when his lady friend wants to marry Lord Edwin?"

"Will he care? He was never one for Edwin, was he? He'll laugh, he will. Passing on his leftovers."

My impulse was to go in and box their ears. They were two evil-minded disgruntled old women. How dared they say those things about Christabel and about my father? It was such nonsense. I would not believe for one moment that Christabel had been my father's mistress, which was what those two old women were suggesting.

I curbed my anger and went quietly away. I did not want to hear any more.

After we retired that evening I was very uneasy thinking about what I had overheard and wondering if there was just an element of truth in it. No! I could not believe that of Christabel . . . nor of my father. If I had discovered that he had had a mistress, I suppose I should not have been so very surprised, but I was sure he had too much respect for my mother and was too fond of her to bring such a woman into the house. Sally and Emily were two malicious old women whose malice had been fostered by a sense of grievance. I understood them in a way. They had passed their usefulness and hated the world for that reason.

I was very apprehensive thinking about Jocelyn and wondering what the outcome of everything would be. I wondered how long he could reasonably stay with Harriet. His sojourn there must be continued as only a temporary answer to our problem.

From the back of the drawer I took out the chain on which hung the ring. I pulled the ring off the chain and slipped it onto my finger. I sat there looking at it. It was the sort of ring which would have been noticed immediately. Leigh was right about that. Not only was the rather elaborate crest etched in gold on the lapis lazuli but inside the ring was the family name. One had to look close to read it but then it was clear enough.

I put my lips to it, thinking of those moments in the cave and the deep tenderness of his voice when he had said he loved me. I had remembered it when I was in the hall and my father had scarcely noticed me. Like Christabel, like Sally Nullens and Emily Philpots and like everyone else I suppose I wanted to be loved.

There was a knock on my door. My mother called softly: "Priscilla."

I hastily took off the ring and picking up the chain pushed both of them into a drawer.

She came in and I could see that there was something on her mind.

"Not undressed yet." She smiled at me tenderly. "I love you in that dress. The lace is so soft and feminine. It suits your brown eyes. It is a little too short though . . . and a little too tight. We must get Chastity to let out a seam and lengthen it. It's worth it and she could do that quite well. I want Emily to get on with embroidering my petticoat. You're growing, that's what it is." She kissed me. "Priscilla, I want to talk to you."

My heart started beating uncomfortably. When one is guarding an important secret I suppose there must be these constant alarms.

"Yes," I said.

"Well, don't look scared. Sit down. Are you all right? You seem a little..."

I looked at her fearfully. "A little what?"

"A little on edge. Are you sure everything is all right?"

"Yes. I'm all right."

"That's good. This is rather a delicate matter. I'm not sure how far it has gone."

"What...matter?" I asked faintly.

"Edwin and Christabel Connalt."

"Oh," I said blankly.

"So there is something. It must be stopped."

"Why?" I asked.

"It's most unsuitable."

"If they love each other..."

"My dear Priscilla, you must not be so childish."

"Is it childish to believe in love?"

"Of course not. But this governess..."

"Dear Mother, she is a governess because she has to earn her own living. She is well educated. You would not be able to tell her from any people who come here. If Edwin loves her..."

My mother's face hardened. It was not like her to be harsh or particularly socially conscious. I thought I understood. She was suspicious of Christabel because of the manner in which my father had brought her into the house. If it were in fact the truth that Christabel and my father had been lovers, it was perfectly understandable that my mother would not wish her to marry her son. I did not believe this for one moment—having come to know Christabel—but I had been confirmed in my opinion that it was what some of the servants believed, and if my mother was suspicious, too, that would explain her attitude.

She said: "It will have to be stopped. She will have to go away."

"Where will she go? You have no idea what the home she came from was like. She has told me about it." I tried to make my mother see something of what Christabel had told me, and my purpose was to reveal to her how impossible it would be for her to have carried on an affair with my father or anyone from such a place.

My mother, who when she had made up her mind usually had her way, was not listening. I could see that she was determined that Edwin should not marry Christabel.

But it would be for Edwin to decide.

I pointed this out.

"Edwin is sensible," said my mother. "He has always listened to me."

"It will depend on what he thinks is sensible," I retorted. "I know he loves you dearly and will always listen to you, but you see there is Christabel."

"So this has gone further than I feared. And it is such a short time that they have known each other."

"Yes, but because of what happened..." I stopped short. How angry Leigh would have been, and how easy it was to betray secrets!

"What happened?"

"Well, I mean Edwin and Leigh came back from service abroad and they looked so splendid in their uniforms... and it was all rather romantic..." I trailed off lamely.

"I just wanted to confirm what Sally Nullens had told me."

"So it was Sally Nullens, was it? That gossiping old woman!"

"You're being unfair to Sally. She loves Edwin and she worries about him. She doesn't want to see him caught by an adventuress. He is far too young to marry in any case."

"He is twenty-one."

"My dear Priscilla, you are very unworldly. Edwin bears a great name and he must marry in accordance with his position."

"I am very surprised to hear you talk like this. I never thought you could be hard and ruthless and socially ambitious. You have always been so different."

"I shall do everything I can to prevent Edwin's marrying Christabel Connalt," said my mother firmly.

"Have you spoken to my father about it?" I asked.

Her colour heightened. I knew then. She really believed this story about the reason for my father's bringing Christabel to the house. It seemed ridiculous. As if he would bring a mistress into the place. It showed that even now my mother was not very sure of him.

She said coldly: "It is not a matter for your father. Edwin is not his son."

She saw how distressed I was and her mood changed. She became the loving mother I had always known.

"Darling child, you must not distress yourself. I shouldn't have bothered you but I thought you would know more than most people did, and we don't have secrets from each other, do we?"

I could not answer that. To have agreed would have been too false. How much easier life had been before I started to grow up.

"Forget it," she said. "It will soon be Christmas. We must start making plans, mustn't we?"

I caught her hands. "Please don't send her away," I begged. "She would be so miserable. It's so wretched . . . that rectory. I don't believe they really have enough to eat. *Please* don't send her away."

"You have a soft heart, Priscilla, and I wouldn't have it otherwise. You can rely on me to do the best thing possible for Edwin and for Christabel."

I threw myself into her arms. I was comforted by her as I always had been. I thought: In time she will accept Christabel. It will all come right.

My mother kissed me and said good night. When she had gone, I sat at my dressing table and looked at my reflection. I wondered if she had noticed a change in me. Perhaps to her I still looked the same girl with the thick straight hair and the rather long brown eyes, the short nose, the wide mouth, the face which owed its attractiveness to its vitality rather than an evenness of feature. I could see a difference though. There were secrets in those eyes where there had been none, a new firmness about the lips. Yes, the last weeks had changed me and it was discernible to those who looked closely.

I hung up my dress—glad to get out of it because it was indeed too tight. A further sign of growing up. I put on my nightdress. Then I remembered the ring and the chain, which I had hastily put into the drawer.

I opened the drawer. There was the chain but I could not see the ring.

It must be there. I took everything out of the drawer and still I could not find it.

But I had put it into the drawer when my mother came in. I was frantic. I knelt down and searched the floor. I could not see it anywhere.

It would be better to search in the daylight. It must have dropped from my hands as I had thought I put it into the drawer. I had certainly done that hastily and it was really the only explanation.

Again and again I went through the contents of the drawer. Gloves, handkerchiefs, collars and frills for cuffs. There was no sign of the ring.

At last I abandoned the search and uneasily went to bed. I could not sleep. I was too upset both by my mother's attitude and the loss of the ring.

I was up as soon as it was daylight, but although I searched in every place, I could not find it.

There was an uneasy atmosphere throughout the house. I saw my mother in the garden with Edwin. They were talking very earnestly. Later I saw her send off a messenger and I wondered to where.

I was still obsessed by the loss of the ring. I was certain I should find it, for it must be in my bedroom.

At first I thought my mother might have taken it, but that was not possible, for she could not have done so without my seeing her.

I grew frantic searching over and over again.

I did not tell anyone of my loss. Only Leigh and Christabel even knew I had the ring and recognized the danger possessing it offered. It must turn up. I had searched every inch of the floor. It was as though it had been spirited away.

Christabel was growing uneasy. She was aware of my mother's attitude. Then four days after I had lost the ring Edwin and Leigh received summonses to rejoin their regiment without delay.

I guessed, of course, that my mother had arranged this and that the message she had sent had been a cry for help to one of her many influential friends in Court circles.

They left. Edwin had made no declaration to Christabel and he had looked so wretched before his departure that I knew he was wavering and considering all the disadvantages which my mother must have put to him. I was sure that she had suggested a separation between him and Christabel so that he could consider very carefully what he was proposing to do quietly and calmly. Edwin was the sort of young man who could be persuaded. That he was especially devoted to my mother I had always known and he could never be happy if he displeased her. When he went away without asking Christabel to marry him, knowing Edwin, I guessed he never would.

Poor Christabel! There was a desperate look in her eyes. She was even more unhappy than she had been before Edwin had come.

We began our preparations for Christmas rather halfheartedly. Harriet very often spent that time of year with us or we with her. This year, however, she made excuses and I knew it was because of Jocelyn. When Harriet played a part she did so with all her heart.

Many of my parents' friends came from Court. They liked to spend Christmas in the country. So there were the usual festivities, and hunting during the day. They were disappointed, though, because the weather was not cold enough to provide skating. There was a great consumption of food, and dancing and games, and everything that we had been doing at that time of the year for as long as I could remember.

Christabel mingled with us as though she were a guest or a member of the family and I was sure many people believed she was.

The Merridews were there and so were the Eghams.

My mother said how unfortunate it was that Edwin and Leigh could not be with them. It was too tiresome of Lord Carson—their fierce old General—to send them off abroad on some duty just over the festive season. She would tell him how she appreciated that when she had the chance!

I understood then. She really would thank him when she saw him.

I went to Christabel's room two or three days after Christmas. It was bedtime and I had thought she looked very sad during the evening.

"I came to see if you were all right," I said.

She smiled at me wanly. "It is not going to happen, Priscilla," she answered. "I might have known it was too good to be true."

I tried to comfort her.

Sometimes I wished that Edwin and Leigh had not come back to stay in the house during my parents' absence. If my mother had been there she would have seen Edwin's affection growing and she would have done something about it before it reached that stage.

Then I thought of the ecstasy when Jocelyn had put his ring on my finger and the agonies I had suffered when I had lost it. I was certain that it had fallen down at the back of the court cupboard which was too heavy for me to move. It was the only answer. At least it was out of sight there and safe, for they could not move the cupboard until springtime when they did the annual turning out. By that time perhaps this stupid persecution would be over and it would not matter who saw the ring.

That was how I comforted myself.

There was a letter for me from Harriet.

My dearest Priscilla,
It seems so long since we have met. I do want you to come and stay for a week or so with me. Just you . . . and perhaps bring that nice Christabel you told me about in your letters. I know your mother

will spare you. We are doing a little masquerade. John Frisby, the young man I told you about—the one who is staying here—is so good in his part, and I have one for you, too. I think he may be leaving soon and I should like you to meet him before he goes. Why not come soon? Don't fail me, dear Priscilla. I am writing to your mother...

I could imagine her. Dear, exciting Harriet, who was the most beautiful and attractive woman I had ever seen. She must have been absolutley irresistible when she was young. When I mentioned this to her once, she laughed and retorted: "My darling, I was never so irresistible as I am now. I have gained experience and I find art quite a good compensation for nature."

It was true that she painted her face with the consummate skill of an artist and gave an impression of dazzling beauty which could dispense with youth.

It was characteristic of her that she should throw herself wholeheartedly into this rescue. I wondered a little jealously whether Jocelyn had fallen in love with her. Most men did.

I went to my mother and showed her Harriet's letter.

"You must go, of course," she said. "It will do you good. You have been looking a little wan lately. You seem as though you are worried about something. Dearest Cilla, don't fret about Edwin. Bless your kind heart, it will all work out for the best, you will see."

She kissed me fondly and I clung to her. I had a great impulse to confess everything and to tell her how worried I was about the lost ring and to explain all we had done about Jocelyn.

That would have been folly. I could imagine Leigh's fury if I had done it.

So I said nothing and just hugged her.

"Harriet and her masquerades!" she went on. "I wonder what it will be this time. I remember long ago before the Restoration when we did *Romeo and Juliet*. Harriet was a bit of a minx in those days. I wonder if she really has settled down. Gregory adores her, of course, and so does Benjie. She was always a collector of men. I think Leigh is fond of her, too."

"I know he is. And so am I."

"Of course he is. She's his mother and she could even desert a child and still keep his love. Well, you go to her and . . . yes . . . take Christabel with you. It will do her good, too. Harriet stimulates people. I wonder what this young actor is like. As I said, Harriet always had a way of collecting men. What are you going to take? You should really have some new clothes now. We'll talk about that when you come back. I don't think you've finished growing yet. You are going to be a tall young woman, I can see."

She patted my arm.

My emotions were mixed: pity for Christabel, apprehension about the lost ring, shame for deceiving my beloved mother, and above all excitement at the prospect of seeing Jocelyn again.

It was mid-January when we arrived at Eyot Abbas. It was a fine old house which Gregory Stevens had inherited when his elder brother had died. It was set in beautiful country, much more lush than that about Eversleigh, for it was not pestered by the cold east winds as we were.

The house was set in hilly country about a mile from the sea, which could be glimpsed from the topmost windows. From there, too, it was possible to see the island known as the Eyot from which the house had taken its name. Once it had been quite a large island—large enough to contain a monastery which had been destroyed at the time of the Dissolution. Now the sea had encroached considerably and there were only a few ruins of the monastery remaining. I had been there on several occasions for picnics. It had always seemed a wild and fascinating place, rather eerie; and there were, of course, the usual rumours of lights being seen there and bells heard tolling.

Eyot Abbas was a rambling old house, Elizabethan. It

had its share of towers and turrets, and with its red Tudor bricks it was delightfully mellow, set in the luxuriant green of the countryside. The grounds were beautiful and not too well tended. There was a delightful orchard next to the paddock where one could go for solitude. During my visits I liked to take a book there and curl up under my favourite apple tree. I had very happy memories of Eyot Abbas. Everything was easygoing there. Harriet reigned like a queen over the household and the servants all behaved as though it were a privilege to serve her. Gregory never seemed to have recovered from the shock of her having married him. Benjie delighted in teasing her and clearly adored her even though she never worried about him, did not seem to care when he came in wet through after riding and that he nearly shot one of the gardener boys when he was practising archery. He was eleven years old and suffered from no restrictions. Perhaps that was why he was so pleased with life.

There were no tensions in that household. Harriet never treated us any differently from the grown-ups. She would not have age mentioned. It was something she preferred to forget and that suited us all.

When we arrived the grooms were expecting us and they took our horses and the bags from the saddle horse and we went into the house.

Harriet was not at home. She was out riding with her guest.

"You know your room, Mistress Priscilla," said Mercer, Harriet's personal maid who had been with her in the theatre. "And I have put Mistress Connalt next to you."

"That's good, Mercer," I replied. "I'll take Mistress Connalt up."

We mounted the stairs to our rooms. The colours were very bright. Harriet had refurbished Eyot Abbas when she became its mistress and the colours she had chosen were scarlet, purples and gold. "Trust Harriet to introduce royal colours," my mother had commented.

My bedroom was in purple—purple hangings on the

bed, purple rugs on the floor, purple curtains. The bedspread was of a lilac shade which toned in perfectly. Christabel's room was in a bluish mauve.

I could see that she was impressed by the richness of everything and delighted to be treated as though she were not a governess. That meant a great deal to her—even more than usual because of what was happening between her and Edwin.

Mercer brought water for us to wash, so we did so and changed; and while this was happening Harriet returned. I heard her voice immediately. It was always like that with her—as though a fanfare of trumpets must greet her arrival.

I ran out of my room to the top of the staircase.

She was in the hall, and beside her, looking even more handsome than I had been imagining him, was Jocelyn. For a few seconds I stood still watching them, my emotions enveloping me.

Then Harriet saw me.

"Ah, my darling child! Priscilla, my love, come down at once. I want to welcome you and introduce you to John Frisby."

I ran down the stairs. She caught me in her arms and I was wrapped in fragrance.

She looked magnificent in her riding habit. It was pale grey and there was a deep blue cravat at her throat which was the exact colour of her eyes. "I never saw anyone with eyes to match Harriet's," my mother had said. "I think they are the secret of her charm." They were beautiful eyes—deep blue and heavily fringed with black lashes; her brows were black, too, very well defined, and her hair, luxuriantly curly, abundant and springing with life, was very dark, too. It was that contrast of blue eyes and black hair with a fair skin, rather impudent nose and perfect white teeth which made Harriet the beauty she was. But it was her exuberant manner, her displays of affection which she bestowed carelessly on all who wanted them—and that was everyone who came within her orbit—that made her the person she was, one who could commit that which in others would be unforgivable and yet in her would be forgiven.

"Harriet is larger than life," Mother had said. "She can't be judged by normal standards."

And that was true. She was scheming, she was selfish, but she was generous. Her great charm was her vitality, her ability to extricate herself from any awkward situations with little cost to herself, and most of all, perhaps, an interest and excitement in life. She lived it fully and with zest, and those about her were caught up in that. No one could be near Harriet and be dull; and this made everyone want to be near her.

Neither of her sons was legitimate. Leigh had been born to her before she was married. His father had been my mother's husband, and it said a great deal for Harriet's charm that my mother, who had been desperately in love with her first husband, now bore no grudge against Harriet. Finding Leigh an impossible encumbrance Harriet had abandoned him when he was a few months old and left him in my mother's care. Years later she married into the Eversleigh family—an uncle of my father's much older than herself. Then she had given birth to Benjie, but it turned out he was not the son of her husband but of Gregory Stevens, who was tutoring at the house at that time. Then when her husband died and Gregory came into his title and fortune, she married him, and Benjie's name was changed from Eversleigh to Stevens, and Harriet emerged as the adored wife and mother.

I was afraid to look at the young man beside her. I said: "Harriet, you look as beautiful as ever."

"Bless you, dear child. I want you to meet my dear friend, John Frisby. John this is my...well, it's a complicated relationship and I should need pen and paper to work it out. But I love her dearly all the same and I want you to get to know each other."

The beautiful blue eyes were mocking as Jocelyn took

my hand and kissed it. We smiled at each other and I thought jubilantly: Nothing has changed. It is just as it was. He loves me still.

And I felt wildly happy.

Christabel was coming down the stairs. I saw Harriet appraising her.

I said: "Oh, here is Mistress Connalt. Christabel, this is Lady Stevens."

Harriet was charming and I saw Christabel flush with pleasure at her reception.

"Welcome, my dear," said Harriet. "I do like to have young people in the house. Priscilla has told me so much about you. Now come and meet John. He's longing to know you."

Harriet whispered to me: "Well done. You play well. We have to be careful. Servants peek and pry, you know."

"Yes," I whispered back. "Thank you, Harriet. Oh, thank you."

She pressed my arm.

"Now, how have you been looked after? Has Mercer given you what you need? I thought you would like Mistress Connalt close by."

"It was kind of you to ask me," said Christabel rather stiffly.

"Nonsense. I am delighted. Has Mercer unpacked for you? You must be hungry."

"Not really," I replied. "We had a pie and cider at the Stag's Head."

"Did you, indeed? Even so we will eat early. John, do go to the kitchens and tell them to put whatever they are cooking forward. We shall eat at six of the clock."

He bowed. His eyes were on me, warm and dancing with excitement.

"Come, my dears," said Harriet, "I want to make sure you are comfortable."

She led the way to my room and ushered us in. She shut the door and leaned against it. Her mood had changed; her eyes flashed with excitement.

"Now . . . we can talk. We have to be so careful.

Servants are everywhere. They have their uses, but in a situation like this they can present difficulties." She turned to Christabel. "My dear, I am so glad you came. I know of your part in all this . . . you and those dear boys, Leigh and Edwin. I am sure Leigh was the leading spirit. He was born to be a leader that one. Now to work. My dear Gregory has been such a help. Who would have believed that he would ever be involved in such a matter!" Again to Christabel. "My husband is the mildest of men. He likes to lead a simple and uncomplicated life. But I am afraid I drag him into the most dramatic situations. Darling Gregory! He is so good about it. But you are longing for news of our friend John."

"Oh, yes, please," I said fervently.

"And I chatter!" She leaned against the door, her hands pressed against it, looking like a queen of intrigue—which she was, of course. How she loved to play a part! "Now listen to me carefully, my dears. They are looking for John. You must never refer to him as anything but John Frisby in this house . . . never . . . *never!* Gregory has his ears to the ground. He was in London recently. This odious Oates is frightened now that he sees his rule coming to an end, but he is determined to let no victims escape him. He and his friends are furious that *our* friend got away. Oates harbours some special grudge against the Frintons. He got the father and is determined to wipe out the family—and that means first of all the son. Our John Frisby is in acute danger."

I caught my breath and put my hand to my throat. Harriet smiled tenderly at me and went on: "I know how you are feeling. I share your anxiety. There is no suspicion in this household at the moment. I am sure of that. But if something should lead them here . . . Well, they would try and question . . . and I am not sure that our disguise would stand up to scrutiny."

"Oh, Harriet, what can we do?"

"You can be sure I would take some action. I have been working on it and I am going to smuggle him to France. I think it is the only thing to be done. We are negotiating now and we hope to have arranged for a boat to take him by the end of the week. I wanted you to come and see him before he went."

"Harriet," I cried, "you are marvellous!"

I felt so emotional that I was afraid I would not be able to hold back my tears, so I threw myself at her and buried my face against her.

She touched my hair. I heard her say to Christabel: "This child has always been a special favourite of mine. Her mother did so much for me. It is something one never forgets."

That helped me a great deal. It made me smile because I knew exactly how she was looking at that moment, posing, of course, as she always did. I often wondered how much of what she said she really meant. It didn't matter. She was Harriet and she fascinated me completely.

"There now," she said, when she felt the scene had been played long enough, and I was now in control of my feelings, "we must be practical. You must not take too much notice of John Frisby ... and yet on the other hand you must not ignore him. You must be interested, yet not too interested. You must be careful but not obviously so."

"I think we understand, Lady Stevens," said Christabel.

"Call me Harriet, my dear. Everybody does." She turned to me. "I know your mother thinks I am the most unconventional being on earth and perhaps I am, but it does not stop people's being fond of me. Isn't that so, dear child?"

"You are the dearest person in the world," I said with vehement gratitude, "and everybody loves you."

"You see how this Priscilla flatters me!" She was smiling at Christabel now. "Never mind. It shows that she loves me."

"Oh, Harriet, dear, *dear* Harriet, how can we thank you for all you have done!"

"I had to do it. Leigh would have wanted to know the reason why if I had not. I am afraid of that forceful son of mine, Christabel."

"I cannot believe that you would ever be afraid of anything," answered Christabel.

"Well," said Harriet, "I must not linger too long. You will want to change and then we'll dine...without ceremony. Gregory will be back for dinner. He should be in shortly. He is helping with the arrangements to get John out to safety. He can stay in France until this nonsense is over, and Gregory says that will soon be. This time next year he reckons it will be forgotten. Come down when you are changed." She turned to the door and whispered: "Don't forget. Careful where John Frisby is concerned. I must go along now and whisper a word of caution in *his* ear. I thought he looked rather like a lovesick Romeo when his eyes fell on you. Romantic and beautiful to behold but highly undesirable in the circumstances."

She went out, leaving Christabel and me together.

"What a beautiful woman!" cried Christabel. "I never saw anyone like her before."

"No one has," I said. "There never has been anyone like Harriet."

* * *

What a wonderful evening that was! It is one which I shall remember forever. We ate in a small room which was used when the family were alone, as we did at home in the winter parlour. It was lit by candlelight which threw shadows on the tapestries of sylvan scenes which hung on the panelled walls and gave them an air of mystery.

Gregory had returned. He was a tall, quiet man who seemed perpetually surprised at his good fortune in marrying such a dazzling creature as Harriet. He was completely her slave. I was sure that the smuggling of a wanted man to France was something he himself would never have undertaken if it had not been her wish that he should do so. He was the sort of man who would have lived to a set of rules from which he had never diverged until he had met Harriet.

I often wondered why she had married him. But she was fond of him as far as she could be fond of anyone, and

93

it was a singularly successful marriage.

Now he was involved in this matter with her and it was one which could bring trouble to his house, and yet cheerfully he undertook what was expected of him because Harriet was the one who expected it.

He sat at one end of the table, Harriet at the other. She had placed Jocelyn on her right hand, I was on her left, so he and I were opposite and could gaze contentedly at each other throughout the meal.

While the servants were bringing in the dishes and serving us, the conversation was of Court matters. The King was seen everywhere with the Queen, Gregory told us. It was his answer to those who accused her of being concerned in the Popish Plot and of planning the death of her husband.

"Dear good lady," said Gregory, "it was the most foolish accusation to bring against her. What has she ever been but a good and loyal wife to him?"

"And brought him Bombay and Tangiers into the bargain," cried Harriet. "My dear Gregory, I could bring you nothing like that."

"You brought me yourself," he answered, like the gallant lover he was, "and that was all I wanted."

She blew a kiss to him across the table. I wondered if she were faithful to him. I knew that she was the sort of woman who would not hesitate to take a lover if the whim came to her. But she would always do it carefully and in a manner to bring the least unhappiness to Gregory. One would always make excuses for Harriet when one was with her. But there was nothing to make excuses for now.

Gregory talked of the theatres and who was playing what and where.

"We've never had one to replace Nell Gwyn," he said. "There are some who regret the King ever saw her and took her away from the stage."

"I doubt Nelly would agree with that," put in Harriet. "She has a great gift but I'm not sure that it was for acting. It was the way she laughed, the way she danced . . . It was inevitable that some connoisseur of women would see that one day. I liked her. Everybody did . . . except those who were jealous of her. People liked her in spite of her good fortune, for she was never one to give herself airs."

"She is urging the King to set up a royal hospital at Chelsea for aged and disabled soldiers," said Gregory. "They say he is interested in the scheme. She is one to ask for others rather than herself."

"A rare quality," said Christabel.

"And one to be applauded," put in Jocelyn.

"We of the theatre owe a great deal to her," said Harriet with a grimace at Jocelyn.

"Oh, indeed," agreed Jocelyn, "I remember . . ."

Harriet silenced him with a look. "For the benefit of anyone with an ear to the keyhole," she whispered to me, "I have to watch those reminiscences of the theatre in that direction. I couldn't have chosen a worse profession for him. It was a good thing I arranged that he should be a child actor who did not fulfill his early promise."

Gregory was saying: "Nelly and Monmouth are not good friends."

"Of course not," agreed Harriet. "She thinks he has his eye on the throne and she can't bear to contemplate his ever reaching it, for that would mean the death of Charles."

"She has given him a nickname and called him Prince Perkin," went on Gregory.

"Plainly referring to Perkin Warbeck, who claimed a throne to which he had no right," added Harriet.

"He retaliated by asking in public how his father can have such a low-bred creature constantly in his company. Then she reminded him that his mother, Lucy Walter, was no better bred than she was. You see, it's a regular battle between them, though they both stand for the Protestant side."

"I know she calls herself the Protestant Whore. Forgive me, dear ladies." Harriet smiled at Christabel and me. "But the Court is far from pure and that means we have to be a little impure when speaking of it. It's a real turmoil of opinions, and I reckon that when the King does die there'll be trouble once more. So...a health unto His Majesty."

The talk went on but what I wanted to hear were the plans for Jocelyn and that, of course, was something which could not be discussed at table. Nor would Harriet allow me to be alone with Jocelyn. She believed at the moment that all was well and that no one suspected that Jocelyn was anything but what he claimed to be; and no one in the household, apart from herself and Gregory, must know that Jocelyn and I had met before.

"We went over to the Eyot a few weeks ago," she said. "It was a beautifully calm and pleasant day. John knows how to handle a pair of oars with real skill. You could row the ladies over tomorrow, John, if the weather is good."

"I should love to go," I said, my eyes shining as I realized Harriet was making our opportunity for us.

"Then we'll pray for a calm day," said Harriet. "I'll have a basket of delicacies prepared for you. There are some really sheltered places among the ruins and you can imagine that the ghosts of the monks are looking after you. Mind you, I don't think they'll appear by day, do you, Gregory?"

Gregory said he doubted they appeared even at night, but according to popular belief they did.

I was longing to be alone with Jocelyn, to talk to him, to make our plans. I wondered where he would go when he reached France. I could see how dangerous it was for us to be too much together, or to talk of these matters in the house. I had to behave as though I had never met Jocelyn before and that was not easy.

I was too excited to sleep when I retired to my room. I put on a dressing gown and was combing my hair when I received the first of my visitors. It was Christabel.

She had changed back to the Christabel she had been when she first came to Eversleigh. That radiant girl I had briefly glimpsed had retreated behind the mask and there she was with her expressionless eyes and that mobile mouth which was a traitor to her.

She sat down. "May I stay and talk just for a few minutes?" she asked.

"But of course."

"It's been such a day... strange and exciting. I think Harriet is the most unusual woman I have ever seen. She is absolutely beautiful and so attractive. I was thinking while I was watching her that she is everything that I am not. I realize how gauche and plain I am when I see her."

"We all feel that beside Harriet."

"It's unfair that some of us..." That little quirk of the mouth was obvious though she sought to control it. She went on: "Some people are born with everything and others..."

"Harriet wasn't. She was poor, I believe. I think my mother said she was the illegitimate daughter of a strolling player and a village girl. My mother said that one could never be sure whether Harriet was romancing. However, I am sure she did make her way in the world."

"Illegitimate! Harriet!"

"So my mother said. I shall know all about it one day when I read my mother's journal. Harriet would always get what she wanted though."

"She has those exceptional good looks."

"Yes, but it more than looks. It's her personality, her vital self. I think she's wonderful. She can be unscrupulous, but somehow you forgive all that. I suppose anyone would forgive Harriet anything. My mother forgave her long ago. I don't think my father ever did. He's different...."

I paused and Christabel said: "So we are going to the Eyot with Jocelyn tomorrow?"

"Yes," I replied. "There we shall be able to talk freely. He will be going away soon. Harriet is wonderful to have helped us so much."

"How lucky you are, Priscilla. Things turn out well for you, don't they? When I think of what your life must have been like... born into that beautiful household and your mother loving you as she did and old Sally Nullens clucking over you... and then this romantic lover comes along and it all works out beautifully... for you."

"But he has to go to France. His life is in danger."

"It'll be all right . . . because it's *your* life. Some people don't have the luck."

The excitement of seeing Jocelyn, my pleasure in being here, was dampened a little. She had reminded me of Edwin's going away and that my mother had arranged it, as I was sure she had. No, life was not going smoothly for poor Christabel, for Edwin was not the sort to go against convention. He was a young man who wanted to sail through life without conflict. He hated to disappoint people. I think he would rather be disappointed himself.

Christabel said: "I won't stay. You must be tired. Let's hope it is fine tomorrow."

I did not attempt to detain her.

It must have been five minutes later when Harriet came in. She looked strikingly lovely in a loose gown of blue trimmed with yards and yards of ribbon.

"Not asleep?" she said. "I guessed you would not be. Too excited, I'm sure. I am so glad you came before he went. It will give you a little time to be together. Two young people in love! It's your first love affair, eh? Does your mother know?"

"No. I cannot imagine what she would say. She thinks of me as a child."

"Darling Arabella! She was always so easily deceived. She didn't understand me one little bit. But I owe her a great deal. My life took a change when I arrived with a band of strolling players at the château where she was in exile. But you'll know about that one day. I had my first lover when I was about your age . . . a little younger perhaps; I was living in a large house where my mother was housekeeper-companion to an old squire who adored her, and one of his friends took a fancy to me. He had charm and though he seemed ancient to me, I liked him. Not as romantic as your dear Frisby, of course, but he taught me a great deal about love and life and I have always been grateful to him."

"It's like you to be understanding, Harriet," I said. "You

always have been. You see, it happened so suddenly."

"It often does."

"We were in the cave..."

"I know. He told me. He adores you. I know exactly what it is like to be young and in love. You must make the most of it, dear child."

"Harriet, do you think we could possibly *marry?*"

"Why not?"

"My parents would consider me too young."

"Girls marry at your age, don't they? Why shouldn't you?"

"My father..."

She laughed. "Your father is like so many of his kind. I'll swear he was adventuring when he was your age. Men such as he is believe there is one law for their sex and another for ours. It is for us to show them that this is not so. I have always snapped my fingers at men like that."

"I hadn't seriously thought of marriage... not yet, of course. I thought we might be betrothed."

"Beware of betrothals followed by separations. They work only in rare cases. However, we have to think of getting him out of the country. That's the first thing."

"When, Harriet?"

"Before the week is out. Gregory has made most of the arrangements. It might well be within the next few days. So make the most of tomorrow. You'll be able to talk in freedom on the Eyot. There'll be only the gulls and the ghosts for company. Christabel will be there with you as chaperone but send her off to explore the ruins."

"She will go willingly. She is completely involved."

"Tell me about Christabel."

I told her.

"So your father brought her into the house." A slow smile played about her lips. "What did your mother say to that?"

"She thought Christabel very suitable for the post of governess."

"Dear Arabella! Well, I'll tell you something, Priscilla.

Mistress Christabel is more than a little envious of you."

"Envious of me!"

"I sensed it. Where does she come from? That rectory, you say. And her father was the rector."

"She had a very unhappy childhood."

"Perhaps that is it," said Harriet. "Well, my dear Priscilla, it is time you slept. Good night. Bless you."

She kissed me tenderly.

I slept little. I was too excited and I was looking forward to the next day with such intensity that I found it hard to think of anything else.

I was up early the next morning. There was a faint mist in the air and the previous night's wind had dropped. It was arranged that we should set out at midday, and Harriet said that a basket of food was being prepared for us.

I was afraid to be too much in Jocelyn's company for fear I might betray my feelings, and I was longing to be able to throw off this restraint and talk freely.

It must have been soon after eleven o'clock when I went to my room to prepare for the trip. I looked out of the window and saw Christabel in the garden talking to one of the gardeners. They were looking up at the sky and I guessed they were discussing the weather. I had been anxious that nothing should stop our going because I knew that very soon now Jocelyn would be crossing the Channel and then how could I know when I should see him again?

At half-past eleven Christabel came to my room.

"I have such a headache," she said. "I woke up with it. I was hoping it would pass but I'm afraid it only grows worse."

I felt apprehensive. Was she suggesting that she felt too unwell to come? There was soon no doubt of this for she went on: "Priscilla, I wonder whether you would mind very much..."

I said quickly: "Of course if you don't feel well enough to come, you can't."

She was deeply concerned. "That it should be now..."

she began feebly. This was the first time I had ever heard her speak of an ailment.

"I have had headaches in the past," she went on. "Awful, blinding headaches. I thought I had grown out of them. The last one came a year or so ago. I had to lie in a darkened room until it passed."

"Go to your room and lie down now," I said.

"But I know what store you set on this. You want to be able to talk to him, don't you?"

"I shall go in any case."

She looked taken aback. Indeed I was a little amazed myself. A few days ago I should have thought it impossible for me to be alone with a young man. I thought of my conversation with Harriet. Harriet would have gone. She knew how to live. If I did not snatch this chance of being alone with Jocelyn I might regret it all my life.

I had definitely decided to go.

There was no doubt about Jocelyn's pleasure when I saw him. He was carrying the basket of food and together we walked down to the shore.

"I'm speechless," he said, "but you know how I feel."

"I'm sure I feel the same."

"There is so much to talk about."

"Let's wait until we are on the island."

"No one can hear us now."

"I shan't feel we're safe until we are there," I said.

We got into the boat. I could see the island but the horizon was obscured by mist.

Jocelyn rowed steadily and within less than half an hour the bottom of the boat was scraping against the sandy shore of the island. As it loomed up before us I had to admit it looked ghostly in the greyish light.

Jocelyn took my hand as he helped me get out. He clung to it for a long time and then kissed it.

I looked over my shoulder furtively and he laughed at me. "There's no one here but us, Priscilla."

"I'm so fearful for you."

"But we're here...alone."

"I mean I'm afraid of what's going to happen."

He released me to tether the boat. Then we walked up the slope to the ruins of the abbey.

"I shall be going to France shortly," he said. "I shall be safe there. You must come to me, Priscilla."

"They'll never allow me to."

"I've talked it over with Harriet. We could be married. Then you could come with me."

"My parents would never agree."

"I meant we would marry and tell them afterwards."

My happiness was tinged with sorrow. My mother would be so hurt if I acted in such a secretive way. It was hard to explain to Jocelyn how close I had been to her. There was a special relationship between us which was in part due to my father's indifference towards me. I knew how deeply grieved she would be if I took such a step secretly, for it would mean I was shutting her out of my life.

I shook my head.

"I'm going to tell you all the reasons why that would be the best thing for us to do," said Jocelyn. "I've talked it over with Harriet."

"Harriet thinks we should marry!" I cried. "She really means we should do it without my parents' consent!"

"Harriet is a wonderful person. That is the sort of thing she has been doing all her life, and did you ever know a more contented woman?"

"She has been very lucky, I think."

"She has been bold. She has taken what she wanted from life and been content with it."

"One cannot always take what one wants. There are others to be considered."

"There are the two of us."

"And my mother."

"She has probably planned some marriage for you. I admit at the moment she would not want to see an alliance between her family and ours. But this madness is going to pass. Then I can tell you the Frintons are not without some standing."

"Oh, Jocelyn, if only we could!"

"We're going to talk about it. It's wonderful that we have this time together."

"Christabel had a headache. Apparently she has them badly now and then."

"Kind Christabel! Perhaps she knew how much I wanted to be with you alone."

We had come to what was left of the wall. We stepped over it. It was an impressive sight—those great stone walls which had once housed the monks now lay in ruins and yet there was enough of the abbey left for one to be able to reconstruct it in the mind. The remains of stone arches through which the grey sky could now be seen left memories of grandeur; here and there were stone flags, some as they must have been before the Dissolution; grass grew in between others. We found a room which was entered through a massive wooden door which had somehow withstood the winds and salt spray of centuries. It was open to the sky, the roof having long ago disappeared, but otherwise it was complete. The long slips of windows looked out on the sea.

"I was fascinated by it all," said Jocelyn, "when I came over a few days ago for the first time. I thought it would be a good place to hide so I went over it very carefully. You get a certain amount of shelter here in this room, though if there was a strong wind it would whistle through those unglazed windows. I suppose that's how they were long ago. The monks lived Spartan lives though, and must have been unaffected by the cold." He turned to me and put his arms about me. "There," he said, "you feel safe now, don't you? We're here alone...you and I on this island. The thought of that thrills me. It has seemed so long, Priscilla, and at times I wondered if I should ever see you again."

I remembered the ring suddenly and a cold shiver ran through me. I had to confess without delay. I told him what had happened.

"Are you sure it's behind this court cupboard?"

"Absolutely. There is nowhere else it could possibly be. They move it only once a year. It is very heavy."

"When you find it, will you wear it?"

"I will. I was afraid to before. That's really why it was lost. Leigh said that it would arouse comment and it did have your family name inside."

"Oh, yes, it has been handed down through the family for generations. That's why I wanted you to have it."

I felt so relieved that he was not put out about the ring and I told myself that I must set aside my fears and enjoy this day.

"Oh, Jocelyn," I cried, "isn't it wonderful to be here...alone together!"

He kissed me tenderly. "And to know we have a few hours here," he added.

"It is only just past midday," I said. "What shall we do first?"

"Explore the island and talk and talk. Then we'll have our picnic and talk some more, and I shall look at you all the time. I want to watch the way you smile. There's the tiniest dimple at the side of your mouth when you do. I love the way your hair falls back from your face. It's so different from those hideous curls they call 'favourites' at Court. I love your brown eyes, and I think how much more beautiful they are than blue ones."

"You're prejudiced," I said. "I think you only like these things because they're mine."

"There could not be a better reason," he replied.

I think we were both a little afraid of the emotions we aroused in each other. I was happy just to be with him, but I could not forget that he was a hunted man and that this was only a temporary refuge. I was tremendously excited by the thought of getting married. It seemed so impossible and yet why should it be? The circumstances were exceptional. I listened to the melancholy screeching of the gulls. It was as though they were warning me that there was not much time.

If he went to France, I told myself, I could go with him. If we were married I most certainly would. But could I leave my family like that?

I wished that Leigh were there so that I could have talked to him. That struck me as strange, for when I was very young, secretly deep down in my heart I had promised myself that when I grew up I would marry Leigh.

We explored the abbey ruins. We found the refectory and the reading gallery.

"This must have been the chapter house," said Jocelyn, but I did not think he was very interested in the ruins. We were both overwhelmed by the significance of our being alone together. I did not know what I wanted to do except cling to him and keep him safe. I wished the boat could come straight to the Eyot and carry us both to France.

There was a strange atmosphere on that lonely island. It was such a still day. The mist hung in wisps which did not move. They looked strange—grey and ghostly.

"There's the church tower," I pointed out. "I wouldn't be surprised if the bells started to ring and we saw the black figures of the monks coming in to complines."

"Not the right time of day," said Jocelyn promptly, and I remembered then that he was a Catholic and that would be a further reason why my family would be upset. My father was firmly Protestant. Not that he was a truly religious man. Religion with him was a form of politics. I knew that he would not be pleased for me to marry into a prominent Catholic family, and that it should be one which was in danger would infuriate him.

Strangely enough, I thought about him as often as I did about my mother. I pictured myself saying to him: "What does it matter to you? You never cared about me. What difference can it make to you whom I marry?" There was bitterness there. I had cared deeply about his neglect of me. And I still cared.

"Where shall we have our picnic?" asked Jocelyn.

I laughed happily. "I seem to be indulging in more al fresco picnics this winter than I ever did during any summer."

"I shall never forget the picnic by the cave . . . you and I together," he said.

"I don't think I have ever been so frightened as I was when that dog came into the cave."

"Neither so frightened nor so happy," he answered. "I knew you loved me in that moment."

"I knew it, too. It took danger to reveal it to me."

"Priscilla, you are very young."

"I am not too young," I answered.

Then he turned to me and kissed me with a mingling of tenderness and passion which moved me deeply.

"Shall we go into that room? I think they would have called it the scriptorium. There would be shelter there. I'll get the rugs out of the boat and we'll spread them out in the flags there. Then we'll eat in our roofless heaven. What do you think?"

"It sounds wonderful. Let's do it."

We laughed together as I spread the cloth and brought out the cold beef and pies which had been packed for us with the cider to quench our thirst.

"There is ample here," I said. "Enough for three. Of course some of it was for Christabel."

"It was good of her to give us this time to ourselves," said Jocelyn.

"Do you think she did it purposely?"

"I do," he answered.

I was thoughtful. I was not sure.

We leaned against the wall of the scriptorium and I looked up at the grey mist through what was left of the roof.

"What a strange place this is," I commented. "The servants say they see lights here at night."

"Servants will say these things. Are you getting frightened?"

"Not with you here."

"That's what I like to hear. You never need be afraid, Priscilla, as long as I am here to protect you."

"What a comforting thought! Have some more of this pie. It is rather delicious."

"Harriet has a good cook."

"Harriet would always have the best of everything."

"We have every reason to be grateful to her."

I agreed.

Then we talked about the wonder of our meeting and the glorious possibility of our marrying. I had heard of girls making runaway matches. There had been one big scandal when a girl had run away with a man twenty years older than herself. He was a fortune hunter and it had been too late for her family to stop the marriage. The girl had been only fourteen at the time.

I was fourteen and I was proposing to marry not a fortune hunter but a fugitive.

I couldn't help it. I was in love. I was going to live my own life. I was sorry because I had to hurt my mother. As for my father he might rave all he liked ... but perhaps he wouldn't. Perhaps he would shrug his shoulders and say, "Well, it is only Priscilla."

We were so happy talking, making plans—although I wondered whether he felt as I did, that there was something unreal about them and that it was hardly likely that they would ever come to pass.

We would go back to the house. We would tell Harriet that we were going to be married. She would find a priest for us and we would make our vows. Then the boat would come and we would go to France. There would be an outcry against us but in due course the wretched Titus Oates would be seen to be the villain he was and my parents would realize that it was no use continuing to fret about an established fact.

"My mother was exiled in France when she was a girl," I told Jocelyn. "How strange! It will seem like history repeating itself."

"This will be rather different."

"I know. Nothing like this ever happened to anyone before."

We went on talking of what we would do when we were married. We would explore the fair land of France together and then we would come home and live in his family house in Devonshire which I would learn was the most beautiful county in England. Nowhere else was the grass so green; nowhere else was there that red earth which meant fertility. There the cream was richer, the beef more succulent. "You'll be a lady of Devon, my dear Priscilla, when you marry me," he said.

And so we sat there, with his arm about me and I lying close to him while we dreamed an hour or so away.

It was I who noticed that it was growing considerably darker. It could not be much more than three o'clock, and if this were so there should be another hour or so of daylight. Gregory had been warned that we should be back before dark, so we should leave the island by half-past four.

I said: "How dark it has grown. It must be later than we think."

I stood up and was immediately conscious of the cold dampness of the air.

"It's the sea mist," said Jocelyn, and as we went out through the door, it was clear that he was indeed right.

"Why look!" he cried in dismay. "You can only see a few feet ahead."

I stood beside him and he put his arm about me.

"We couldn't even see to find the boat," he went on.

"We'd better try," I answered.

I tripped over a jutting stone and he caught me in time to prevent my fall.

"We shall have to be careful," he warned. "You could have hurt yourself badly then."

"You saved me, Jocelyn."

"I'll always be at your side to save you, I trust."

I took his arm and clung to him. There seemed to be an ominous warning in the air. It was indeed an eerie spot, with the mist enveloping everything and the stark grey ruins around us like the landscape of another world. There was no wind at all—no sound of the sea. It seemed as though Jocelyn and I were alone on another planet.

We looked at each other in dismay as the realization of our position struck us. I saw the moisture on his lashes and brows, and I felt waves of emotion surging over me because it occurred to me then how acute was the danger he was in, and that this time on the island was very precious indeed, for if his enemies captured him they might sever that fair head from his shoulders. Or they would put a rope about it. I had never asked how his father had died. I did not want to know. I wanted to forget it had happened and make Jocelyn forget.

"What are we going to do?" I asked.

"There's nothing we can do. We'd better get back inside the scriptorium. We've got our rugs and at least we shall be sheltered to some extent there. We had no idea how thick the mist was because we were shut in by those four walls."

"Don't you think we ought to try to get to the boat?"

"We might not find it and you saw how a moment ago you slipped. It would be difficult to see which way we were going. No, it's safer to stay here until the mist clears. Even if we found the boat, it would be folly to try to reach the mainland. We might drift right out to sea."

He was right, of course. We went back to our rugs. It was certainly better within the walls of the scriptorium. We sat down on the rugs and he put an arm about me.

"The Fates are with us," he said. "Here we are alone . . . isolated from the rest of the world, shut off by a blanket of mist. Don't you find that an exciting prospect, Priscilla?"

"Of course, but I am wondering what will happen."

"They know where we are, and they'll know what has happened. They won't be worried about us. They know we'll have the good sense to stay here until the mist lifts."

"That could be a very long time, Jocelyn."

"Hardly likely. The wind will rise soon and carry it away."

"I wonder what the time is?"

"It's afternoon."

"How long were we talking?"

"Does it matter?"

We sat close, leaning against one of the walls, and we talked again of our marriage which should take place without delay when we returned to the mainland. Everything seemed credible there in that quiet atmosphere of strange, whirling mist.

We had no idea what the time was but we realized that

it was getting late because it was growing darker and we could not even see the mist. But we were aware of it—damp and clinging. It was growing colder; Jocelyn held me tightly against him.

He said: "Suppose we spent the rest of our lives here? It doesn't seem such a bad prospect."

"How could we?"

"We could build a house and grow our own food. We could live the simple life like Adam and Eve."

"It's hardly the garden of Eden."

"It would be paradise for me while you were there."

It was lovers' talk. There was no sense in it; yet it soothed and comforted, and there was something inevitable about the mist. We were held here by the forces of nature and we could not be blamed for taking these hours together.

I think that in our hearts there was a sort of desperation, a looming fear that life was not going to be as easy as we had deluded ourselves into believing it would be.

We ate the remains of the picnic; it was dark by now and the mist was more dense. There was a deep silence all around us. It was strange to be so near the sea and not to hear even a murmur.

It was night now and growing colder.

Jocelyn spread out one rug and we lay on it. The other he wrapped round us. He took me into his arms and we lay close together.

I suppose what happened was inevitable. We were young, and there was passion in our blood.

"We shall be together for the rest of our lives," said Jocelyn. "We are married, you and I, sweet Priscilla. Is a ceremony so important? There will be one when we get back. Immediately we shall be married. We shall tell Harriet and she will help us. You will come to France with me."

I believed it fervently, because I wanted to.

I did resist a little . . . at first. It was the thought of my mother. I wished I could forget her. But when I thought of my father, I felt defiant. What had he ever cared for me!

Why should I think of him now? But I did think of him with a kind of exultation. I should be married. He would no longer be burdened with a useless girl.

Jocelyn was kissing me fervently.

"Priscilla, sweet Priscilla," he was saying, "shall I tell you what bliss is? It's a mist-shrouded island when I am alone with you."

And there on that island we were lovers in truth.

I was a little bewildered, exalted and exultant. I felt as though I had left all that I had been before behind me. I was no longer Carleton Eversleigh's daughter. I was Jocelyn Frinton's wife.

I awoke to hazy sunshine. It was morning. My limbs were stiff with cold. Jocelyn was still sleeping and I was overcome by tenderness as I watched him. He looked so young, so defenceless without his periwig. I thought inconsequently: I know why men wear them. It gives them importance. Without his Jocelyn looked like a beautiful boy.

I leaned over and kissed him.

He caught me in his arms. "My Priscilla," he murmured and drew me down beside him.

I said: "The morning has come. The mist has almost cleared."

He sat up. "It's over then..." He looked at me wonderingly. "Oh, my love," he went on, "you and I together for the rest of our lives."

"It has to be a long lifetime," I said. "Oh, Jocelyn, I'm frightened."

"Don't be. I'm determined now...more than I ever was. There are two of us now, my darling. You don't know what a difference that makes."

"I do. Because I am one of the two."

He kissed me.

"We must be going," I said.

"Just a little while yet."

"Look at the sun breaking through. They'll be expecting us."

"Just a few more minutes," he pleaded. He held me against him. "My bride," he went on, "tell me you regret nothing."

"I regret nothing."

"We'll tell Harriet. She'll help us. She must now."

"She would in any case. I know what she'll say. Be bold. Be adventurous. Take what you want and if it doesn't work out as you had hoped don't complain. I think that's her motto."

"It's served her well. Darling, don't let's go yet. Let us stay awhile . . ."

I lay down beside him and his arms were tight about me. There was a desperate passion between us as though the daylight were telling us that the dreams that came in the mist might disappear under the searching light of reality.

I raised myself. "We *must* go," I said. "It may be they will be looking for us. They'll know we have not been back all night."

"Perhaps they won't. Harriet will see that they won't."

I shook my head. "Come, Jocelyn. We must not delay."

We took the rugs and basket back to the boat. I think we were almost hoping that it would be gone so that we would have an excuse to continue with our island idyll. But it was there just as we had left it. He unmoored it and in a short while we were rowing to the mainland.

He helped me out and tied up the boat. We started to walk towards the house.

We had not gone far when we saw Christabel running towards us. Her eyes were as expressionless as ever, but her mouth showed the stress of great emotion.

"Come in at once," she said. "There has been trouble. Where have you been?"

"My dear Christabel, surely you were aware of the mist?"

"They said you shouldn't have gone. You have to leave at once. Harriet and Gregory are quite disturbed. The boat is in . . . waiting for you. It was there early this morning.

112

Why didn't you come back sooner? The mist had cleared at dawn. They're very anxious."

We started to run towards the house.

As we entered, Gregory came out to meet us.

"Thank God you're here," he said. "They're on the trail. I've been warned. You have to get going without delay. They could be here at any minute."

Harriet came into the hall, looking like the heroine in a play of adventure.

"My dear boy," she cried dramatically, "you must go at once. You should have left at dawn. There isn't a moment to lose. Go at once. That's so, eh, Gregory?"

Jocelyn said: "I'll get my things together. I'll change quickly."

"Your things are ready," replied Harriet. "I have them waiting. You can change in France."

Gregory said: "You must get out of the house quickly or we shall all be involved. Harriet's right. There's not a moment to lose. A few of your things are here in a bag. Get down to the shore as fast as you can. You know Lime Cove. That's where the boat is. Get in and get off as fast as you can."

I said: "I must go . . ."

"You must come with me, my child," replied Harriet. "You are cold right through. The mist is dangerous and you have been out in it all night. Go now, dear boy, and God be with you."

That was how it happened. He had to go straight down to the cove and he had to go alone.

There at the cove his enemies were waiting for him. They seized him as he was making his way to the boat.

One of the servants told us that he had been seen, hands tied, riding on a horse in the midst of a company of soldiers who were taking him back to London.

The weeks which followed were the most wretchedly tragic in my life up to that time, for it soon became clear that I should never be Jocelyn's wife. His trial was brief;

his sentence was carried out almost immediately. His guilt was clear, they said. Why else should he have run away? I had nightmares. I dreamed I was there at the scaffold when he laid his fair head on the block. In my dreams I saw the executioner's bloody hands as he held up that beloved head now severed from the body which I had loved.

I was stunned. There could never have been such misery as I was suffering. Jocelyn ... dead! Never to see him again! Never to feel his arms about me!

How I wished I had been beside him. I wished they had taken me with him. I wished that I had died beside him, for there seemed no point in living on without him.

How quickly everything could change! I had been so happy. I had dreamed of our going to France together, living there so blissfully happy, and coming back later ... husband and wife.

I should never know peace again. I had lost my dear one. My life was finished. There could never be any happiness for me again.

I could not eat. I could sleep only fitfully and then I was haunted by nightmares. In these I was at the scaffold. I saw the executioner with that beautiful, well-loved head in his hands—a head without a body. The voice echoed through my dreams: "Behold the head of a traitor."

He was no traitor. He was just a good, kind man ... the man I loved.

I thought: My life is finished. I shall never be happy again.

Harriet was wonderful to me. She looked after me through those weeks. She would not allow me to return home.

Gradually I learned what had happened and it did not relieve my misery to know that I was responsible for his capture.

It was Harriet who broke it to me. "You'll have to know how they were led to him," she said. "Now you mustn't blame yourself in any way. You gave him the greatest happiness any one person can give another. I know that. You loved him and he loved you. So you must not fret. You will grow out of this. One does. You remember the ring he gave you... plighting your troth?"

"The ring!" I cried. "Yes, the ring. It will be there beneath the court cupboard. I shall treasure it forever."

"You will never see it again, my child."

"What do you mean, Harriet?"

"It was not behind the cupboard."

"Then it was found! But it couldn't have been. I searched everywhere."

"Your mother has told me what happened. She took a dress from the cupboard and gave it to Chastity to lengthen or alter in some way. Chastity was to take it home with her. She went into the kitchen to have a word with her mother. The dress was over her arm, I imagine. There was a ring caught up in the lace."

I felt sick with misery. Why had I not examined the dress! Why had I been so foolish, so careless as to have deluded myself into thinking the ring had fallen behind the cupboard!

"Jasper was in the kitchen at the time," went on Harriet.

"Oh, no, no no!" I cried.

"Alas, yes. He seized the ring. He thinks all such baubles sinful. He examined it, saw the crest and the name inside. Then it was remembered that food had disappeared from the pantry... and conclusions were drawn. He told no one in the house what he intended to do. He took the ring to London and went to see Titus Oates."

"I hate Jasper," I cried. "I hate his black, bigoted soul."

"He said he was doing his duty. Of course you can guess what happened. You were under suspicion immediately. Your parents did not know about it then because Jasper had acted without telling anyone. Oates's men wanted to know where you had gone and that led them here. They have been asking questions in the neighbourhood. They discovered that a young actor calling himself John Frisby was here. The description fitted Jocelyn."

"Did they come here, Harriet?"

"They did not because I had friends who did not wish to involve me. So they took him after he had left, and there

115

have been no inquiries about our involvement. I daresay your father had something to do with it, too. You are only a child so they would not be harsh with you ... particularly when you have a father who is so friendly with the King. So, dear Priscilla, this tragedy has struck you. You have lost your first lover but you must learn that life goes on. You are so young. You do not yet really know what it means to love."

"I do, Harriet. Oh, I do."

She took my hands and looked at me searchingly. "My poor child," was all she said. Then she put her arms about me gently, as though I were a baby.

"You know you have me always, Priscilla," she said.

"Yes, I know it."

"Now you must not fret."

"I shall never forget that it was my carelessness which brought them to him."

"He should never have given you the ring in the first place. He brought it on himself. It was too obvious a form of identification. But it is done. Dear Priscilla, in time you will have to go home. They will expect it."

"I know, Harriet. I wish I could stay with you."

"You must come back soon."

"At home ... they know ..."

"They know, of course, that he gave you the ring."

"My father will be very angry."

"He has had his adventures. He has done what he wanted to. And so have you. As for helping the fugitive, you were not the only one, were you? Leigh, Edwin, myself ... we were all involved."

"Oh, Harriet, you are so good!"

She laughed. "You might find a number of people to disagree with you on that point. A *good* woman is a compliment rarely applied to me. But I know how to live, how to enjoy life. I don't want trouble for myself, nor for others. Perhaps that is rather a good way of living—so I may be good after all."

I clung to her, for into my misery had crept a new

116

emotion: a dread of going home. But I realized I had to face it.

I would soon be fifteen years old and I had already had a lover. Was that so unusual? He would have been my husband had he lived.

I shall never marry now, I thought. I have been married all but ceremonially to the one I loved and whom I shall love forever.

Christabel was with me a great deal. She seemed to have grown more fond of me in my misfortune. Perhaps those hard days at the rectory and Edwin's lack of purpose seemed less tragic now that she could compare her lot with mine.

On the day before we were due to leave for Eversleigh, I went down to the gardens and walked round. There was a faint mist in the air which reminded me of that other day.

One of the gardeners was digging, and as I approached he leaned on his spade and looked in my direction.

"Good day to you, Mistress Priscilla," he said.

I returned his greeting.

"You be leaving us I hear, mistress."

"Yes," I said.

"'Twere a sad matter," he went on. "There's many of us here as would like to see that Titus Oates get a taste of his own medicine, that we would. Oh, yes, 'twere a terrible business. If only the mist hadn't come up so bad you'd a been back that day and your gentleman would have been over the seas afore they got here. Why did you go out, mistress, when I warned you?"

"Warned me? Warned me of what?"

"I've lived in these parts all my life and that's nigh on fifty years. I can tell what the weather's going to be . . . and never wrong . . . well once or twice maybe. I said there'll be heavy mist long before nightfall. Unless the wind comes up sudden . . . which it can do, winds being something you can't count on. Given no wind, though, that mist will be in from the sea and Eyot will be wrapped up in it. 'Don't you go out today, mistress,' I said."

"You didn't tell me. I didn't see you on that day."

"No. 'Twas the other one. She were going, weren't she? There was to be the three. Mary said she'd make a hamper for three."

So he had told Christabel!

"Yes, I see that we shouldn't have gone," I said. "Good day to you, Jem."

"Good day to you, mistress. And I'll look to see you again in happier times."

I went into the house. I wondered why Christabel had not told me that she had been warned about the mist. How very strange.

Of course she had a raging headache. Perhaps it had made her forget. Hardly that, though, when the headache was the reason why she had decided not to come. Surely the thought of our going must have reminded her.

It seemed strange, so I sought her out at once and asked her.

She flushed painfully and her mouth moved with emotion.

"I have suffered such remorse," she said. "I did see Jem and he did mention the mist. My head was throbbing. I only remembered it when you didn't come back. I feel responsible . . ."

"It's no use worrying now," I said. "It's over and done. He is dead. He is lost to me forever."

"But if you had not gone to the island he would have got away in time."

"Yes. If I had not lost the ring . . . If I had not taken it in the first place . . . So many ifs, Christabel. But what is the use of all this remorse? It's over. There is no going back. I have lost him forever."

My father was away when I returned to Eversleigh Court. I think my mother was relieved. She was anxious and sympathetic, I knew, but at the same time deeply shocked that I could have become so involved in such a dangerous situation without her knowledge.

The very first day she sought an opportunity to be alone with me and she wanted to hear everything that had happened. I was so distressed that I found it difficult to talk at first.

I could only keep saying: "I loved him. I loved him. And now they have killed him."

She took me into her embrace as she used to when I was very young, but I did not feel comforted, only impatient. It was almost as though she thought it was a matter of "kiss and make better" as it had been when I had fallen and scratched myself.

"Dearest Cilla," she murmured, "you are young... so young."

I wanted to shake myself free of her. I wanted to say: I am not young. I am grown up. Some people are, you know, at fifteen—and I am nearly that. I have loved. I have lived. And I am not a child anymore.

She went on talking. "It seemed very romantic. He was very good-looking, I believe. And the way he came here.... He had no right to come."

"He was looking for Edwin. Edwin was his friend."

"Edwin should not have tried to hide him."

"What should he have done? Given him up to that brute Titus Oates?"

She was silent, stroking my hair.

"You know your father is most put out. You know his feelings."

"He has never shown me much of his feelings," I said. "All he showed me was indifference."

"My dear child..."

I cried: "It's no use talking to you. You don't understand. Jocelyn came here. We helped him. We're not ashamed of it. We'd do it again... all of us. He and I fell in love. We planned to marry."

"Oh, my darling! But it's all over now. We must try to make you forget."

"Do you think I shall ever forget!"

"Yes, my dearest, you will. I know how it feels now."

119

"You do not know and I wish you would stop talking about it. I have nothing to say to you. You don't understand in the least. Harriet..."

"Harriet, of course, understood perfectly."

"Harriet was wonderful to me."

"And kept him there and sent for you! It's what one would expect of Harriet. She is completely without thought for others."

"I don't agree."

"Oh, she fascinates you as she does everyone else. I know that."

"Harriet has been kind to me. I shall never forget what she has done for me. Please, Mother, leave me alone. I want to be by myself."

The reproachful look she gave me touched me deeply and I threw myself into her arms. She did not say anything. She just held me and it was as it had always been between us.

Carl was very upset by what had happened. It was his first experience of real grief and I loved him for it. He just looked at me blankly and said: "They can't have done that to Jocelyn!"

I turned away and he came and took my hand and pressed it.

"I wish I'd been there," he said. "I wouldn't have let it happen. You ought to have told me he was with Aunt Harriet."

"There was nothing you could have done, Carl, nothing."

"I *hate* Titus Oates."

"So do countless others."

Oddly enough Carl comforted me more than my mother had been able to.

My father returned and he was very cool towards me. He hardly addressed me at all during the first evening. During the next day I went into the gardens and he followed me there.

"A nice mess you got yourself into," he said.

I looked at him defiantly. "In what way?" I asked.

"Don't be silly. You know what I'm talking about. This romantic adventure of yours. Fools... the whole lot of you. You particularly. Taking an incriminating ring and then leaving it for others to find."

"You wouldn't understand," I retorted.

"One would have to be half-witted not to. A pretty young man comes along and you think it would be great fun to hide him and feed him and accept a ring from him with his crest and name on it. And he is suspected of taking part in a plot against the King's life."

"You know very well that there was no plot. You know it was fabricated by this friend of yours... this Titus Oates."

He seized me by the wrist and I cried out in pain. His grip was like iron.

"He is no friend of mine," he said. "I despise the man. But I have the sense not to entertain those against whom he brings accusations. Who can say who will be the next? And, by God, we might have been! You could have put the whole family into danger. It has not been easy extricating you, I can tell you. All this trouble because of a silly girl's prank."

"It was no prank." I jerked myself free. "And I would do it again."

"I shall have something to say to the others when I see them. If they want to risk their lives that's their own affair, but they should not have involved a foolish girl who could bring trouble tumbling about our ears with great risk to our necks, I might tell you."

"So you blame me for everything?"

"If you had taken his ring you should at least have kept it hidden."

"It was an accident."

He laughed. "I'm sure it was. Now a word in your ear. If you attempt any more of these follies don't rely on me to get you out of them."

"I'm surprised that you bothered."

"It was necessary to save us all."

I turned away and ran into the house. I shut myself in

121

my room. I had never felt so unhappy in all my life. If only he had given me one word of tenderness. If only he had been concerned for *me!* But he had made me feel that had I alone been involved he would not have taken the trouble to save me.

He had looked at me with a certain contempt and I wondered why a man such as he was who was fond of women—some said too fond—should find nothing to care about in his own daughter. I wondered what he would say if he knew the extent to which I had been involved with Jocelyn. He would be horrified, I was sure. Yet according to what I had gathered he had had adventures at a very early age. What was natural for him and those who shared his pleasures was shocking in his daughter. This was strange, for he was a logical man in other matters.

A few days passed, and when the possibility that I might be going to have a child came to me I was jerked out of my misery momentarily. I had not thought of this. I had been so wrapped up in my grief. Now I was faced with a problem. If it were to be so, what should I do?

I could not marry because the father of my child was dead. I did not want to tell my mother. I could not bear to think what my father's reaction would be. If Leigh or Edwin were here I might confide in them. They would help me, both of them. But they were far away and I did not even know where.

My emotions were in turmoil. I did not know whether I was glad or not that this had happened. I was filled at one moment with the wonder of it and the next with a fearful foreboding.

A child—the result of that night we had spent on the mist-shrouded island! Our wedding night, Jocelyn had called it. And our marriage was to have taken place as soon as we returned to the mainland.

Oddly enough a change had settled on me. I was more serene, which seemed strange in view of the enormity of the problem which was arising before me. It was almost as though Jocelyn were speaking to me from beyond the grave in which they had laid his poor mutilated body.

Then I was certain. It *was* to be.

I tried to work out what I must do. I needed help, but I did not want my mother to know. As to my father—I shivered at the thought. I could not talk to Christabel. Since our return I had avoided her. I kept wondering why she had not told me that it would be dangerous to go to the island and I could not completely convince myself that she had forgotten. She had played a big part in the tragedy and I felt unsure of everyone, including myself.

There was, of course, Harriet. I wrote to her, carefully disguising what was wrong but wondering whether a woman of her worldliness might guess. I had to see her, I said. I wanted to talk to her, as I could not talk to anyone else. Would she invite me please?

Her response was immediate.

My mother came to my room holding a letter in her hand. "It's from Harriet," she said. "She wants you to go over for a visit. She thinks it would be good for you. Would you like to go?"

"Oh, yes," I said fervently.

"Perhaps it would be a good idea."

"I should like to get away for a while."

She looked at me sadly, and I went on angrily: "I think my father would be delighted not to have to see me."

"Oh, Priscilla, you must not say that."

"But it's true."

"It is not true."

"It is. Why do we have to pretend? He has never wanted me. I was of the wrong sex. He wanted a boy who would be just like himself. I am expected to go through my life apologizing for not being a boy."

"You are overwrought, my dearest."

"Yes, I should like to go away," I said firmly.

I could see how hurt she was and I was sorry.

She put her arm about me and I was stiff and unyielding. She sighed and said: "Christabel should go with you."

I did not protest although I would rather have gone alone.

123

At Eyot Abbas, Harriet greeted me warmly.

"I was afraid you would not want to come here again," she said. "I feared it might bring it all back too clearly."

"I had to come," I told her. "And I want to remember...I want to remember every minute."

"Of course you do."

Harriet greeted Christabel with warmth but I did not think she greatly liked her. Harriet was a superb actress though, and one could never be sure.

I knew it would not be long before we were alone together and Harriet soon contrived that. I had been in my room only five minutes when she arrived. She had given Christabel a room on the next floor and I guessed there had been a purpose in this. Harriet anticipated many an uninterrupted talk.

She came in conspiratorially, her lovely eyes alight with speculation.

"Tell me, my dear, just tell me."

"I am going to have a child," I said.

"Yes. I thought that was it. Well, Priscilla, we must see what can be done. There are people who can be of assistance."

"You mean get rid of it. I don't want that, Harriet. I should hate it."

"I thought so. Well, what do you propose? What will your parents say?"

"They'll be horrified. My father will be quite contemptuous."

"He would. Having himself played the masculine role in dramas of this nature, he would be deeply horrified at his daughter's taking the feminine one. Such men always are. I want to snap my fingers at them."

"You don't like him, Harriet, I know. He is one of the few people I have heard you speak quite vehemently against."

"No, I don't like him. To be perfectly honest I think it's because he never liked me."

"All men like you, Harriet."

"Most of them," she agreed. "He hardly looked at me. He was all for your mother. She was the one he wanted."

"I know he has a very special feeling for her. I wish they were more gentle with each other."

"He's not the kind. But what are we doing talking of him? We have our problem."

It was typical of Harriet that she should call it "our problem." That was the charm of her. She was not in the least shocked and she was going to summon all her ingenuity to help me.

I felt the tears come to my eyes and she, seeing them, patted my hand and said practically: "We've got to get down to serious planning. You're sure, are you?"

"Yes."

"And you are going to keep the child?"

"Oh, yes."

"Have you thought what this will mean? The child will always be there in your life. You see, this matter does not now end with Jocelyn's death. He will always be there through this child. Now, you have your own life before you. It has scarcely begun. You should ask yourself whether you want this child to be there for the rest of your life. It is possible to get rid of it. I know how that can be done, but it will have to be now. It is dangerous later. In fact it could be dangerous now. I hope you won't want to do it, Priscilla. But if you decide..."

"I couldn't. I want the child. It has already made a difference to me. I no longer feel as though I died with him. I now feel there is something for me in the future."

"Very well, that's settled. But what are we going to do? Are we going to tell your parents?"

"I don't want to. I'd rather go away."

"Does anyone else know this? Does Christabel?"

"No. No one."

"So at the moment it is our secret...yours and mine." I nodded.

"You could go to your mother and tell her. She would consult your father. They might decide on two alternatives: to send you away where you could have your child in secret and then get it adopted, or marry you off to some willing young man who will take you for a price and it will be pretended that your child was born prematurely. No one will believe it, of course, but it helps the conventions. Do either of these prospects appeal to you?"

"I wouldn't agree to either."

She smiled at me. "You are a very determined young woman, Priscilla. I understand your feelings. Now when I had Leigh I had no such fine feelings. You see how much easier it is for a woman like me. I'm bold and I snap my fingers in the face of convention and everyone thinks I am rather a wicked woman. But I get along very well. I have been thinking about you so much. I shall never forget your dear stricken face when you heard the news. I knew what had happened on the island. It is often easy to see in a young girl's face when she has taken a lover. I saw it in yours and I was glad for you. He was a charming boy and young love is beautiful. Well, now it is over and I do not regret it. You have had a taste of life and found it first sweet, then bitter. But that is life, my dear. I must stop philosophizing and we must plan."

"You are going to help me, Harriet, I know."

"Of course I am going to help you. You have always been dear to me. I am very fond of your mother. I have treated her badly at times. It was wicked of me, was it not, to go off with a lover and leave little Leigh—my own child—for her to look after? I was trapped, though. Her parents knew me for the adventuress I was and so did the Eversleighs. They didn't know then that Leigh was an Eversleigh. They had pinned that indiscretion on some poor, defenceless young man. Oh, it is so complicated and when you read about it you will understand, perhaps. You may not like me much then. I come out in a very bad light."

"I shall always love you whatever the lighting is like."

"Bless you, child. But let us be serious and clever. We have to be, you know, for this is a mighty problem."

"Harriet, what can I do?"

"An idea came to me when I received your letter

because, as I said, I guessed at once what your dilemma was. Would you be prepared to deceive your mother?"

"I don't understand, Harriet."

"If your mother knows, so will your father, and I gather you don't want him to."

"I dread that more than anything."

"You are very close to him in a way, Priscilla."

"I! Close to him! He doesn't care anything for me."

"Perhaps that's why you care so much about him. You want him to love you. You always did. You admire him. Oh, yes, you do. He is the sort of man women desire. Strong, ruthless, virile ... completely a man, if you know what I mean. I can assure you that my quiet and loving Gregory is easier to live with. I myself have felt the attraction your father exerts over women. I am not indifferent to him. Oh, understand me, I have no designs on him. I would like to score over him, to snap my fingers at him. I like the fact that his daughter should come to *me* for help and that I should know what is happening while he remains in ignorance of it. I am talking a lot of nonsense."

"No. You're talking sense. I understand, and I think you realize my relationship with him better than anyone else ever has ... more than I do myself. I could not bear him to know what has happened. He is the sort of man who would shrug his shoulders if he knew we had been lovers, but rant and rage against me if I were to have a child. I could not bear him to know."

"Then my plan might appeal to you."

"Harriet, tell me."

"It may not work. It is rather wild. It will need a great deal of careful planning ... a certain intrigue."

"And you love intrigue."

"Working it out, yes. The carrying it out is going to make life very interesting in the next year."

"You're keeping me in suspense."

"It is very simple. *I* will be the mother of the child, not you."

"How could that possibly be!"

"I am not sure yet. I have to work it out. Gregory would be in the secret of course. It would be impossible if he were not. He will be the father."

"Harriet, what are you saying!"

"Now don't dismiss it. Don't be one of those people who see defeat everywhere before they have explored the possibility of success. You will have to spend a lot of time with me. Why not? I will tell them that you are in need of a change of scene. You are not well. You are fading away. I will take you away with me for a few months. Then we will go to France . . . to Italy . . . Benjie is going away to school. That helps. I shall miss him. So you and I will travel. It is just what we both need. When we have left I will write to your mother and tell her that Gregory and I are in a state of bliss because we are going to have a child. I, who had thought my childbearing days were over! You must be my companion during those waiting months. In due course my/your child will be born and we shall return to England."

"Harriet! What an idea!"

"I can see nothing wrong with it, if we play our cards well. And we shall, never fear. I have played a great many parts and I shall play this one with my usual skill. You will do well, too."

"And when we return to England?"

"The child will live at Eyot Abbas and you will be devoted to it. You will love it as your own and I shall laugh with your mother and tell her that I believe my little Gregory or Harriet, whichever it is, has given you a new interest in life. You will come and stay with me more and more and no one need ever know the truth unles you wish them to."

I went to her and hugged her. "Oh, Harriet, you think of the most fantastic ideas!"

"They work—and so will this. The most difficult part, I believe, is now. You'll have to go back to Eversleigh. Then we'll start planning. I don't want you there too long. You have a household of prying servants. No one must guess your condition, no one. No one knows as yet. Let us keep it that way. Don't tell anyone."

"I was wondering about Christabel. If I come to you..."

"Christabel should not come. The fewer people who are in a secret the safer it is. Christabel will have to go."

"She comes from a wretched home. She is always afraid that she will be sent back there."

"I shall have to think about her. I am a little unsure of her. The way in which she came into the house is a little mysterious and she is not treated like a governess, is she? At the moment not a word to her. This is a secret ... yours and mine. I shall start working on what we must do. In the meantime you will have to be on your guard. The servants must not guess. You have that hell-raising Jasper and his ninny of a wife and their chaste daughter. You must take special care. I shall not write anything of this to you. It is never safe to put things on paper. I shall in due course ask you to come and visit me. And I will prepare the way."

Her eyes sparkled with anticipation.

"I feel so much better," I said. "It is wonderful to know that you are here."

"We'll do it; I am so excited. I feel pregnant already. I am so looking forward to this child. And dearest Priscilla, you and I will play this to perfection. Remember this: you are not alone."

I was caught up in the excitement of it. It was the best thing that had happened to me since Jocelyn's death. I felt that he was watching over me and that he had given me this to help me over my sorrow.

Harriet and I talked constantly about our plan during that visit. Then I returned to Eversleigh.

~Intrigue in Venice~

My mother noticed the difference in me on my return and I think she was a little hurt that Harriet could comfort me in a way which was beyond her powers. She was glad, though, to find me roused a little from my wretchedness. She did not understand as Harriet did. She could only see me as a child.

It was only a few days later when she came to my room with a letter she had received from Harriet.

"Harriet is going away," she said. "Some friend of hers has offered her a palazzo in Venice. She may be away several months."

I lowered my eyes. I knew what was coming.

"She is very fond of you, Priscilla. She always was. She is suggesting that she take you with her."

"Take me with her!" My voice sounded flat. It was difficult to play my part before my mother.

"Listen to what she says:

I must have mentioned the Carpori family to you.

I met them years ago during my stage career. The Contessa was always a friend of mine. Now she has offered me their palazzo in Venice. I did visit it once and it is quite a pleasant spot. The fact is I think they would like me to inhabit the place while they are away.

Gregory thinks it would be a good idea. He will spend part of the time with me. It will be rather a quiet life, I fancy. Now I am going to ask a great favour of you. Could you spare me our dear Priscilla? Perhaps it is selfish of me to ask but I really do think a change is what she needs just now. She has suffered a great shock so recently and I myself was quite worried about her when she was here a short while ago. This unfortunate matter has hit her hard, I fear. I believe this jaunt might be exactly what she needs. Could you put it to her? Ask her what she feels about it. Of course, she may hate the idea—in which case, please don't press it. I should like the choice to be entirely hers. . . .

She stopped reading and looked at me. I stammered: "Venice! A palazzo!"

My mother was wrinkling her brows. I knew that she wanted the best for me and would be wondering whether Harriet was right and this trip would help me to recover from the blow which she realized had shaken me severely.

"For . . . how long?" I asked.

My mother looked back at the letter. "She doesn't say, but I daresay it would be for several months. I doubt she would plan to go so far for a short stay. And she says Gregory will be coming back to England and she will be alone for a while. What do you think about it, Priscilla?"

I was silent for a while. I must not seem too eager.

I said slowly: "I . . . don't know. It's so . . ."

"Unexpected," finished my mother. "But one can always rely on Harriet to do the unexpected."

After a brief silence I said: "I think I *should* like to get away."

She nodded. "And you are very fond of Harriet and she of you . . . as fond as she is able to be of anyone apart from herself."

I had to defend her. "She has always been good to me. Gregory and Benjie adore her."

"She has special gifts. So you really feel you would like to go?"

"Yes, I would. I should love to see Venice. I believe it's very beautiful."

"It is said to be."

"Mother . . . what about Christabel?"

She frowned slightly. "If you were going to be away you would still have to continue with your lessons."

"I should like to go alone," I said.

"I will see what your father says," she answered.

I felt my lips curl bitterly. "Oh, he will not care what I do. I dare swear he'll be glad to be rid of me."

"You don't understand him, Priscilla."

"I do. I understand perfectly."

She could see I was becoming emotional so she just shook her head, kissed me and left me.

My father agreed that I should go to Venice with Harriet. There was one stipulation. Christabel should come with me. I remarked bitterly that he seemed more concerned for Christabel's welfare than he was for mine.

"Nonsense," retorted my mother. "He wants her to go for your benefit."

I did not argue the matter. I thought how fortunate I was to have Harriet, and sometimes I would break into a cold sweat wondering what I should have done if she had not been at hand to suggest her preposterous plan. But because she was Harriet it did not seem impossible to carry it out, as it would have done if anyone else had thought of it.

It was now the end of February and Harriet wrote constantly of what she called "plans." I was sure she enjoyed writing these letters which she couched in innuendo—references which I could understand and no

133

one else could. Intrigue was the breath of life to her.

We were going to leave at the end of March.

"A very appropriate time," she wrote, meaning that the existence of my baby, conceived in mid-January, could without a great deal of subterfuge be kept secret until that time. "It will be springtime, the time of growth when the flowers and the trees begin to blossom. We shall be there through the summer, which I believe is delightful, and the sunshine more reliable than it is here."

"I believe," said my mother, "that you really are getting excited about this trip."

"Venice is said to be so beautiful and I long to see it."

She was pleased. I knew she was thinking that I was getting over what she thought of as "that unfortunate episode." Christabel, too, was excited. They seemed to have forgotten—though I did not—that she had an unfortunate episode of her own to get over.

I was concerned about her, though. Sooner or later she would have to be in on the secret. I had told her nothing yet. I wanted to wait until I had consulted Harriet.

There was news from Court. Titus Oates was losing his importance. People were growing less afraid of criticizing him. He had made a big mistake in talking so disparagingly about the Duke of York and in such a way that it appeared he was preparing to make him his next victim.

"He is a fool," said my father, "if he thinks the King would see the end of his own brother. Oates should have realized what dangerous grounds he was on when he tried to attack the Queen. The King showed it clearly. It seems to me the man is riding for a fall."

I hoped so with all my heart, and then I felt bitterly angry because it was too late to save Jocelyn and my happiness.

There was comfort, though, in thinking that this wicked man who had caused such misery might now be seeing the end of that power which had been bestowed on him in such a ridiculous manner. It seemed incredible that Parliament could have made the Duke of Monmouth responsible for his safety, the Lord Chamberlain for his lodging and the Lord Treasurer for his food and such necessities. I had heard that he had three servants in constant attendance and two or three gentlemen—after the manner of royalty—to wait on him and wrangle over the honour of holding the basin for him to wash.

But as such men will do, he had gone a little too far. Voices were being raised against him. My father brought home a pamphlet which had been written by Sir Robert L'Estrange that demanded to know how much longer the country was going to allow Titus Oates to drink the tears of widows and orphans.

"He has made many enemies, that man," said my father. "They are waiting to rise against him."

I fervently hoped they would rise, and this man who had brought misery to so many would be called upon to answer for his sins.

But that would not bring Jocelyn back.

At the middle of March we were ready to leave for Harriet's. It had been decided that I should stay with her for two weeks before leaving for Italy.

I said good-bye to my mother who was very sad at my leaving. I think she realized how eager I was to be gone and she construed that as meaning that I was happier with Harriet than with her. I almost felt like telling her the real reason why I had to go away but stopped myself in time.

The countryside was beautiful on the day we set out. It was a sparkling morning, though still cold. Spring was in the air and a certain exultation in my heart. I was very much aware of the growing life within me, and although the way ahead was fraught with difficulties, I could not regret what had happened.

Only my child could compensate me for what I had lost, and I longed for its birth.

I looked at Christabel beside me. She was happier than she had been since she had realized that Edwin was not going to defy his parents and offer her marriage. She, too, was getting over her sorrow.

Harriet received us with that exuberant welcome she bestowed on all her guests, but which was heartening all the same. She took my hands and pressed them with special significance. We were conspirators.

Soon we were in our rooms—the same as we had occupied on the previous visit—and Harriet was with me within five minutes.

She put her hands on her hips, her eyes sparkling with excitement.

"Let me look at you. No sign. No sign at all." She put her head on one side. "Except, perhaps, a serenity of countenance which comes, so they tell me, to all expectant mothers. My dear child. I have such plans. All is prepared. Gregory will play his part as well as he can. He is not the world's greatest actor... but never mind I shall be there if he fluffs his lines. Your part will be the most difficult... with the exception of mine... but of course I have played different parts before. I shall sustain the role with never a false step, you will see."

"But it will only be necessary until we get to Venice."

"I don't plan it that way. This has to be the complete deception. A good name for a play, don't you think? But this *is* a play... a masquerade. We can never be sure what might happen if things were known to be as they are. Life is full of coincidences. You cross the Grand Canal on the Rialto Bridge and you run straight into someone you knew at home. 'My dear Priscilla, how are you? How *well* you look. I do declare you have put on considerable weight!'"

I couldn't help laughing. She had assumed the part of an inquisitive and malicious gossip.

"'People at home will be *so* interested to hear that we have met and how you are looking!'" she went on. "You see what I mean? No. We are going to play this as it should be played, and that means playing it safely."

"Do you really think we can disguise my condition from everyone right to the end?"

She nodded. "I have designed some delightful gowns. They are going to be the latest fashion in

Venice . . . because I shall wear them and that will be enough. It will be believed that they are designed to hide my pregnancy, which I shall discuss endlessly. Do you get the idea?"

"Harriet, you are wonderful."

"My dear child, you have seen nothing yet. This is going to be one of my most successful roles. The only sad thing is that no one will realize how successfully I am playing it. One of the ironies of life, my dear child."

"I don't know what I should do without you. I was thinking that as we came along. What *should* I have done, Harriet?"

"There is always something. But I am glad I am here to help you."

"You are so good."

"Let us keep our eyes on the facts. There is little good in me. I am fond of you. I always have been. I owe your mother something for looking after Leigh. I owe your father something for his contemptuous attitude towards me and his refusal to be friends. So it gives me great pleasure to be closer to his daughter than he can ever be. My motives are mixed—some unworthy, as most motives are, but I think the chief is my love for you. I never had a daughter. I *should* have had a daughter. A daughter would have been to me what a son is to a man, what Carl is to your father. You see, I should have wanted her to be like me . . . made in my own image as they say. It's the vanity of women . . . which almost rivals that of men. But what a lot of nonsense we are talking! We must get down to practicalities. Now, there is Christabel."

"My father insisted that she come with me. I have to go on with lessons."

She nodded. "He has a special interest in Christabel." She smiled wryly. "Well, we have her here. Either she goes or she is told. Has she guessed anything?"

"She has given no indication that she has."

Harriet was silent for a moment. Then she said: "That's a deep one. I am unsure of her."

"I think I understand. She had a miserable childhood. Then she hoped Edwin would marry her. It has made her a little bitter."

"I get impatient with people who are bitter about life. If they don't like the position they are in they should get out of it."

"All have not your ingenuity, Harriet, to say nothing of your beauty and charm."

"You know how to please. You are right, of course, and we should not be too hard on Christabel who lacks my ingenuity, beauty and charm."

"It means she has to know."

She shrugged her shoulders. Then she added: "We will wait, though, until we are in Venice and delay the telling until the last moment."

It was a long journey but we were too excited at the prospect of seeing new countries to think very much about the exhaustion. We had crossed the Channel and made our way across France to Basle. Harriet had many friends in France, for she had lived in that country before she joined my mother at the Château Congrève before the Restoration. It was true that most of her friends had been players. Some had married into rich families and we often stayed at châteaux. Sometimes we sojourned as long as two days. Gregory accompanied us and was very kind and considerate, which was pleasant, as naturally sometimes the journey could be irksome. We had two menservants with us, too, so we had good protection should we need it.

Harriet had written to my mother after we had left England, telling her that she believed she was going to have a child. She had shown me the letter.

As you can imagine, my dear Arabella, I am uncertain about this. The mother in me rejoices. The worldly woman I am is not exactly singing the Magnificat. Gregory, dear, foolish man, is beside himself with joy. Had I been wise I should probably have cancelled my trip, but as you know full well, my dear, I am not always wise.

"There," she said, sealing the letter. "The first step in our campaign."

It was at a château close to Basle that I took Christabel into my confidence. The decision was forced on me, for I had delayed it as long as I could. I was standing by my dressing table when suddenly I fainted.

It was all over in a few minutes. She helped me to my bed and watched me anxiously, and when I opened my eyes I saw that she guessed.

"You know then?" I said.

"I have wondered for the last week or so."

"You wondered!"

"Well, there was that night you stayed on the island." She lifted her shoulders. "These things happen. There were one or two signs...But, Priscilla, you should never have come here."

"It is precisely because I am in this condition that I am here."

"You mean Harriet..."

"Harriet planned it."

"So she knows!"

"She was the first to know. I went to her because I did not know what else to do."

"I would have helped."

"How?"

"I would have thought of something."

"Harriet made these plans and she has the money to carry them out. She has told my mother that *she* is pregnant. When the child is born she will take it and care for it, and I shall be with her often. It is a wonderful plan."

"It seems rather wild."

"Because of Harriet it will succeed."

"Oh, my poor Priscilla!"

"Don't pity me. I loved Jocelyn. I had that. We should have married and then it would have been wonderful. But this happened..."

"I wept for you, Priscilla. I knew how you felt. You see ..."

"Yes, I know. You and Edwin."

"At least," she reminded me, with a quirk of her lips, "Jocelyn did not desert you. I had the idea that you did not want me to come with you."

"If I gave that impression it was only because of the difficulties. I did not want more people involved than was necessary."

"You might have known I should want to be with you."

"Thank you, Christabel."

She looked almost happy. It was as though she was pleased by what had happened. Perhaps she, too, felt the need to get away from Eversleigh.

It was well into April when we arrived at the Palazzo Carpori. I had heard Venice called the Pearl and the Queen of the Adriatic, but I was unprepared for its unique charm and beauty. We had stayed at Padua and arrived in the afternoon; and there it lay before us ... those islands of the lagoons connected by their stone bridges while countless brightly coloured boats, each with its gondolier, plied through the canals or waited hopefully for those who might need them. It was like a fairy city; the light was golden; the sun seemed to have scattered diamonds on the waters and the houses and palaces were like enchanted castles.

Harriet accepted our wonderment with a kind of smug contentment. She was in excellent spirits and this was partly due to what she called "the plan," which was so wild that she was sure no one but herself would have attempted to carry it out. But she was going to make it succeed.

Gregory, Harriet, Christabel and I were taken in a gondola to the palazzo; the rest of our group followed with our baggage.

Our gondolier had a smattering of English, which was quaint and musical to listen to, and he obviously wanted to use it on us. I noticed that his eyes were on Harriet with undisguised admiration, which did not displease her, though, heaven knew, she must have had a surfeit of it. He kept addressing himself to the bella signora, and as we shot under the bridges he declared himself very happy that we had come.

Venice was the most beautiful city in the world. "Look, bella signora . . . bella signorina . . . here the Rialto. Carpori soon. Very nice palazzo; La Contessa very nice lady. She use my gondola . . . sometime. Very kind!"

He was implying of course that `he expected similar kindness from us and I was sure he would get it. Harriet always believed in being generous to those who served her.

"Carpori close to St. Mark's. Leave to me. I show."

The gondola came to rest and we alighted before the palazzo. In the sunlight it looked like a piece of confectionery. Everything seemed touched by that golden light and I felt as though I were stepping out of reality into an enchanted world.

The Conte, who with his wife, the Contessa, owned this beautiful palace must, I suspected, be a man of some wealth. At each end was tower with a row of arches in the centre opening onto a long veranda. The walls were covered in marble of delicate shades of pink. Behind the veranda was a large hall with exquisite murals and paintings on the ceilings. The floors were paved with marble in beautiful colours of blue and gold.

Christabel caught her breath in wonder and I understood her feelings. I had never imagined anything so lovely.

A beautiful staircase led to the next floor. Here window arches, extending from end to end, formed a continuous arcade.

As soon as we entered, the house servants came to greet us, headed by one whom I guessed to be the majordomo, a garrulous, important-looking man with black sparkling eyes and an ingratiating manner, who was Giuseppe. He clapped his hands and others ran to do his bidding while he fussed around us.

Rooms had been made ready for us. Mine contained a

bed with silk hangings, which was very charming, and I was delighted to be able to step out onto the veranda and look out over the canal.

Harriet was soon with me, her eyes dancing with excitement. She had come to see how impressed I was with her cleverness in arranging such lodgings for us.

"But it is so luxurious!" I cried.

"What did you expect? Did you think I would bring you to a hovel?"

"You have some very good friends."

"Ah, yes. I once did the Contessa a great service. She was a merry girl, but she has become fat—a fate which sometimes overtakes us and I must watch it does not catch up with me. She loved good food, my dear Contessa. She was Marie Gissard. French. She was in our company . . . not exactly beautiful . . . nor even pretty, but she had this . . . *je-ne-sais-quoi* about her. Do you know what I mean? Men liked Marie and Marie liked men. She liked them so well that they could not resist her. She had so many lovers, and she was like a butterfly, flitting hither and thither. But she became a wise butterfly when the Conte Carpori came along. Now he was serious. He wanted a wife and Marie was deeply involved with André . . . I forget his other name . . . and André was determined that Marie should be his. You understand? She might have lost her Conte. He was ready to kill anybody, including herself and himself. And André was out to make trouble. But I took over André at precisely the right moment. It is a simple story. Because of my prompt action Marie was left free to give up her life and settle down with the Conte. It worked well. She became the Contessa. She has two sons and she will never forget the good services of her dear friend, Harriet. So when I tell her that I need to get out of the country for a while, there is the palazzo at my disposal. 'Stay there as long as you like,' wrote Marie. They have palazzos all over Italy. The favourite one is in Florence, and there is another somewhere, to say nothing of several country estates. You see the extent of her gratitude to me for making it all possible. Marie was never one to forget her friends."

"Oh, Harriet, you have had such an exciting life!"

"It may well be, dear child, that you will also have an exciting life. After all, you have not begun so dully, have you?"

I found myself laughing with her, and if it was slightly hysterically, it was better than crying. My emotions were so involved that I was not at all sure what I was feeling.

The first weeks in Venice passed like a dream. I think Christabel felt the same as I did. We had never seen anything like this city where one must travel everywhere by boat. We quickly formed the habit of getting in and out of the gondolas, as there were several of them belonging to the palazzo and two gondoliers to look after them and to be at our disposal to take us wherever we wanted to go.

There were times when I almost forgot the reason I was there, so overcome was I by the unique beauty of the place. What struck me most was the use that had been made of marble and porphyries which had rendered the city one of the most colourful in the world. I learned that these had been brought from various countries to adorn this city—green porphyry from Mount Taygetus, red and grey from Egypt, Oriental alabaster from Arabia, white marble from Greece and red from Verona. There was also blue marble, amber-coloured and a delightful variety with purple mottling.

How I revelled in this city during those few weeks. I would linger on the Rialto Bridge and gaze along the Grand Canal. I spent hours in and around St. Mark's. I was enchanted by mosaics of colourful glass tesserae. I stood before the Doges' Palace overawed by its magnificence; I gazed up at the saddest bridge in the world—called by the evocative name, the Bridge of Sighs, and thought of the prisoners who came from the Doges' Palace and, crossing the bridge on their way to prison, took their last lingering look at the beautiful city.

There were many little shops which were like Aladdin's cave to me. In them I found the most exquisite pieces of glass and enamel; there were rings and brooches made from precious stones and semiprecious stones and ribbons and silks of enchanting colours. There were beautiful tapestries and slippers intricately worked. I think both Christabel and I forgot our sorrows for short periods of time.

It was one gloriously sunny day when Marco, our gondolier, had taken us to St. Mark's Square and Christabel and I were revelling in the shops there. I was buying some slippers and there were several of them laid out on the counter. I could not decide between those with lavender-coloured flowers worked on a background of black silk or a dark russet brown with deep blue flowers. I looked up suddenly and I saw a man at the window watching me. I felt an unmistakable apprehension. I was not sure why except that he was watching me so intently.

He was a little over medium height and exceptionally handsome. Elaborately dressed in what were called petticoat breeches adorned with rows of lace and blue ribbons, he was something of a dandy. His coat was so scanty in order, I was sure, to show off the magnificence of his white ruffled shirt and most elaborate cravat. The buttons glistened with jewels and his hat over his dark periwig was set off with a blue feather.

I flushed and looked down at the slippers. Rather hastily I selected the black and lavender. While the transaction was completed I was very much aware of the man watching me.

As we were about to leave the shop he came in. He stood aside for us to pass, bowing deeply.

I had to pass too close to him in the narrow space so I saw his face clearly. His eyes looked straight into mine and there was in them a suggestion of admiration which was too bold to be called complimentary. It even held a trace of insolence.

I was very glad to get into the street. I said to Christabel: "I should like to go back to the palazzo."

"So soon?" she replied. "I thought you wanted to do some more shopping?"

"I feel a little tired. I would rather go straight home."

We went to the gondola.

"Back to the palazzo?" asked our gondolier in surprise.

"Yes, please," I answered.

As we moved along the canal, I saw the man who had come into the shop. He was standing still, watching us.

Perhaps I should have forgotten him within a few days, for there were a number of bold young men ready to ogle unattended females. My mother, of course, would not have allowed Christabel and me to go out alone, even though we were together. Venice was said to be a city of romance and adventure but I sometimes thought there was a sinister ambience about those little alleys and byways. Life could be violent even in the quiet villages of England. But here I had a feeling that disaster could spring out unexpectedly.

It was early evening just after dusk. I had rested in the afternoon. Harriet had insisted. She said I must remember what lay ahead of me. We did not want complications. It was necessary to the plot that everything run smoothly. I had succumbed to her persuasion, and I would lie in my bed reading or thinking of my child and wondering what the years ahead held in store for me.

I had risen and changed into a long loose gown which I had bought in the square the day before. It was part of Harriet's scheme to introduce loose-fitting garments into our wardrobes, and to do so before they were necessary, she said.

I was brushing my hair, and with the brush in my hand, I had the impulse to step onto the veranda. Sunset was beautiful over Venice. I never failed to watch and delight in it. And as I stepped out, I saw him ... the man who had been outside the shop. He was in a gondola which was not moving along the canal. It was motionless immediately below the palazzo, and he was looking up at the veranda.

I felt a shiver run down my spine. It was almost as though he had willed me to come out and see him.

145

He made no sign. Indeed I did not wait for him to do so. As soon as I realized who he was, I stepped back into my room.

My heart was beating absurdly fast. He knew where I was staying!

I went on brushing my hair. What was I afraid of? I was not sure.

But I certainly was afraid.

Harriet was excited. We had received an invitation to a masked ball at the Palazzo Faliero. The Duchessa herself had called on Harriet, and like everyone else had been enchanted by her. She and Gregory must attend the ball and bring with her the two girls whom she was chaperoning. Harriet had accepted on our behalf without consulting us.

"I have told the Duchessa of my interesting condition and it amused her very much," Harriet told us. "She has recommended the best of midwives. One who brought her own offspring into the world. I shall investigate the woman thoroughly, for I have yet to work out the last act of your play, which will of course be the most hazardous. However, later for that."

"Harriet," I said, "sometimes I think it would have been better if we had gone to some quieter place. Wouldn't it have been easier to have done it that way?"

"Nonsense," she retorted. "The best way to keep a secret is to make no apparent effort to hide it. Had we gone to some remote place, we should have immediately become the focus of attention. And people in little quiet places have nothing or little with which to occupy themselves. Therefore they display a great interest in others around them. The simplest yokel becomes a shrewd detective. Here, my dear, everyone is concerned with his or her own affairs. The Duchessa is mildly amused by my pregnancy today. She will have forgotten it tomorrow because she will be thinking exclusively of her new lover. I have heard that there is a succession of them. You may trust me to do what is best."

146

"I do. I should never have questioned it."

She kissed me. "Now, my darling, what are we going to wear for the ball? I think it would be a good idea to introduce a new fashion. Loose Grecian robes. It may well be that the French are still wearing tight-peaked bodices and tiny waists. But we shall return to the Grecian styles which are so much more becoming and so all concealing. We shall choose our materials with the greatest care because in these styles material will be everything. I shall be in deep blue silk the colour of peacocks' feathers. My eyes tie me rather to that colour. And you, my dear . . . for you I have thought of a delicate rose. There is Christabel, too. My dear, she lacks your charm. There is that burden of bitterness which she cannot throw off. It detracts from any attractiveness she might otherwise have. If she would only be less angry because she has missed something in life, she might begin to gain something. Never mind. Perhaps it will come. Green for her, I thought . . . green for envy."

There was great excitement selecting our materials, and what exquisite colours we had to choose from. Elaborate black silk masks were made for us, and we were all growing very excited. I did once or twice see the man who had filled me with apprehension. He appeared again when we were shopping, but as he ignored us completely, I was able to dismiss him from my mind. There was, however, one other occasion when I saw him in his gondola looking up at the palazzo, but I soon forgot about him.

A few days before that fixed for the ball, we had a great surprise. Leigh came to Venice.

Christabel and I were not at the palazzo when he arrived. We were shopping and when we returned Harriet was waiting for us impatiently.

"Leigh is here," she cried. "I sent him off to look for you. He has gone to the Rialto."

"We were in St. Mark's Square."

"I know. That's why I sent him to the Rialto. I wanted to see you first. This may be tricky. Leigh must not know why we are here."

I saw the point, but it would be difficult not to tell

Leigh. He and I had always been completely frank with each other.

"You will have to be careful, Priscilla. He won't suspect anything though. It wouldn't occur to him... provided none of us betrays anything." She was looking steadily at Christabel. "I do not want anyone to know of this... except us and Gregory. The fewer who know the better. Leigh would be absolutely trustworthy but he is hotheaded and I know how upset he would be. He is devoted to you, Priscilla. Well, I just know in my bones that it must be kept from him. So... be careful."

We promised we would, but I was very uneasy.

Leigh was very soon with us. He had scoured Venice, he said, looking for us. He picked me up in his arms and looked searchingly at me.

"You look... blooming."

Harriet smiled on us benignly.

During lunch Leigh told us that he could only be in Venice one week. He had wasted some time of his leave by going to Eversleigh, where he had heard that we had left for Venice; and more time was spent getting to us as more would be going back. Edwin was envious of him. Poor Edwin, he had been unable to get away.

"You will be able to attend the masked ball," said Harriet. "I am sure the Duchessa will be most put out if you do not accompany us. She especially welcomes dashing young men."

Leigh thought it would be amusing. He told us that that villain Titus Oates was beginning to show a certain reticence in his discoveries, and there was a feeling that the tables might really be turning against him. He had been a fool to slander the Duke of York, who was far more powerful than the poor little Queen who relied on her husband's natural benevolence to save her from disaster.

It was when I was alone with Leigh that I had to be most careful.

But it was wonderful to be with him again. He had always given me a sense of security and I had turned to him for that affection which I had lacked from my father.

In the past I had taken my difficulties to Leigh and he had so much enjoyed coming up with the solution. And now this great secret must be kept from him.

We were on the veranda watching the boats pass by on the canal when he said to me: "You mustn't grieve over Jocelyn Frinton. I know about the ring."

I could not answer. Those simple words had brought it all back to me with startling clarity.

He patted my hand as he used to when I was a little girl.

"He shouldn't have given you that ring. It's over now. I'm glad you're with Harriet. She'll be best for you now."

"She has done so much for me. I don't think I shall ever be able to repay her."

"My dear Priscilla, the last thing friends want from each other is payment. Harriet wants you to get over this thing . . . and you'll do it."

"Yes, Leigh."

"Of course," he went on, "it was all rather a romantic adventure, wasn't it, and you are so young."

"I don't feel young anymore," I said tersely.

"But you are. And I'm glad you came to Venice with Harriet. By the way, has she told you her news?"

"News?" I said uncertainly.

"She's going to have a baby."

"Oh," I said faintly.

"She's delighted. Can't wait, she says. I must say I was surprised. I never thought of her as the maternal type. Fancy Harriet! Everyone will be amazed. She'll be telling you all about it. By the way, I went to see Benjie at his new school. He says he hopes you will all be in Venice for his holidays when he wants to come out here."

I felt apprehensive. It was even harder than I had believed it would be.

"You look worried," he went on. "Harriet will be all right. She's a natural survivor."

"And I'm glad you'll be here for the ball," I said.

"Gaiety in Venice, eh? As for you, I'm not sure you should go. You're not really old enough for balls."

It was the old theme with him. He regarded me as the

perpetual child. I wondered what he would say if he knew the truth, and although I hated having to be secretive with him, I was glad in a way that he did not know.

It was the night of the ball. How romantic it was sailing down the canal to the Palazzo Faliero in our flowing gowns and our masks. The great hall of the palazzo was lighted with flaring torches. Its marble walls—mauves, greens and gold—gave it the appearance of a fairy palace. The water below the palazzo was crowded with boats and the sound of music was in the air.

It seemed as though everyone in Venice was going to the masked ball.

There was no formal reception by the Duchessa because everyone was supposed to be unrecognizable behind their masks, which added to the excitement. At the hour of midnight all would assemble and unmask.

Gregory said that he thought there would be several uninvited guests.

Leigh's comment was: "You must keep with me, Priscilla. I really think you are too young for such affairs."

"Nonsense," retorted Harriet. "One is never too young for such affairs. Priscilla passed out of babyhood some time ago."

"Leigh will be calling me his *little* sister when I am fifty," I said.

His voice was close to my ear. "I intend to call you something else then."

We alighted and mingled with the guests.

There was an intoxication about the soft lighting and the music. From the veranda on the palazzo the torches shone out on the water and I felt I had come a long way from Eversleigh.

Leigh was close to my side. We danced together...not very well. Neither of us was exactly skilled and there were too many people to make it easy for the most practised performers.

Leigh said: "I don't know why people come to these

affairs, except of course to meet strangers."

"Perhaps that is what you should be doing," I suggested.

"I'm going to look after you."

"Really, there's no need to make such a task of it."

"My dear child, do you think I would leave you alone . . . here!"

"I could look after myself."

"There are some shady characters around, I do assure you. Adventurers, robbers, seducers . . . And *I* don't think you *can* look after yourself. You've shown . . ."

I said quickly: "You mean Jocelyn."

"Well," he said gently, "you are so young."

I wanted to shout at him: Stop harping on my youth. I am not young anymore. I shall soon be a mother. That would startle him.

I felt impatient with him. I don't know what it was about Leigh but I was always happy in his company. I wanted him so much to think highly of me. I had laughed and felt really happy when I was dancing with him; and I was gratified—while at the same time impatient—that he should insist on taking care of me. But I was irritated by his constant references to my youth, and I wanted to jerk him out of his belief that I was still a child.

In a room leading from the hall, tables had been set up and loaded with delicious meats, wines and fruit to which the guests were invited to help themselves when they felt in need of refreshment. Leigh and I took ours out to the veranda and found chairs there. We sat watching the lights on the water and the gondolas going back and forth, and at the same time listening to the clamour which came from the hall.

"It's a little more peaceful here," said Leigh. "I am sorry I shall have to leave you the day after tomorrow."

"How is Edwin? Is he happy?"

"Do you mean that affair with Christabel?"

"Poor Christabel!"

"It would have been quite unsuitable."

"Why should it have been?"

151

"She is not the one for Edwin."

"You mean not rich enough? Not of the right background?"

"I meant nothing of the sort. She is a strange girl. She broods so much. I don't understand her. Edwin needs someone lively. He is rather quiet. He needs someone who is entirely different from himself."

"Did he really love Christabel?"

"He liked her very well. I think he was sorry for her. Edwin would always be moved by pity."

"You think it was pity then?"

"It could have been."

"He didn't help her much, did he? It's no use feeling pity for someone for a while and making it worse than it was before."

"He was persuaded that it was not right to continue with it and I think he realized that."

"She was very unhappy, you know."

"She will recover. It's better for her to be unhappy for a few months than for the rest of her life."

"I wish he had not taken so much notice of her in the first place."

"We all wish we had not done certain things at some time in our lives, my dear Priscilla."

"Even you?" I asked.

"Even I."

After a while we went back to the ballroom, Leigh keeping close to me all the time. I did not know what came over me then. Perhaps it was the sight of a couple embracing in a sequestered corner of the ballroom. It seemed to me that many people had come here to meet romance, to enjoy an adventure, to revel in the anonymity which their masks gave them. I had come here because Harriet had suggested it, and Leigh had come to take care of me. He could not get out of his mind the belief that I was a child. I felt a sudden urge to show him I was quite capable of taking care of myself.

There was such a press of people in the ballroom that I managed to escape from him. I had to choose my moment, of course, but it came and I took it.

I pushed my way through the crowds and went back to the veranda. There was no one there and I found it pleasant to inhale the fresh air. I stood for a moment thinking of the strangeness of everything that had happened, and suddenly I was aware of a touch on my arm. I turned, expecting to see Leigh. I was looking into a masked face. I gave a little exclamation of surprise and the man who was standing there lifted his mask briefly and then let it drop. He had shown me enough. He was the man I had seen in the shop in St. Mark's and who had watched my window from the canal.

"At last me meet," he said.

There was no doubt of his nationality. He was as English as I was.

"Who are you?" I asked.

He put his hand to his lips. "At the moment let me remain your mysterious admirer," he said.

"For what reason?" I asked.

"Oh, just because it makes our meeting so much more interesting. Romance thrives on mystery."

"I don't understand you," I said coldly, preparing to walk back into the ballroom.

"Not so fast, elusive lady," he murmured. "I wish to speak to you."

"*I* wish to return to the ballroom."

"First listen to me."

"I would prefer to return to the ballroom."

"Sometimes even charming ladies have to do what others prefer."

I was beginning to be alarmed. This man had inspired me with apprehension from the moment I had seen him. Now I realized that my misgivings had not been without some foundation.

He held my arm in a grip which was firm and which belied his ingratiating manner. I attempted to wrest myself free but his grip tightened and I knew I was in danger.

"You will take your hands from me," I commanded.

He brought his face close to mine. He smelt of a delicate perfume—musk or sandalwood. There were several rings on his fingers and jewels in his cravat. "Is that an order?" he asked.

"It is," I replied.

"How charming!" he murmured. "But it is time for me to give the orders."

"You speak in riddles, sir. And I have no wish to learn the answers."

"You have a sharp tongue, dear lady. I like my ladies to have spirit. First I demand beauty; then they must love me dearly; but I am not averse to a little acidity on the tongue. It makes a diversion."

"You are talking nonsense."

He had bent me backwards and put his lips, hard, against mine.

I fought him off. "How dare you?" I stammered indignantly.

"You must be mad."

"Mad for you. You are so young and youth is so appealing. I do so much enjoy the company of young ladies."

I turned but he held me firmly. He had great strength and agility. He had doubtless had a great deal of experience in this kind of adventure. I was unable to withstand his attack, and in a short time he had dragged me from the veranda and down the steps to the very edge of the canal.

I called out: "Leigh! Leigh! Come quickly . . ."

A gondola was bobbing about below me. I was lifted up suddenly and caught by a man who was waiting in the boat.

It had all happened so quickly that I could not believe that I was actually being abducted. I screamed, but my screams were futile and were drowned in the noise of the music which came from the palazzo. One or two gondolas went past, but no one seemed interested in the struggling girl who was clearly being taken away against her will.

154

My captor leaped down into the gondola beside me.

"Ready, Bastiani," he cried and we started to move.

I cried out but his hand was over my mouth.

"Too late, little bird," he said. "You are trapped now. Oh, so haughty you were. Not one smile for me! Well, now I am going to make you smile. I have ways, you know. I like a little reluctance at first ... but only at first."

My intended fate was obvious. I felt sick with fear, and anger against myself. What a fool I had been! Leigh was right. I *was* a child ... unable to look after myself. I had meant to teach Leigh a lesson. And what a bitter one I was learning myself.

I would fight, though. I would never give way to this man. He had to get me out of this gondola and carry me to his horrible, sinister place. He would not do that easily. I should fight him with all my strength.

We had left the wide canal. It was darker now. We shot under a bridge and I heard the gondolier say something.

"Go on. Go on," commanded my captor.

We went on.

I called out but a hand was immediately placed over my mouth.

The gondola stopped.

My captor had leaped out and was waiting to receive me. I refused to get out. Just then a gondola shot past us. I did not see it stop because I was by then struggling in the arms of the gondolier who was trying to hand me up to my captor who was prepared to drag me up to him. I was very frightened, for I knew that I could not hold out indefinitely.

Suddenly I saw a dark figure spring upon the man. He spun round and I heard him give a cry of pain and anger. I could see the two figures struggling and then there was a cry as one of them fell into the canal.

The gondolier had released me. He was attempting to move away when a voice cried: "Wait." I felt joy sweep over me, for it was Leigh's voice.

The gondolier seemed to be struck with terror. The

man who had tried to abduct me was clawing at the gondola; but Leigh was reaching for me and I sprang up into his arms.

He did not say anything. In a few seconds we were getting into the gondola in which Leigh had followed me, and were swiftly moving away down the canal.

I looked back fearfully and saw that my would-be abductor was being pulled into the gondola by his accomplice.

"Oh, Leigh!" I cried.

He put his arm about me and directed the gondolier to take us to the Palazzo Carpori.

We did not speak until we were in the palazzo.

Then he said: "Thank God I saw you."

"You saw me dragged away?"

"Yes. I came to look for you. Thank God I was in time."

"I was so frightened, Leigh."

"I'm not surprised. I told Harriet that you should not have gone to the ball. You're too young for affairs like that. These people ... well, you don't understand. They are capable of all kinds of villainy."

"Who was that man?"

"I know his reputation. I regret to tell you he is one of our own countrymen. He has been involved in scandals at home. He's a friend of the Earl of Rochester—and you know what that means. Abductions of young ladies is one of their favourite games. I'd like to break his neck. I would have given him something to remember tonight but I was thinking of getting you back."

"Oh, Leigh, you are a comfort to me." I put my arms about his neck. "If you hadn't been there ..."

"But I *was* there. You've nothing to fear while I'm around. How did you come to miss me?"

"It was my fault."

"Idiot!" He spoke tenderly. "I'm going to talk to Harriet. There are to be no more masked balls for you. I don't want you attending such dens of iniquity when I am not there to protect you."

He kissed me tenderly and I longed to tell him of my

love for Jocelyn and why I was here, but it was not only my secret now. It was Harriet's as well and she had distinctly said that Leigh was not to be told.

I was upset and nervous. I must be very careful.

Leigh told me that the man's name was Beaumont Granville and that he was a gambler, a profligate and rake. "He has got through a fortune and is now on the Continent in disgrace. He abducted an heiress . . . only fourteen years old. He hoped to marry her. He needed her fortune. By good luck, her father caught him in time. He had to get out of the country quickly."

"Oh, Leigh, how lucky I've been that you were there."

"It makes me mad with fury to contemplate the plans he had for you."

"I'm no heiress."

"He likes to amuse himself with young girls. It's only the heiress he wants for marriage. You have no idea what wicked people there are in the world, Priscilla. You have learned a lesson tonight. Where was Christabel? Surely she was supposed to be looking after you?"

"You were doing that. She must have discreetly vanished when you took over. They will miss us at the unmasking."

"Not they! There is too much of a crush."

"Harriet . . ."

"She'll presume I brought you here. I told her I would if it became too rowdy."

I smiled gratefully. This was one of the occasions when I enjoyed being looked after.

"You're very shaken," he said. "That was more of an ordeal than you realize."

I flushed slightly. If he knew of my condition would he be so concerned with my innocence? But that sweet and tender love with Jocelyn had been so different from what might have happened tonight.

I said: "You yourself couldn't have emerged without a scratch."

"That's just about all I did get. I had him from behind and he was in the water almost immediately. That'll cool

157

him down a little I imagine. I'm sorry he got off so lightly."

"We shouldn't want trouble. He was all right. I saw him getting back into the boat."

"Now listen to me, Priscilla. You must be very careful in this place. It's not Eversleigh, you know. I shall speak to Harriet and Christabel. I don't want you ever to go out without one of them."

"I don't."

"You have seen tonight that it is necessary to take especial care. It's unfortunate that I have to leave the day after tomorrow."

"I shall remember, Leigh."

"You must look on this as a lesson," he went on. "If it helps you to be more careful it will have been worthwhile."

"I *was* careful. From the moment I saw him I tried to escape. He frightened me so much."

"The devil! There are many like him at Court nowadays, I'm afraid. The King is too lenient with such men. They are witty. They amuse him and he shrugs aside their rakish adventures. Anyway, Beau Granville is not going to forget easily his attempts on my little sister."

"Leigh, I am not your sister."

He laughed lightly and kissed me on the brow.

Again I put up my arms and placed them round his neck. He held my hands there for a moment. Then he said: "Look. There are bruises on your arm. I could kill him for these."

"They will go."

"I think," he said, "that you should go to bed now. It's late."

"Time for little girls to be asleep?" I said mockingly.

"Exactly. It's been a shock. You don't realize it now. I'll get them to send something up to you. Good night, Priscilla."

"Good night, Leigh, and thank you."

"It's my pleasure to look after you now and always," he said.

I went. My emotions were in such a turmoil that I did

not trust myself to remain. One of the servants came up with some warm wine. I drank it and was soon asleep.

I awoke late next morning and so did everyone else. I did not see Harriet until the afternoon.

Leigh was making his preparations to leave and everyone seemed heavy-eyed and rather listless. I said nothing to anyone about what had happened the previous night. I could not bear to talk about it. It was a subdued household and when Harriet did appear, she told me that Leigh had been at the palazzo when she and Christabel with Gregory had come back at three o'clock in the morning.

"He had already told me that he would bring you away just after midnight." She grimaced. "He didn't think it suitable for little girls to be out after that hour."

Leigh left early the next morning. He was subdued and very sorry to go. I knew he was anxious about our remaining in Venice and Harriet told me that he had tried to persuade her to go back to England.

"He thinks it unnatural to have the child here. He believes—good Englishman that he is—that none but the English are capable of delivering babies. How he imagines the rest of the world became so well populated I can't imagine. I must confess, though, that in ordinary circumstances I should have wanted to have the child at home. But it will be rather amusing, I think, to give birth in Venice."

She was, as she would say, working herself into the role and talked as though she would indeed bear the baby. Even when we were alone she kept this up. I had found it a little disconcerting at first but I was getting used to it.

It was after Leigh had left that we called on the Duchessa to thank her in person for the evening at the ball.

As we left the gondola and went up the steps to the veranda and into the great hall of the palazzo, my memories were such that they set me shivering. I wondered whether Harriet, Gregory or Christabel would notice the change in me.

They said nothing.

The Duchessa was full of the latest gossip. Had we heard? she wanted to know. It was most exciting. Did we know that wicked, wicked Beau Granville was in Venice? A fascinating creature . . . really quite irresistible, but oh, so wicked. No one was safe within a mile of him. He had a habit of scenting out the prettiest girls and he was insatiable for virgins. "They send him wild. Well, my dears, it will be interesting to discover who did it. Some husband, it is thought. Or perhaps a lover. However, our Beau is not looking quite as pretty as usual. Are you sure you haven't heard?"

"No," said Harriet, "we haven't heard."

"He has been thrashed within inches of his life! A pretty mess, they tell me. Attacked . . . in his own house. They have had to get doctors to him. He will not be chasing women for some time, I imagine. It is rather amusing. Of course, they are saying he has brought it on himself. And of course it is true. It was certain to happen to him sometime. I wonder what effect it will have on him. I'll swear he will rise from his convalescence every bit the rake he was. It'll be fun to see."

"It will be the greatest fun," agreed Harriet. "And, Duchessa, we are so grateful to you for giving us such an entertainment. There hasn't been anything like it for years, they tell me, even in Venice."

"If it was a success it was you dear people who made it so."

"Alas," said Harriet, "I shall be living a quieter life from now on. Necessity, my dear Duchessa. But we are not unhappy about it, are we, Gregory?"

Gregory said it was the greatest joy to them and he was going to be very stern and forbid his wife to exert herself.

"What a fierce husband you have, my dear," said the Duchessa somewhat maliciously.

"I live in terror lest I displease him," replied Harriet, smiling affectionately at Gregory.

Christabel was silent, but then she usually was. She

160

murmured her thanks to the Duchessa, who showed little interest in her.

When we returned to the palazzo, Harriet came to my room.

"You know it was Leigh, don't you?" she said.

"I . . . I guessed."

"He told me what happened. He was so furious he couldn't contain himself. He said he only gave Beau Granville a taste of what was to come at the time because his one idea was to get you to safety. He went back last night to settle the score."

"Yes," I said faintly.

"I'm glad he's left. Beau Granville could be vindictive, I'm sure. Leigh says I have to take special care of you. He wanted us to leave here. I couldn't tell him, of course, why we couldn't. But he has given me and Gregory very special instructions. I daresay Granville will leave Venice when he's able to. He'll feel humiliated and he won't like that. Leigh will be able to take care of himself, I know. But I'm glad he's gone."

"It's all so horrible."

"There's something else. Gregory knows what happened and he's afraid it may have done some harm to you."

"Harm?"

"Yes, the baby and all that. He thinks that we should have you looked at. It's all rather difficult but I do agree with him. The Duchessa has recommended a midwife . . . a poor woman who will be ready to serve us well for a good payment. You will be Lady Stevens during the examination. We have to change identities. Never mind. It will be a little rehearsal."

I was thinking too much about Leigh and wondering what the result of this affair would be to worry much about the encounter with the midwife.

Harriet staged it perfectly. She had touched up my face to add a wrinkle or two and make me look older. She had assumed the character of a young girl and so good was she that she played the part to perfection. Christabel and Gregory were helpful.

I was examined by the midwife in one of the small rooms and quickly informed that all was well with me and I could expect a normal delivery in due course.

Harriet was delighted with the result—not only with the midwife's verdict but the way in which we all played our parts.

"You can be sure," she told the midwife, "that we shall follow your instructions and look forward to the time when you come to help Lady Stevens bring the little one into the world."

Like many of Harriet's dramatic announcements it resembled the last line of the act. And indeed it seemed so. Leigh had gone and Beau Granville must have recovered from the attack, for we heard a month later that he had left Venice.

"He won't come back," said Harriet. "I doubt he'll ever want to see Venice again."

I hoped that would be so.

I must settle down now to the quiet time of waiting.

The summer was beautiful. It was hot, but by nature of our mission we lived quietly. Harriet and I were often together. I developed a desire to make clothes for the baby and I did so under Christabel's guidance. Harriet would smile at us benignly and I marvelled that she who had such a taste for gaiety should be content to shut herself away in this manner. She was playing a part, and how well she played it!

She rested in the afternoons, she walked rather slowly about the palazzo and discussed symptoms of pregnancy with Caterina, the chief of the women servants who was the mother of five children, and she deceived her completely, for if she were in any difficulty she would always pretend that it was due to her imperfect knowledge of the language.

Gregory had to return to Court and was loath to go, but she insisted. He was not necessary to the plan now that he had given his blessing to his wife's pregnancy which, said Harriet, had strengthened the case considerably. It was arranged that he would return as soon as he was able and perhaps by that time the child would be born and we would all return to England.

"We should be back before Christmas," said Harriet. "The child is due in mid-October, and by the beginning of December it should be old enough to travel."

It was August when Gregory left. In two months my child would be born and I was beginning to find it difficult to hide my condition. The loose gowns we wore were a great help and I kept to my rooms and those of Harriet a good deal. I think she made a better job of being a pregnant woman that I did of attempting to deny I was one.

In a way they were happy months. I had never felt quite like this before. A serenity had settled on me. I thought almost exclusively of the child. I forgot Jocelyn and my heartbreak over his death for weeks at a time. I forgot the terror I had suffered at the Duchessa's ball. All that seemed to fade away and there was only this life which was growing within me—making itself felt every minute of the day. I longed for my child.

I did not even think very much of what could happen after its birth. I knew it was going to be close to me for the rest of my life. I thought I had loved Jocelyn with all my heart but I loved this child beyond anyone I had ever known.

I liked to sit with Christabel and talk about the wonders of motherhood. She was wistful. Poor Christabel! She told me she would have loved to have a child.

She would one day, I told her.

She said rather bitterly: "If what happened to you had happened to me, there would have been no kind friend to help me out of my troubles."

It was almost as though she resented the fact that Harriet had gone to such pains to help me.

But this was not really so. She was careful of me and had done a great deal to help me. She had made some exquisite

163

garments and I should treasure them even more than those which Harriet had bought for the baby. Harriet had sent to one of the shops and asked them to call on her. She received the proprietress in her bedroom where she reclined on the bed. I was present, seated on a chair close by.

"Put the things on the bed," commanded Harriet, "where I can see them. Oh, that is beautiful. You understand, signora, how it is. Sometimes I feel I must keep to my bed. My time will soon come."

The saleswoman nodded sympathetically and said that Lady Stevens must take great care. When was the little one expected?

"In October. I can hardly wait."

"The waiting is so irksome," said the woman. "I have two of my own."

"Is that so? Then you must know all about it. I have two boys, you know. Of course, I am not so young as I was when they were born!"

"Lady Stevens will always be young," was the answer.

Harriet smiled, well pleased, and spent lavishly.

Did she hope for a boy or a girl? asked the saleswoman.

"You know well how it is. One hopes for a boy. One hopes for a girl. And when it comes it is always what you wanted most. Is that not so?"

It was agreed that it was.

So they chattered; and knowing exactly how I felt as an expectant mother, I could not help but congratulate Harriet on a superb performance.

So the days passed.

September came. It was still very warm. I did not go out at all now. I felt it better not to. Christabel shopped for me. She liked to go into the square and buy ribbons and the things I needed.

I did lessons now and then as my mother would have expected us to, and it seemed incongruous to me that a mother should be in such a position. I had been fifteen on my birthday in the July just past.

I urged Christabel to go out more. There was no reason

why she should not. Some protégée of the Duchessa—a certain Francesca Leopardi—became friendly with her and the two went out together now and then. Francesca asked permission for her to visit the Palazzo Faliero, which Harriet immediately gave, and it became a practice of hers to go there. She even spent a night there occasionally, which I thought was good for her because she blossomed noticeably during that time. I believed it was because at last someone was interested in her for herself and not because of her association with us.

But to tell the truth I gave very little thought to her. I was absorbed by my baby; and Harriet was of course the same because she was completely wrapped up in her part.

By the beginning of October, Harriet began to have certain qualms about me. It was the first time she had faltered.

I was young, this was my first child, and she was suddenly afraid that all might not go well. So far she had succeeded in playing her part to perfection. The only tricky moment had been the examination by the midwife. Now she wanted the midwife to move into the palazzo and it would mean, when she did that, that there could be no more pretence.

Harriet talked about it a good deal. She went to see the midwife and came back elated.

"My dear Priscilla, she lives in a hovel. Yes, nothing more than a hovel. There is one way to deal with her. Money. She will have to be in the secret. It is no use my pretending that I am pregnant to her. The time has come when a good performance must be supported by factual detail. Naturally she would be well paid for coming to the palazzo and spending a week or so here when the birth becomes imminent. But if we take her into our confidence—which we shall have to do in this case—and offer what will to her be a fantastic sum of money if she keeps our secret...I am sure she will do so."

"Do you think she can be trusted?"

"I shall mingle bribes with threats. An irresistible combination, I assure you."

"Harriet, you have been so wonderful to me."

"Nonsense, my dear child, it has been my pleasure."

"All these months when you have lived so quietly..."

"Enjoying every minute. My dear, I intend to see you out of this trouble. It has been an exacting role, but worth it."

I went to her and kissed her, which pleased her. She liked demonstrations of affection.

"You are as my own child, Priscilla," she said. "As I have said, I always wanted a daughter. And you are like my own. I was so involved with the Eversleighs. I was one myself once. So no more talk of gratitude and who owes this one what. As I've told you, I owe a big debt to your mother and I find it very gratifying to discharge my debts. Now let us be practical. Yes, I shall send for the midwife and have a little talk with her. You shall be present."

She did so without delay. "For," as she said, "I shall not feel happy until the woman is here. I want her to be on hand the moment she is needed."

The midwife was rotund and pale faced, with lively black eyes, a patched gown and a cloak which showed signs of past grandeur and must have been presented by a client some years before. Her name was Maria Caldori and she was the mother of five children, which, said Harriet, was a good point, as it was always well to have firsthand knowledge of a subject.

Harriet brought her up to my bedroom and closed the door firmly.

"Now," she said, "I have something of great importance to say to you. If you were paid well to keep a secret would you be prepared to do so?"

The woman looked startled. A faint tinge of colour had crept into her cheeks. Harriet mentioned a sum of money which made her blink. I had a notion that she had never heard of such a sum in the whole of her life.

"You would do a great deal for so much, I don't doubt, signora."

"I would do nothing which could set the law on me," said the woman, visibly trembling.

166

"This is nothing to do with the law and all you will be asked to do is say nothing. It is your silence which can put this money in your pocket."

"What is this, my lady? Please tell me what it is."

"First I want your promise to be silent. There is nothing wrong in what you are asked to do. In fact it can only be good. All you need to do is say nothing. No one will ask you questions."

"It is about the . . . baby, my lady?"

"You shall have half the money now," said Harriet, ignoring the question, "and half when the matter is over. But first I must have your word on the name of God and the Holy Virgin that you will in no circumstances tell of what you learn in this house."

"My lady, I swear. In my profession there are sometimes secrets. I have always been discreet."

"You will need to be discreet now. You may think that when the money has been paid and we have gone, you are free to speak of what you know. If you do so, you will have broken your word and you will be punished. Do you know what happened to an English gentleman not so long ago? Have you ever heard the name of Granville?"

The woman was trembling a little. I saw the sweat on her forehead.

"I heard, my lady. He was very bad . . . because of what happened to him."

"It could happen to you, signora, if you betrayed a trust. It will not, I know. You are too wise. You are going to take the money, which is more, I vow, than you earned in the whole of your life before bringing babies into the world and now and then waiting on the nobility. What is it to be?"

The woman lifted the cross which she wore about her neck and swore on it. Nothing on earth should drag the secret from her.

It was dramatic, another of Harriet's scenes, and naturally she played it to perfection.

"I trust you," she said. "And now you will find the matter very simple. When you came here before you did not examine me but this young lady. She is the one who is

167

to have the child. For certain reasons we do not wish it to be known that the child is hers. All you have to do is attend her, make sure she has the best of care, bring a healthy child into the world with as little inconvenience to the mother as possible and *hold your tongue.*"

Relief spread across the midwife's face.

"My lady," she said, "it is nothing... it is little..."

Then she stopped, obviously afraid that if she made it sound too easy the fee might be lowered.

She went on: "Your secret is safe with me. There are many such in my work. I shall say nothing. I shall let it be believed that the child is yours, my lady. Oh, my lady... and signora..." She looked at me apologetically. "It often happens there are certain secrets."

"I am sure that in your profession it is one secret after another, and remember how well you are being paid to keep this one and remember too that Venice will not be a very healthy place for you if you fail to keep it. Now you are free to look after your patient."

Harriet left me alone with Maria Caldori, who asked me a great many questions, examined me and declared herself delighted with my condition.

"Two weeks perhaps," she said. "It may be sooner. Babies like to choose their own time."

Harriet had arranged that I should sleep in her room and had had a small bed brought in. The fact was that she occupied this and made me sleep in the large one in which the child was to be born.

Maria Caldori occupied a room close by and was in constant attendance. I think she enjoyed her part in the conspiracy and whenever we had visitors I would leave her and Harriet together and Harriet said she did her part very well. "Mind you," she pointed out, "I carried her along. But I must say she played with a certain conviction."

Christabel was very kind and eager that I should not be put to any strain. I had never seen her so contented as she was at that time. She was out a good deal with Francesca and again and again I was struck by the change in her.

The weather was still warm and I was feeling the heat

very much. As I did not go out a great deal I liked to sit at the doors of my room which opened onto the veranda and watch life pass by on the canal.

It was just after sundown, and as I sat there, I saw a gondola shoot by. There was a bright moon that night so I saw the gondolier quite clearly in his yellow coat and brown breeches, but it was his passenger who held my attention.

As they passed he looked up at the palazzo and I saw his face distinctly.

It was Beaumont Granville.

I felt a sudden wave of terror wash over me. I stood up, turned abruptly and went into my room.

Then I felt the pain take hold of me.

My child was about to be born.

For the next hours I forgot all about Beaumont Granville. There was only the agony to be endured; and yet all the time I was thinking of the child and assuring myself that soon I would emerge from the pain and would have the baby I longed for.

I was aware of the candles that flickered and threw shadows over the room, the sound of voices. Maria Caldori soothing, Harriet tense and anxious.... No longer in her role, I thought, in the midst of my pain.

It was not an exceptionally difficult birth, but it seemed a long time to me before I heard the cry of a child.

I was aware then of a wild exultation. I was a mother. That was all I could think of. I was more exhausted than I had ever been, but I thought: I'm happy.

Harriet was at my bedside—dear, protective Harriet.

"All is well, dear child," she whispered. "A lovely little girl ... *our* little girl."

A little girl! That was what I wanted more than anything in the world.

I held up my arms.

"Sleep first," commanded Harriet. "That's what you need. Maria Caldori says so. Maria has been wonderful. Now rest, my darling child, rest ... rest and then we shall

169

have the little rogue made presentable to meet her mama."

I was about to protest but an utter weariness came over me and I slept.

It was late afternoon when I awoke. Harriet came quickly to my bedside. She kissed me. "You were wonderful. Now you want to see our little angel. Maria is a tigress. She hates me to go near her. You'd think it was her baby. Maria, I insist. Give me the child."

Harriet brought my baby to the bed and placed her in my arms. I felt weak with happiness. I knew that nothing had ever been so important to me before as this red-faced child with the scanty dark hair and its button of a nose. She had been whimpering slightly, and when I took her into my arms she stopped and something which might have been a smile crept over her face. How I loved her! I examined her tiny fingers and marvelled at the minute nails. I looked at her little feet.

"She's perfect in every way," cooed Harriet. "We could wish she had a slightly less lusty pair of lungs but Maria is overcome with admiration even for them. If you ask me she spoils the child."

I lay there holding her in my arms.

This was my daughter, the result of my love for Jocelyn. I thought then: Everything was worthwhile for this.

Harriet and I spent a long time discussing the name. At length we decided on Carlotta. It seemed to suit her. She was going to be dark-haired and she had the most enchanting pair of blue eyes. "As though," said Harriet, "she knew she had to be my daughter so therefore her eyes should be the same colour as mine." Harriet's were that rare violet blue and her most startling feature. I wondered whether Carlotta's would be the same.

Harriet took charge of her. The midwife left with her money and made protestations of her loyalty and gratitude. Never, never should anyone know from her who the mother of the child really was.

All the women of the household wanted the privilege of being the child's nurse. Harriet chose the most likely, a middle-aged mother who had had several children of her own.

Christabel showed great interest in the child and was clearly moved by her. Christabel was always surprising me. Despite what she had told me I should not have thought she cared greatly for children.

A few weeks passed by. I was completely absorbed by the child and I was dreading the day when we should leave Venice, which meant that Harriet would take Carlotta and I would have to return to Eversleigh.

"I shall tell your mother that you have been so helpful to me, and I am not really cut out to be a mother, and that she must spare you to me often."

"Harriet, you are a darling, but even so I shall have to leave her for long periods."

"We'll work something out, never fear," said Harriet.

Oddly enough Carlotta managed to bewitch Harriet, who admitted that before the coming of this infant, young children had had no great charm for her. Perhaps all the effort we had made for Carlotta had given this child something extra.

She was going to be a beauty, Harriet declared. "Look at those eyes! That deep sparkling blue. And that adorable button of a nose. It is just right. She knows it, too, I am sure. See how determined she is to have her own way."

"Really, Harriet," I chided, "you positively drool over this baby."

"I find her excessively drool-worthy."

She talked of the nursery at the Abbas which would have to be completely refurbished. "Would it be a good idea to get old Sally Nullens over?"

"She's an old gossip."

"There'll be nothing to gossip about and your mother says she is wonderful with children."

"Perhaps it would be a good idea," I said. "We were fond of her when we were little."

"Old Nullens it shall be. I've had enough of this place. It's romantic enough if your sense of smell is not too strong. I believe they throw all sorts of rubbish into the canals. I

171

shouldn't care for it in winter, and I do really think we should be making plans."

She was right, of course.

When Gregory returned to Venice at the end of October, he, too, seemed to fall victim to the baby's charms.

He agreed that we should start the journey home almost immediately. To leave it later could mean that we might run into really severe weather.

I was sure that he had been prompted to such a comment by Harriet who, now the baby was born and the real difficulties of the initial stages of the project were over, was growing tired of the monotony of life and was determined to return to England.

So with some misgivings I made my preparations to leave. While I was packing with Christabel, I remembered seeing Beaumont Granville on the night before Carlotta's birth. Strangely enough, in view of everything that had happened I had forgotten the incident.

I said to her as she was helping me put my things together: "I had a shock on the night my pains started. I thought I saw Beaumont Granville."

"Beaumont Granville," she repeated, as though she were trying to remember who he was.

"The man who tried to abduct me. The one whom Leigh nearly killed."

"Do you think you really did?"

"I was sure of it. I saw him clearly. He was going past in a gondola, and he looked up at the palazzo."

"You could have been mistaken. Do you think he would come back here after what happened?"

"I shouldn't have thought so."

"You haven't seen him since?"

"No."

"Well, you were in a state of tension, you know. You were expecting the baby at any moment . . . and I imagine it could have been someone who looked like him."

"That could be so," I agreed.

And I believed that might be true.

$\mathcal{O}$ The Price of a Life $\mathcal{O}$

Christabel and I arrived back at Eversleigh in time for that Christmas of 1682. I had stayed for two weeks with Harriet, but could not in reason stay longer; and to tear myself away from my child—even though I knew she would receive the best of care—was heartbreaking.

I was certain that Carlotta was an exceptional child. Christabel might smile benignly when I mentioned the fact, but Harriet agreed with me wholeheartedly. My baby really took notice of what was going on, had a definite will of her own and was ready to scream until she was blue in the face until she obtained what she wanted.

I was with her constantly during those two weeks with Harriet, but I knew I had to go. To be parted from my daughter from time to time was the price I had to pay for my unconventional behaviour.

My mother welcomed me warmly.

"How could you stay so long away from us!" she said reproachfully. "Let me look at you. You've grown thinner. You've grown up."

173

"Dear Mother, did you expect me to remain a child forever?"

"And to have travelled so far and lived abroad so long! You will miss all that now you are home. I suppose Harriet will want to be off again shortly. She was always a wanderer. It's amusing about the baby. I'll swear she wasn't very pleased when she first discovered her condition."

"Harriet loves Carlotta dearly. Oh, Mother, she is the most lovely little girl."

"One would expect Harriet to have a beautiful daughter. If she is only half as good-looking as her mother she will be the toast of the Court."

"She is going to be a beauty, I am sure."

"She seems to have charmed you, at any rate. Come into the house. Oh, Cilla, it is good to have you home."

I wanted to say it was good to be home, but it wasn't. No place could be good unless Carlotta was in it.

I told my mother that Harriet had suggested Sally Nullens go over to Eyot Abbas as nurse to the baby.

"That's a wonderful idea," she said. "Sally will be mad with joy. She's been going round like a shepherd who has lost her sheep ever since Carl escaped from the nursery."

"Shall I go and tell her right away?"

"Do. There's no point in withholding such good news."

I went up to Sally's sitting room. It was just as it had been before I went away. She was sitting watching the kettle which was beginning to sing and was close on boiling; and Emily Philpots was with her. They looked startled to see me and I thought they had aged a little since I last saw them.

"Well, if it's not Miss Priscilla," said Emily.

"Back from foreign parts," added Sally. "Why people want to go off like that I can't make out, and to bring a little baby into that sort of place . . . it's likely to affect it for the rest of its life. It's heathen, nothing more."

"I am sure you will soon make a nice little Christian of her, Sally," I said.

There was a hint in my words which made her perk up

her ears. She looked at me rather breathlessly. Babies were to Sally Nullens what lovers were to romantic young ladies.

I said quickly: "Lady Stevens suggested to me that you might be prepared to go over to the Abbas and look after her child. I thought it was a good idea."

Sally's nose had turned slightly pink at the tip. I heard her whisper something like "a dear little baby."

"Would you consider going, Sally?"

It was an unnecessary question. I could see that in her mind she was already getting the nursery together.

She pretended to consider. "A girl, is it?"

"The most beautiful little girl in the world, Sally."

"I never cared much for beauties," said Emily Philpots. "They give themselves airs." I could see by the way she screwed up her face that Emily was growing sick with envy. She was seeing a dark future when she hadn't even Sally Nullens to complain to.

I was overwhelmed with pity for them suddenly. I thought how sad it must be to be old and unwanted.

"The child is going to need a governess, too," I said. "I believe a child cannot begin to learn too early."

"It's true," agreed Emily Philpots fervently, the red colour suffusing her face by now. "Children need the guiding hand even before they can walk."

"I think it is very likely that Lady Stevens will ask you to go along with Sally to the Abbas."

"Well, I never!" cried Sally, beginning to rock vigorously in the rocking chair which she always used. "A little baby again."

"May I write to Lady Stevens, and tell her that you accept, Sally?" I asked. "At the same time I'll suggest that Mistress Philpots goes with you."

Happiness had suddenly arrived in that room. I could tell its presence by pink-tipped noses, watery eyes and the squeak of the rocking chair.

Life was unsatisfactory. The periods I looked forward to were those when I could go to Eyot Abbas. Naturally I could not go too frequently. Even going as I did aroused comment.

Harriet contrived that I should see Carlotta as much as possible; she visited us and stayed for quite a long time. Sally Nullens was already installed in the nursery and Emily Philpots was there too, fussing over the baby's clothes and adorning all her garments with the most exquisite stitching.

Carlotta had soon become aware of her importance. As she lay in her cradle, kicking a little and smiling contentedly, she was like a monarch receiving her courtiers, and she would look with what must surely have been a certain complacency on the adoring throng who gazed down at her in rapture. Benjie was her devoted slave and worshipped with the rest. He thought it was exciting to have a little sister and he was very glad because his mother was home again. Gregory doted on her and I believed that Harriet had willed him to think the child really was his. Harriet continued to play the proud mother and Sally Nullens looked younger every day and grew more and more aggressive towards the rest of us, declaring, "I'm not having my baby kept from her rest!" and trying to shoo people out. Oddly enough, almost as though she had some extra sense, she never tried to turn me out of the nursery. She said it was as pretty as a picture to see me sitting there petting the baby. Mistress Carlotta had taken a real fancy to me, she told me. "And that's something with Mistress Imperious, I can tell you!" Then there was Emily Philpots, fussing if her clothes were not immaculate.

"They'll ruin the child between them," said Christabel.

Carlotta took all this adulation as her right.

My father scarcely looked at her. I wondered what he would have said if he had known she was his grandchild.

He once made a comment on her. "She'll be another such as her mother," he said, and that was not meant to be a compliment, for as I have said there was a definite antipathy between him and Harriet.

176

We passed into the unsatisfactory summer when I made an effort to continue with my life as it had been before the great adventure. Christabel and I made a show of taking lessons together but my thoughts were always at Eyot Abbas with my child. Christabel, too, was absentminded; that unhappy look had come back to her and I could tell by some of the bitterness of her comments that she was dissatisfied with her lot.

Once she said: "What will become of me when I am no longer required to teach you?"

I answered: "You could stay with me as long as you wished to."

"I'd be a sort of Sally Nullens or Emily Philpots, I suppose."

"You would never be like that. You and I have been friends." She turned away and I saw her lips move in that pathetic way which always upset me. In spite of her aloofness there was a closeness between us. After all, she knew a great deal more about me than anyone else in the house did.

There was a great scare that year and my mother was very anxious. Ever since the Popish Plot had been the great event of the time, showing us that our comfortable lives could be easily and tragically interrupted, an uneasiness had settled on her. I knew it concerned my father.

He was a very forceful man and not inclined to keep his opinions to himself. He had grown firmly anti-Catholic, and as the heir to the throne was James, Duke of York and *he* made no secret of his leanings, she could see trouble ahead. My father was a great friend of the Duke of Monmouth and my mother always said that he was one who was born for trouble.

Monmouth, son of Charles the Second and Lucy Walter, was the most colourful man at Court . . . next to his father. He had good looks, which his father lacked, and he had a certain charm; he did not possess his father's shrewdness and clever devious mind, though he was bold and reckless—brave enough, but careless of his own safety and that of others.

The King loved him dearly, and while Charles lived, Monmouth would be forgiven a hundred indiscretions. Yet those about him feared that he might go a little too far one day. And during that summer it seemed he had.

It was understandable that my mother should view with disquiet my father's friendship with such as Monmouth. It was not so much that my father was devoted to the man; it was rather what he stood for. My father said he had not lived through the Commonwealth and upheld the Royalist cause for the sake of a Catholic bigot who before long would have the Inquisition installed in England.

He would grow very fierce when he talked of such matters and I noticed that my mother, who normally would have indulged in verbal battle with him, was unusually silent.

When we first heard about the Rye House Plot she became almost ill with anxiety.

It was a foolish plot, doomed to disaster. The plan was to assassinate the King and his brother as they rode back to London from the Newmarket races. The road led past a lonely farmhouse, near Hoddesdon in Hertfordshire, known as Rye House, and from this the plot took its name. It was owned by a man named Rumbold, who was one of the chief instigators.

Two events worked against them. There was a fire in the house in Newmarket where the King and Duke were staying, and they decided that rather than bother finding another lodging they would return to London. Thus they travelled along the road past Rye House Farm before the conspirators expected them.

Meanwhile a letter was found addressed to Lord Dartmouth in which the plan was set out.

Having just emerged from the excitement of the Popish Plot, which had now petered out like a dampened fire, the people were eager to give their attention to another plot. The Rye House Plot was discussed with animation throughout the country. A proclamation was issued for the apprehending of suspects and there was a reward of a hundred pounds to any who succeeded in bringing any of the conspirators to justice.

This was when my mother began to grow uneasy. She was terrified that my father might be involved and that for the large sum of one hundred pounds someone might be tempted to betray him.

I heard them discussing it together.

"I tell you," he said, "I was not involved. I had no part in it. It was a foolish venture, in any case... doomed to failure. Besides, do you think I would agree to a plot to assassinate Charles?"

"I know of your affection for him... and his for you..."

"And you think I am in the habit of plotting against those for whom I have affection?"

"I know your strong feelings for Monmouth and your desire to see him on the throne."

"Oh, Bella, you surprise me. I want Monmouth on the throne only if there is a question of James taking it. What I want is what is best for the country... for you... for me... for every one of us... and that is that Charles shall stay where he is for the next ten or twenty years."

"I could not believe that you would want to harm him."

They walked together in the gardens arm in arm—not hiding their tenderness for each other on this occasion.

Being so absorbed in my child and my constant thought being how we could be together, I had little time to brood on plots. As long as I knew that my father was not involved I could forget it. There had been an attempt on the life of the King; guilty men had been brought to justice; and that was an end to it.

It was disconcerting to discover that this was no rustic conspiracy contrived by a mere maltster in a country farmhouse. It was revealed that quite a number of rich and influential members of the nobility were concerned in it. Lord Howard of Escrick and William Lord Russell were two of them. Heads began to fall and I could see that my mother was growing more and more apprehensive.

It was not long before the name of Monmouth was beginning to be mentioned.

The King was taking his usual diffident attitude towards the whole affair. My father said that Charles was more interested in intrigues with his mistresses than attempts on his life. His attitude was: It has failed, so why be concerned about it? He was a man who disliked conflict and wanted to live in peace. He enjoyed witty conversation and the company of beautiful women far more than bringing his enemies to justice.

"He is a man," said my father, "who regards death without concern. His idea of heaven would be a Whitehall where there were no plots or tiresome issues. It should be all pleasure which he finds in the women who surround him."

"Yet they say he can be wily enough in his dealings with France."

"Ah," said my father, "he leads the French King where he will, and what is amusing, he also leads him to believe that the leading strings are in French hands. Quite a feat, really. Charles is shrewd, Charles is clever, but above all he is lazy and can never really give quite the same concentration to anything as he gives to the seduction of women. If only he would make up his mind and legitimatize Monmouth. It seems the sensible thing to do."

"And now what?" asked my mother. "Monmouth is involved in this ..."

"Jemmy would never agree to kill his father. That I know."

"How will he prove it?"

Monmouth did convince his father that although he had known of the plot he would never have agreed to the killing of his father. Whether the King believed him or not no one was certain. Whether Monmouth would be prepared to commit parricide for the sake of the throne no one was certain either. What was certain was that Charles could not bring himself to execute his own son—traitor though he might be.

The King could not of course ignore what had happened, and as a result Monmouth was banished from Court. When we heard that he had gone to Holland my mother was intensely relieved. My father laughed at her. She was like an old hen, he said, clucking round her family.

But they were close, those two, and I liked to see them thus.

Two people who lived near us were involved in the plot. They had visited us now and then in the past, being near neighbours. It was a shock, therefore, to hear that they had been arrested.

There was John Enderby, who had lived in a rather fine house called Enderby Hall with his wife and son, and even closer to us there was Gervaise Hilton of Grassland Manor.

There was a great deal of talk about it. The properties would be confiscated and doubtless sold to other families. I wanted to call on them but my mother forbade it.

"It might be said that your father sent you. We have to keep outside all this."

I obeyed her, but I wondered about the families.

They disappeared, and the houses stood there looking more and more desolate as the months passed.

Time had indeed passed. Carlotta was now over a year old—a very definite personality and growing prettier every day. Those startlingly blue eyes—not quite as dark as Harriet's—attracted everyone's attention, and I was amazed that people could say how like her mother she was growing. Harriet was very amused by this.

"Trust Carlotta to play her part," she commented. "That child will be an actress, mark my words."

I think Harriet's interest in the baby had waned a little. One could not expect her to become completely absorbed in a child—particularly someone else's. Moreover, Sally Nullens mounted guard over the nursery like some fabulous dragon breathing fire on anyone who dared approach her baby. I did not mind this, for I knew that Carlotta would be tended with the utmost care. Any little ailment would be detected at once and dealt with. Sally had become a different woman from that disgruntled, ageing female who had crouched over her singing kettle and rocked herself angrily before her fire. Life had meaning for her now. It was the same with Emily Philpots. Carlotta was not just an ordinary child. She was a saviour. They doted on her, but I knew that Sally would not allow any spoiling which, good nurse that she was, she knew was bad for the child. She had her rules, which must be obeyed, and at the same time nothing was spared in the devotion she bore the child.

Carlotta could not be in better hands and I should have been satisfied, but how I longed to have her for myself!

That Christmas, Harriet and Gregory came to us at Eversleigh, so I had the baby under the same roof, which was wonderful. Harriet did warn me that I must not behave as though there was nothing in life but Carlotta.

"It might set minds working," she said. "After all, it *was* rather unconventional to go to Venice to have my child. Try to be a little restrained, dear."

I knew what she meant when I heard my mother's comment: "Priscilla will make a good mother. Just look at her with Carlotta. You would think she was the mother—not Harriet."

Yes, I could see that Harriet was right. I was on dangerous ground.

That was an exceptionally cold Christmas and during January my father said that we were all to go to London. There were invitations from Court and they could not be ignored.

He was looking at Christabel and me rather speculatively and I fancied he was thinking that I was no longer a child. I was sixteen years and would be seventeen in July. I could see how his thoughts were working, and although he was as indifferent to me as ever, he did remember his duty as a father and that would be to get me suitably married.

The idea was repulsive to me. It horrified me. How could I marry without telling my husband that I had a child?

I began to feel very apprehensive.

It was the coldest winter within living memory. There had been a hard frost since the beginning of December and when we arrived in London it was a different city. The Thames was frozen so hard that salesmen had been able to set up booths on it, making it look like a fair. It had changed the face of the city and newcomers marvelled. The inhabitants were now used to it and they just went out walking and shopping on the river.

There was a great deal of merrymaking. It seemed to be an occasion to celebrate. There had never been anything like it and doubtless there never would be again. The ice was as hard as stone; this was proved because they had started running coaches from Westminster to the Temple; and when they roasted an ox on the ice, the fire made little impression.

Some of the Puritans—and there were still many around—declared that the weather would grow colder still and we should all be frozen to death—except the righteous. God had sent the plague and the great fire and this was another warning.

The watermen were dour. This was taking away their trade. Many of them set up stalls and turned into salesmen. "What is good for one is bad for another," was the philosophical comment.

My mother, with Christabel and myself, would go and shop on the Thames. The cold was intense but the stall holders were very merry, and we had to be very careful how we walked across the ice. But it was so hard that it was like walking on stone and so much traffic had made it less slippery than it would otherwise have been.

Everyone was watching for the thaw; but so thick was the ice and so long had it been there that it seemed unlikely that it would thaw quickly even when the weather changed.

It was on the ice that we made the acquaintance of Thomas Willerby. He was a middle-aged man with a somewhat portly figure and a round rosy face. He was standing by one of the stalls drinking a hot cordial. There were many sellers of hot drinks on the ice, for they were a very welcome refreshment in such weather.

It so happened that as we passed the stall, Christabel slipped and slid right into Thomas Willerby. The cordial was almost thrown into his face; it missed that, however, and went streaming down his elaborate coat.

Christabel was overcome with horror. "My dear sir," she cried, "I am so sorry. Oh, dear! It was my fault. Your coat is ruined."

He had a pleasant face, this Thomas Willerby. "There, there, my pretty," he said, "don't you fret. 'Twas no fault of yours. 'Tis this unnatural ground we're treading on."

My mother said: "But your coat..."

"'Tis nothing, lady. 'Tis nothing at all."

"If it is not washed off immediately it will leave a stain."

"Then, my dear lady, there will be a stain. I would not have this lady"—he smiled on Christabel—"worried about a coat. It was no fault of hers. As I say, it is this unnatural ice."

"You're very kind," said Christabel quietly.

"Now I told you not to fret."

"You must come to our house," said my mother. "I insist. There I will have the coat sponged and we will do what we can with it."

"My dear lady, you are too good."

But it was clear that he was very eager to accept the invitation. We took him to our London house, which was close to the Palace of Whitehall, and there my mother made him take off his coat and sent a servant to bring out one of my father's. This he put on while his own was taken away, and mulled wine was served with cakes which we called wine cakes—spicy and hot from the oven.

"Bless my soul," said Thomas Willerby, "I'll say it was a lucky day when I was bumped on the ice."

My father joined us and was told the story of the encounter. He clearly took a fancy to Thomas Willerby. He had heard of him. Wasn't he a London merchant who had come up from the country ten years before and done very well for himself?

184

Thomas Willerby was a man who clearly liked company. He also liked to talk about himself. He was that very Thomas Willerby, he assured my father. He had suffered a bereavement a year ago. He had lost his dear wife. They had had no children, a great sorrow to them both. Well, now he was thinking of retiring from business. He had made his fortune and would like to settle in the country...not too far from the town...within reach of London. Perhaps he would like to do a little farming. He was not sure. What he needed was the right house.

They talked awhile of the country's affairs and the Rye House Plot, of course. They agreed that it would be a sad day for England when the King died, there being no heirs but the King's brother and the questionable one of his illegitimate son.

Thomas Willerby did not wish to see the country go Papist and in this he was in complete accord with my father.

By the time the coat was brought in, sponged and looking fresh and as clean as it had been before the wine was spilled on it, we had become very friendly and my father had suggested that Thomas Willerby might like to look at two properties not very far from our own Eversleigh Court.

These were Enderby Hall and Grassland Manor, which had been confiscated when their owners were caught in the Plot. My father believed that these could be had by the right buyer.

The outcome was that Thomas Willerby decided that he must come and look at them.

That turned out to be quite an eventful morning.

There was no sign of the thaw until February. Then the booths disappeared from the river and gradually the ice began to crack.

By that time Thomas Willerby had bought Grassland Manor, which was only about half a mile from us. My father seemed very pleased to have him as a neighbour and showed great friendship towards him.

He visited us frequently and paid a great deal of

attention to us all, but I fancied particularly to Christabel. He was clearly delighted to have made a contact which brought him into our family.

My father was, of course, a man who was rather sought after. He was rich and influential in Court circles, being such a close friend of the King and the Duke of Monmouth—not that the latter was a favourable thing to be at this time since the Duke was in exile. But it was known that the King showed special favour to my father because he amused him.

Thomas Willerby was a man who had not moved in the highest echelons of society. He was rich, though he had not inherited a penny. He was a countryman who had come to London to seek his fortune, which through hard work and honest dealing he had found in good measure. Having a deep respect for those born in a higher grade of society than himself, he was delighted to be received as a friend at Eversleigh.

He and Christabel were often together. There was that trait in Christabel's character which made her constantly imagine that she was not quite acceptable—though had she not assumed this, no one would have doubted it. But this attitude did not naturally extend to Thomas Willerby; and one day she came to me in a state of obvious pleasure.

"I must speak to you, Priscilla," she said. "Something wonderful has happened."

I begged her to tell me without delay.

"Your father sent for me. He has told me that Thomas Willerby has asked for my hand in marriage and that he thinks it would be a suitable match. I am going to marry Thomas Willerby, Priscilla."

"Do you . . . love him?"

"Yes," she said fervently, "I do."

I embraced her. "Then I am so happy for you."

"I don't really deserve this happiness," she said.

"Oh, nonsense, Christabel, of course you do."

She shook her head. "You see, this will make everything come right."

I was not quite sure what she meant. She hesitated for a

moment, then she said: "He has admitted it now. And you should know. I always guessed, of course, when I came here..."

"What are you talking about, Christabel?"

"I am not the Connalts' daughter. My father is yours and my mother was Lady Letty."

"Christabel!"

"Oh, yes," she said, "theirs was an affair which had unfortunate consequences—myself. Our father was then married to his first wife, and it was unthinkable—as you yourself know—that an unmarried lady should produce a child. So I was born in secret like your own Carlotta and then I was given into the care of the Connalts to be brought up as their daughter. Lady Letty arranged the living for them and they came to the rectory with the newly born child."

"My dear Christabel!" I put my arms about her and kissed her. "Then we are sisters."

"Half sisters," she corrected me. "But what a difference! You were acknowledged, accepted, born in wedlock. That makes all the difference."

I immediately thought of Carlotta and I said to myself: It shall make no difference to her. She shall have every advantage.

"And you knew this, Christabel."

"Not for certain. I guessed, though. Our father used to come to the Connalts sometimes and he would watch me. I was aware of that. Lady Letty took an interest, too. She used to send things for me... although they weren't supposed to come from her. And when I came here and was treated as I was... not like a governess really and at the same time not like a member of the family... I felt certain."

"I wish you had told me before."

"Suppose you had betrayed me? I might have been turned away."

I understood it all now... the bitterness, the moods of dejection. Poor Christabel!

"It's strange," she said. "They call us... people born as I

was . . . the love children. Yet love is something which we so often miss."

Carlotta, too, I thought. My love child. Carlotta was not going to miss love. That I should make sure of.

"It is wonderful to discover a sister," I said.

"I have been so jealous of you."

"I know."

"It was hateful of me."

"No. I understand. You won't be jealous now, though."

"Oh, no, no. I'm not jealous of anyone now. Thomas chose me right from the first. I shall always remember that."

"I think he is a very good man, Christabel," I said.

"He is," she answered. "Oh, Priscilla, I am so happy."

There was nothing to delay the marriage, said my father, and so it took place almost immediately. Christabel blossomed. She was clearly very happy. She was busy furnishing Grassland Manor and she often came over to see us, bustling about in a state of ecstatic domesticity. She had her still-room and her flower garden and she fussed about Thomas Willerby in a manner which astonished me. She had always seemed a little cold before, never very demonstrative in her affections. I had never seen anyone change so much. Of course, her husband was delighted with her and no one could doubt that it was the happiest of marriages.

Within a short time she came over to Eversleigh to confide in me that she was going to have a baby. It seemed all she needed to make her bliss complete.

With great pride she showed me the nursery, and Thomas purred and puffed and gazed at her as though, as Carl rather irreverently remarked, she were the Virgin Mary.

It gave me great pleasure to see their happiness and it was my turn now to feel a pang of envy. I thought how different everything would have been if Jocelyn and I had married and I had been able to make my preparations openly as Christabel did, instead of indulging in what, looking back, seemed a quite incongruous farce. More-over I was separated from my child for long periods so I could not be very contented with my lot. I thought about consulting Harriet, asking if she could think up another plan in which I adopted Carlotta.

That December, Christabel's child was born. Both my mother and I went to Grassland Manor and were there during the birth. We had to comfort Thomas, who was in a panic lest anything should go wrong. His devotion to Christabel was heartwarming, and I thought what a marvellous trick of fate's it was to have sent us out on the ice that morning.

The birth was long and arduous. In due course though we heard the cry of a child. The look of joy which came over Thomas's face moved me deeply.

We sat tense, waiting. Finally the midwife emerged. "It is a boy," she said.

There was silence. Thomas was too overjoyed to speak. Then he said: "And my wife?"

"Very, very tired. She cannot see you . . . not yet."

There was a warning in her voice and a terrible fear struck me. I looked at Thomas and saw the joy fading from his face.

My mother said: "It was a long labour. She will be all right when she has rested."

During the few days which followed there were grave fears for Christabel's survival. She had developed a fever and needed the greatest care. My father sent our doctor to her and he also brought down one of the Court doctors. I was glad he did. It showed that he had some feeling for his daughter.

My mother and I were at Grassland Manor more often than at Eversleigh Court. Together we nursed her and great was our joy when at last we began to see signs of improvement. My father had told my mother that Christabel was his daughter. She said she had guessed and wanted to do everything she could make up for those early days at the rectory.

"She's going to get well," I told Thomas.

He just put his arms round me and clung to me. I was touched and surprised to think that Christabel had inspired such devotion.

As for the baby—christened Thomas—he thrived, quite unaware of the near tragedy his coming had brought with it.

The doctors said that Christabel must go very carefully and must not think of having more babies for a long time...if ever.

Christmas had passed almost unnoticed and the New Year was upon us. A wet nurse had been found for Master Thomas and he gave little trouble. He was a contented child, healthy in every way and a great delight to both his parents.

This was what Christabel had needed all her life—to be loved. She was ready enough to give love in return and I have never known any woman more contented with her lot than Christabel was with hers at that time.

One cold January afternoon when the north wind was buffeting the walls of the house and it was comforting to be sitting before a warm fire, she confided in me.

She said: "How strange life is, Priscilla. Only a short time ago I had nothing. The future looked bleak. I dreaded it. And then suddenly everything changed. Happiness such as I had never dreamed possible came to me."

"That is life, Christabel. It's a lesson, I suppose. One shouldn't ever be too despondent."

"Or too elated, perhaps."

"I don't agree. When we are happy we should live it fully at the time and give no thought to the future."

"Is that what you thought when you were on the island with Jocelyn?"

"I didn't consciously think it. I suppose I was just happy to love and be loved by him. I accepted that moment and did not think beyond it."

"With what consequences!"

I said: "I would not be without Carlotta for anything."

"I understand that, Priscilla. I'm rather wicked, I'm afraid."

"Oh, nonsense! What are you talking about?"

"I don't deserve all this."

"Of course you do. It wouldn't be yours if you didn't. Do you think Thomas would be so completely in love with the sort of person you're trying to make out you are?"

"I'm different with him. I loved him from the moment he was so charming about the coat. He loved his first wife but she couldn't give him children, and now we have little Thomas. He is so happy about it. He always wanted children and now he has a son. He says he can't believe all this could come to him because of a piece of slippery ice."

"Well, it has come and now all you have to do is appreciate it and keep yourselves happy."

"I intend to. I wouldn't do anything to spoil it."

"Then don't talk of spoiling it. Don't even think of it."

"I won't. But I can't be completely happy until you have forgiven me."

"I forgive you? For what?"

"I was envious. I think I sometimes hated you. You were so kind to me, yet I couldn't stop it. I was fond of you often, but there was this strong resentment inside me. It was horrible. It was so strong it made me want to harm you."

"What are you talking about?"

"I was so conscious of being the outcast, the unwanted one, the child whose existence had been an embarrassment . . . like something you hide under a stone. To be put out by your parents, Priscilla, is heartbreaking to a sensitive child. I never had any love at all. The Connalts had none to give to anyone. They were the worst possible foster parents for a child like myself."

"It's all over, Christabel. It's done with. You're out of it. You have your son and your husband who adores you, and you have this lovely home. Never mind what you suffered to get here . . . you're here now and it's going to stay this way."

"You will understand me, Priscilla, I know, but let me confess. It will ease my conscience."

"Very well. Confess."

"There was a horrible need in me to humiliate you as I had been humiliated. You were the legitimate daughter, I the illegitimate one. I have a very unpleasant nature, you see. I knew what was happening between you and Jocelyn. I knew how innocent you were. I knew how people feel when they are desperate. We were going on the island, remember . . . all three of us. Then I pleaded a headache and I didn't go. I knew it was going to be misty. One of the gardeners told me. I deliberately let you go alone . . . the two of you."

"But why?"

"It occurred to my devious mind that what would happen was what did. My mind was twisted. Envy does twist the mind. It's the deadliest of emotions. It hurts the one who feels it more than the one it is directed against. Somehow I believed that it would happen as it did. You were two desperate people and it was inevitable that you should snatch at a few hours of happiness while you could. I did not think there would be a child, but this, of course, was a possibility. You see how my mind worked. I am really evil. And that I should have worked against you who have always been so kind to me . . ."

"Is that all your confession?" I asked.

She nodded. "Isn't it enough?"

I kissed her. "Please forget it, Christabel. I knew it long ago. Carlotta is so important to me that I cannot brood on how she came to be here. I can only rejoice that she is."

"It would have been better for you to have married Leigh. He loves you. Then you could have had children and they would have been with you. There wouldn't have been all this secrecy."

"You have always built up trouble, Christabel. You look for it. You look for slights. I noticed that from the first. Edwin upset you."

"I never really cared for Edwin. I know that now. I just wanted to escape from my poverty and insignificance.

Edwin is weak. I like strong men."

"And now you have your husband and child. Be happy, Christabel. You must be happy. You must make the most of what life has given you. If you don't, you might lose it."

She shivered and I put a shawl about her shoulders.

"I am wicked, Priscilla," she said. "If you only knew . . ."

I kissed her.

"No more of this morbidity. Shall I ask them to bring young Thomas in?"

She held out her hand to me and nodded.

When we returned to Eversleigh Court a shock awaited us.

My father was pacing up and down the hall, clearly in a state of tension and excitement.

"What has happened?" cried my mother.

"The King is dead," he replied.

My mother put her hand to her heart and turned pale.

"Carleton, what will this mean?" she whispered.

"That, my dear, remains to be seen."

"What are *you* going to do?"

"That also depends."

"Oh, God," prayed my mother fervently, "don't let this mean trouble.

"It was not unexpected," she went on. "Of course he has not been well of late."

"No," added my father. "For a year or more he has been unwell and not the man he was. He was so full of health before that, tiring his friends out at walking and sport. But of late he has been mildly irritable . . . so rare before with him. I think I saw it coming, but not so suddenly as this."

"He is not old. Fifty-five is not an age to die."

"He has lived too well perhaps. He has had the appointed span albeit he has packed into less years more than most men do."

They were talking round the real issue which was how would Monmouth act now, and more important still, what did my father intend to do?

My father went on talking about the King's death, how

the evening before he became ill he had been in the midst of the company and seemed well enough. He had supped with his concubines—the Duchesses of Portsmouth, Cleveland and Mazarin—and had given them many caressing displays of affection as was his wont. There had been the usual gambling and music, and they had all been enchanted by the singing of a little French boy who had been sent over by the courtesy of the King of France.

The King had visited the apartments of the Duchess of Portsmouth and had been lighted back to his rooms, where he had joked in his usual benevolent manner. The gentleman-in-waiting, whose duty it was to sleep on a mattress in his room along with the spaniels which were the King's constant companions, had said that the King had groaned in his sleep and when he arose did not seem well. He had taken a few drops of the medicine he had invented himself and which was called "The King's Drops." My father had had it given to him on more than one occasion and the King had described the ingredients to him: they were opium, bark of elder and sassafras all mixed up together in wine. Fifteen drops of this in a glass of sherry was considered to be a cure for all ailments. It had failed to cure the King, and when his servants were shaving him they were horrified to see his face grow suddenly purple, his eyes roll to the ceiling as he lolled forward in his chair. They could not understand what he was trying to say. They thought he was choking. He tried to rise and fell back into their arms. They feared death was imminent.

The Duke of York—the heir—came running to his brother's bedside with one foot in a slipper and the other in a shoe. They had not known whether Charles had recognized him.

"York!" cried my father angrily. "It is a sad day for this country with such a King. Charles knew the people did not want James. Didn't he say once: 'They'd never get rid of me, James, because that would mean having you. Therefore the crown is safe on my head.' Oh, why didn't he legitimatize Monmouth!"

"There would still have been those who stood for James."

"The Catholics, yes," retorted my father angrily. Then he went on to tell us how attempts had been made to save the King's life. Every remedy known had been used: hot irons pressed to his forehead, a liquid made from the extraction from skulls of dead men and women forced down his throat. He had been in great pain, but he had regained control of his speech and managed to joke in his wonted manner.

"We thought he was going to live," said my father. "You should have seen the joy in people's faces. They wanted to light their bonfires everywhere. Alas, it was a little too early to rejoice. There was a relapse and then there could be no doubt that he was dying. He showed more concern for his mistresses and his illegitimate children than anyone else."

"And Monmouth?" asked my mother.

"He did not mention his name."

"So now James the Second is King of England."

"God help us, yes."

"Carleton, you will not become involved. You will stay here in the country."

"My dear Arabella, you know me better than that."

"Does all this mean nothing to you? Your home, your family . . . ?"

"So much," he answered, "that I shall protect it with my life if need be."

They seemed unaware of me. I turned away and left them. He was comforting her, easing her fears. But I knew him well. He was a man who, when he had made up his mind that a cause was right, would stop at nothing to work for it. He had been the one who had stayed in England during the Commonwealth to work for the return of the King. He had lived in the midst of his enemies, posing as a Roundhead, he, the greatest Royalist of them all.

He had risked his life every minute of the day. He would do it again.

I was very uneasy.

We knew little peace from that moment. My mother went about the house like a pale ghost. My father was often at Court. I noticed how nervous my mother was becoming. She was startled every time we heard the sound of horses' hoofs in the courtyard.

We learned that the new King had heard Mass openly in the Queen's chapel. The Quakers sent a deputation to him in which they testified their sorrow in the death of Charles and their loyalty to the new King. The wording of the petition was significant.

We are told that thou art not of the persuasion of the Church of England any more than we, and therefore we hope that thou will grant unto us the same liberty thou allowest thyself.

In April the new King and Queen were crowned. James showed his leanings clearly by arresting Titus Oates, and although none felt any great sorrow about that, it did indicate that the King wished for no voice to be raised against the Catholics. Titus Oates was made to pay a fine of one thousand marks, was defrocked and condemned to be whipped publicly twice, and every year of his life to stand five times in the pillory. This would perhaps be the worst ordeal of all, as he had gathered many enemies during his reign of terror.

It was May—a beautiful month. Twenty-five years ago Charles had come back to regain his kingdom, and for those years the country had been lulled into a sense of security and rich living. The Puritan rule was over; the meaning of life was pleasure. The King had set the example and the country was only too happy to follow. The reign had been marred only by the Popish Plot and the Rye House Plot; and both of these had been formed at the instigation of foolish, evil men.

Now the days of soft living were over. There was a new King on the throne, and he was a Catholic King in a country which was dedicated in the main to Protestantism. It was said that Charles himself had been a Catholic; if he had been, he had also been too wise to show it openly. James had no such cynical wisdom, and in that beautiful month of May the menacing clouds hung over our house.

My father said quite casually, but I could tell he was hiding his excitement, "The Duke of Monmouth has sailed from Texel with a frigate and two small vessels."

"So," replied my mother blankly, "he is coming to England."

My father nodded.

"He will not be such a fool..." she began.

My father said: "He is the King's son. Many say Charles was married to Lucy Walter. Most important of all, he will stand for the Protestant cause."

"Carleton!" she cried, "you will not..."

"My dear," he answered very soberly, "you may be sure that I shall do what I consider best for us all."

He would say no more than that. But he was waiting. And we knew that one day the summons would come.

It was nearly three weeks later when it did.

Monmouth had landed at Lyme in Dorset and was appealing to his friends to join him. He was going to make an attempt to take the throne from James.

On the day my father left for the West Country a Bill of Attainder was issued against the Duke and a reward of five hundred pounds offered to anyone who could bring him to justice, dead or alive.

My mother was inconsolable.

"Why did he have to do this!" she cried. "This will be civil war. Why do we have to take sides? What does it matter to me what King is on the throne?"

I said: "It matters to my father."

"Does it matter more than his home... his family?"

"He was always a man for causes," I reminded her.

She nodded, and a bitter smile touched her mouth. I knew she was thinking of her arrival here when she had come with her first husband—Edwin's father—and how she met my father, who was then living at the utmost risk... for a cause.

197

"Monmouth will never succeed," she said vehemently
"I know it."

"And I know," I assured her, "that my father is a man
who will win through."

It was a grain of comfort . . . nothing more. There was
little we could do but wait. It was then that she gave me the
family journals to read and I learned so much about her
and him that I was filled with a new tenderness toward
them both.

News came from the West Country. Monmouth had
taken Taunton and it seemed that the West was ready to
declare for him. Flushed with victory, he had issued a
counter proclamation to that of the King, offering five
thousand pounds for the head of King James and declaring
Parliament a seditious assembly.

"It was the braggart in him," said my mother. He was
young and reckless. He might be Charles's son but he
would never be the man his father had been.

"How can your father! How can he? Monmouth is
doomed to failure. He has failure written all over him. I
pray to God to guard your father."

There was a jubilant message from my father.
Monmouth had been proclaimed King in Taunton and was
marching on Bristol.

We heard later that he did not reach Bristol, as the
King's army was approaching. So he went back to
Bridgwater and there prepared for the great battle.

My father wrote to us on the eve of the battle and sent a
messenger to us.

Be of good heart. Ere long there will be a new King
on the throne and though his name will be James he
will not be James Stuart. This will be James Scott,
King of England.

Reading the letter my mother grew angry.
"How foolish of him . . . to write thus. The risk he runs
Oh, Priscilla, I fear for him. I fear so much."

198

I repeated my belief that he would always win through. "Whatever happens, he will be all right. I know it."

She smiled wanly. "He always got what he wanted," she agreed.

The outcome of that fateful battle of Sedgemoor is well known. What chance had Monmouth against the King's forces led by the Earl of Faversham and his second in command, John Churchill? Monmouth's army consisted of rustics and men such as my father who, for all their bravery and dedication, were not professional soldiers.

Monmouth's army was easily defeated and Monmouth himself, seeing the day was lost, was more intent on preserving his own life than standing to fight with those who had so loyally supported him.

Many people had been taken prisoner—among them my father.

We were stunned, although my mother had been expecting disaster ever since the death of the King, but that our pleasant lives should be suddenly so devastated was something we found it hard to accept.

The news grew worse. My father was imprisoned in Dorchester, and when my mother heard that the Lord Chief Justice, Baron George Jeffreys, would preside at the trial, she was overcome by a frenzy of grief.

"He is a wicked man," she cried. "He is cruel beyond belief. I have heard such tales of him. And your father will be at his mercy. He said at the time of his appointment that he could not understand why Jeffreys had been given the post. Charles disliked him. He once said he had no learning, no sense, no manners and more impudence than ten carted streetwalkers. I know he opposed the appointment for a long time. It was a sign of his weakening strength that he at length gave way. Oh, I am so afraid. He hates men like your father. He envies them their good looks, their breeding and their boldness. He will have no mercy. There is nothing he enjoys more than condemning a man to death."

My mother's grief was more than I could bear. I kept thinking of wild plans to rescue my father. The thought of his being herded into prison with countless others was horrifying.

Thomas and Christabel came to see us as soon as they heard the news; they were genuinely grieved. Thomas had a grain of comfort to offer. "Jeffreys is a greedy man," he said. "It is hinted that he will be lenient in return for some profit. They say he is hoping to make a small fortune out of these assizes, for there are some rich people involved."

"Then there is a chance!" cried my mother.

"It would have to be done very tactfully and he would want a good deal, I daresay."

"I would give everything I have," she replied fervently.

Clearly the Willerbys had raised her spirits, for she came to my room that night. She looked very frail and there were dark shadows under her eyes. She stood against the door and I longed to comfort her, for I knew that without him her life would not be worth living.

She said: "I have made up my mind. I shall leave for the West Country tomorrow."

"Do you think it possible to bribe this judge?"

"It is obviously possible and I am going to do it."

"I shall come with you," I answered.

"Oh, my dearest child," she cried, "I knew you would."

"We will make our preparations early in the morning," I said, "and leave just as soon as we are ready."

What followed is like a nightmare to me—and still is.

We went by stagecoach, which seemed the easiest way. It was a sombre journey and at the inn where we rested there was constant talk of what was being called the Monmouth Rebellion. The name of Judge Jeffreys was spoken in low whispers. It was clear that everyone pitied his victims.

It was said that he not only passed the harshest sentences which he could, but he did so with relish and could, with his wicked tongue, turn innocence into guilt.

As we approached the west, the mist grew more intense. Monmouth's army had been active only in Dorset and Somerset, and the prisoners were all judged in those counties.

Jeffreys, with his lieutenants, was in his element. He delighted in his grisly work. There should be no delay once a man was sentenced. In twenty-four hours from his condemnation he was swinging on a gallows or suffering whatever the bloodthirsty judge had decreed for him.

"Oh, God," prayed my mother, "let us get there in time."

I think perhaps I pitied her more than I did my father. If he were sentenced, his death would come quickly. *She* would be haunted by the tragedy for the rest of her days. She was almost demented with grief. We would save him, I promised her. We must. It was not impossible and she must not allow herself to think so. We were going to get there in time. We were going to give everything we had if necessary to save my father's life.

It was so irksome for her when we stayed in the inns on the way. She would have liked to drive through the night.

As we came nearer to our destination, so did the horror increase. The judge, whose name was on every lip, and was spoken of with disgust and repugnance, had ordered that it should be brought home to the people what happened to traitors. Often we passed limbs hanging on trees and corpses of hanged men. The smell of death permeated the air.

"What shall we do?" demanded my mother. "What can we do when we get there?"

At an inn one night they were talking about the case of Lady Lisle whose crime had been to give food to two of Monmouth's followers who had escaped from the battlefield.

Jeffreys' manner towards the poor woman had been so cruel even for him that the case was being discussed everywhere.

He had a way, this judge, of bullying his juries into giving the verdict he wanted. If they seemed inclined to be lenient he would fix them with a glare from the most wicked eyes in the world so that they shivered in their seats and wondered what case would be brought against them if they did not do the judge's bidding.

This poor lady was called a traitor; she should suffer the death of traitors. He sentenced her to be burned to death.

This was too much to be accepted. Moreover, it was being said that the harshness shown to Lady Lisle came at the instigation of a higher source, for she was the widow of John Lisle, who had been one of the judges at the trial of Charles the First.

This seemed like the King's revenge on the murderers of his father, and friends of Lady Lisle were pointing out that the lady herself was guilty only of two things—giving food to men who happened to be flying from Sedgemoor and being the wife of a man who, with others, had condemned Charles the First.

James should consider. What would his brother Charles have done? He would never have allowed a woman to be treated so.

James was not inclined to enjoy being compared with his brother, but he did have enough sense to see that to submit a frail woman to one of the most barbaric deaths conceivable for no real crime would not redound to his credit. At the same time he wanted everyone to know that they would be ill advised to take up arms against him.

Lady Lisle was saved from the stake to lose her head on the block.

My mother had scarcely eaten since we left home. She was very pale and had lost weight. I was fearful for her health.

There was more news. Monmouth had escaped to the New Forest even before the battle was over. He had hidden there for a few days but had been captured and taken to London. There he had implored the King to save his life. "For my father's sake," he begged. "You are my uncle. Remember that."

But James only remembered that Monmouth had tried to take the crown from him. There was no point in delay, he said.

We had reached the town of Dorchester when news was brought to us of Monmouth's death. He had deserted his army; he had cringed before the King; but once he knew that death was inevitable, he had met it bravely, affirming on the scaffold his adherence to the Church of England. It must have been a gruesome scene because the executioner struck five times before he completely severed the head and brought about the end of the Duke of Monmouth, reckless, ambitious and lacking in principle.

At least he died a brave man.

This was small comfort to my mother.

We came to lodge in an inn in the ancient market town—a busy one, for through it passed the road to Devon and Cornwall. The earthworks, known as Maiden Castle, relic of four thousand years before when the land must have been little more than a forest, brought many people to look at it. But we had no thought of such matters.

My mother, frantic with anxiety, frustrated because she had no idea how to set about the task of freeing my father, was in a desperate state, and the very night we arrived at the inn was smitten with a fever and was delirious. I was really frightened and the next morning sent for a doctor. He came and said she must rest and nothing must be done to disturb her. He gave her a potion to make her sleep.

"You are here because you have a relative prisoner?" he asked.

I nodded.

The doctor shook his head sadly. "Let her sleep as long as you can. It is acute anxiety which has brought this on. I have seen much of this since our town was turned into a court and a shambles."

I was grateful for his sympathy. I asked myself what I should do. How could I set about this delicate task? To whom did I offer my bribe? I must not run into trouble, for there was my mother to care for.

I was in a state of great anxiety.

When the doctor had left I went down to the inn parlour. I wondered if I could speak to the innkeeper. There might be someone here . . . someone from the army, perhaps, who could help me. Edwin and Leigh were in the army. It was ironical to think that they might have been fighting against my father had they been in England.

We had at least been saved that.

My grandfather, my mother's father, now dead, had been General Tolworthy; the Eversleighs were connected with the army, too. Yes, I decided there must be some high-ranking soldier in this town who would be ready to help me.

I came into the inn parlour. A man was sitting there. He was in uniform, so he was a soldier and a high-ranking one. My heart beat fast. My prayers might be about to be answered.

I said, "Good day."

He turned. I was looking into the face of Beaumont Granville.

A shiver of terror ran down my spine.

I muttered: "I'm sorry. I thought I knew you."

Then I turned and ran quickly up the stairs.

I was trembling. I felt sick with fear. The nightmare was indeed growing worse.

I looked at my mother lying there sleeping. She was pale and very still. I knelt by the bed and hid my face in the bedclothes.

I felt very apprehensive.

After a few moments I arose. He wouldn't have recognized me, I assured myself. He had said nothing. I should have to be watchful now. I must keep out of his way.

What evil fate had brought him here to Dorchester? I had not thought of his being a soldier—one of the King's men. This town was full of soldiers.

I looked at myself in the mirror. I must have changed since those days in Venice. No, he would not have recognized me, for I had hurried from the room almost as soon as he had looked at me.

I sat down and thought of it all—those days in Venice, that night of the ball when he had come very near to kidnapping me, the birth of Carlotta; I thought of Harriet, lively, energetic, relishing a situation which was full of pitfalls.

What can I do? I asked myself.

I felt the situation was growing more and more desperate every minute.

There was a knock at my door. I started up, crying: "Who is there?"

It was the innkeeper.

I opened the door and he stood there with a letter in his hand. "A gentleman asked me to give you this," he said.

I took it and said: "What gentleman?"

"He is below, my lady. He awaits an answer."

"Thank you." I shut the door and listened to his footsteps as he went down the stairs.

For some moments I was afraid to open the letter. Then I took it to the window and read:

I know who you are and why you are here. I think I may be able to help. Will you come down to the inn parlour and discuss this?

Beaumont Granville

I stared at the paper. So he had recognized me. What did it mean? He could help me? My impulse was to tear up the letter.

I stood for a moment hesitating and then I looked at my mother's face.

I must at least not let the opportunity pass by. All my instincts called out to me not to trust this man. Yet what would I do? I did not know which way to turn. At Eversleigh it had seemed easy enough to say: "Offer a bribe. Others have done so with success. They say Jeffreys is becoming rich out of the Bloody Assizes." Yet how did one offer a bribe? It was a delicate procedure. It was something which must not be mentioned in actual terms. There would have to be hints. Ways had to be found to give the bribe as though it were not being given at all.

I knew I would see this man. I must. There was no alternative.

I went down to the inn parlour.

He turned as I came in. He was smiling with what I can only call triumph. He rose and bowed low.

"So," he said, "we meet again."

"You had something to say to me?"

"Indeed I have. Won't you sit down? I have told the innkeeper we must not be disturbed."

I sat down. There was a table between us. I looked into his face. Beau Granville. The name suited him. He had those excessive good looks which had no doubt led him to believe that the world was his for the taking. I guessed he took a great pride in his appearance. His linen was scented with the smell I remembered at once. It was a mingling of musk and sandalwood, perfumes I did not like.

"I know why you are here. Your father is in prison in this town. His trial will be in two days' time."

"Two days," I repeated.

He smiled. He had perfect teeth and clearly liked to show them.

"That gives us a little time," he said.

"Yes," I answered quietly.

"I could help you, you know."

"How?"

He lifted his shoulders. "My country estate is on the edge of this town. I know the judge well. I have often entertained him here. I believe that a word from me would go a long way."

"We will pay," I said eagerly.

He put his hands to his lips. "Do not speak so," he replied. "It could be dangerous."

"I know these things are done. I have heard . . ."

"My dear young lady, you are reckless. If these things are done, then it is natural that they should be, but to *speak* of them, that is a crime."

"Please be serious. This is very important to me . . . to us . . ."

"Of course. Of course." He spoke soothingly. "Your

father would meet the worst possible fate. He is just the sort my friend dislikes. Given a chance..."

"Please...we will do anything."

"Will you?"

"We will do *anything*," I repeated.

"It will rest with you."

"What?" I said faintly.

I knew, of course. I saw those eyes, sly, lascivious, assessing me.

"I admired you from the moment I saw you," he said. "It was a great regret to me that we did not become better acquainted in Venice. It is my urgent desire that we should repair that unfortunate state of affairs."

"Will you please say clearly what you mean."

"I should have thought it was clear."

I stood up.

"Don't be hasty," he warned. "You will regret it all your life if you are. Think of your father. Think of your mother."

I closed my eyes. I was thinking: I shall have to save him. I shall have to save them both. I must. And this man knows it. Oh, Leigh, where are you?

Yet what could Leigh do to save my father?

"Come," he said, "be reasonable. Sit down. Listen."

I sat. I felt hypnotized by those cruel golden eyes with the long, almost feminine lashes and the beautifully marked golden brows.

"You cheated me...in Venice," he went on. "That brute came and snatched you from me. If you had only come to me then I should have so delighted you that we should have been happy together. But I lost you, and ever since I have thought of you. Then I saw you today and I knew your father was here. I can save him. I can bring many favours to people who seek them. My family is an influential one. I *will* save your father. I promise you...but I need my reward."

"And your reward is..."

"You." He leaned forward and spoke almost breathlessly. "I will send a carriage for you at sundown. You will be brought to my house. You will stay with me until the dawn. During that time you will be my beloved little slave. You will be mine entirely, denying me nothing, wishing only to serve me."

"I think you are despicable. You are in a position—so you say—to save a man's life, and you ask payment for that!"

"Oh, come, you are a young woman who would be too proud to accept charity. You would want to pay your debts, would you not?"

"I hate you."

"That may be, but it is not a question of your emotions, but of mine. I am the one who has to be paid."

"It . . . is not possible," I said.

He shrugged his shoulders. "So you will let your father die?"

I looked at him wretchedly. "Is there nothing else? . . . We could pay."

"I need money. I always need money. They say I am rather extravagant. But in this case there is something I want more, and I am afraid it is the price for this particular service."

"How could it be brought about . . . my father's release, I mean?"

"I would see that he walked into the inn on the day that followed."

"Can you be sure?"

He nodded.

"But how can *I* be sure?"

"It would be a gamble," he said.

"Then I shall have to find some other means."

"How? What will you do?"

"I will find some way."

"There is not much time. Do you propose to seek out the judge and say, 'Fair sir, I offer you this . . . or that . . . for my father's life?' I warn you his price might be the same as mine."

I felt dizzy. I kept thinking of my father and imagined him, swinging on a rope . . . or worse still. I thought of my mother and I realized how dear they both were to me—he no less than she was—and that I had wanted my father's love all my life. I had longed to shine in his eyes; I had wanted him to be proud of me and his indifference to me had not really changed my feelings towards him. Perhaps it had made me more eager for his approval.

"What if you do not keep your part of the bargain?" I asked.

"I give you my word that I shall. I can and I will do it."

"How can I trust you?"

"You can't be sure, can you? You will have to take that chance. I am not, as you may have guessed, noted for my virtue, but I have a deserved reputation for paying my gambling debts. When I give a promise to pay I consider it a point of honour to do so."

"Honour. *You* talk of honour?"

"Honour of a sort. We all have our standards, you know. Well, what is it to be?"

I was silent. I could not bear to look at him. But even while I hesitated I knew I had to save my father.

"I will send a carriage for you at dusk," he said. "It will bring you back the following morning. The next day you will be able to return with your parents."

I felt numb. I had prayed for a solution, and here it was offered to me, but at what a price!

He was regarding me with glittering eyes. I thought of the first time I had seen him in St. Mark's Square and how this had really grown out of my love for Jocelyn and had begun when I discovered him in the haunted flower garden.

I turned and hurried from the room.

My mother's fever had not abated and the doctor came again.

"How ill is she?" I asked. "Is there not something that can be done?"

"What she needs is her husband safe beside her."

I thought: Everything is telling me that I must do this. I could save them both. Surely what happened to me was nothing compared with their future happiness. I *must* save them both, no matter what it cost me.

I hated this man with an intensity I had never felt before. It was in his power to save my parents, yet to do so he insisted on my utter humiliation. One moment I wished I had never seen him, and then I remembered that if I had not there might not have been even this opportunity of saving my father.

I thought of the tangled web of my life and how one event was so closely interwoven with another. I tried to think of anything but the coming night.

For one thing I was thankful. There would have to be no explanation to my mother. She would sleep deeply through the night and if she needed anything there was a bell rope by the bed which would bring one of the serving maids to her. I trusted she would not wake and find me missing.

There seemed no fear of that. The doctor had given her a potion which he said would make her sleep, for forgetfulness was what she needed more than anything.

So, as the shadows were falling I put on my cloak and went down to the inn parlour to wait.

I did not wait long. A liveried servant came asking for me, and there was the carriage waiting to take me to my doom.

We rode through the streets of that old city which had been built hundreds of years before when the Romans came to Britain. The streets were full of strangers and there were soldiers everywhere. It was a town of roystering and tragedy, for many a Dorset man would come to a sad end within the next few days. Through the town he went, past the almshouses known as Nappers Mite, past the grammar school founded by Queen Elizabeth, and the old church with its tower which was two hundred years old.

I saw these things as though in a dream. If I save my father, I thought, I shall never want to see this place again. Then I was praying silently for help to get me through this night.

210

On the edge of the town was a mansion. We turned in at the gates and went up the drive. The house loomed before us—sinister, I thought, like an enchanted dwelling conjured up by evil spirits.

I tried to appear calm as I stepped down and entered the hall.

It was not unlike our hall at Eversleigh—the high vaulted roof, the long refectory table with the pewter utensils on it, the swords and halberds hanging on the wall—a typical baronial mansion.

A woman came forward. She was rotund, middle-aged and heavily painted, with a patch on her cheek and another on her temple.

"We are waiting for you, mistress," she said. "Please follow me."

With a heavily beating heart and a warning within me to be prepared for anything terrible and strange which might happen to me, I followed her up a staircase lined with family portraits.

We went along a gallery to a door. I was taken into a room at the end of which was a dais; curtains were half drawn across this.

The curtains were then pulled right back and a serving girl with her sleeves rolled up was waiting there. There was a hip bath and two tall pewter jugs from which rose scented steam. I guessed they contained hot water.

"I am ready, mistress," said the maid.

The woman who had brought me in nodded. "Fill the bath," she said; and to me: "Take off your clothes."

I said: "I don't understand."

"You are here to obey orders," said the woman with a smile, which was the first of the humiliations I was to suffer that night. I saw her in the role for which she was ideally suited; she was a pander, a procuress. I had heard of these matters.

The maid had filled the bath and turned to me giggling. I felt an impulse to turn and run. Then horrible images came into my mind. My father...my mother...And I knew then that whatever happened to me I must accept because it would be a means of saving them from tragedy.

Time passes. It will be over, I promised myself. Whatever it is I must bear it.

"Come, my dear," said the woman. She had a deep, hoarse voice like a man's. "We have not all night." She laughed and the maid laughed with her.

"There is no need for a bath," I said. "I am clean."

"This is the way it is wanted. Are you ashamed to take off your clothes? Are you deformed or something? Oh, come, you look pretty enough to me. Now let us undo these buttons...quietly, gently. We don't want to pull them off, do we?"

So I was stripped of my clothes.

"Quite commendable," said the woman. The maid continued to giggle.

I stepped into the bath and washed myself.

The maid stood by with a big towel with which she dried me while the woman stood by smiling.

When I was dry she brought out a bottle of lotion which was rubbed into my skin. It smelt of musk and sandalwood which I had noticed before and reminded me of Beaumont Granville. The scent was mingled with that of roses.

"And now," said the woman, who was growing more and more odious to me with every passing moment, "one which is to be especially for you. He has chosen for you the rose. He likes different ones for different people." She rubbed another lotion into my arms and about my neck.

"There," she murmured, "that will please, I have no doubt." She turned to the maid. "The robe."

It was wrapped about me. It was a cloak of fine silk—pale pink with black roses embroidered on it.

"There! Now let us go. My lord is impatient."

I felt as though I had been brought into some eastern harem. The whole procedure was more hideously distasteful to me than anything I had ever known. I was trying hard not to think of what lay before me.

I followed the woman up another flight of stairs; she knocked on a door, pushed it open and led me in.

She left me there and went out, shutting the door behind her.

He came forward. He was wearing a cloak not unlike my own. The smell of musk and sandalwood was strong.

He took my hand and kissed it.

"I knew you would come. Have they treated you well?"

"Humiliatingly."

He laughed. "It is simply the way in which you regard these matters. They did not ill-treat you?"

"Only insult me. But that was on your orders, wasn't it?"

"I am a great believer in the bath," he said. "And I have studied perfumes. I make my own, you know. Do you like the rose?"

"I do not like anything I find here."

"There is one thing you have to remember about our little adventure. You must please me."

"Yes," I agreed, "I know that."

"That is what you have come here to do. You must not be upset because you have taken a bath and been anointed. Tonight is going to be one you will never forget."

"That is something I can be sure of, although I shall do my best to put it out of my mind as soon as it is over."

"Don't talk of its being over when it is only just beginning."

"Will you swear that you will save my father?"

"I have given my word. I told you, did I not, that I pay my debts? I promise you that if you give me what I want I shall give you what you want. Have no fear of that. I will tell you that I already have the matter in hand. Your father has been removed to a small room in the prison. He will spend the night there. In the morning, if you are good to me, the door of that room shall be unlocked and he shall go forth a free man. I have put our plan into action so far."

"You must have great power and influence with this man who is murdering those men and women whose only fault was that they supported the losing side."

He put his fingers to my lips. "You talk too freely. You must be careful, you know. We want you and your parents

213

to be riding home within the week, don't we?"

"Yes," I said, "more than anything I want that."

"Very well. You have come here to me. I appreciate that. Virtue in ladies is to be admired—but not above all things, eh? Tonight is mine. You belong to me tonight . . . completely. That is understood, is it not?"

"In exchange for my father's life, yes."

"You shall be paid for your services, never fear. Come close to me. How delightful you smell. I chose the rose for you to mingle with the musk. It's a clever idea really. You are an attractive creature, Priscilla. I like your name. It is a prim name, you know. Primness can be very attractive as long as the owner of it knows when to discard it. You are aware of that, I am sure. First I am going to show you some of my pictures. I am an artist, you must realize. I am a man of great talent. There are many things I might have done if I had not been born a gentleman with no compulsion to do anything. I can blend my perfumes. I might have set up shop and supplied the Court. Scents to delight ladies in their boudoirs; scents to disguise evil odours, and there are plenty of those in the streets. Scents to titillate the senses and to arouse the passions of jaded gentlemen. Then I am an artist. I shall show you my pictures now. Come with me."

The evening was taking an unexpected turn. I had not been prepared for these preliminaries. Although I was aware of the lust in him and I knew what the climax must be, I could not understand why all this cruel dallying was taking place beforehand.

There was a room leading from this one and he took me through to it. It was a small room and the walls were lined with pictures. He lighted candles and led me to the wall. There were drawings of women, all naked and in various positions which showed their physical differences clearly.

"Ladies I have loved," he said. "I sketch them. You must admit there is a good deal of the artist in me."

"I suppose so," I said turning away.

"You would be surprised what a good aid they are to the

214

memory. I come to this room and relive the hours I spent with each of these."

"An occupation which doubtless gives you some gratification."

"A great deal. You see this space on the wall."

I felt great waves of horror sweeping over me, for I knew what was coming.

"It is reserved for you," he said smiling.

"No," I cried fiercely.

"You have forgotten our bargain already?"

"What purpose would it serve?"

"It would please me, which is the sole purpose of this occasion, is it not?"

"I was not told of this. It was not in the bargain."

"You were told that you must do as I ask. I am rendering you a great service. It is not easy at a time like this to snatch a man from the hangman's rope."

"I must go."

"Very well. I shall make no effort to detain you. Shall I ring for the woman? She will give you your clothes and I'll send the carriage back with you to the inn."

He was watching me sardonically.

"My poor Priscilla! In two days' time it will be over. You can return to your home . . . fatherless but virtue retained. You see, I make no effort to hold you. There shall be no force, although in your present vulnerable position that would be easy. No. I have promised myself, She shall come of her own free will. That is the bargain and we shall keep to it."

"Where will you do this . . . drawing?"

"I will show you."

There was yet another room leading from the picture gallery. This was small. There was a couch on it covered with black velvet.

"The contrast of the blackness of the velvet and the colour of the skin is delightful," he said. "Now. Your cloak, my dear."

He took it from me and studied me with glinting eyes. I

thought he was going to seize me then, but he restrained himself. He just let his hands slide over my body and taking a deep breath said: "Later. This first."

He made me lie on the couch and put me in the required pose, which I found loathsome. There was an easel at the end of the room.

It was like something out of an impossibly wild dream—myself lying naked on a couch and this strange man, who I was sure was mad, sitting there in the flickering candlelight sketching me.

I wondered what else the night would bring forth.

Whatever it is, I said to myself, I must endure it. Was it true that my father had already been removed from the terrible prison which he would have shared with many others? Had I succeeded even so far in bringing him a little comfort? I could not let a chance of saving my father pass by. I kept telling myself that it was going to succeed.

I heard him speaking. "It is a rough sketch only. I will complete it later. Then we shall know each other more intimately. That is important to the artist."

I did not look at the sketch. I did not want to see it and he did not offer to show me.

"Now we shall sup," he said. "It will be ready for us now. You must be hungry."

"I never felt less hungry."

"You must not allow the anticipation to spoil your appetite."

I put on my cloak and we went back to his bedroom. There was a small fire in his bedroom although it was summer. I stared blankly at the blue flames. Several candles had been lighted, and a table set up. Food was set out most tastefully and there was a flask of wine.

He indicated that I should sit down opposite him.

"This is a great occasion for me," he said. "I have never forgotten you, you know. You looked so young, so innocent, there in St Mark's Square ... so different from the women one meets so frequently in such places. When I saw you in the shop I had a great desire to be your lover."

216

"Should that be marvelled at? Has not such a thought occurred to you a thousand times with a thousand women?"

"I admit that I have a fondness for your sex and I have always had a partiality for the virginal. The young are so appealing. There is an urge in us all to instruct, and if we are skilful at some art, that urge is greater. I have loved women from the time I was ten years old, when I was seduced by one of my family's servants. I had discovered my métier in life."

"To be seduced?" I asked.

"You could call it that. But I have become such a master at the art of making love that I have ceased to become the pupil and have taken on the role of tutor."

"And seducer?"

"When it is necessary. But a man of charm is somewhat sought after, as you can imagine."

"It is difficult for me to imagine, for no such urge would ever come to me as far as you are concerned."

"I see I shall be on my mettle. Who knows, you may fall in love with me, and it will not be I who offers rewards for your company, but you for mine."

"That is completely impossible."

"Who shall say? This is not quite what you expected, is it?"

"No."

"You thought I should seize you, debauch you, and that would be all that was asked."

I was silent.

"But I am a man of cultured tastes," he went on. "You and I shall share this bed throughout this blessed night, but our encounter shall be one of refinement."

"Please," I replied, "if you are a man of refinement and culture, let me go. Show your gallantry, your courtesy, your perfect manners by behaving like a gentleman and generously give me my father's life and ask nothing in return."

He stood up and began to pace the floor.

Wild hope surged up in me. I thought: He is strange. Perhaps he is mad. Could it really be that I had touched a softer side of his nature?

He took off his golden wig. He was, as I had thought in Jocelyn's case, more handsome without it. His short hair curled about his head, and he looked younger, less sinister.

But when he came to the table and I saw him clearly, I was aware of a fanatical gleam in his eyes.

"Look at me," he said. "Look closely."

He put his fingers to his brow and I saw the scar from the roots of his hair almost extending to his eyebrow. This had been hidden by the curled wig.

"You see this," he explained. "I received it in Venice. The night after the Duchessa's ball. You may remember it."

I stared at him. I knew that my hopes of getting out of this house unscathed had completely gone. He wanted more than my body. He wanted revenge.

"It was a frolic," he went on. "A light adventure. A young girl...made for love...unawakened, I thought, adorably innocent. I would initiate her into the ways of love. There would be nothing rough about it."

"Nothing rough," I cried. "You dragged me from the ball. I was covered in bruises. And you say nothing rough."

"I would have been tender to you. You would have been in love with me before the night was out."

"You have too high an opinion of your powers and no knowledge at all of me."

"I learned a great deal about you, my prim Priscilla. This man came to rescue you. He took you from me and threw me into the canal. That was not all. The next night he came. I do not care for this kind of brawl. He had me at a disadvantage. This is not the only scar I have to show you. He prated about innocent girls...his little sister...still in the schoolroom...innocent virgin...and so on."

"It was a wicked thing you tried to do."

"And for it I am marked for life. And then I discovered the truth."

"What truth?"

"Surely you know. Our innocent virgin schoolgirl is in Venice for a purpose. She has been guilty of an indiscretion. Now young ladies are often guilty of indiscretions and sometimes they have alarming consequences. Then, if the girl is of good family, heads are put together to discover how best the little matter can be kept secret. The Virgin of Venice was in such a position, so while I was being scarred for life for having made overtures to this saintly child, she was in Venice to bear the little bastard...the result of an adventure with one ...perhaps more..."

I had risen from the table. "How dare you!" I cried. "Stop this lewd talk."

"My dear little would-be virgin, this is my night. I call the tune. Do you remember?"

"How do you know of these matters?"

"That is unimportant. The fact is that I know. But I did not discover until afterwards. At the time I took my punishment, thinking that perhaps it had not been undeserved. Outraged brother...or close relation...who has doubtless had his own adventures is incensed because someone might wish for a similar adventure with his sister. We understand. And then to learn that the girl is nothing but a little harlot...and at her age!"

"It's untrue."

"No, it is not, my dear. I learned all I wanted to know. Oh, I had a very good informant."

"Who was it?"

"That would be telling. The child was born and your good friend, Lady Stevens, pretended it was hers. What a drama! But that does not concern me. What does is that my prim little harlot was posing as an innocent young girl."

This was becoming more and more like a nightmare. I heard myself saying: "I was going to be married. He died..."

"Yes," he said, "they always do. So inconsiderate of them. They might wait until after the ceremony before they die. It saves so much trouble."

"I can see it is no use talking to you."

219

"The time for talking is past. Let me fill your glass. Let us drink to the night. I am not sorry. You and I will have much to give each other, I am sure."

"I shall give you hatred and contempt."

"Well, that can be very interesting. How angry you are! And surprised, too. It has put a colour into your cheeks, like the roses with which you are so delicately scented. They come from Bulgaria where they are the very best. If I had time I would show you my laboratories. The late King and I shared an interest in them...only he was more interested in pills. We had many interests in common— perhaps the chief was the delights of love. He was a connoisseur, God rest him. But no more so than I, you will discover. You shiver. Is that meant to be with repulsion? I promise you, you shall shiver with delight."

"I could never delight in you. You have done nothing but insult me from the time I saw you."

"And in return you deceived me...at first that is. A naughty little girl, pregnant, and posing as an innocent child. Who would have believed it! You owe me something for that and for this"—he pointed to the scar—"and for the other which I shall show you. But come, eat. This is the finest venison, captured in my woods. And drink."

"Anything at your table nauseates me."

"I think you are dreading what is to come."

"I should not be here were it not for my father."

"You will discover that you have never had a lover such as you will have tonight."

"It is a discovery I would rather not make."

"I am making everything so easy for you, am I not? You have been bathed in scented water, anointed with perfumes. Do you like the musk? It has very special properties. It is said to touch the senses and arouse desire. Did you know that?"

"I did not and it certainly has no effect on me."

"I told you I have my laboratory. Do you know what musk is? It comes from the musk deer. It is a glandular secretion. This deer is found in the mountains of India. It is a scent he carries most strongly during the rutting season and it is irresistible to the female deer. You see that it has these special properties. Of course, we do not use it in the crude form. Ladies are not female deer, are they? But they have the same desires and they can be aroused just as those of the deer can. There is a little pod which is inside the animal's body. A little hole is made in the skin... just enough for a man's finger. Thus the pod can be extracted. Don't look so disgusted. It does no harm to the deer. He goes on living but he probably wonders why he finds it so hard to get a mate. Never mind. His musk is making a beautiful scent to lure some lady from the path of virtue."

"It is revolting and so are you. I loathe the smell more than ever."

"That's what you tell me, but you don't always tell the truth, do you? What a spectacular piece of acting, to play virgin when you were so clearly different from that. I am pleased with you though, naughty Priscilla. I think I like you better as the scheming woman than as the virgin. You are sly, of course, very sly. But you please me. I am getting impatient now. Come, drink some of this wine."

I shook my head.

"It has aphrodisiac qualities... like the musk. If you are really not looking forward to the night, it might help you."

I still shook my head.

"Drink it," he said, and his manner had changed. "I say drink it. You are here to obey me. Is that not part of the bargain?"

I suddenly felt that it was no use caring any more what happened to me. I was here for a purpose and that must be carried out. There would be no one to rescue me this time and I could not ask to be rescued. I *had* to save my father.

I drank the wine. I had had nothing to eat and I felt a little dizzy. He was right. The wine would help me endure what had to come.

I heard him laugh softly.

"Come," he said, "I am ready now."

I stood up. I felt his hands on my cloak. It slid to the ground. He took off his cloak and stood before me. He touched the angry mark across his chest. "Inflicted by your protector," he said. "You have to pay a good deal for that." There was a savage note in his voice. I had to suppress a desire to turn and run. But he had picked me up and thrown me onto the bed.

Even now I cannot bear to think of that night. He was determined to make me pay in full for the thrashing Leigh had given him and for the fact that he, who prided himself on his knowledge of women, had been deceived into thinking a pregnant girl was an innocent virgin. This was what I was paying for, although the bait he offered me was my father's life.

The man was amoral. He had no feeling for right or wrong. Again and again during that night he reminded me of my need to submit to his will—and every time I dared not disobey.

I tried to disengage myself, to be as one looking on at my other self partaking in these activities. I knew that he was trying to subdue my spirit as well as my body, and it irked him—while it aroused a certain admiration in him—that he could not. He was a strange man. Oddly enough, I trusted him to keep his part of the bargain, although from everything I knew of him, it seemed foolish to expect it. But I did. He was, as he had said, in some ways a man of refined tastes. His scented linen, his well-washed body bore this out. At least I did not have to endure an unwashed lecher. I felt bruised bodily and mentally, and all the time I was telling myself that it must soon pass.

When I saw the first streak of dawn in the sky, I knew my ordeal was coming to an end.

He made no attempt to stop my leaving. I wrapped myself in the cloak and pulled the bell rope. The woman whom I had seen when I arrived came into the room. She looked different without her false pieces of hair and her patches. But she was clean. I was sure that everyone near him must be that.

She took me without a word to the room where I had bathed. There were my clothes. I dressed and she led me out. The carriage was waiting and I was taken back to the inn.

I went straight to my mother's room and with great relief saw that she was still sleeping. I prayed to God that she had not missed me during the night.

I took off my outdoor clothes and sat down. I shut my eyes. Images from the previous night kept crowding into my mind.

My father will come today, I told myself, and then it will all have been worthwhile.

Yes, it would. What was a night's humiliation compared with a life, and my father's life at that!

I thought about him. He was another strange man, a man who had known many women before he married my mother. I believed he had been faithful to her. Christabel was his daughter. He had admitted that. Perhaps he had other children here and there.

Thinking of my father stopped those images. I saw him instead of the handsome, lascivious face of Beaumont Granville which I was sure would haunt me for the rest of my life.

I thought then: I love my father. I love him dearly . . . perhaps more than I do my mother. Always I had wanted to impress him, to have him take notice of me, to look for me when he came home after an absence. He never had. He never would. I was only the daughter and sons were important to a man such as he was.

Then suddenly I was elated because when he came through the door I could say to myself: I saved you. I brought you home. The daughter you have never thought of much account was the one who saved your life.

I did not care at that moment what I had done. I was glad of it. I had suffered humiliation for his sake and I would do it again.

My mother stirred uneasily during the morning. I sat beside her with a sickening fear in my heart.

Would Granville keep his word? Why should I trust such a man? Was he laughing now because he had deceived me as he had been deceived about me in Venice?

He had sworn that he paid his debts and I still believed he would pay this one. I must believe it. But as the morning wore on terrible doubts came to me.

I thought fiercely, If he has failed me, I will kill him.

It was early in the afternoon when my father walked in.

He was dirty and unkempt. He smelt of the prison. There was death in that smell. He was pale and had lost a great deal of weight. But he was there. He was safe.

"Oh, father!" I cried. "So you are back!"

He nodded. "Your mother . . ."

I looked towards the bed and he was kneeling there. She opened her eyes. I shall never forget the smile on her face. She was young and beautiful again and they were in each other's arms.

I stood watching them, but they were unaware of me.

‿❧ Carlotta's ❧‿
Cupboard

My mother's recovery was rapid. The doctor had been right when he had said that all she needed was to see my father safe and well.

We made hasty preparations to leave, for she said that we should not feel safe until we were back in Eversleigh. There was a determined look about her mouth. I could see that she had made up her mind that there would be no more dabbling in rebellions. We had King James the Second on the throne; he was a Catholic, and my father, in common with a great many English men and women, did not want a Catholic King; but my mother's theory was that he was there and there he must stay and we must put up with him. We were running no more risks.

I think seeing her so ill and anxious had affected my father deeply. During the days which followed they would not allow one to be out of the other's sight. It was moving, and in spite of my bruised and humiliated body, I felt exultant because but for me it would have been a very different story.

We took the first coach back and went by stages. My father thought it best to travel as simply as possible in case there had been a mistake.

When we were back in Eversleigh they talked more freely.

"I cannot think who my benefactor was," said my father. "It happened so suddenly. I was taken to a room where I spent the night alone. It was a relief. The conditions were appalling. I shall never get that stench out of my nostrils. Just to be taken away from it was a blessing. And the next day I was free."

He was convinced that my mother had paid a heavy bribe to someone. She assured him that she had not. Indeed when we had arrived in Dorchester she had been in a fever and had not even known where she was.

"It must have been someone," said my father. "I wonder who. I shall discover. I certainly have a very good friend somewhere."

"Someone for whom you once did a service," suggested my mother.

"I should remember. But I can think of no one. It would have needed a great deal, I am sure. Jeffreys—the devil—is becoming rich through the assizes."

Neither of them noticed me, and it occurred to me that after the experience of that night there *must* be a change in me. I felt I should never be the same again. It had been utter degradation, complete submission to a man who mingled his sexual desires with a passion for revenge. I would never forget his gloating laughter, and I had known that he was thinking of Leigh and his own humiliation in being severely thrashed. How that must have offended what he called his refined tastes! What lotions he would have needed to heal his wounds! But what had affected him most deeply was the humiliation. I guessed he had soothed that a little after what he had done to me.

And yet, to witness the love of my parents and their joy in finding themselves together again filled me with exultation because but for me their lives would lie in ruins.

226

I had saved my father's life, and my mother from a living death, so I could not regret what had happened.

My mother insisted that we celebrate my father's return. Harriet must come over with the child.

"I know how you love to see them," said my mother. "My dear Priscilla, this has been a great ordeal for you, too."

"But he is safe now," I said.

"My dearest child, I want to go down on my knees and thank whoever did this for us. It is such a mystery. But I think we shall know one day."

"I am sure it will be reward enough for this... benefactor to see your happiness."

"Your father and I are like one person," she confided. "If one was lost to the other there would be little in life left for the one who remained."

I felt too emotional to speak.

"And you, dear," she want on, "we are forgetting you. It has been such a terrible time for us both. You looked after me so well. It was such a comfort to have you with me."

I thought to myself: If you only knew! But I could never tell them. I wondered, though, what their reaction would be if I did. There was no one to whom I could talk of what had happened. Not Harriet... not Christabel... no one. My great desire was to wipe it from my memory. I should never do that completely. Every time I smelt that hideous musk smell I would remember him... his eyes gleaming as he talked of the deer.

How different from that night of tender love which I had spent with Jocelyn. That had produced Carlotta. The fear hit suddenly. What if there was a child born of that night of horror! What should I do then?

It could not be. That would be too much. I had paid for my father's life. Surely I had paid in full.

At times I would wander out into the garden. I would go to the bed of red roses and think of when I had first met Jocelyn and I would say to myself: If it should be so, what can I do?

I was, however, spared that.

There would be no child of that shameful night.

Now, I said to myself, I must try to forget.

There was not, after all, to be a great show of rejoicing on my father's return.

"From now on," said my mother, "we must live quietly."

There would be no journeys to and from Court. We were out of favour there. We must not remind anyone that we had favoured Monmouth's cause. We had a new King on the throne, and if we did not like him, we must make the best of him.

My father was restive. It was his nature to be, and I was sure that if it were not for worrying my mother, he would have been involved in some plot or other. They were uneasy days which followed the death of easygoing Charles. Charles had been so popular since the days of his restoration but James had not the gift of winning people to his side.

"It is no concern of ours," said my mother firmly, and as she showed signs of becoming ill every time she saw the lust for adventure in my father's eyes, he would regretfully turn away from whatever he was planning.

He loved her dearly. There was no doubt of that.

So his return was not a matter for an open celebration. We did entertain friends. Harriet came over with Gregory, Benjie and Carlotta and they stayed for several weeks. I could forget my experiences in the company of my daughter. She was now nearly four years old and she was going to be a beauty; her blue eyes were growing more and more like Jocelyn's; they had not that deep violet shade which was Harriet's great beauty; they were clear, like cornflowers; her dark hair was a lovely contrast, and her short, pert nose was adorable. Her skin was like flower petals and she was enchanting. But her chief attraction was her vitality. She was so lively that Sally Nullens said that it was one body's work just to keep pace with her. Emily Philpots saw that she was always exquisitely dressed and had already started teaching her to read, which she quickly learned. Emily said she had never known a child to learn so quickly. To those two women Carlotta was the centre of life.

And being a child with a quick and shrewd mind, Carlotta had rapidly become aware of her importance. She could be imperious, and then she would be very loving; she could stamp and kick when forced to obey, and at the same time she could burst into tears if she saw anyone or -thing in distress. She was a child of moods, which could change so quickly that it was hard to keep pace with them and assess her nature.

Benjie loved her and was teaching her to ride. Gregory accepted her as though she were truly his daughter, and and had recently bought her a beautiful little pony which he considered safe for her to ride. Harriet treated her with a sort of mild tolerance; she never went out of her way to make a fuss of her as the others did, but I believe that Carlotta loved Harriet best of all. From the others she accepted homage as her right, but there were times when I noticed her trying to please Harriet.

When they arrived I went down to the courtyard to greet them. My eyes went at once to my daughter—so beautiful in her red cloak, the colour of her cheeks, her blue eyes sparkling and her dark curls in disorder as she pulled off her hood. She flung herself at me and hugged me. I felt so emotional that I feared I should not be able to hold back my tears. She always had this effect on me.

It was almost as though she knew of this special relationship between us. She put her hand into mine as we went into the house.

My mother greeted them warmly, my father less so. He was always slightly hostile towards Harriet. I saw the corners of her mouth turn up with amusement. She resented him as one of the few men who had refused to be overwhelmed by her charm.

"This is a happy day," said Harriet. "We were all so anxious."

"We don't speak of it," my mother told her. "It is over now and best forgotten."

"You are back home, Carleton," added Harriet, "and here you must stay."

Benjie told my father how far he could shoot his arrows now and he wondered whether we should be practising archery on the lawns. He was sure he could beat Carl. Carl immediately challenged him and they went off chattering.

"Are you going to have Carlotta in your room this time, Priscilla?" Harriet asked me. "She likes that, don't you, Carlotta?"

Carlotta looked at me and nodded.

"It would be a help," said my mother. "That small bed could easily be put up."

"I've already had it done," I assured her.

Carlotta ran over to me and gripped my skirt. She smiled at me as though there were secrets between us. I felt overwhelmed by happiness. How I loved this child!

My father said: "I should have thought she was old enough to sleep in the nursery. I am sure Sally thinks so, too."

Carlotta scowled at him and said: "I don't like you."

My father guffawed. "What shall I do about that?" he asked. "Go out and jump in the sea?"

"Yes," cried Carlotta excitedly. "Yes, yes. You go and jump in the sea. Then you'll be drownded."

Harriet burst out laughing and my mother said, "Now that is no way to talk to your Uncle Carleton."

"It's my way to talk," retorted Carlotta defiantly. She put out her tongue at my father.

I feared he would order her to be whipped, but I saw that he was trying hard to control his laughter. Even he, who had no great love for children, and especially female ones, could not but be charmed by my daughter. "That child is spoiled," said my mother. "She should be restrained."

"She's all right," replied Harriet. "She says what she means. She has not yet learned to dissemble."

I was terrified that my mother might suggest some

punishment. I would not allow that. I picked up Carlotta, who put her arms about my neck. "What's restrained?" she whispered.

I said: "I'll tell you later."

"You won't let that man and her, will you...?"

"No," I whispered.

She laughed and nuzzled close to me.

Harriet watched us, looking as near sentimental as Harriet could look.

"Come on," I said, "we'll go to our room."

I set Carlotta down and she put her hand in mine, looking triumphantly over her shoulder at my parents.

How happy I was to have her with me! She jumped up and down on my bed and she said: "I'll sleep here, won't I?" And I knew it would be as it had been on other occasions. She would be put to bed by Sally Nullens and when I came up she would be awake. She would watch me undress and when I was in bed creep in with me. I would tell her a story and she would be asleep halfway through it and I would lie there and hold her in my arms and my love for her would overwhelm me.

Of course, Sally Nullens, as my father suggested, said it wasn't right. There was room in the nursery and the child should sleep there where she could keep an eye on her. But I soon subdued Sally. She remembered that I was the one who had recommended her to Harriet, and so did Emily Philpots. They soon accepted the situation and raised no more objections.

It was during that visit that Carlotta showed the extent of her powers to fascinate. She shared a certain characteristic with me, which I suppose was not surprising since she was my daughter, inasmuch as because my father was unimpressed by her charms she must feel an urge to impress him.

I saw her often watching him; and if she had a chance, when she thought he was not looking, she would put out her tongue at him. I warned her not to do this, for I was afraid that if she were caught some punishment would be considered necessary. I wanted to protect her from that. I knew that Sally was too good a nurse not to inflict punishment now and then and Carlotta accepted the occasional slap. I had seen Sally turn her across her knee and apply a light cane, which made Carlotta roar with anger, but I noticed that Sally was very soon afterwards given a good-night kiss without rancour, so I presumed she took punishment from Sally without its impairing their relationship.

My father was of a different calibre. I was terrified to think that he might want to punish Carlotta for her insolence.

Carlotta was fearless.

We were in the garden where she was running about with her shuttlecock. My father was sitting on a wooden seat by the pond; he had shouted to her once not to make so much noise.

She stood looking at him and then went on batting her shuttlecock in silence.

He appeared to be asleep and I saw her creep up to him. She stood watching him for a moment. I was about to call her away but hesitated. She was breaking no rules by looking at him. She crept closer. I saw her hand on his knee. Then to my amazement she scrambled up and put her arms round his neck—not in a gesture of affection, but to steady herself. She waited a few seconds, looking into his face as though examining every detail. Then I heard her shout: "You're a nasty old man!" And then she attempted to jump down.

I saw him catch her in his arms. I did not know what I expected but I heard him say: "What was that? What was that, eh?"

She was silent, looking into his face so closely that I was sure he could not see hers very clearly.

"You're a bold child," he said, "when you think the old ogre can't see you. You thought he was asleep and you could tell him what you think of him. It's different now, eh?"

"It's not different!" she shouted.

"Then say it again."

"You're a nasty old man!" she shouted.

"So you're not afraid of me, then?"

She hesitated.

"You are!" he cried triumphantly. "You're afraid I'm going to whip you. Till the blood runs, eh? That's what you think. And you still say it."

"You're a nasty old man," she repeated but more quietly.

"And you're not afraid of me?"

I could imagine those beautiful blue eyes as they looked into his. She was frightened of him, but she was fascinated too. He was the only one in the world who did not think Carlotta must be cherished.

"You are afraid of me," he insisted.

She nodded.

"And still you come right up to me and tell me I'm a nasty old man."

She nodded again.

He started to laugh. "I'll tell you something," he said. "You're right. I am."

Then she laughed and the sound of their mingling laughter was very sweet to me.

I knew she had won him as I had never been able to.

I crept away. Half an hour later she was still seated on his knee telling him the story of the wicked Roundheads who had cut off the King's head.

That visit was memorable because Edwin came home.

There was great rejoicing in the household. My mother was always delighted when Edwin came. He was subdued on this occasion, and it was, of course, because of what had happened. It was clear that he thought my father had been ill-advised to join Monmouth because as a soldier he knew that the Duke had never had a chance. It was true that the country was not in love with its new King, but rebellion by such as Monmouth who, many would say, was not an improvement on James, was not the way to help matters.

But Edwin was never one to force his opinions on others. The army had not changed him. He was still gentle, unassuming, malleable. I wondered what would happen when he met Christabel because as such near neighbours we saw a great deal of each other.

Their meeting passed off easily. He was clearly pleased to see Christabel so happy. As for her she was so contented with her present state that she had completely forgotten her disappointment of the past.

Young Thomas was thriving, and according to Christabel and Thomas Senior, he was the most marvellous child that had ever been born.

She was still discussing the anguish we had suffered in the Monmouth Rebellion.

"It was like a miracle," she said, "when you all came back safely. Thomas could scarcely believe it. We were so anxious for you. It just shows that miracles do happen."

She was thinking of herself; and indeed when I saw her looking almost beautiful, the centre of her happy home, I thought that perhaps she was providing the greatest miracle of all.

My mother was eager to see Edwin married. He was now past twenty-five—so was Leigh—and neither of them married. I was occupying her thoughts too, for I was nineteen. Now that she could keep my father at home she planned entertaining so that we could meet families like our own among whom there might be a husband for me and a wife for Edwin. Jane Merridew had always been a favourite of hers. Jane must be about twenty-five—a rather handsome girl, serious-minded, practical, just the girl for Edwin.

The Merridews came and stayed. They were stern Protestants and viewed the new reign with disquiet just as my father did; so they had a great deal in common. Before the end of the visit Jane and Edwin were betrothed.

"There should not be a great deal of delay," said my mother. "Soldiers should marry quickly. So much of their married life is spent away from their wives, so they must make the most of the time."

The Merridews were not averse to a prompt wedding either. Jane was not so young that they wanted to wait.

It should be in six months' time, decreed my mother, when Edwin believed he would have leave and Leigh would be present, too.

Harriet walked in the gardens with me. "Your turn will come soon," she said. "You're no longer a child, Priscilla. You can't go on grieving for a dead lover all your life."

I did not answer.

"You'll fall in love one day, my dear child, and you'll be happy then. I know you will. There's one I've always wanted for you. I think you know who. But I wouldn't press it. You have to discover each other for yourselves. You mustn't let what happened colour your future."

"But surely, Harriet," I replied, "what happened *must* colour my future, mustn't it? Something happens and we go on from there."

I thought of the steps which had led me to that musk-scented bed and my crushing humiliation at the hands of Beaumont Granville. The discovery of Jocelyn, our love, its consummation, Venice and all it entailed, and there he was, the evil genius who had done something to me which I could never forget and which in spite of Harriet's injunctions must colour my life and would hang over me for as long as I lived.

"If we make mistakes," said Harriet, "we must never brood on them. We should accept them as experience."

Experience! I thought. A musk-scented bed and a man who demanded everything from me, who humiliated me in such a way that I could only find peace of mind in forgetfulness.

I was almost on the point of confessing to Harriet, but I restrained myself in time. It was my shameful secret. It was better locked away in my mind. It must never come out to the light of day. I wouldn't let it. I could not bear it.

So she thought only of my love for Jocelyn, which was something I did not want to forget.

"Your mother has the light of battle in her eyes," went on Harriet. "Edwin today, Priscilla tomorrow. She wants grandchildren playing at her feet. Dear Arabella, she was always a sentimental creature. I know exactly what she feels and thinks. I love her dearly. She has meant a lot in my life. And now there is you and our little devil-angel Carlotta. *There* is one who is going to live an exciting life. I hope I live to see it."

Of course, Harriet was right about my mother. She was delighted by Edwin's betrothal. She said to me one evening: "Priscilla, I am so happy about Edwin. I am sure Jane will make him a good wife."

"You always wanted Jane for him," I reminded her. "You stopped his marrying Christabel."

"And how right that was! Christabel has found complete happiness with Thomas. He was just right for her. And they have dear little Thomas. That is a happy household."

"But she was very unhappy when Edwin allowed himself to be persuaded."

"My dear child, if he had really cared for her he would not have been persuaded. And if she had really cared for him she could not be as happy as she is with Thomas. So it was all for the best."

She looked at me wistfully.

"You were meant to marry, Priscilla," she said. "Your turn must come."

"I hadn't thought of it," I replied.

"To see you with that child Carlotta...She is a little minx, I think. She has even fascinated your father. To see you with her makes me feel that you should not delay too long before marrying. You can't go on being a child forever. I thought only this morning when I watched you with Carlotta, Priscilla was meant to be a mother."

I smiled at her. Dear Mother, I thought, I wonder what you would say if you knew that Carlotta is my daughter, and that I also gave myself so utterly, so completely and so shamefully to a wicked man in exchange for my father's life.

It was April in the following year that Edwin and Jane were married. The Merridews lived not more than five miles from us and there were great celebrations in their country house.

Edwin seemed quite happy and Jane certainly was. My mother was contented too. She and Jane had become very good friends, which was as well, for, when the celebrations were over, Jane would come to live with us at Eversleigh which would be her home from henceforth. Eversleigh Court belonged to Edwin, as he was in the direct line, although my father had always managed the estate and I was sure looked on the place as his. Edwin was of such a temperament that it never occurred to him to stress otherwise.

It was a good match for the Merridews—providing, of course, that there was no trouble through my father's involvement with the Monmouth Rebellion. Estates and fortunes could be lost overnight through such activities.

The Merridews, like ourselves, were keeping away from the Court at this time, remaining in the country, which was some way from London. We were hoping that recent events would soon be forgotten, although we did hear rumours that there were many who did not care for the new King's views and that trouble was brewing in various quarters.

"Whatever it is," said my mother firmly, "*we* are keeping out of it."

And I think that in view of my father's recent experiences, her words carried weight.

At this time there was nothing to think about but the wedding and we travelled to the Merridews for the ceremony, which took place in the chapel in their house. There was a banquet and much toasting of the married pair, after which they went back to Eversleigh, for it was considered fitting that they should spend the first night of their married life in the traditional bridal chamber which my mother had prepared for them.

We stayed at Merridew Court for two nights before returning, and as we were riding home side by side my mother said to me: "It is a great pleasure to me to see

Edwin happily married. Jane is such a pleasant creature. I am sure they will be happy."

"Yes," I agreed, "they suit each other. It wouldn't occur to either of them to be anything but happy together."

"Now what do you mean by that?"

"Well, I think they would always do what was expected of them and everyone expects them to be happy."

"That is not such a bad thing, is it?"

"No. But it doesn't always work out so neatly for some."

I wished I had not said that for it gave her an opening.

"My dear Priscilla, I should like to see you as happily settled."

I was silent.

"I know," she went on, "that you felt some romantic attachment to that poor young man, but it is quite a long time ago and you were only a child then."

Still I said nothing.

"It was only a childish fancy, my dear. You mustn't let it colour your life. You must meet more people. You seem so serious sometimes . . . almost as though you are brooding. You have been different since we came back from Dorchester."

It would have been so easy then to have shouted the truth, to tell her what I had done, to explain the mystery of my father's release. I wanted to laugh mockingly at her references to me as a child. A child who had borne a child, who had lived through that night with Beaumont Granville! *She* was an innocent compared with me. I was the worldly one, the woman who had lived.

We had been back at Eversleigh Court two days when Leigh arrived. He had been unable to get back in time for the wedding.

It was a great pleasure to see him. He had grown visibly older. He had seen service abroad and there was a certain uneasiness in his manner. Later he told us the reason for this. Trouble was in the air. The King was favouring Catholics in all walks of life and a large proportion of the people did not like it. Leigh very much feared there would be rebellion in the country.

"Another civil war would be disastrous," he said, when we sat over dinner. "Englishmen against Englishmen as it was not so long ago. It is different if it is one country against another. I don't want to fight my fellow countrymen on whatever pretext. I wish I were not in the army. Perhaps I'll retire and settle down."

"That," said my mother fervently, "would not be a bad idea. But if James were not King, who would be?"

Leigh lowered his voice. "There is the King's son-in-law, William of Orange."

"William of Orange!" cried my mother.

"Why not? He is married to Mary and she is the King's eldest daughter. He has a claim of his own. Wasn't his mother the eldest daughter of Charles the First? He is a Protestant and a steady man, a brave one too if not a very likeable one. But charm is not one of the necessary qualifications of a ruler "

"This is strange talk," cried my father, "but, by God, it would be a good day for England if ever this came to pass."

"There would be a certain amount of conflict before it did," Leigh pointed out. "I don't like it at all. If only Charles had lived."

"Ah, there you express the sentiments of us all," said my father.

In spite of the happy occasion of the wedding a gloom had crept into the house. I think my parents were remembering the days of the Civil War when no man had known who was his enemy and my father had entered into a great charade, playing the character of a Roundhead while serving the Royalist cause. I had heard many a tale of those times.

Leigh and I went riding. We rode down to the sea and there tethered our horses. We walked together along the beach and suddenly he said: "Will you marry me, Priscilla?"

I suppose I had always believed that one day he would ask me. In the old days before I had known Jocelyn, I had hoped he would. I had had a kind of hero worship for him

239

when I was a child. He had always been my champion. Until Jocelyn had come along I should have said that Leigh was the one with whom I should want to share my life.

But I wasn't that simple, innocent girl anymore. I had fallen in love with Jocelyn and then...there was Beaumont Granville. I should never really get him out of my mind. That night with him had made me feel I had no desire for marriage.

And yet here was Leigh...and I loved Leigh. I trusted him. He was my protector. He was the one who had thrashed Beaumont Granville for daring to attempt my abduction.

I was silent for some minutes, and I sensed Leigh's disquiet.

"I've been waiting for you to grow up," he said. "And I have been away so much. Priscilla, you do love me, don't you?"

"Of course I love you. I've always loved you."

He stopped and joyfully took my hands. He looked into my face. "Then what is it?" he asked.

"I am not sure," I answered.

"Not sure! But you have said you love me. You always did. When you were tiny you used to come to me first...with everything. *I* was the one you always wanted."

"Yes, I know. You were like my brother."

"Your brother. Yes that, but more besides. It wasn't like Edwin, was it?"

"No, it wasn't. Yes, Leigh, you were the hero, the one who saved me when I was in difficulties...the shining knight in armour."

"Now you are getting poetic. Why do you hesitate, Priscilla? There is no one else, is there?"

I shook my head.

I wish we had not come to the beach. I could remember so much. Jocelyn and I sitting there near the cave...the man who had walked along with the dogs and the awful fear that had possessed me then...groundless fear as it had turned out to be.

"Then what is it?" asked Leigh.

"It is not quite what it seems, Leigh. There are things you would have to know."

"Then let me know them," he said.

"I am afraid this will be a shock for you. Carlotta is my daughter."

He stopped still and stared at me.

"You see, Leigh," I said, "when you know everything you may not want to marry me."

He said slowly: "It was Jocelyn...but I thought that was just a child's admiration for a handsome young hero."

"You always insisted on my childishness. You have made me a child for too long. I was not a child. I was young, but I fell in love with him, and when we were marooned on the Eyot we were lovers. He was taken the next day and, as you know, executed. I have Carlotta to remind me of him."

"But Carlotta is supposed to be my mother's daughter."

I shook my head. "Harriet helped me. What I should have done without her, I do not know."

"So you went to Venice. It was you who were going to have the child."

"It was like a play to her and she played it magnificently. Harriet was wonderful to me. I shall never forget it."

"Carlotta..." whispered Leigh. "I can't believe this. It's preposterous."

"It would be with anyone but Harriet. She was determined to carry it out and she did."

"Is this why you do not want to marry me? You are still in love with a dead man?"

"I love you, Leigh. Nothing can alter that. I always did. If I married anyone I should want it to be you. But what has gone before changes everything."

"It does not change my feelings for you."

"Oh, Leigh," I said. I put my head against him and he held me tightly. I felt at peace there. I listened to the rise and fall of the waves and the melancholy screeching of the sea gulls. These were the sounds which had accompanied my meetings with Jocelyn. But this was different. This was

Leigh, the strong man, the protector. I realized in that moment that I had loved Jocelyn because I had felt the need to protect *him*. I knew that if I had Leigh beside me I should draw on his strength and perhaps in time forget my fears. He knew the secret of Carlotta's birth. It was a great relief.

I loved Leigh. Of course I loved him. Our future would be built on strong foundations—a love and trust which had existed since my childhood. I felt a surge of happiness such as I had not known for a long time, and an urge to tell him everything. I wanted to explain our fears for my father, my mother's sickness which was born of heartbreak. I wanted to make him see that I had done what I did because I had to. If I could tell him, the memories would begin to fade. I could be happy again. That was what Leigh meant to me.

But I could not tell him. I could imagine his fury. It would be a cold rage such as that which had sent him to Beaumont Granville's apartments where he had thrashed him to a dangerous degree. If he knew of this, he would kill Beaumont Granville. Of course I dared not tell. It must remain my secret.

"You should have told me before," he said.

"You understand, Leigh?"

"Yes, I understand. It was a romantic adventure. He was in danger and we were all helping him. I understand it, Priscilla. And the result was . . . Carlotta. That of course makes a difference. We must see what can be done about that."

"What do you mean? What can be done?"

"I know how you must feel about the child. Perhaps we could take her. She needs a father."

"She has that in Gregory. He adores her."

"She needs a mother. Harriet was never very maternal."

"Carlotta loves her dearly, all the same. But how I should love to have her all to myself."

"We will see what can be done."

"Oh, Leigh," I cried, "I am happier than I have been since . . . since . . ."

He took me in his arms and said: "It's coming right now,

Priscilla. It always had to be. You and I...I always knew it."

He kissed me solemnly. We had plighted our troth.

Then we went back to the horses.

My mother was delighted.

She kissed me and then Leigh. "It is what I always hoped," she said. "You always looked after her, Leigh. I remember you as a boy. You felt you ought, in the manly tradition, to despise girls, but you never could quite manage it with Priscilla, could you?"

"Never," agreed Leigh. "Of course Priscilla was no ordinary girl."

My father showed little enthusiasm. He quite liked Leigh, who was not unlike himself and different from Edwin, of whom he had a very poor opinion. I thought resentfully: I suppose he is glad to have his daughter taken off his hands.

"There should be no delay," said my mother. "I daresay you will be called away, Leigh, all too soon."

Leigh agreed that it might be so and arrangements went afoot with all speed.

Christabel came over from Grassland Manor to congratulate me. She had left plump Thomas Junior in his nurse's charge. She hated to leave him for long but she had to come and wish me well.

She came to my room for a tête-à-tête.

Leigh had always loved me, she said. She had been envious because he had never looked at her. She lowered her gaze and said: "Priscilla, what about Carlotta?"

"He knows. I told him. I wouldn't marry him without his knowing."

"And he...understands?"

"Yes, he understands. He said...Oh, Christabel, this makes me so happy...he says that we must work out some plan to get her with us, so that she can be with her mother. He knows me so well. He knows exactly what I want."

"He will be a good husband to you, Priscilla, and there is nothing so wonderful in life as a happy marriage."

"You should know," I said. "You are one of the fortunate ones who have achieved it."

"And I don't deserve it. That's the point."

"Nonsense. Ask Thomas whether you do or not. You have made him a very happy man."

"Yes, he is happy, and that is something, isn't it? At least I am responsible for that."

"You must stop reproaching yourself, Christabel. You still do it, you know."

"I was so envious. Envy is a deadly sin, Priscilla."

"Well, you are rid of yours now. Wish me happiness like yours."

"I do," she answered, "with all my heart."

Harriet came over a few days before the wedding accompanied by Gregory, Benjie and Carlotta.

That Harriet was delighted was obvious.

"It was what I wanted for you and Leigh," she told me. "I can't tell you how happy this has made me. I was an Eversleigh once...when I married Toby...and I was proud to be one. Now I shall have an Eversleigh for a daughter-in-law and I tell you this, there is no one I would rather have."

"You have always been so good to me, Harriet. I have told Leigh about Carlotta."

She nodded.

"It makes no difference. He still wants to marry me."

"I should not think much of him if he did not."

"He says that in time she should come to live with us."

She took my hand and pressed it. "He's right. Oh, isn't this a lovely solution to our little drama? Wedding bells. It was always a popular finale. And so they lived happily ever after! That was always my favourite line."

"A fairy tale ending," I said. "But life is not a fairy tale."

She looked at me sharply and again I had that impulse to tell her about Beaumont Granville. I must not. Nobody must know. I promised myself that I was going to forget he had ever existed. I was going to wipe out the memory of that night forever.

Leigh had to go to London. He would not go to Court

but he would frequent the coffeehouses there where it was possible to pick up the latest news, for in these shops men of the Court, soldiers, politicians, wits and gossips, gathered and talked together with the utmost indiscretion.

I didn't want him to go. I was afraid that something would happen to him. With every passing day I realized how important he was to me. I was even beginning to see that what had happened with Jocelyn was not the grande passion I had imagined it to be. Jocelyn had been a handsome boy in danger. We were alone on an island...two young people...and we had loved in a natural way. It happened so quickly. We were in love and we knew we could quickly be parted, so we foolishly snatched at those moments. We had talked of marriage. For a night we were as married people. Now I began to wonder what would have happened if he had escaped, if we had married. I was realizing that this growing emotion I felt for Leigh was strong and steady, unwavering, the sort of love I had seen between my mother and father. It was the true love, the love of endurance which nothing could change...not the flimsy stuff which is airy romance.

It was Leigh whom I loved. That was why I feared for him when he went to London, why I attempted to gather news of what was happening, why I began to fear another civil war, a rebellion...just as my mother did. And this was not due to patriotic fears for our country but simply that we were women who wanted to protect our men.

It was a great revelation. I loved Leigh and we were to be married. He knew about Carlotta and he understood. He was going to help me. He would be a wonderful father to her. I was happier than I had been for a long time, but soon I began to be haunted more than ever by memories of Beau Granville. I would dream of him. Leigh would be in that dream, and suddenly as he came towards me he would change into Beaumont Granville. I began to experience a vague apprehension.

My wedding day had almost come. The house was in a bustle of excitement. From the kitchens came the smell of roasting and baking. My mother was in a blissful state. She refused to think of possible trouble coming to the realm. Her family was about her. Edwin was married to a girl of her choice and she told me she had always wanted it to be Leigh for me. Leigh was a strong man, she said. He was not unlike my father. Such men needed special care.

"He shall have it," I assured her.

"Leigh is a man in every way . . . just like your father, and you'll be happy with him. He will take care of you and he has loved you for a long time. I am so glad, dear child, to see you settled."

Carlotta was sleeping in my room. She was very interested in all the preparations and spent a lot of time in the kitchens watching the baking and now and then slipping a finger in some bowl to extract a delicacy, I was sure.

They pampered her down there and I knew that Ellen liked to have her seated at the table and even showed her how to stone raisins.

Old Jasper, of course, was immune to her charms. I daresay he thought her a devil's imp with her bright colouring and obvious beauty of which he would not approve. She did not like Jasper and made no attempt to hide the fact. She told him that she did not think God would like him very much either, which I believe shook Jasper more than anything that had happened for a long time.

At night she would creep into my bed and talk to me. When I was married, I told her, she would not be able to come. I should be in the bridal chamber where lots of other brides had slept.

She listened entranced.

"When shall I marry?" she wanted to know.

"It will be years yet," I told her.

"Will you have a baby?" she asked.

"I don't know."

"Promise."

"Promise what?"

"When you do, you'll still love me best."

"I shall always love you, Carlotta."

"But best," she said. "I want to be *best*."

"Promises like that can't be made. You have to wait and see."

She was thoughtful, and pondering that fell asleep.

I had many gifts. Christabel had made some fine pillowcases for me, delicately embroidered as she knew so well how to do. I had more embroidered linen from Emily Philpots. Sally Nullens was delighted at the prospect of more babies, both from me and from Edwin. My mother gave me some beautiful silks, which could be made up into bed gowns and wraps as well as dresses.

"From your father and me," she said, but I knew he had had no hand in the gift.

There was one present which was brought to the house by a messenger who would not wait for a reply. One of the servants brought it in. The messenger had said that it was to be delivered to me but would not say who had sent it. It was a flat, square package. I was very curious. I took it up to my room and opened it.

It was a picture, painted in delicate colours, of St. Mark's Square in Venice, and the shop where I had bought the slippers was represented in it.

I knew who had sent it and if I had had any doubt, there were the initials in the corner to confirm my fears: B.G.

I felt sick with fear. What did it mean? It was clearly a reminder. He was telling me that he was still there in my life and I must not think I was rid of him.

The picture was lying on my bed. I turned away from it. I could not bear to look at it. My apprehension was growing with every minute.

What could he do to me now?

I thought then of what Leigh's fury would be like if he ever knew. I believed he would kill Beaumont Granville. He had nearly done so once before for a lesser offence.

Leigh must never know.

I wondered if any member of the family had seen the messenger arrive. My mother might ask what had been brought. Could I show the picture? "It was someone we met in Venice," I could say.

Leigh would see it. He would see those initials in the corner.

My impulse was to destroy it, but I decided not to do so just yet. I put it into a drawer with some kerchiefs and collars on top of it. In a few days I would destroy it, for if no one had mentioned its arrival by then, they would not do so later.

I had to compose myself before I went downstairs. I managed to do so, but a terrible shadow hung over me.

No one had seen the messenger come, and as nothing was said about what he had brought, a few days later I tore up the painting and burned it in the grate. I felt better as soon as I had done so.

It was just a mischievous gesture, I assured myself. But I was uneasy that he had known about my coming marriage. Leigh had been in London and there was no reason why our marriage should be kept a secret. He was known by too many people and naturally they would want to know whom he was marrying. I was the granddaughter of General Tolworthy, a very well-known soldier, who had distinguished himself in the Royalist cause. My father was Carleton Eversleigh, who had been a close friend of the late King. It was to be hoped that not too much had been said about the Monmouth Rebellion, but I gathered that so many people were disillusioned by the present King that there would be little rancour against my father.

In any case, I felt better when the picture was no longer there, and I tried to forget it on my wedding day.

And so we were married in the Eversleigh chapel, and even as we emerged, my arm in Leigh's, I was deeply conscious of the secret which lay between us and I longed to tell Leigh of that fearful night, but I knew that if I did he would not rest until he had taken revenge on Beaumont Granville and that could result in the death of one of them.

I could not escape from Beaumont Granville. I loved Leigh, I was capable of passion, but Beaumont Granville was there all the time. Leigh was conscious that something was wrong. He was puzzled and hurt. I think he believed that I still hankered for Jocelyn. I could not explain that I loved him, that I wanted him only, but there was something else I could not do and that was drive from my mind the memory of that night in Dorchester.

Leigh still thought of me as not quite grown up in spite of the fact that I had a child. He was uncertain of me and I knew vaguely disappointed. I guessed he would be uneasy when we were apart. He talked a great deal about the future and said that he did not think it was good for married people to be apart as they inevitably must if one was a soldier. When the situation was more stable he thought it would be a good idea to get out. We could not stay at Eversleigh Court for the rest of our lives, for that was the home of Edwin, his wife and the children they would have, as well as my parents and Carl. But there was the old Dower House. It was a fair-sized Elizabethan house—Eversleigh Court on a smaller scale. He would buy it from the Eversleigh estate and we could live there. Already he had plans for enlarging the house and farming some of the land. There was quite a large area of land which he could acquire.

"It would keep me home with you," he said; and I was aware of the disappointment he felt in our marriage and I longed to tell him of that terrible night which had scarred me forever. I wanted him to know that it was due to no lack of love on my part, that all that had gone before had shown me that I could never love any man as I loved him. But when I thought of what the consequences might be, I dared not.

Harriet stayed on with Carlotta, Benjie and Gregory. She said she wanted to be with her son as long as possible and of course I was delighted, not only that Harriet should stay—she was always an asset at any gathering—but because Carlotta remained too.

Carl was sixteen now, Benjie a year or so older, so they were really quite grown up and were going to the university together in the autumn.

Leigh was talking about the Dower House, a favourite

topic of his, and my father was pointing out that some of the land there would need a good deal of treatment before it offered good crops.

Carl said suddenly: "Why don't you have Enderby Hall, Leigh? That's a grand house...or was..."

"Enderby Hall," echoed Leigh. "Hasn't anyone taken it yet?"

"No," replied my mother, "and not likely to. It has the reputation of being haunted."

"What nonsense!" cried Leigh. "It was all right when the Enderbys were there."

"Oh, that was a great tragedy," said my mother.

"He was involved in the Rye House Plot with Gervaise Hilton of Grassland Manor," added my father. "The houses were confiscated then."

"First, though," said my mother, "the men were taken away. Poor Grace Enderby was heartbroken. She tried to hang herself. It was in the great hall and she tried to do it from the gallery. The rope wasn't long enough and she fell to the ground instead of swinging as she had intended to. She didn't die immediately. Some of the servants said she laid a curse on the place and that her cries can be heard as you pass by at night."

"So that's how it got the reputation for being haunted, was it?" asked Leigh.

"No one has heard the cries," put in my father. "It is always someone who knows someone who did."

"I think it is often like that with these haunted houses," Leigh said.

"We always thought it was a strange old place though," added my mother. "The family had been ardent Catholics and there are said to be hidden places where they used to hide the priests."

"What a sad story," said Jane. "I don't think I should like to go there after dark."

"Surely you're not affected by such nonsense," chided my father.

"It's all very well to be brave by daylight," said my mother. "It is a gloomy old place now. The garden's

250

overgrown. It's for sale. But who will buy a house where that sort of thing has happened?"

"I think it passed into the hands of some distant cousin of the Enderbys and he wants to get rid of it as fast as he can. He'll never sell until he clears the garden, which would do a great deal to dispel the gloom and make sure that all that gossip about a ghost is put a stop to."

"I'd like to go in and look at it," said Benjie.

"You'd never dare," challenged Carl.

"Don't be silly," retorted Benjie, "of course I would."

"Well," I said, "it has stood empty for a long time. If someone would take it and let in the sunshine, it would be just a normal house."

The conversation turned to the affairs of the country, which were always uppermost in our minds, and the ghostly house and the Enderbys were forgotten.

It was late afternoon of the following day when Sally Nullens came running into the garden, where we were all sitting enjoying the sunshine, with the disturbing news that Carlotta was nowhere to be found.

I was immediately afraid.

I turned to Sally and cried: "But where can she be?"

"She was in her bed having a nap, so I thought. I went in to rouse her and she was not there."

Carlotta had returned to the nursery when I was married and had been a little resentful about that and was inclined to blame Leigh who, she was afraid, was usurping her place with me.

"She's probably in the garden somewhere," said my mother.

"I'll go and look," I replied.

"And I'll come with you," said Leigh.

We searched the garden, but there was no sign of Carlotta. Then we went into the house and searched every room.

Now I was really alarmed.

"Where can she have got to?" I cried frantically.

Sally Nullens was muttering: "The imp. She didn't want

251

to go to bed. I had trouble with her. She's getting above herself, that one. Wants her own way all the time. Said she wanted to go with Carl and Benjie. Young men like them don't want a baby at their heels."

"Where are Carl and Benjie?" I asked.

"I don't know," replied Sally. "They went off somewhere together about two o'clock. I haven't seen them since."

I felt a faint twinge of relief. "She must be with them."

"She was pestering and they said they wouldn't take her. And then I came along and said Bed."

"I think she must have gone with them, Sally," I said anxiously. "They relented perhaps and took her."

"I don't know, I'm sure. I'll have something to say to her when she comes back, mark my words."

Sally was worried, I could see.

We went back to the group in the garden.

"Did you find the mischievous creature?" asked Harriet.

"No," I replied. "Sally thinks she went off with Carl and Benjie."

"Oh, that's it. She's always trying to link up with them."

"She's like you, Priscilla," said my mother. "You always wanted to go where Edwin and Leigh went."

"Sally is put out. She is supposed to be in bed."

"Carlotta has an adventurous nature," put in Harriet. "There will always be some excitement where she is."

"She's a spoiled child," said my father, but there was a hint of indulgence in his voice. I never ceased to marvel at the way she had bewitched him.

We talked of other matters: what was happening at Court, Continental affairs. The name of William of Orange was mentioned as it was frequently nowadays.

It was about an hour later when Carl and Benjie returned.

I ran to meet them.

"Where is Carlotta?" I cried.

They looked puzzled.

"Wasn't she with you?"

They shook their heads.

Now I was really frightened.

"We had better start searching at once," said Leigh.

"She can't have gone far," Harriet pointed out.

I thought of her wandering in the woods lost. I was terrified of what might befall her. Occasionally gipsies camped in the woods. I had heard stories of their stealing children. I felt sick with horror.

My father said: "We'll soon find her. We'll have two separate parties and we'll scour the neighbourhood. She can't have gone far."

I went off with Leigh, Carl and Benjie; my father headed another party.

"I reckon," said Leigh, "that she has gone somewhere and fallen asleep."

"Either that or she's lost," I said blankly. If the gipsies found her, her clothes would be taken from her. The gold chain which Gregory had given her and which she always wore round her neck would be worth something. Her outstanding beauty would attract them. I imagined their gloating over my beautiful child. What would they do with her? I pictured her, dirty and unkempt, selling clothes pegs and telling fortunes. That would never suit her imperious nature. How rebellious she would be. And what would they do to her?

Leigh was comforting me. "We'll find her soon. She's somewhere close. She couldn't have gone far."

We searched all round the house and beyond. I said I wondered whether she had tried to get to the sea. She was talking about it yesterday.

"She wanted to come with us," said Carl. "She was here when we left."

"What time was that?"

"It was just after two o'clock."

"But she was supposed to be resting then. Sally had sent her to bed."

"She said she wanted to come with us and I said, 'You can't. We're going to the haunted house.' She kept saying she wanted to come. So we went off and left her."

"You don't think . . ." I began.

"The house is nearly a mile from here," Leigh pointed out.

"She knows the way," said Carl. "We rode past it only the other day. She said she wanted to see a ghost."

"She's been listening to gossip," I said. "That's where she's gone. I'm sure of it. Carl and Benjie were going and she wanted to go with me. Come on. We're going to Enderby."

Leigh said we should ride there, for we should get there more quickly that way, so we ran to the stables and in a short time we were on the road to Enderby.

We tethered the horses and dismounted. The drive was so overgrown that we had to pick our way carefully. I must confess to a little shudder as we passed through the gates. There was something eerie about the place which seemed more than the state of the grounds warranted. The house rose before us—red Tudor brick—centre hall with east and west wings; the walls were covered with creeper, which hung over some of the windows.

It was easy to imagine why it had been called haunted.

Eager as I was to search the place I felt a great repugnance about entering it.

"Creepy," commented Benjie.

"You can get in quite easily," said Carl. "You just unlatch the door. We didn't see any ghosts," he added.

"No," put in Benjie, "but you felt they were there . . . watching you."

"We must go in," I insisted. "We have to search the place."

Then I felt my blood run cold, for I saw a light flicker in one of the windows and then disappear.

"Someone's there!" I gasped.

"I'm going in," said Leigh.

We unlatched the door and stepped into the hall. The door shut with a bang behind us. Only a little light came through the dirty windows. I looked up at the great, vaulted ceiling; the stone walls were damp; there was a great staircase, which must have been beautiful once, and over which the lady of the household had tried to hang herself.

Yes, it was a haunted house. It repelled me. It was almost as though there was an atmosphere of hostility, something which warned me to keep out.

Then we heard a noise above. The opening and shutting of a door. Someone was there. There must be. We had seen a light.

"Carlotta," cried Leigh in a loud voice, "are you there? Come here, Carlotta. We have come for you."

His voiced echoed through the empty house.

"Carlotta! Carlotta!" I cried in anguish.

Could she really have come here alone? I had a terrible premonition that we were going to discover something fearful.

"Listen," said Leigh.

We distinctly heard the sound of footsteps and they were not those of a child.

"Who's there?" called Leigh.

There was a movement from above and we saw a face on the balcony...the balcony over which the rope had been thrown.

A man was standing there.

"Have you come to see the house too?" he asked.

He started to descend the stairs. There was nothing ghostly about him. He was by no means young and was quite soberly dressed in a frogged coat and grey velvet breeches; his clothes were quiet, well cut and of good quality.

"We are looking for a lost child," said Leigh. "We thought she might be here."

"A lost child," he repeated. "I have seen no one."

I felt ill with disappointment and anxiety.

"We have reason to believe she may have come here," said Leigh.

"Yes," went on Carl. He turned to Benjie. "You remember I said I heard something. You said I thought it was the ghost."

Benjie nodded slowly.

"We must look for her," I insisted. "We mustn't waste any time. She'll be frightened."

"I have been over the house," said the man. "Some of it is very dark. But I had a lantern which I have left up there." He pointed upwards. "I haven't seen a child, but of course there are so many rooms. I doubt I have seen everything."

"We shall search every corner," said Leigh.

"I will join with you," the man replied.

"Let's all keep together," suggested Leigh, "and we will search from top to bottom. She may be shut in somewhere. Come on, we'll waste no more time."

We searched the hall and the kitchens. We went into the outhouses, and it was in the washhouse that I found a button lying on the floor. It had come from Carlotta's coat.

I pounced on it. It was the most hopeful sign we had had. I was sure now that Carlotta was in the house and I was not going to leave it without her.

"This is her coat button. She has been in here," I cried. "She must be in this house now. She must."

We went up the stairs—those sad, haunted stairs which creaked protestingly under our feet. There was the balcony where the minstrels had once played in the days when it had been a happy home with tragedy undreamed of.

There were heavy curtains at either side of it and an alcove in which musical instruments had been kept. There was a door in it. I opened it and there, lying fast asleep, was Carlotta.

I swooped on her.

She opened her eyes. "Hello, Cilla," she said.

I just held her in my arms and stepped out onto the balcony.

Everyone cried out joyfully at the sight of us. Carlotta looked at them all in surprise.

"Did you come to see the haunted house?" she asked. She looked at the stranger. "Who's that?" she said.

I said: "Carlotta, we have been looking for you. You have been naughty again. You were supposed to be in your bed."

She laughed. She was so enchanting when she smiled and I was overcome with such happiness to have her safe that I could only laugh with her.

"I wanted to see the haunted house," she explained. "They went." She pointed to Carl and Benjie. "They wouldn't take me with them."

"Well, we'll get home now quickly," said Leigh. "Do you realize that they are all worried about you? Sally will have something to say to you, I can tell you."

Carlotta was momentarily sober.

"A happy conclusion to our search," said the stranger.

"We are sorry to have intruded on you," I replied. "And thank you for your help."

"It was a very interesting encounter. I shall always remember the charming young lady who was asleep in the cupboard. If I take the house I shall call it Carlotta's cupboard."

"You must have the house!" cried Carlotta. "I want it to be called Carlotta's cupboard. You will have it, won't you?"

"Just to please you, I am sure that the gentleman will," commented Leigh.

"My name is Frinton," said the man. "Robert Frinton."

I felt my senses swimming. Frinton! Jocelyn had been a Frinton. It was not an unusual name, and yet on the other hand it was not a common one.

"I am Leigh Main and this is my wife, her brother and my half brother. There are rather complicated relationships in our family. Come back with us and have a meal. That is, if you have time. We must hurry now because they are all anxious about this errant child."

"What's errant?" asked Carlotta.

"What you have been," I replied fondly.

"Is it something nice?" she asked complacently.

Robert Frinton was saying how happy he would be to accept our invitation. He felt almost inclined to buy the house since it would mean that he would acquire such pleasant neighbours.

His horse was at the back of the house, which was why

we had not seen it when we arrived, and soon we were all mounted, Carlotta riding with Leigh, and on our way back to Eversleigh.

There was great rejoicing when we arrived. Sally Nullens and Emily Philpots were waiting in the courtyard, and Sally pounced on Carlotta and demanded to know what she had been up to, the bad, wicked girl, giving us all the fright of our lives and going off like that.

Emily said: "And look at your gown. All dirty. And you've caught that lovely stitching. I shall never be able to get that right, you see."

Harriet smiled on the child benignly; my mother was beaming with delight and my father was trying to look stern and failing completely, while Carlotta smiled at us and said: "He's going to call the cupboard Carlotta's cupboard. It's after me... because I went to sleep in it."

"People that goes off and worries the life out of everyone don't get cupboards named after them," pronounced Sally. I burst out laughing. It was rather wild laughter, I suppose, because Leigh put his arm about me and said, "We're forgetting to make the introductions." And he told Robert Frinton who everybody was and my mother said how delighted she would be if he stayed and ate with us, and she would love to hear what he thought of Enderby.

Carlotta was put to bed with a scolding from Sally and Emily. I went in to see her when I was ready for dinner. She was in bed by then. I think the walk to Enderby's had tired her out, which was why she had promptly fallen asleep, after the manner of children.

She was none the worse for the adventure, but it struck me that she was growing up fast and we should have to be watchful of her. She was going to be wayward. I had always known that. I would talk to Sally about her the next day.

I kissed her and she smiled happily as I did so; she was half asleep but aware of me. I loved her so much and I wondered how I should feel when I had Leigh's child, which I supposed I would in time.

I did not believe I could ever love any child as I loved this one.

Over dinner we learned that Robert Frinton was of the same family as Jocelyn.

"There was trouble in our family," he told us. "A great tragedy it was. My brother and nephew were the victims of that archvillain, Titus Oates."

"Ah, yes," said my father, "I remember that well."

"They confiscated much of his property. My brother was older than I and had the family estate. We lost it all. I have been compensated now but shall never go back to the old place. I was wondering about this Enderby Hall. It has possibilities."

"It used to be a delightful place," said my mother. "Once the garden has been cleared up and the house cleaned out, I think it should be all that it used to be in the past."

"I think so, too," said Robert Frinton. "I have a fancy for this part of the world." He looked at us rather shyly. "It was a strange way that we met this afternoon, but the fact was I was hoping to call on you. I wanted to thank you for all you did for my nephew."

He was looking at my father who said: "Don't thank me. I knew nothing of it until it was over."

I said: "It was Leigh, my husband, and my brother Edwin . . . and, of course, Lady Stevens who did so much. It could have worked. We could have saved him . . . but circumstances were against us."

"I know. He was taken and murdered. Yes, it was murder and I will call it nothing else. That man Oates deserved the worst possible fate and so do all those who were afraid to stand up against him. What misery he caused while his brief reign of glory lasted. But I do want to thank you for what you did. It is something I shall never forget."

Harriet put in: "He was such a charming young man. We all loved him. What we did for him was so little. If only we could have saved him!"

"My lady, you have earned my eternal gratitude."

"Well, you must repay us all by taking Enderby Hall and becoming our good neighbour," declared Harriet.

"I feel very much inclined to do so."

"We will all drink a toast to that," said my father. "Let the goblets be filled."

So we drank, and in due course Jocelyn's uncle bought Enderby Hall.

The next two years were, I think, some of the most momentous in English history and I never ceased to marvel at how quietly we lived through those events. Leigh was still in the army, serving under the Earl of Marlborough, whom my father had known in the days when, as John Churchill, he had been a rival of the King's for Barbara Castlemaine's favours. Leigh had a great admiration for him as a soldier and there could be no question, at this time, of his leaving the army.

It soon became obvious that trouble was inevitable, for the King was at variance with so many of his subjects.

The belief in the Divine Right of Kings which had brought his father to the scaffold was there in James, and my father said he could see disaster creeping nearer and nearer. He simply could not believe that he could be turned off the throne, although one would have thought that what had happened to his father would have been a lesson to him. Poor James! He lacked not only his brother's wit and charm but his common sense.

There was a great deal of talk about the number of Catholics he was appointing to important posts, and when he issued the Declaration for Liberty of Conscience, this was seen as a scheme to establish Papal Supremacy in England.

It was discussed over meals. There would be Thomas Willerby, Gregory and my father all earnestly asking themselves and each other what the outcome would be. Robert Frinton sometimes joined them, and although he came of a Catholic family and would have welcomed freedom for all opinions, he could see that Catholicism would never be accepted in England, for the people had sternly set their faces against it since the reign of Bloody Mary. They still remembered the Smithfield fires when so many Protestants had been burned at the stake. It had happened more than a hundred years before, but the memory remained.

The King should have seen disaster approaching, but blithely he pursued the course, turning his face away from the will of the people; and when the seven bishops, who refused to accept the declaration, were arrested and taken to the Tower, there was a general murmuring throughout the country.

On the day of the trial my mother implored my father not to go to London, and to please her he desisted; but it was against his nature. He was born to fight and to fight recklessly. One would have thought his experiences in the Monmouth Rebellion would have taught him a lesson; but he was the sort of man who would never learn from that kind of experience. When he supported a cause, he did so wholeheartedly.

Everyone now knows the outcome of the trial, how the verdict was not guilty, and how those in court cheered until they were hoarse, how the people waited in the streets to welcome the seven bishops, how the whole of London was en fête.

Foolish James, he should have known; but so much did he believe in his right to the throne that he could not conceive that it could be taken away from him. The Queen had just given him a son, and the country must surely be delighted with a male heir, but a baby could not save him now.

I was getting anxious about Leigh at this point because there was so much talk about William of Orange and his wife Mary, and there were hints that they were to be invited to England to take the throne. It was three years since James had been crowned, and in that short time his actions had brought him to this state. There could not be a more unpopular man in the country than its King.

"The trouble with him is," said my father, "that he is not content to be a Catholic—which the country might have accepted. He wants to be a Catholic reigning over a Catholic country. I know that certain ministers have been in touch with William."

"As long as they don't start fighting," said my mother, "I don't care what King we have."

"Then you should care," retorted my father. "James will try to turn us all Catholic . . . gentle persuasion at first and then . . . not so gentle. I know the methods. Englishmen will not endure it. James has had every opportunity to reign in peace, but he is obsessed not only by practising his religion but imposing it on the whole country."

There came the day in the summer of 1688 when a party of men led by Lords Danby, Shrewsbury and Devonshire, and including the Bishop of London, sent an invitation to William inviting him to prepare to come to England. William arrived at Torbay, whither he had been driven by storms at sea, and his ship bore a flag on which were the words: "The Protestant Religion and the Liberties of England"; and beneath this was the motto of the House of Orange: "I will maintain."

In the September of the year 1689 I gave birth to a daughter. I called her Damaris for no other reason than that I liked the name.

Edwin's wife, Jane, had a child—a boy whom she called Carleton after my father. He took quite a fancy to the boy and was far more interested in him than in my Damaris.

Sally Nullens was in a fine state about the births because she did not like the thought of new nurses being brought in, although she was now with Carlotta at Eyot Abbas. She reckoned that young Carleton and Damaris were really her babies.

"And what's to be?" she moaned. "I can't split myself in two, can I?"

Harriet brought Carlotta over to stay when the babies were born so Sally took over the nursery—temporarily, as my mother said.

Emily Philpots was busy giving lessons to Carlotta and embroidering for the babies.

Harriet was greatly amused. She waylaid me in the garden one day and laughingly said: "I think this is the time to bring our little scheme into motion."

"How?" I asked.

She put her hands on her hips and gave a good imitation of Sally. "'I can't split myself in two, can I?' Sad, but true," she went on. "Well, then since such division is impossible, and Sally can't be in two places at once, all the children must be in one place."

I laughed with her, my spirits soaring. "You mean Carlotta will come here?"

"That's what I was thinking."

"It's an excellent idea."

"Of course she will have to come visiting her supposed mamma quite frequently. Do you know, I should miss her if she didn't."

"Oh, Harriet, isn't she the most adorable child you ever saw?"

"She is one of the most scheming, selfish little brats I ever saw. She is full of wiles, already aware of her attractions, which I admit are considerable. She has the art of attracting the opposite sex already at her fingertips. You see how she is throwing her web around Robert Frinton, who is becoming quite besotted . . . naming his cupboard after her! All this is going to her head."

"But she is unusual. You must admit that, Harriet."

"She will have to be guarded carefully; otherwise we shall have trouble there. She will mature early. You know, she is amazingly like me. Sometimes I think fate is having a little joke. She might be my daughter more easily than yours."

"I suppose it is living so near you."

"She lives nearer to Sally but I see no resemblance between them—thank God. But is this not a heaven-sent opportunity?"

"You mean she shall come over to our nurseries and be looked after by Sally who, with Emily, will move back to us?"

"A very sensible arrangement. Then, my dear Priscilla,

you can glory in your offspring to your heart's content."

"Oh, Harriet, you are so good."

"For heaven's sake, child, you must be blind. I am only good when it is no trouble to be. I'm a little tired of the role of mother. I never thought I played it very well. Though I was very good as the expectant mother. But expectancy is always so interesting. It is the reality which can pall. I'll speak to your mother about it. Then I'll tell Sally. She will be filled with bliss. Greedy old thing! She wouldn't give up one of her babies to some poor deserving nurse. Emily Philpots is such another."

She kept her word and did speak to my mother.

My mother gravely came to me at once to tell me what had been arranged.

I said: "It is really an excellent idea. Sally will be delighted and so will Emily."

"It saves having two nurseries where one will do. And I am sure Sally would have been unbearably critical about everything that happened in the nursery. You're delighted, I can see. You can have your Carlotta under your eyes every day."

I laughed. "She is an adorable child," I said.

"Handsome, yes, but quite spoiled. She needs more discipline. I shall speak to Sally. You know, Sally is as bad as everyone else where that child is concerned."

"Sally loves her."

"Sally loves all babies. But I must say I think Harriet is rather an unnatural mother. She always was. When I think of her leaving Leigh as she did . . . when he was only a few months old . . ."

"Harriet is a good friend, though."

My mother shrugged her shoulders. Although she agreed that it was a good, practical idea for the children all to be under one roof, she did not approve of Harriet's action.

That was why that year was a happy one for me. What I had so desired had come about in a natural way. I had my new baby and my own Carlotta and I was with them every day. Leigh was away a good deal and I was anxious for him, but I had the comfort of my children and I was happier than I had been since Jocelyn's death.

Then there was consternation in our household. My mother knew that if it came to war she would not be able to prevent my father's sharing in it. One day he was missing and she found he had gone, leaving a note for her.

I found her seated in the window, the letter in her hand and a look of blank despair on her face.

"He's gone," she said. "I knew it was in his mind. I knew I kept him against his will."

I took the letter from her and read:

My dearest,
I could not tell you. I knew you would unnerve me.
You would have made me stay. I cannot. I must go.
So much is at stake. Our future depends on it . . . the future of our grandchildren. Understand, dear Bella, I must go. You will be in my thoughts every minute. God bless you.

Carleton

She murmured: "It is like an evil pattern. Oh, God, if he should be taken again . . . as he was before . . ."

"Perhaps this will be over soon. They say the King hasn't a chance."

"He defeated Monmouth."

"It was before he had shown that he was not a good King."

Then a terrible thought struck me. Leigh would be involved in this. He was in the King's army. My father would be on a different side from my husband. I knew that Leigh had no great respect for the King, but he was in the King's service and a soldier's first duty was loyalty.

I could not bear to think of what might be the outcome.

As for my mother, I was afraid she was going to be ill again as she had been in Dorchester.

The coming of William of Orange had set James attempting to rally men to his cause. There would be war, and the people remembered that other war of not so very long ago. The last thing they wanted was civil war—Englishmen fighting Englishmen. There was little glory to be gained and a great deal of sorrow. "No war!" declared the people.

I rejoiced when I heard that the Duke of Marlborough had deserted the King and gone over to William. That meant that Leigh and my father would not be on opposing sides. Everybody was deserting the King. I could feel sorry for him, although I knew he had brought this on himself by his obstinacy and foolishness. His daughter was the wife of the man he would call the usurper; his second daughter, Anne, with her husband, the Prince of Denmark, had turned against her father and was supporting her sister and brother-in-law.

That must have been a bitter blow for James. He would know then that the day was lost.

As disaster and defeat descended upon him, our spirits rose. It looked as though the war was over. James had fled to Ireland, where the Irish rallied to him because of religious sympathies. But William was a brilliant general, and James had little chance against him.

Both Leigh and Edwin fought in the Battle of the Boyne, which was decisive.

The war was over. The revolution was successful. Few kings had been turned from their thrones with such ease.

We had now moved into a new era. James was deposed and in exile. William and Mary reigned in England.

~ A Visit to London ~

Now our lives had set to a pattern. Leigh continued in the army and we waited eagerly for those times when we could be together. The children were growing up. Damaris was six years old; Carlotta, thirteen. I was twenty-eight years old.

"There is plenty of time to have more children," said my mother.

She was contented. My father was at home and she was glad that he was getting old.

"Too old for adventures," she said with a chuckle.

But my father was the sort who would always be ready for adventure, as Leigh was. My mother and I were closer than we had ever been. We shared each other's anxieties. She told me what a comfort I had always been to her. "Though when you were born," she said, "I was disappointed because you weren't a boy. But only for your father's sake, of course. He always wanted boys."

"I know," I said, with a trace of bitterness, "he made that clear."

"Some men are like that," replied my mother. "They think the world is made for men . . . and so it is in many ways. But some of them can't do without us."

I felt very tender towards her. Beside her, I felt worldly beyond imagining. She had lost her first husband when he was very young and had lamented for him over many years, deceived into thinking that he was the perfect gentle knight when, all the time he had been professing devotion to her, he had been Harriet's lover. Yet my mother had overcome that to walk into a lifelong romance with my father. In a way life had protected her as it never had me. I had loved and borne a child out of wedlock; I had been caught up in intrigue and had spent such a night with a man who seemed to me like a monster of iniquity; and now I was living the quiet country life like a matron who has never strayed from the conventional paths. There was so much which I could not explain to my mother.

But now we both feared for the men we loved and that brought us together. There were times when I almost told her what had happened to me, but I restrained myself in time.

So, there were those occasions when Leigh came home and we planned for the future, but although I longed for him while he was away, when we were together we never quite reached that blissful contentment which I knew should have been ours. Always the memory of Beaumont Granville would be there to torment me, to jeer at me, to remind me of my humiliating submission. If I could have disguised this from Leigh I should have been happier, but he was aware that something was between us and deeply hurt by it; and I began to fear that in time it could corrode our relationship and ruin our marriage.

Damaris was a quiet, reflective child. She was clever at her lessons and Emily's favourite. I was glad of that. Emily's devotion to Carlotta had waned a little, which was largely due to the behaviour of Carlotta.

Carlotta was wild, impetuous, given to flashes of

temper when she would say whatever came into her mind. Damaris was gentle and never hurt anyone. I remember the day during a very hot summer when she came running to me in great distress, telling me that the poor world was broken. She had seen cracks in the parched soil and it had distressed her because she thought that anything which was broken must be painful. She loved animals and more than once had brought me a wounded bird to heal. One was a gull she had found on the beach. "It had a broken wing," she cried, "and the others were pecking at it."

Damaris was a pretty child, but before the blazing good looks of Carlotta, any child must seem insignificant.

There was no doubt that Carlotta was going to be a great beauty. She had never gone through any plain stages as so many beauties-to-be do. That outstanding colouring was always there. The soft, dark, curling hair and the vivid blue eyes. Her hair was not as dark as Harriet's and her eyes were of a lighter blue. I had only seen one person with those violet eyes and near black hair and that was Harriet herself. But Carlotta had the same sort of beauty, and many people remarked that Carlotta took after her mother, which never failed to amuse Harriet.

Carlotta at thirteen was well formed, in advance of most girls of her age. She had been born with the art of attracting people, and I had to confess this gave me some cause for alarm. She was a little like my grandmother, Bersaba Tolworthy. They had something apart from beauty which drew men to them. Harriet had it even now when she was a little plump, and my grandmother had retained it all her life.

Carlotta was often at Eyot Abbas. She was very fond of Harriet, still believing her to be her mother. But it was not so much this supposed relationship which held them together as the fact that they were two of a kind. Harriet gave entertainments at her house and often staged plays. Carlotta always wanted the chief part in these and Harriet was content to give these to her.

"For the sake of the play," she said. "Carlotta should have gone on the stage. Of course it's looks mostly. She would have brought them in! If King Charles were alive he would move heaven and earth to get that one into his bed." She laughed at me. "Now you are looking like Prim Priscilla. That child will have lovers, mark my words. What we have to make sure of is that it doesn't happen too soon and with the wrong one."

Carlotta had escaped from Emily Philpot's jurisdiction and we had engaged a governess for her, a pleasant young woman who, like Christabel, had come from a vicarage. "Always the best background," said my mother.

So Amelia Garston entered our household, and Carlotta spent certain reluctant hours in the schoolroom. Emily did not resent this because she had long realized that Carlotta was too much for her to handle, and in any case she had my dear, gentle Damaris, who responded so cleverly to learning and was a good child into the bargain.

Carlotta never liked to be in one place too long. She visited Christabel now and then. Young Thomas adored her, in common with other members of his sex. I liked going to Grassland Manor. It was such a happy household. I had never seen anyone change as Christabel had, and the change never failed to delight me. Envy had spoiled her life and now it had completely disappeared. She was deeply contented.

She admitted to me once that there was nothing more she wanted, then she qualified that. "Yes, just one thing. I'd like to have another child. Thomas would love another. Of course, we are lucky to have young Thomas—who is the most wonderful child in the world, although I don't expect you to agree with me—but I should like to have given Thomas several more children."

"Perhaps you will," I said.

"No." She shook her head. "You know I nearly died with Thomas. The doctor said that to have another would be dangerous. I think my dear husband would rather have me than another child . . . even if I could have it."

"I'm sure of that."

"I'm so glad it turned out the way it did, though I don't deserve it. I really don't."

"I never heard such nonsense," I said; and she just smiled at me and shook her head.

Carlotta was a frequent visitor at Enderby Hall. She had completely charmed Robert Frinton and I was glad that she went to see him, for he was a lonely old man. I often wondered what he would say if he knew of the relationship between them. I was sure he would be pleased.

He had made a habitable residence of Enderby Hall but he never quite succeeded in dispelling the gloom. I could never enter that hall without feeling a faint twinge of apprehension, and on the rare occasions when I had been there alone, I would find myself taking furtive looks over my shoulder because I felt I was being watched.

He had brought a small staff of servants with him and lived quite simply. He often visited us, for my mother was constantly inviting him. I noticed that as soon as he arrived he would look round for Carlotta, and if she were not present—for she often decided that she would go and stay with Harriet—he would be unable to hide his disappointment.

Of course Carlotta was wayward and bent on having her own way, but she only had to smile at us and we were her slaves. All except Harriet, who made no attempt to please her and somehow managed to do it as well as any of us could.

It was a sunny day in the June of the year 1695 when Harriet and I sat in the gardens of Eyot Abbas overlooking the sea, and as I made out the island just rising out of the sea mist, I remembered, as I could never fail to, that night I had spent there with Carlotta's father. I thought of my youth, my innocence and the tenderness of our love, so beautiful in itself and the beginning of everything which had happened afterwards, culminating in that night of horror which still haunted my dreams and coloured my life. It was like a black cloud, ever present, menacing my happiness.

Leigh and I were, of course, happy together, but the complete intimacy for which we both longed still eluded

271

us. It was a mystery to Leigh, but I knew full well what it was. I could never feel completely at peace while the memory lay between us.

I knew Leigh well—the kindest of men where his loved ones were concerned, but he was capable of a reckless fury over what he considered injustice. He had gone over easily to the side of William because, although he had sworn allegiance to the King, he did not respect him. His commanding officer, Churchill, had his wholehearted support; and if Churchill went over to William, then he believed it was morally right for him to do so. I often thought of the way in which Leigh had brought me back to the palazzo and then cold-bloodedly gone off the following night and half killed Beaumont Granville. He must never know. I was certain that if he did there would be no half measures. That would be the end of Beaumont Granville.

"You're thoughtful." Harriet was watching me closely. "Thinking back to long ago? You shouldn't brood on the past, Priscilla. You have to look ahead to the future. I want to talk about Carlotta."

"Oh, yes?"

"I feel she is my responsibility as well as yours. After all, I am her mother in a way. I feel my duty towards her, although you may not believe it."

"Of course I believe it. You have always been good to her. She loves you."

"She admires me, yes. I think we are a little alike, Carlotta and I. I'm thinking of her future. She'll marry young."

"She's a child yet."

"Some of us stop being children early."

"She is thirteen years old."

"How old were you, dear Priscilla, when you stayed the night on the island with your lover?"

"It was unusual circumstances."

"Unusual circumstances are sometimes quite usual, which sounds a contradiction but is oddly true. They arise, these unusual circumstances, and catch us unaware. I am sure that a girl like Carlotta will attract such occasions as she attracts every male creature who comes within a few yards of her."

"I agree that we shall have to be careful with her."

Harriet laughed. "The more careful she sees us to be, the more reckless she will become. I know her kind ... none better."

"Well, if we are going to be careful, what are we going to do?"

"We'll guide her ... with invisible hands."

"Harriet, what do you mean?"

"I have a bridegroom for her. One I have always wanted her to have."

"Harriet!"

"Yes, my son Benjie. He adores her ... but he doesn't really know how much yet. Besides, he thinks she is his sister. He'll have to discover that she is not, that she is no relation. It reminded me of you and Leigh ... although he knew all along that he was not related to you. But he was brought up with you like a brother. You see, it makes a complicated situation. Suppose Leigh had not been looking on you as his dear little sister all those years, you would have been together from the start. It is Leigh you really loved. I always knew it. That idyll on the Eyot was the awakening ... if you see what I mean."

"I see, of course, but it is not necessarily true."

"It is true. You and Leigh would have been lovers when you were fourteen ... after all he was a man then. Then all those complications would not have occurred. Well, that's all finished. Carlotta is in the picture now. I want Benjie to know that she is not his sister. It was wise of you to have told Leigh."

"You know I couldn't marry him without telling."

"Of course you couldn't, and he understood. After all he is my son. I am very happy that you and Leigh are together, Priscilla. It makes you my daughter in a way. I could be very sentimental about that ... if I were a sentimental woman. But what I am really thinking about is Carlotta's future."

"Somehow I could not bring myself to tell my parents."

"Why not? Your father has not exactly lived the life of a holy monk."

"I know it, but he has always been rather contemptuous of me. No, that's too strong a word. He has been indifferent to me."

"That has hurt you. There are times when I should like to give your father a talking to. He really is the most obstinate of men."

"I shall never forget what you did for me, Harriet . . . you and Gregory."

"He is a dear man and played his part well. He would do anything for me. But it is Carlotta whom we are discussing. You are not anxious to disclose the truth to your parents. . . . Perhaps not, but there is someone else who should know."

"You mean Benjie?"

"Yes, later. But I was thinking of Robert Frinton."

"Robert Frinton!" I cried. "But why should he know?"

"Because the child's father was his nephew."

"But . . ."

"You are depriving the man of his family. He loves Carlotta. He is a lonely old man. That was a terrible tragedy in his family. Just imagine what it would mean to him to find he had a family in this enchanting child."

"I don't think it would be wise."

"Why not?"

"We have guarded this secret so long. You, Leigh, Gregory, Christabel and I are the only ones . . ."

I stopped suddenly in horror. There was one other who knew. I saw again vividly those lascivious mocking eyes. "Posing as a virgin when all the time you were there to have your little bastard!"

Harriet had risen and put an arm about my shoulders.

"The secret will still be safe," she said. "The only difference is that Frinton will know. Think how happy it will make him. You owe it to him, Priscilla."

"No," I cried, "the fewer who know the better."

Harriet shrugged her shoulders. "Well, I have to tell you. He knows."

I stared at her. "You told him!"

"Yes, I told him."

"Harriet, how could you!"

"It was my secret as well as yours. I thought it best to tell him." She went on quickly: "What I have done is the best for everybody. He will be here shortly. I asked him to come. He wants to see you. He wants to talk to you."

I was dumbfounded. It was no use reproaching Harriet. It was so like her to do something she wanted to and then tell about it afterwards. I wanted to shout at her: This is my affair. But that was not entirely true. She had made it hers.

It must have been an hour later when we heard the sounds of arrival. Harriet and I went down alone to greet Robert Frinton.

When he saw me he put out his arms and we were both so overcome by emotion that I went straight into them and we clung together for a few moments.

He released me and looked into my face. "You have made me so happy," he said. "So very happy. For me this is like a miracle. Something I never dreamed could possibly be. I loved the child from the first. I cannot tell you what this means to me."

When I realized his happiness I felt reconciled to what Harriet had done.

We were together a great deal during that visit and he talked continuously about Carlotta. He had brought a gold chain with a diamond pendant for her. She delighted in it. Carlotta loved gifts and she had a passion for jewels.

Robert Frinton and I travelled back to Eversleigh together. He talked all the time of the joy it gave him to know that Carlotta was Jocelyn's daughter.

"The fact that he fathered a child—and such a child—makes him seem less lost to me," he said. "How I wish it could have been in different circumstances. There is no one I would rather have seen him married to, dear Priscilla. And Carlotta delights me. I want to watch her all the time. I want to listen to her. She is the most enchanting child that ever was. This has been like a new life to me. How I thank my good fortune that I decided to come to Enderby Hall. It was like fate, wasn't it? And there she was in the house . . . in Carlotta's cupboard. Oh, how glad I am! You need have no fear. This shall be our secret until you wish it to be divulged. I would not cause you, who have given me such wonderful happiness, one moment of grief."

So he talked and I thought that no harm had been done. He was such a delightful man and there was no doubt that the revelation had brought him great happiness.

But when I went to see him soon after at Enderby Hall, I was more than ever aware of the sense of foreboding in that house. It was a house of shadows; there was an eeriness in spite of the bright furnishings and the smell of beeswax and turpentine which his servants used so lavishly.

When Robert appeared, the mood of the house seemed to change, but when I stood alone in the hall, I seemed to sense something evil, something which was like a warning. I wondered whether it was the shadow of past tragedy, but somehow I could not get out of my mind the feeling that it was a warning of some impending disaster.

After that I saw a great deal of Robert. We had naturally moved closer together. He was a frequent visitor at Eversleigh Court and I was often at Enderby Hall. He was so pathetically eager to see me, and Carlotta often came with me. That was indeed a red-letter day for him.

I was glad that Carlotta liked him and went out of her way to charm him. She need not have bothered, she did it effortlessly. Such was her nature that the more pleasure he showed in her company, the more she liked him. I was glad to see that he inspired a certain gentleness in her nature which I had not noticed before. There was nothing she liked better than to serve us with coffee or chocolate, which was becoming so fashionable in the London coffeehouses. Carlotta would preside at the table and we

ould watch her with pride as she brought the beverages
o us.

"My father and mother took tea when they were in
London," she told us. "It is a strange outlandish herb, they
say. They didn't like it much, but it is being drunk by all the
notable people."

Her eyes sparkled. I knew she longed to go to London
and mingle with the notables.

"My mother says that when I am fourteen, which is this
year, she will take me to London."

I could never become accustomed to hearing her refer
to Harriet as her mother, although I should by this time.

"What do you want to do in London?" asked Robert
indulgently.

"I want to go to balls and to be presented to the King. It
is a pity the poor Queen died. It means the Court is very
dull. And of course there is no heir to the throne except
Princess Anne. It makes rather a dull Court. Still the balls
must be gay, mustn't they? And I should love to see it.
Benjie says it is fun to go to the coffeehouses. Important
people meet there and talk and talk. Then there are the
shops. How I should love to go to London."

"And what would you buy in the shops?" asked Robert.

"I would buy beautiful materials to be made into ball
gowns. I would buy a riding habit in pearl grey with a hard
grey hat with a feather that has a little blue in it . . . but not
too much . . . bluey grey. Then I would buy a diamond
brooch."

"It seems," I interrupted, "that you would spend a small
fortune within a few hours. You should be happy to buy
just one of those things to start with."

I saw Robert calculating and I knew what the outcome
would be. We should soon be seeing Carlotta in a grey
riding habit; silks would be arriving at the house; and
before long there would be a diamond brooch.

I remonstrated with him. "You give her too much," I
protested. "She will wonder why."

"Carlotta will never have to wonder why people want
to please her. I never saw such a delightful girl."

It was her fourteenth birthday—a dull October day—and when I awoke I thought, as I always did on this anniversary, of that day in Venice when I first heard the cry of my child.

My mother liked to celebrate our anniversaries. She was very sentimental and eager to preserve the family feeling. Carlotta's birthday was a very special occasion, for Carlotta was looking upon it as a coming of age. It was to be held at the Abbas, for although she had spent a great deal of time at Eversleigh, that was reckoned to be her home. She had added her governess, Amelia Garston, to her admirers and a friendship had sprung up between them, much as had existed between Christabel and myself. Harriet said it was a good thing for her to have a friend nearer her own age and Amelia had come from a desirable background; the only thing her family lacked which ours had was money.

The great hall at the Abbas was decorated with as many plants as could be mustered at that time of the year. I arrived with Damaris, my parents, Jane and her son, plus Sally Nullens who regarded herself as indispensable to the children.

Robert Frinton was naturally there. He had looked forward to the event for weeks, he told me. I was sure that he had brought rich presents for Carlotta who, I was glad to say, always thanked him charmingly and made rather a point of what she called "looking after him," which surprised me because she was usually so involved in her own affairs; but I supposed she found his devotion especially touching.

I had never seen Carlotta more lovely. She was, of course, the centre of attraction. After all it was her day. A large birthday cake had been made and this Carlotta ceremoniously cut. She was dressed in a gown of deep blue—the silk had been one of those which Robert had sent her—and at her throat sparkled the diamond brooch—his present. She wore a string of pearls threaded through her hair—the gift of Gregory and Harriet—and on er finger a sapphire ring from Leigh and me. Rather an xcess of jewellery for one so young perhaps, but this was er birthday and she must please all the donors by wearing ieir gifts.

She was completely happy, and when she was, it was a leasant trait of hers to want everyone else to be the same.

She danced a great deal with Benjie, who was now well dvanced into his twenties. I agreed with Harriet that, in pite of the fact that she was quite a few years younger, he ould make a good husband for Carlotta. Benjie always boked slightly bewildered when he was with Carlotta. I ondered about him. He had never thought of marrying s yet. Was it true that he was in love with the girl whom he elieved to be his sister?

What complications arose when one stepped outside he rules of convention. If Benjie suddenly knew that Carlotta was not his sister, what would his reaction be?

It was becoming more and more clear to me that sooner r later I should have to disclose the truth. I could have told ny mother. I was sure she would understand. But for some bscure reason I did not want my father to know. That eemed absurd. Why he should think worse of me when he ad never thought very much about me in any case, I did ot know. But he would be critical. He had entered into nany relationships lightheartedly, I was sure. There had been results in at least one. My half sister Christabel was vidence of that. So why should he stand in judgment on ne! And yet I could not bear him to know. He dominated ne as he always had done. The fact that I had saved his life hould have made a difference... if he had known. I ometimes played with the idea of telling him. I heard nyself saying: "Carlotta is my daughter. Yes, I have an llegitimate daughter just as you have. I should have narried her father had he lived. Your relationships were lifferent. You entered into them to satisfy your lust. Can ou criticize me? And let me tell you, you who never vanted a daughter and thought little of the one you had, if t had not been for her, you would be dead now... and you vould have died horribly. I paid dearly for saving your life, and what happened to me is something which has scarred me forever."

I wondered so often what he would say if he knew. Yet I told myself that he never should.

Now there were Carlotta and Benjie to think of. I saw Harriet watching them, and then her eyes were on me. Harriet would tell Benjie, I knew, just as she had told Robert Frinton.

Perhaps she was right. If one stepped aside, others must not suffer because of it.

The dance had stopped. Carlotta was taking a goblet of wine to Robert Frinton. She sat beside him. He was smiling with pleasure as he fingered the brooch at her throat, and I knew she was telling him how much she liked it and thanking him for it. She leaned forward and kissed him.

He took her hand and held it. She did not remove it but let it lie in his. I think she was really quite fond of him.

The music started and she took the wine from him and set it down. She pulled him to his feet and went out with him to lead the dance.

He was not very agile and I thought how old he looked, but perhaps that was in contrast to Carlotta's glowing youth.

They led the dance round the hall and others fell in behind them. Then suddenly Robert Frinton turned and swayed. There was a gasp through the hall; the music stopped, and for a few seconds there was complete silence. Carlotta was kneeling down beside him, pulling at his cravat. My father hurried over.

"Get a doctor," he said to Harriet.

That was the end of Carlotta's fourteenth birthday party. Robert Frinton was carried to his bed at once. He died during the night. He was just conscious and able to see Carlotta beside his bed. His hand curled about hers and she knelt, looking at him with the tears falling down her cheeks.

I heard him murmur: "Beautiful child...you have made me so happy."

He was taken back to Enderby Hall and buried in the Eversleigh churchyard.

We learned that he was a very rich man and that he had left everything he possessed to Carlotta.

She was to inherit on her eighteenth birthday, or when she married, if that were earlier, and then she would be one of the richest women in the country.

The day after he was buried—Harriet and Gregory had come to Eversleigh for the ceremony—she and I walked to his grave and laid a posy there.

"Dear Robert," she said, "he so loved Carlotta. She was a symbol to him that his family lived on. I did right, you see, to let him know who she really was."

"Harriet," I asked, "did you know how rich he was?"

"Well, one can never be sure, of course."

"But you did know."

"It was reasonable to suppose he was not poor. I knew that he received compensation for the estates which had been taken from his family, but he was of course a rich man in his own right."

"And you thought this might happen?"

"It seemed a natural conclusion."

"I see. It was another of your schemes."

"But how could I be sure?"

"You couldn't be. But you thought it likely."

"My dear Priscilla, don't take up that high moral tone. If a fortune is around and a family has a certain claim to it, they would be foolish not to make themselves known."

"Harriet," I said, "from the moment you stepped into the château where my mother was in exile, you started to shape our lives. You have gone on doing it."

She was thoughtful. "There may be something in what you say," she agreed. "But this little bit of shaping is very good for all concerned. Beautiful Carlotta, who would have had no great fortune, is now a considerable heiress. What could be wrong with that?"

"I don't know," I replied. "I shall have to wait and see."

Dear Robert Frinton! If he could have foreseen what effect his action would have, he might have decided against it.

I shall never forget Carlotta as she was when she heard the news. A look of great wonder spread across her face. She said: "He must have loved me very much."

No one spoke, and for a few seconds her face was tender as she thought of how much this old man of whom she had been so fond had loved her. Then the realization of what this meant came to her. She was rich. The whole world was open to her. She had only to wait four years before this great fortune was hers.

I could see plans forming in her mind. She would go to London. She would travel through the world. She would have a house of her own. She would escape from every restriction.

I said: "Don't forget you will have to wait until you are eighteen. Everything will go on much as before until then, and by that time you will have made up your mind what you have to do."

"Four years!" she cried.

"A short time really," soothed Harriet.

And she shared Carlotta's excitement. Harriet was a schemer and her schemes were almost always for her own advantage. She wanted Robert Frinton's fortune for Carlotta partly because she intended it to come to her son Benjie.

I should have known. Harriet had schemed throughout her life. It was a habit she could not discard now.

In my heart I was afraid of this money. I had a sudden feeling it would bring no good.

Carlotta wanted to go to London.

"It is so sad here now that he is dead," she said. "He would have wanted us to go."

Harriet thought it was a good idea and it was agreed that she, Gregory and myself with Carlotta should go for a brief stay to London.

"Mind you," said Harriet, "the Court is dull these days.

How different from Charles's time! What fun it was then! And how gracious he was! Between ourselves William is a boor ... a Dutch boor. They say he scarcely speaks at all."

"The people admire him for he is a good King," replied Gregory. "And that is what we need."

"If the Queen had lived ... or he had married again ..."

Gregory shook his head. "He won't and it will be Anne who follows him ... or perhaps her boy William, though he is very delicate."

"Well, let us hope she will make a more lively Court than the present one," said Harriet. "I like not these dour rulers. Charles was so different. I for one shall never stop regretting his passing."

It was the middle of December when we set out. Harriet had said we should go before the really cold weather set in which was usually after Christmas. Carlotta was very excited at the prospect, though every now and then she would remember Robert and a certain sadness would settle on her. Knowing her so well I realized that she felt guilty because she found it possible to be happy in spite of his death.

I was pleased to see this sensitivity in her. She was not completely selfish—only young, full of vitality which deplored inaction, and if she took admiration as her right, it was because so much of it had come her way.

We had arranged to stay at the Eversleigh town house which was very close to Whitehall. It was not Carlotta's first visit to London, but she seemed to be seeing it all through different eyes. She was now an heiress. Her eyes danced with pleasure and there was a wild anticipation in them. I was sure she was contemplating all she would do when she reached the magic age of eighteen.

It was difficult not to get caught up in the excitement of London. Those of us who lived quietly in the country could not but be amazed by the vitality, the bustle, the sheer joy of living which was generated in those streets.

They were less unsavoury, Harriet said, than they had been before the great fire, and some of the new buildings which Christopher Wren had set up were very fine. It was no less noisy, no less colourful than before the plague and fire had decimated so much of it.

"How beautiful it is!" cried Carlotta as we rode along the Strand past the large houses with their gardens running down to the river. Little boats rocked at the privy stairs and all along the waterway, craft of every description passed by. The songs of the watermen wafted towards us, vague and haunting among the noise of the streets.

Harriet pointed out some of the new coffeehouses which were springing up here and there and taking the town by storm. "Mind you," she explained, "beverages stronger than coffee can be obtained there. The company can get a little wild as the night wears on."

"Shall we go to a coffeehouse?" asked Carlotta.

"I hardly think it would be the place for us," I said.

Carlotta grimaced at me. "Dear Priscilla," she said, "you would be perfectly safe with me." She glanced at Gregory. "You would take me, wouldn't you?"

Gregory gave a little laugh and murmured: "We'll see." He always found it hard to give Carlotta a direct refusal.

We had come into the Mall and Harriet was again sighing for the days of Charles's reign when he himself could often be seen here watched with admiration while he played the game which gave the thoroughfare its name.

"You should have seen him," said Harriet. "No one could drive a ball as he could. It would go halfway down the Mall, as I heard it said by an old soldier, 'As though it were shot from a smoking culverin.' One cannot imagine his present Majesty performing such a feat."

"It is no use sighing for the old days," I said. "Let us be thankful that we have a King who appears to know how to govern."

"Even though he keeps the dullest Court in Europe."

"The parks are beautiful," sighed Carlotta.

"Yes," said Gregory, "I always enjoyed the parks, and we have our share of them. I think the people would cause a riot if anyone attempted to take our parks from us. St.

James's is beautiful, as you say, and there are Hyde Park and Spring Gardens and Mulberry Gardens."

"But not to be entered after dark," interposed Harriet. "Even though one was masked, one would be suspected of being there for a purpose—but enough of that."

Flower girls and orange girls threaded their way through the crowds, and there were milkmaids laden with their wares. Coaches passed us in which sat patched and powdered ladies; occasionally we saw a dandy pull down his window and chat with a lady in a passing coach.

We had come into Town just after noon, which was the busiest time of the day. At two o'clock the streets would be quiet, for two o'clock was dinnertime for most people, and at four o'clock the streets would be full again with people making their way to the playhouses.

Carlotta had difficulty in keeping her eyes from the displays of ribbons and laces and fine garments which were displayed on the stalls and in the booths. Harriet promised her that they would do a great deal of shopping during the visit.

We reached our house where everything had been made ready for our coming. Dinner was served and Carlotta immediately wanted to go out. I reminded her that it would soon be dark and I thought that we should wait until morning. She was disappointed, and after dinner went to a window and sat there looking out on the Town.

The following day we went shopping in the New Exchange in the Strand. This was almost like a bazaar, with an upper gallery full of stalls displaying the most exciting merchandise. Carlotta cried out with delight as she examined the silks, ribbons and laces; and we bought material for new gowns.

Ladies, some of whom I was sure were of questionable virtue, sauntered through the Exchange. They glanced from right to left and were clearly looking for interested gallants. Some of these were very glorious to behold in their velvet cloaks, silken breeches and feathered hats, and very often they carried Toledo swords at their sides. Many of them were followed by their pages and looked very grand indeed. I saw many glance Carlotta's way and I was glad that she was too interested in what she was buying to notice them.

We had come to a booth where fans were on display. We paused, for Carlotta wanted to buy a fan. There was one she found which was very beautiful and decorated with brilliants. She opened it and began to fan herself.

"I must have it," she said. "It is lovely. It will match the new silk I have bought."

Then I found myself turning quite cold, as though someone had thrown a bucket of icy water over me. Standing at the next stall was a man whose face I should never forget if I lived to be a hundred. It was a face which still came to me in my dreams and filled me with terror.

Beaumont Granville was buying cravats at the next stall.

"What do you think of it?" I heard Carlotta's voice from a long way off. Time seemed to have stood still and everything was happening very slowly, for Beaumont Granville had turned at the sound of Carlotta's voice and he had seen me.

I saw the smile of recognition turn up the corners of his mouth. I saw his gaze go from Harriet to Carlotta and rest on her fleetingly. She was holding the fan up to her lips and gazing at me over the top of it.

I was saying: "I want to go home. I feel . . . er . . ."

I was aware of them all looking at me. Harriet's deep blue eyes curious, Carlotta's anxious.

I turned sharply. I had to get away from that amused stare, from those eyes which would always be for me the most cruel in the world.

I caught my foot in the cobblestones and I should have fallen if Harriet had not caught me. A sharp pain shot through my ankle.

"What happened?" asked Harriet.

I did not answer I stooped and touched my ankle.

Then I heard his voice, which I remembered so well—musical, gentle, beguiling, and I felt as if I were in one of those nightmares which had afflicted me since that night I had spent in his odious company. "If I can be of any assistance..."

He was bowing to Harriet, to Carlotta, to me.

I said very quickly: "Thank you. Everything is all right."

"How kind of you!" Harriet's voice was extremely courteous. I had realized that he was still as handsome as ever. Harriet always changed subtly at the advent of a man, of whatever age, however unattractive. It was Harriet's way.

"I am perfectly all right," I insisted hastily.

"You've hurt your ankle," said Carlotta.

"It's nothing...absolutely nothing. I can feel nothing..."

"I have a friendly apothecary close by," said Beaumont Granville. "He would look at it and verify that you had not injured it. For if you have a broken bone it would be dangerous to walk on it."

"I feel nothing at all."

"You have gone very pale," said Carlotta. "Hasn't she?" Her lovely face betrayed her anxiety. I was too worried to think clearly. I reminded myself that at all costs I must not show agitation, but how could I be calm when I feared him so much?

"You must allow me to help," he went on. "My apothecary friend is here in the Exchange." He had taken a parcel from Harriet. "Allow me." He laid a hand on my arm and his eyes looked mockingly into mine. "I really think you should see this man. A bandage may be necessary even if it is only a strain."

"You are very kind, sir," said Carlotta.

"I am delighted to be at your service."

"It would be churlish to refuse such kindness," added Harriet.

"Yes, Priscilla," said Carlotta, "you must see this apothecary. It hurts. I can see that."

"Then," added Beaumont Granville, "the matter is settled. May I lead the way?"

I was limping badly. I had twisted my ankle but I was

unaware of the pain. I could only ask myself what cruel trick of fate this was which had brought him back into my life.

I did not trust him for one moment. I wanted to tell him to go, to explain to them that I knew from experience that this man was no fit company for decent people.

Carlotta had slipped her arm through mine.

"Does it hurt, Priscilla?"

"No, no. This is nonsense. I'd like to go home without delay."

Beaumont Granville was standing on the other side of me.

"Would you care to take my arm, to lean on me?" he asked solicitously.

"It is not necessary, thank you."

"Well, it is only a few steps," he said and led the way.

There was a smell of scents and unguents in the apothecary's shop. We took a step down into the dark exterior and a man in a yellow coat came hurrying to meet us. He bowed low when he saw Beaumont Granville and was prepared to be extremely subservient. It was clear that he was a most respected customer.

"My lord," he asked, "what can I do for you?"

Beaumont Granville explained that I had hurt my ankle and he wanted the apothecary to look at it and see what damage had been done and perhaps supply an unguent and a bandage or whatever was necessary.

He would indeed. He looked round and found a stool on which I was immediately seated. He then knelt and probed my ankle. I caught my breath with pain.

He looked up at Beaumont Granville who was watching me intently.

"No bones broken," he said. "Just a little twist ... nothing that cannot be cured quickly."

"Have you something to put on it?" asked Harriet.

"The very thing. I'll bind it up and then the lady should rest for a day or so ... and all will be well."

"Then get to it," said Beaumont Granville. He turned to Harriet. "You ladies were shopping. Why do we not leave

288

our patient here to be bandaged while we continue with what we have to do? We can return when she is ready to leave. Have you a coach? She should not walk."

"We could return home and bring it," Harriet explained. "As we were shopping and we are but near Whitehall, we came on foot."

"She must not walk far. Leave it to me. I will take you back in my carriage."

"You are too good to us, sir," cried Harriet.

"It is my pleasure to serve you," he answered.

"It seems a good idea, Priscilla," said Harriet.

I did not answer. I felt sick with anxiety.

The apothecary was shaking something in a bottle. I was thinking: Granville can do no harm yet. But what does it mean? What can it mean?

"Then we shall see you later," said Harriet.

"Say half an hour?" suggested Granville.

The apothecary agreed that I should be ready to leave by that time.

"It seems the best thing," said Carlotta. "And then we must get you home."

I watched them leave. At the door he turned and looked back at me. I could not guess what was in his mind, but I was deeply conscious of that mocking amusement.

I was nauseated by the scents of the shop. I sat on the stool and removed my stocking. My ankle was very swollen.

The apothecary knelt at my feet and put something cooling on the afflicted part. It soothed my ankle but nothing could soothe my mind.

What could it mean? Why had I hurt my ankle just at that moment? I had turned clumsily because the sight of him had made me numb with horror.

Well, he would take us home in his carriage. I should have protested about that. He would be invited in and given wine or some refreshment. Harriet was impressed by him. I could see that.

I must remind her who he was. Perhaps she would remember when she heard his name. There had been a great deal of talk about the thrashing Leigh had given him in Venice. But that was fifteen years ago. I would remind her as soon as possible that he was a man whose acquaintance we should do without.

The apothecary was talking about his unguents and lotions. He was trying to sell me some of his aids to beauty. There was a face wash he had which could make a lady's skin look like a child's. There were lotions to disguise grey hairs. There were exquisite scents to please the gentlemen. His shop was a magic cave of delights.

I lay back and closed my eyes. My thoughts were far from the apothecary's shop.

In half an hour they returned. Carlotta was very excited. They had been taken to the most wonderful shops. Their kind friend knew all the best shops in the Exchange and he had made sure that they got the best bargains.

"Are you feeling well enough to walk?" His voice was tender though his eyes still mocked.

"I should like to go home," I answered.

"My carriage is here. All you have to do is to get out of the shop."

"First," I reminded him, "we must settle our account with the apothecary, who has been so good."

He waved his hand. "I have a standing account with him. This shall be my affair."

"I shall not hear of it," I replied.

"Oh, come, come, such a small matter."

"Pray tell me your charge," I said to the apothecary.

"I forbid it," commanded Granville.

The apothecary looked at me and lifted his shoulders.

"I cannot and will not allow this," I said firmly.

"So you would deprive me of this pleasure?"

I took some money from my purse and laid it on the counter. The apothecary looked at it helplessly. I could see he was very much in awe of Beaumont Granville.

"You will at least allow me to give you the comfort of my carriage."

"There is no need," I replied. "We could wait here for our own."

"What has come over you?" said Harriet, laughing. "It is ungracious of you to refuse such kindness so graciously given."

He helped me into his carriage. We sat facing each other—Harriet beside him, Carlotta beside me.

Carlotta cried: "What an adventure! How is your ankle feeling, Priscilla?"

"Much better, thank you."

"It was such an exciting morning. First all those lovely silks and now this. . . . Oh, I did not get the fan. I forgot all about it."

"Never mind," said Harriet, "you have had a very interesting morning. But what of poor Priscilla? My dear, I hope it is not painful."

I said it felt better after the apothecary's attentions.

"I'm sorry," cried Carlotta instantly, "I didn't mean it was fun that you hurt yourself."

"I understand," I told her and she gave me her lovely, dazzling smile.

We had reached the house and Beaumont Granville had leaped down to help us out.

"You must come in and drink a glass of wine with us," said Harriet.

He hesitated and looked at me. I said nothing.

"Yes, please," cried Carlotta. "You *must* come."

He turned his gaze on her. "Are you sure I am not encroaching?"

"Encroaching! After all you have done. We are very much in your debt."

And so Beaumont Granville came back into my life and the nightmare began.

I said to Harriet, "You know who this man is. He is Beaumont Granville."

"Yes, that is his name."

"Have you forgotten Venice?"

She wrinkled her brows.

"Don't you remember? He tried to take me away from the ball and Leigh went to his apartments the next day and nearly killed him."

Remembrance came back to her. She burst out laughing.

"It was nothing to laugh at, Harriet. It was a very serious matter."

"It must be fifteen years since it happened."

"It is something that will never be forgotten."

"My dear Priscilla, you are behind the times. Men fight duels one day and forget it in a week or so. It was a bit of high spirits on his part."

"He almost succeeded in taking me away. If he had . . ."

"But Leigh was there. That was so romantic. Leigh saved you and then went round and there was trouble. Yes, I do remember it well. All Venice was talking about it."

"I don't want to know him."

"So that's why you were so cold . . . and really quite discourteous, I thought. After all, he was offering to help."

"Harriet, I don't like the man. I don't want him in this house."

"We had to ask him in after what he did."

"Well, let's hope that this is the end of it and we don't have to see him again."

"He seemed so eager to please, and you must admit he did help with the apothecary."

"We could have managed without him."

"Oh, Priscilla, you really are holding this prank against him, are you not?"

I wanted to shout at her: If you knew everything you would understand.

I almost told her, yet I could not bring myself to speak of it. If she knew she would readily understand why I never wanted to see him again.

Carlotta burst in on us. She was carrying the fan she had seen on the Exchange stall and waving it before our eyes.

"You have been out to get it," I cried. "Oh, Carlotta, you must not go out alone."

She shook her head. "Three guesses. Now how did I come by this beautiful fan?"

"Gregory went out and bought it for you," said Harriet. "That man spoils you."

"Wrong," she retorted. "Try again. Not Gregory but . . ."

She was flourishing a note in her hand. Harriet snatched it from her.

She read:

I did not like to think of your losing the fan, so I crept back and bought it. Do please accept it. B.G.

I wanted to shout at them both. I wanted to say: It must be sent back. We want nothing from this man, not even a trifle such as this.

"A charming gesture," said Harriet.

"It was so *thoughtful* of him," added Carlotta.

"I think he is a very charming man," added Harriet, almost defiantly.

I was filled with foreboding

❦ *The Elopement* ❧

For the next few days I could not go out. On the morning following our visit to the Exchange my ankle was very swollen and Gregory said I should see a doctor. He called one in and the verdict was the same as that of the apothecary. I must rest it and in a few days I should be able to walk on it.

I felt frustrated. Fervently I wished that we had not come to London. Gregory and Harriet took Carlotta to Mulberry Gardens one afternoon so that she should not be disappointed. They took her to Spring Gardens one evening where they supped. Carlotta came in to tell me all about it, her eyes sparkling with the wonder of it all. They had walked through the gardens where they had eaten a collation of fish and venison pie followed by tarts and syllabub; and with it they had drunk a fine muscatel wine.

They had watched the masked ladies parading through the paths and the gallants who had pursued them. Harriet had declared that it was nothing compared with what it had been in the days of Charles when people knew better how to enjoy life. But they had seen some of the players from the theatre walking there, and Carlotta had enjoyed it greatly.

I would wait breathlessly for some mention of Beaumont Granville, for I had a notion that he would not allow the acquaintance to peter out. I was sure that he was bent on some mischief, and those days when I lay on my bed resting my foot, or sat at the window watching people pass by, were for me filled with frustration and fear.

As the days went on I began to think that I had perhaps attached too much importance to the matter. After all, what had happened was no credit to him. Perhaps he wanted to forget it too.

Yet he had looked at me with that sly mockery which had set the fear rising in my heart. I must hope that he had forgotten, and I would suggest that we return to Eversleigh sooner than we had planned.

At length I was able to hobble about, but I still had to take care, and Harriet suggested that a visit to the theatre would not be too taxing and this was arranged.

"After all," she said, "you only have to walk to the carriage and then from it into the theatre."

It seemed a good idea and I was glad to be able to get about. I had said nothing more about Beaumont Granville and I presumed the incident had been forgotten.

It was always exciting to be in a theatre—particularly with Harriet, who knew so much about it, having, of course, once been a player herself. The play was William Wycherley's *The Country Wife*, which even Harriet had never seen, and I felt my spirits rising.

We had a box near the stage and Carlotta was chattering rapidly, asking questions of Harriet as to who was that and who was this, which delighted Harriet, though she admitted she had been stagnating in the country for far too long.

"We really must come to Town more often, Gregory," she said.

"Oh, yes, please, we must," cried Carlotta.

The smell of orange peel was strong in the air; it mingled with the apothecaries' scents and the less pleasing odours of humanity. It was all part of this somewhat unreal but intriguing world of the theatre. The orange girls proffered their fruit to the young men in the pit who were clearly, and not successfully, aping the nobility and doubtless making assignations. There was a great deal of giggling and general noise until some elegant lady, masked and accompanied by an exquisite dandy, entered one of the boxes. Then there would be a brief silence while the company studied her in awed curiosity.

The play began. It was quite amusing and I felt better than I had since I had seen Beaumont Granville. Perhaps I had exaggerated, I told myself. It was just a passing encounter. What could he want with me now? I was no longer the young girl I had been when he had cast his lecherous eyes on me. Moreover, he had not made any effort to renew the acquaintance. It was just that initial shock which had unnerved me and that, having led to this silly accident, had made me feel that trouble was looming.

Then suddenly I noticed that Carlotta's attention was not on the stage. She was gazing at the box opposite, which a short while before had been empty.

It had an occupant now. At first I thought I was imagining this. He had been so much in my thoughts. But there was no doubt. Of course it was Beaumont Granville. He had come late to the play and there he was smiling at Carlotta. My fears were intensified. He looked strikingly handsome. He certainly lived up to his name. He was dressed in the latest fashion. His square-cut coat of thick silk material was braided across the front in many rows and the buttons were rubies. He wore one of the very fashionable wigs which I had noticed since coming to London. They were profusely curled and heavily scented. The curls fell about his shoulders, almost obscuring the most elegant of white silk cravats. The air of worldliness, combined with that Grecian perfection of feature, showed the world that he was a man who would have few rivals for good looks.

297

I would have preferred to see the ugliest man possible sitting in that box instead of that exquisite dandy.

I glanced at Harriet. She had seen him, too. I was aware of the smile at the corner of her lips.

Suddenly I knew. They had told him we were coming to the theatre and he was there to see us, to torment me as he was well aware he did, to amuse himself with what to him would seem a piquant situation.

I had ceased to concentrate on the play. I was only aware of the secret looks which crossed between my party and him.

I gave no sign—at least I hoped I did not—that I had seen him. I tried to keep my eyes on the stage and pretend to be absorbed by the action; but I could not have told anyone, had they asked me, what the play was about.

After the first act he came to our box.

"What a delightful surprise!" He was bowing over our hands, his manners matching his appearance.

I realized by the looks exchanged between him and Carlotta that it was no surprise; it was an arrangement between them.

Oh, my God, I thought, what does this mean?

"I am hoping," he was saying, "that you are going to sup with me after the play."

"What a lovely idea!" cried Carlotta.

"That would be delightful," said Harriet. "How kind of you! One should always sup in good company after the play. One of the delights of playgoing is to pick the piece apart afterwards. Don't you agree?"

"I do with all my heart," said Beaumont Granville. "Would you care to sup at my place or go somewhere else?"

"I really think we should decline this kind invitation," I said.

They were all looking at me. He was forcing an expression of concern onto his face, although trying not to show that he was suppressing amusement.

"It is my first outing," I stammered. "I really feel..."

It sounded so hideously selfish. Because I wanted to go home I was stopping their pleasure.

Gregory, always kind, said: "I'll take you back if you like, Priscilla."

They were all looking at me and I thought: No, if they are going to be with him, I must be there to see what happens. I could sense the situation becoming more and more dangerous.

"We will cheer you up," said Beaumont Granville, looking at me pleadingly. "I have a very fine malmsey wine which I should like you to try. Do come. The company will be incomplete without you."

"You will certainly not be able to refuse an invitation so graciously given," said Harriet.

"You *must* not!" cried Carlotta passionately.

"Ah," put in Beaumont Granville, "I believe she is wavering."

"It is good of you all to be so concerned whether I come or not."

"Then it is decided," said Beaumont Granville. He sat down and we started to discuss the play. When the interval was over he returned to his box, but I was aware that throughout the play he was watching us.

There was some diabolical scheme working in his mind.

He shepherded us out of the theatre, through the crowds to our coach. He had sent his home and said he would share ours if we would permit it. I noticed how people made way for him; some called a greeting. He was clearly well known and many were in awe of him. He had an air of importance which I could see had aroused Carlotta's admiration. In fact I was beginning to realize that Carlotta's admiration was great and that he very much enjoyed this.

His house was only a short distance from ours.

"See what near neighbours we are!" he said. "A town house is so necessary. I have an estate near Dorchester, but I confess I spend more time in London than in the country."

299

"I have never been to Dorchester," said Carlotta.

"I hope to change that one day," he answered.

The house was furnished in a manner to be expected of one with such elegant tastes and he was clearly proud of it.

Supper was ready for us, which showed he had had no doubt of our accepting his invitation. His servants waited on us silently and efficiently. The malmsey was indeed excellent, and so was the food, and I could see that he enjoyed playing host.

He spoke of the play and the players knowledgeably, and he and Harriet were engaged in spirited conversation.

Carlotta listened, hardly ever taking her eyes from his face. Now and then he would look at her and smile tenderly. I was stricken with horror. This was the ultimate nightmare. I could not believe it. She was giving him that kind of hero worship which young girls sometimes feel for older men.

It could not really be what I feared. He must be over thirty years older than she was. My imagination was in a fever. I was suffering from some form of hallucination.

I said: "You have a very fine establishment here, sir. Is your wife in the country?"

He turned his false smile on me. "I have no wife. No, I have never married. I have been too much of a romantic."

"Oh, is that so? I should have thought your romantic ideals might have led you to marriage."

"I suppose I was always looking for the perfect woman. Nothing less would suit me."

"Then it is not to be wondered at that your search was fruitless," put in Harriet.

"I am not disturbed that life may have passed me by." He was looking at Carlotta now. "I think my good angel was preserving me. Do you know, it is a belief of mine that if you want something and are determined to get it, and will not allow yourself to be diverged from the main object, it comes to you in time. I am not old yet. In fact I feel fresher and more vigorous than I did in my extreme youth. No, dear ladies, I do not despair."

"You have travelled a great deal?" I asked.

"I have seen much of the world. But having seen it I want most of all to settle down here in England . . . living my life between this city and Dorset. A little of the country is good now and then. It makes you appreciate how much more invigorating is life in the town."

"Oh, I do agree," said Carlotta. "I wish we could come to London more often."

"Perhaps you will . . . now that you are becoming a young lady of fashion."

She laughed. "Oh, do you really think I am that!"

"In the very best sense. I deplore those people who follow a fashion slavishly, particularly if it is ridiculous and does not suit them." He had turned his admiring gaze on Carlotta. "You are too young to remember the hideous manner in which women wore their hair in Charles's time. How they could endure those little rows of curls on the brow I cannot understand. *Crève Coeurs*, they called them. Heartbreakers! At least that's what I suppose they meant. Surely there was little less designed to keep a man's heart intact. I like to see ladies follow their own styles, as you all do so admirably, and not become slaves to the mode of the moment."

"The lady we saw in the Mulberry Gardens . . . do you remember?" Carlotta was smiling at him. "She really did look ridiculous."

"She had so many patches that they looked like a heavenly constellation," he replied.

In Mulberry Gardens! Carlotta had betrayed the truth to me. During those days when I had been confined to my room, they had been meeting!

I do not know how I lived through that evening. I tried to hide my fears. I tried to be as merry as they were, and all the time I was endeavouring to discover how much they had seen of each other, how far this acquaintance had progressed.

If only we had not come to London!

It was late when we returned home. He put us into our

301

carriage, kissed our hands with grace and charm, and as we made the short journey from his house to ours, my thoughts were in turmoil.

When we stepped out of the carriage and went into the house, Carlotta slipped her arm through mine.

"How is the ankle?" she asked.

I had forgotten it. I could think of nothing but this fearful thing which was looming up over me.

"I scarcely feel it," I answered.

"I thought it must be painful. You were so quiet this evening."

"Well, perhaps I felt a little...shut out."

"Shut out! What do you mean?"

"You have apparently been seeing a great deal of that man while I have been incapacitated."

"Oh, we have met once or twice. He always seemed to be where we were."

"By arrangement?" I asked.

She flushed a little.

"Oh, come," I said, "he knew we were going to be at the theatre this evening."

"I told him we were going. Why shouldn't I? It was no secret."

"You seem to be on very good terms with him."

"Why not? He is so kind. And is he not amusing? I think he is the handsomest man I ever saw."

"You mean among the old men of your acquaintance?"

"Old? Oh, one never thinks of age in connection with Beau."

Oh, God help me, I prayed, it has gone further than I thought.

"He is so much more interesting than young men," said Carlotta. "He has the experience of the world which they lack."

"Did he tell you that?"

"Why have you taken against him! He was so kind to you in the Exchange. I think you're rather ungrateful."

"So you have seen him more than once or twice when you have been out with Harriet?"

302

"Yes . . . a few times . . ."

"And have you ever seen him when you have been alone?"

She turned to me almost angrily. "When have I been allowed out alone? You all seem to think I'm a baby. Well, I'm not. And I don't intend to be treated like one."

I felt desperately uneasy. It was worse than I had thought.

I had to see him alone. I had to discover what he was planning, for that he was planning something seemed obvious to me.

Carlotta! Could it really be that he was leading her into seduction? What had he said? He had a passion for young virgins. He was cynical in the extreme, I knew. Oh, yes, he was planning something. I could sense that. There was an air of triumph about him when he looked at me. He would be remembering that night when he had forced me to submit to his will, when he had humiliated me beyond endurance. If there had not been so much at stake I should never have agreed to such a bargain.

I imagined that his life had been full of adventures such as that. He would revel in this. It was his nature to wish to subdue people mentally and physically. He was proud, arrogant, vain and cruel. He saw himself as the only person of any importance in the whole world. His desires must be granted and if he had to contrive to achieve that end, he was only too pleased to do so. Intrigue was the breath of life to him. There had been one time when he had lost and he bore the scars to remind him.

Oh, God help me, I prayed. If he attempts to ruin Carlotta's life there will be a second time. I will do anything . . . anything rather than that shall happen.

I thought I would first speak to Harriet and see what she had to say. She was a woman of the world. She must have some idea of his intentions.

It was midmorning. She was not yet up but was in bed sipping a dish of chocolate which one of the maids had brought to her.

"Priscilla!" she cried. "So early! And skipping around like a young lamb. That's a good sign, I'll warrant. The ankle is behaving in that seemly manner which all good ankles should."

She was clearly in a good mood and was just about to launch into a comment on the Wycherley play when I said: "I'm worried about Carlotta."

"Worried! Why, the child is having a wonderful time. And what a little beauty, eh?"

"It's this man ... Beaumont Granville."

"What a charmer! He has enlightened the days, I'll admit."

"How much has he been seeing of Carlotta?"

"Oh, it is Carlotta, is it?"

"Harriet, you don't seem to understand what sort of man we are dealing with. Yet you know what happened in Venice."

"My dear Priscilla, as I have said before, that was all those years ago. Most of us have adventures in our youth which might be considered shocking. We grow out of them and if we are wise we forget them."

"Carlotta is still in the schoolroom. I don't want her to see this man. He is old ... old in years and old in iniquity. I want her removed from him."

"She adores him. It is amusing the way in which her eyes light up at the sight of him."

"It doesn't amuse me."

"Of late it has become increasingly hard to amuse you. Don't grow old before your time, Priscilla."

"I'm worried about Carlotta and that man. I want to go back home. She is my daughter and I want you to help me as you did before."

"Of course I'll help you. But really, Priscilla, you are like one of those fearsome Puritans. It's good for Carlotta to have this little flutter. It is preparing her for life."

"I don't want that man to have a hand in the preparations. He's dangerous. I don't like him."

"You've made that obvious."

"I thought you wanted her to have Benjie."

"Of course, she's going to have Benjie, but she has to grow up a little more. Stop fretting, Priscilla. Everything will be all right."

I could see that I should get little help from Harriet, but something would have to be done. What?

An impulse came to me. I had to discover what his plans regarding Carlotta were, and I had an idea that he might tell me, out of bravado. He was so sure of himself and already he was weaning her from me. I had always been impulsive, and no sooner had the idea occurred to me that I must talk to him than I began making my preparations to do so.

I left Harriet, and within an hour had put on my cloak and hood and was walking the short distance between our houses.

I was admitted by one of the servants I had seen the previous night. He showed no surprise at the sight of me. I supposed he was accustomed to women calling on his master.

I was shown into a small room leading from the hall and asked to wait.

He came almost immediately—exquisitely dressed as ever—his square-cut, mulberry-coloured velvet coat open to show his very fine waistcoat; his knee-length breeches were of the same shade of mulberry; his shoes had high red heels, which made him taller than he actually was; and he carried a jewelled snuffbox in his hand. I don't know why I should have noticed his clothes at such a time, but the manner in which he wore them always made one notice. He was one of the leaders of fashion and well known for it throughout Court circles.

He bowed, holding the snuffbox in his left hand, and taking my hand in his right, kissed it. I shrank visibly.

"What a pleasure!" he murmured. "Once you came to visit me in Dorchester. Now you come to London ... of your own ardent wish in both cases."

"I have come to talk to you," I said.

"Dear lady, I had not the temerity to imagine that you had come for any other reason this time."

305

"What is your object in making yourself so agreeable to my family?"

"I am always agreeable," he answered, "and my object is to extract as much enjoyment from life as it will offer."

"And what does this particular enjoyment involve?"

"Pray be seated." He laid the snuffbox on the table, and brought out a gilded chair for me. He sat on another close to the table. "It is a very interesting situation," he went on. "It is all very clear to me. So the delightful Carlotta is the result of that peccadillo of yours. A most delightful result, I must say. And her father was Jocelyn Frinton. That is most interesting. Poor fellow, came to a bad end through that low-born monster, Titus Oates. But not before he gave us this delightful creature."

"Us?" I said.

It was then I realized the extreme cruelty in him. He knew how tormented I had been and he gloated on it . . . just as he had on my shame and humiliation on that other occasion.

"You will not be allowed to be greedy, dear lady, and keep all that sweetness to yourself."

"Please explain."

"I find her enchanting."

"She is a child."

"Some of us love children."

"Depraved people like yourself, you mean."

"You could say that, I suppose."

"Then you must turn your eyes elsewhere."

"My dear Priscilla . . . I always loved the name. It sounds so prim. Remember I told you that during that ecstatic night we spent together. You haven't forgotten? I never did. I often wanted to remind you of it. You are not really in a position, are you, to tell me what I should do about your daughter? I have a charming picture of you. You didn't see it completed, did you? You must come to Dorchester sometime. It is the kind of picture only a lover could produce. Now listen to me. I have a great fondness for your daughter. My intentions are absolutely honourable."

"Good heavens! You mean you want to marry her! This is too foolish for words."

"By no means foolish. It is very sensible. The whole of London is talking about the Frinton fortune. Our delightful, beautiful, desirable Carlotta is not only a beauty, she is a considerable heiress."

"You're monstrous."

"I enjoy revealing myself to you as I did on that night . . . that memorable night. I kept my word, did I not? Were you not surprised? What a gamble you took! You should be grateful to me really. But for me your father would have been long since dead. To seduce a woman is a venial sin, but to save a life a great virtue. For what I did that night, surely I will have a place in heaven."

"I would be ready to gamble on the fact that it will be hell for you."

"Where all the interesting people will be, so they tell me. But we stray from the point. It is not the hereafter that you are concerned with; it is the present."

"Will you leave my daughter alone?"

"No," he replied firmly, "I am fond of her. You yourself said I should marry and so I always intended to when I met the lady who had all the necessary qualifications."

"And Carlotta's fortune puts her into that category."

"Exactly. I appear to you to be rich. So I am in a way. I have the credit of the whole of London, but bills do have to be paid in time. There are a great many of them and my life-style is expensive. You see, everyone looks to me to lead the fashion. My tailor's bills are so long that it takes half a day to read them. I need money. I need that fortune badly. And the Fates have given me a very pleasant way of acquiring it."

"She is not fifteen years old yet."

"A delectable age. Moreover she is mature for her age. She is a warmhearted child, longing for love."

"When I tell her of your cynical proposition what do you think she will say?"

"She will never believe you. She will think you are jealous."

"She is not so foolish as that. What will happen when I tell her certain things about you?"

"She will tell you that she knows I am a man of experience. That is what she admires. A man who has known many women and selects her for his wife. What greater compliment could there be?"

"The compliment might not be so great if she knew it was her fortune that made her so sought after."

"I will convince her that I am in no need of a fortune and that the sordid suggestion comes from those who are jealous of youth and happiness."

He took a pinch of snuff from the box and held it in between his well-manicured finger and thumb. He smiled at me as he took it.

I stood up.

"So," he said, rising, "our little tête-à-tête is over."

"This shall never come to pass," I declared. "I will do anything . . . anything to prevent it."

"My dear Priscilla, you are being most unworldly. Let the child be happy. After all, how old were you when you had your first fling?"

"How dare you . . ."

"I dare much, my dear mother-in-law-to-be. Is that not amazing? You . . . my mother-in-law. All I ask you, who at the age of fifteen—Carlotta's age—slipped secretly into Venice to give birth to your bastard child, not to hold up your hands in horror at a man who has had a few adventures which an enlightened society would call normal for the times."

"For the last time I ask you. Will you go away? Will you promise not to see my daughter again?"

"I will promise you two things. I shall *not* go away and I shall see your daughter again."

I faced him and said: "If you attempt to put this evil plan into practice, I will stop at nothing to prevent you. I would kill you."

The slow smile spread across his face.

"What an intriguing situation," he said.

I turned away and walked out of the house.

I walked through the streets without seeing anyone or anything. I went straight up to my room and all the time I was asking myself what I could do now.

To whom could I go for advice? Harriet did not understand the horror of the situation. How could she? She did not know what had happened that night in Dorchester. The escapade in Venice she dismissed as a youthful frolic. That was something Harriet could understand. Gregory was kind; he would do anything he could to help, but he was not the most resourceful of men and I felt this would be a situation he would not be able to grasp.

Carlotta? Suppose I talked to her? I thought of Benjie—dear Benjie, who had a great deal of his father in him. When I considered him, I did agree with Harriet that he was the one who would make Carlotta happy. He was steady, he was honest, he would be faithful and love her devotedly. I wanted her to be young for a while, to continue her lessons with Amelia Garston; I wanted her to have a gradual awakening to love and marriage. If this fearful thing which threatened was ever to come to pass, it would be complete misery for her. I could not bear to think of her being submitted to his lust as I had been.

I went to her room. She was getting ready to go out. She swung round and looked at me.

"Whatever is the matter?" she asked.

I touched my face.

"You look so pale and your eyes are wild. You look as if you've seen a ghost."

"Carlotta," I said, "I want to tell you something."

She came to me and kissed me. Then she pushed me into a chair and drawing up a stool sat at my feet. She put her head against my knee. For all her youthful arrogance, she had endearing ways.

"I've thought for some time that you had something to tell me," she said. "In fact, I fancy you have been on the verge of it now and then. Is it very important?"

"Carlotta, I am your mother."

She turned and stared at me. "What . . . do you mean?" she stammered.

"I, not Harriet . . . am your mother."

"My mother! But . . ."

"I have wanted to tell you often. I think you ought to know. Your father was Jocelyn Frinton."

She continued to stare at me, and then understanding dawned on her.

"So that was why . . ."

"Robert knew," I answered. "Harriet told him."

"Wait a minute," she said. "It's all rather bewildering. Tell me everything right from the beginning."

So I told her how Jocelyn had come to us . . . a fugitive, and how we had sheltered him and he and I had become lovers.

"We should have married," I told her, "but he was taken prisoner when we came off the island."

"Oh, you poor Priscilla! Mother . . . I suppose I shall call you that now. It's strange. I hardly ever call Harriet that. She likes to be called Harriet, which is odd . . . but then Harriet is not like other people."

"She was good to me. It was her idea. It seemed wild at the time and yet it worked."

"Harriet loves planning and playacting. She is doing it all the time. And you are my mother. I always loved you. I expect you always loved me, too."

"Oh, my darling child. I have wanted so often to have you with me. I schemed to have you with me."

She put her arms around me and held me tightly. "I'm glad," she said. "Yes, I am glad. I'm what they call a love child, am I not? It's a beautiful expression in a way. Conceived in love . . . reckless love I suppose it means, the kind of love that takes no count of the cost." She paused and then she said suddenly: "Benjie is not my brother."

"No," I said happily, "no."

"He won't be able to bully me anymore."

"He has always been so fond of you."

"What will happen now? Shall you tell people?"

"I shall tell my mother and I suppose she will tell my father. Gregory already knows, of course."

"Dear Gregory, he has always been such a nice father. One doesn't tell him things...but I know that he would always be kind and understanding if one did."

"He is a good man. Christabel knows. She was with us in Venice."

"Christabel! I never think much about her. She is just...there. And all *she* thinks about is that son of hers."

"She helped look after me in Venice."

"Yes, I was born in Venice and I always thought that rather romantic. And there was all that fuss about my arrival."

"You've always liked fuss, haven't you, Carlotta?"

"Well, can you wonder...considering my birth."

She kissed me again and I could see that the news had stimulated her. She was not in the least shocked at having been born illegitimate. She thought it all romantic and exciting, and the fact that I was her mother gave her a certain pleasure. I couldn't help commenting on it.

"Yes," she said, "I *am* glad. You're the sort of mother I want. That sounds unfair to Harriet. She's a most exciting mother...but somehow not like a mother. One wants a mother to be a little fussy, caring in a way that makes you impatient...someone you feel will always be there no matter what you have done...someone who'd die for you."

"Oh, Carlotta," I said, "I would do that willingly for you and Damaris."

"Damaris is my sister, of course...my half sister. Everything is turning about. Leigh is my stepfather. Does he know?"

"Yes, he knows."

"I thought so. You told him, did you?"

"Yes. Before we were married."

"Obligations, I daresay."

"You could call it that."

"Who else knows?"

I hesitated and then I said: "Beaumont Granville."

She stared at me in amazement. "Beau knows?"

"Carlotta, it is this which made me decide that you must know without delay. I don't like your friendship with this man."

"What do you mean, you don't like my friendship with him!"

"He is not a good man. In fact he is a very wicked man."

I saw the hard look creeping over her face. The tenderness of a few moments ago was fast disappearing.

"You hated him from the first moment in the Exchange," she said.

"I hated him before that. I had met him before."

"You didn't say so."

"Did he?"

"No."

"He was in Venice before you were born . . . and I think at the time of your birth."

"Why?"

"He was there . . . adventuring, I suppose. Doing what he has done all through his useless life."

"How can you say his life is useless? He has done many things. He was once in the army."

"I am sure he looked very pretty in his uniform."

"Please do not sneer at him."

"He is a wicked man. He tried to abduct me in Venice. Leigh thrashed him. He bears the scars still. That is his life. He seduces girls when he can . . . preferably young and innocent ones."

"You are so behind the times, dear Priscilla. You have lived too long in the country."

"Unlike you who have been in Town for a week or so."

"I understand him," she said earnestly. "He has told me so much about his life. Oh, yes, he has had adventures. There have been lots of women. They chased him, you know, and he couldn't hurt their feelings by refusing them when they were so persistent. But now he has finished with that."

"Since when?"

"Since we met."

312

"Are you telling me . . ."

She interrupted: "I am telling you I love him and he is in love with me."

"He is in love with your fortune. Has that occurred to you?"

"He has never mentioned my fortune."

"He has mentioned it to me."

She stared at me blankly. "He . . . has spoken to you!"

"Yes," I replied, "he wants your fortune. He appears to be wealthy, but he has to keep up appearances and that requires a great deal of money. Yours will be useful."

"This is so silly."

"On your part, yes. On his, it is quite clever."

"How you hate him. Is it because I love him?"

"No. It went back before that."

"Because he once liked you?"

"He doesn't like anyone but himself, Carlotta. And he is so besottedly in love that no one else matters."

"So you have seen him, and because you thought he would tell about Venice you thought you ought to tell me first."

"Yes, that might be so."

"You told him, when you were in Venice, that you were going to have me . . ."

"I did not tell him. I had no conversation with him . . . in Venice. I was dragged away from a masked ball. Fortunately Leigh was at hand and rescued me."

"Then who told him?"

"He discovered somehow . . . I never knew how. He had people who worked for him perhaps. I never found out."

"And you hate him for knowing it?"

"Not for that . . . for other things."

"Well, you will have to stop hating him because I am going to marry him."

"No, Carlotta. It's impossible. You are too young for marriage. Good heavens, child, you're not fifteen years old yet."

"Many people have married at fifteen. Princesses . . . queens . . . always do. As for you, you may not have married, but it would have been more acceptable to society if you had been."

"It's a different case."

"How? You loved my father. I love Beau."

"He is so old."

"So you think I want a silly boy?"

"He must be at least thirty years older than you are."

"I don't care if he is fifty years older. He is the most exciting person I have ever met, and I am going to marry him."

"No, Carlotta, you are not. You cannot marry without your parents' consent."

"Considering I have only just discovered who my parent is that seems a poor argument to put forward. You have only just acknowledged your relationship."

That hurt me. As if I had not wanted to claim her all these years!

"Carlotta, do understand. Everything I do is for your sake. You cannot marry this man"—I clutched at some respite—"yet."

She responded at once. "How long would you expect us to wait?"

"Till you are sixteen."

"It's too long."

"A year then," I conceded. "Six months at least..."

She appeared to consider that.

Time, I thought. Time will help. As long as she does not rush into this there may be hope.

"All right," she said, "perhaps we could wait for six months."

I felt exhausted and desperately unhappy.

The very worst which I had feared had happened. But at least she knew now. That was like a burden lifted from my shoulders.

I went to Harriet and said: "I have told her. She knows now."

Harriet nodded. "That is as well," she said.

"And now, Harriet, I want to go back to Eversleigh. I don't want another day here."

314

She looked at me with that understanding which came to her at rare moments.

Then she said: "We will leave tomorrow."

The next day we began our journey home. Carlotta looked sullen and scarcely spoke to me. At least, I thought, she will not see him for a while. Surely Harriet will not ask him to the Abbas, and I shall certainly see that he does not come to Eversleigh.

We arrived first at the Abbas, and I was hurt when Carlotta said she would stay there for a while and come over to Eversleigh later.

I went back alone.

I knew that I should have to tell my mother about Carlotta's birth. The secret was out really, and I wanted her to hear it first from me.

She was a little concerned when I arrived. She said I did not look well. Had I had too many late nights? I told her how I had sprained my ankle and she insisted on calling Sally Nullens to look at it.

Sally prodded it and shook her head and said it was all that gadding about. But she could not really see anything wrong with it, and to satisfy her and my mother I promised to rest it every day.

My mother followed me into my bedroom and that gave me the opportunity I needed to be alone with her.

I began as I had with Carlotta. "I have something to tell you."

She was all concern immediately. "What is it, my darling?"

The gentleness of her voice brought sudden tears to my eyes. I hastily blinked them away. I said: "I am afraid this is going to be a shock to you. I have hated keeping it from you but I was afraid to tell."

She looked startled. "Surely you are not afraid to tell me anything?"

"I was only afraid of causing you pain."

"My dearest, are you ill? Please tell me quickly. Can't you see how you're frightening me?"

315

"No, I'm not ill. It's not that. Something happened to me long ago. I had a child."

She stared at me incredulously.

"Carlotta is my daughter," I said quickly; and I told of what had ensued on my night on the island with Jocelyn and of its aftermath.

"Oh, my dear, dear child," she cried, "you should have come to me. I was the one who should have looked after you."

"Harriet had this idea."

"Harriet!" I saw the lights of anger in her eyes. "Harriet *would* interfere. You and I should have gone away quietly to a little English village in the Midlands... or the North... somewhere where they didn't know us. Harriet! Venice! That is just like her."

"I was very grateful to her. She helped me so much, and she pretended that Carlotta was her child."

"It was crazy. Melodramatic in the extreme."

"It was better than having the child put out with a foster mother, which is often done in such circumstances."

"I would have arranged something. We could have adopted her. I would have seen that she was brought into the household."

"I know you would have helped me, but it seemed better to do it that way then. I told Carlotta about it when we were in London."

"And Leigh?"

"Leigh knows. He knew before we were married. I told him."

"Thank God for that! I shall tell your father."

"I doubt whether he would be interested."

"But of course he will. Carlotta is his granddaughter. You are his daughter."

"He has never been the slightest interested in me."

"Of course he has. It is just his way."

"Then tell him if you wish. It is a relief that you know."

"So this is why Carlotta has come into money. It's from her father's family."

I nodded.

She reached for my hand and held it fast. "Oh, Priscilla, when you were little, we were so close."

"Because my father resented me."

"He didn't resent you."

"He just ignored me. I was a girl and he wanted a boy who looked just like he did. I always knew it. It did something to me. I used to like to go to Harriet's where Gregory was always so interested in me. He used to show me pictures and tell me stories about them. One day I said to him, 'I wish *you* were my father.' And he said, 'Hush, you mustn't say that.' And I said, 'Why not? It's true. We're supposed to tell the truth.' And what do you think he said to that? 'You mustn't tell the truth when it hurts people.' Then I said, 'My father would never be hurt because I didn't want him for a father, because he didn't want me anyway.'"

She put her arms about me. "I didn't know you cared so much about him," she said.

"I don't care about him."

"Oh, but you do. My sweet daughter, you *do* care about him. You should have come to us with your trouble. Oh, how I wish you had come to me!"

"I suppose I might have done. But Harriet seemed the best one to confide in and she was so interested at once and so was Gregory." Then I was laughing, a little hysterically perhaps. "You seem to care more that I went to Harriet than that I had a child when I was fifteen born out of wedlock."

"Never mind," she said, "it is all done with now. I'm glad you told me. Carlotta is my grandchild ... like dear little Damaris. There must be no more fretting, no more secrets. We have to forget the troubles and learn to be happy. This has been worrying for you, and is worrying you still. I can see it in your face."

But how could I tell her the real reason for my worry? How could I ever tell her what happened while she lay in a fever in a Dorchester inn?

She told my father that night.

He said nothing to me about the matter. I did catch him

317

once or twice looking at me intently, as though he saw m
in a different light. I could imagine that he was thinkin
that his daughter, whom he had scarcely noticed, was
woman after all. She had perhaps inherited something o
her father. She had had a lover when she was in th
schoolroom; she had borne his child.

I fancied that he was a little more interested in me tha
he had been before. But he was as aloof as ever.

Christmas had come, and as usual Harriet and Gregory
with Benjie and Carlotta, were to spend the holiday wit
us. I was eager to see Carlotta again and deeply hurt whe
I received her cool greeting. She was blaming me fo
having shown a lack of understanding about her lov
affair.

The house was decorated in the usual manner—holl
and ivy and some other green plants. The carol singer
came and Harriet devised a play in which we all took pa
on Christmas Day.

Not a word was said about Beaumont Granville, an
but for Carlotta's coolness to me I should have thought h
had been forgotten.

I noticed my father watching Carlotta with a certai
twitch of the lips which indicated amusement. I suppose
he was proud to have such an attractive granddaughte

I felt a great longing for Leigh who had been absent s
many months. He was still on the Continent where th
King was deeply involved in the matter of the Spanis
Succession, as Louis the Fourteenth was trying to secur
the crown of Spain for his grandson. This was o
importance to England and to Europe, and William kep
troops in Holland. Leigh was in command of one of th
companies and Edwin of another. We did not know fro
one moment to another when fighting would break ou
but at least they were temporarily not at risk.

I thought a great deal about my marriage with Leigh.
had never been completely satisfying; yet I loved Leig
and Leigh loved me. I knew that I was to blame.

I could not forget Beaumont Granville. So often whe

318

Leigh embraced me I would see the mocking face of that man, and the beloved body of my husband would seem to change to that other. Beaumont Granville had not only bruised and humiliated me on that night; he had done so forever. That was the price I had paid for my father's life.

Sometimes I wanted to tell Leigh, to explain to him my emotions. I thought if he knew we might grow towards an understanding. I wanted to tell him that I loved him, that I wanted perfect union between us. I did not shrink from passion, as I knew he sometimes believed I did. It was simply that I could not forget.

I was sure that if only I could bring myself to tell him, he would understand. He would help me overcome this barrier which I had set up between us. He was a man of a passionate nature. I often wondered about him—those long separations were dangerous, particularly as when we were together our relationship lacked the ultimate satisfaction which it should have had.

At the back of my mind was the niggling fear that one day he might turn from me.

What a price I had paid for my father's life!

And now . . . Carlotta.

Twelfth Night had come and gone. We had had the traditional cake and the ring had fallen to Harriet who had been Queen of the Night. She had, of course, made us perform all kinds of charades which we mimed under her direction.

I thought wistfully how I should have enjoyed it if Leigh had been there and I had never heard of Beaumont Granville.

The day after Twelfth Night, Carlotta was missing.

I shall never cease to be grateful that we discovered her absence almost as soon as she had gone.

Emily Philpots had come to her room to take a petticoat which she had been embroidering for her, and had found her gone. Emily went in search of her and by great good fortune she met me on the stairs.

"I've just been to Mistress Carlotta's room," she said. "Is she still sleeping?"

"No. She is not there. I wonder where she could be this hour."

She was not an early riser so it seemed strange that sh should be about already. We breakfasted at no given tim but came down when we wanted to between half-pa seven and nine o'clock to help ourselves from th sideboard—except Harriet who took a dish of chocolate her room. I had been down at eight and had not see Carlotta.

I felt a twinge of apprehension and went up to h room.

To my relief I saw that the bed had been slept in. So sh must have gone out in the early morning.

I went out into the garden. Jasper was already workir near the haunted patch.

I paused to chat with him. He said the weather w unseasonable, too warm. What we needed was a touch snow to keep the bulbs warm.

He shook his head mournfully. "I don't know what th world's coming to."

"You mean...no snow in January."

"This is a wicked world," he went on. "People pay f their sins. Everyone has to be accounted for."

"That's a gloomy thought," I replied. "We're none of so pure that some price won't be extracted for them. Ev you, Jasper, will have an account rendered."

Irony was lost on him. "I've served the Lord as best know," he said grimly.

"Has it occurred to you that many of us do that? B what we consider best might not be what God does."

"You was always one to try and twist right and wror around with words. I mind you as a little girl."

"Well, Jasper, we are as God made us, as you know f well, and if He doesn't like us the way we are, well...H shouldn't have made us that way."

"I can't listen to blasphemy, mistress. It's sinful to op the ear to what may offend the Lord. Besides, I've got t much to do. A fine mess that carriage has made out there the drive. It's this damp and the rain. Carriage ruts right into the grass."

"When was this done?"

"Well, 'tweren't yesterday. No rain then ... but we had a real downpour in the night."

I went with him to the end of the drive and saw the ruts made by a carriage. A sudden horror overwhelmed me. This morning ... early ... a carriage had drawn up there. For whom? Carlotta?

I went at once to Harriet. She was sleeping; the empty dish which had contained her chocolate was beside her bed.

"Harriet," I cried. "Wake up, Harriet."

She opened her eyes and stared at me.

"Do you know where Carlotta is?" I asked.

She looked puzzled and yawned.

"She's gone," I cried. "A carriage came this morning. Have you seen Carlotta? What has she told you? What is going on? I must know."

She sat up. "I have no idea where she is," she said. "I know nothing."

I was convinced that she was speaking the truth. I was frantic. Carlotta had run away and I could guess to whom she had gone.

I questioned the servants. No one had seen her leave. Ellen thought she had heard a carriage at about seven o'clock. She wasn't sure.

It was Amelia Garston who confirmed my fears. When I questioned her, there was something furtive about her. I guessed that Carlotta had confided in her.

At last I made her tell me, although she tearfully protested that she had promised not to.

Carlotta had eloped. Beaumont Granville had come for her early that morning. He had had the carriage waiting at the gates. They were going to London where they would be married.

I thought we should never arrive in time. I insisted on going with them. We took the most fleet of the horses—my father, Gregory and I. I was glad my father had come because I believed he would know how to deal with Beaumont Granville. Carlotta was too young to marry and Gregory, who had always been as a father to her, and I, her mother, and her grandfather must carry some weight. My father was no longer out of favour at Court and his presence would give us the influence we needed. I doubted Beaumont Granville was the kind of man who would find much favour with the King.

We were in sight of London. It was a misty day with a drizzle in the air. I could just see the towers and spires of the city rising up through the mist. The distance seemed twice as long as it normally did, and I was in the deepest despair before we had the greatest stroke of luck.

There in the road less than a mile from the city was the carriage. One of the wheels had gone into a ditch and the coachman was doing his best to get it out.

"Thank God," I cried, "we are in time."

My father took charge.

"Good day, sir," he said. "And what are you doing on this dull morning? Stuck in a ditch, eh? That's justice. You have no right, sir, to take this young lady from her home."

Carlotta had appeared. I saw the blank dismay on her face. She had flushed scarlet and she cried out: "I was not taken from my home. I came willingly."

"You will return with us ... albeit less willingly," said my father. "This is no way to behave."

She clenched her fist, but she looked uncertain. She had always been slightly in awe of my father, although he had been softer to her than he ever had to me. There was an affinity between them. She was wild, passionate and self-willed. He was all that, too.

Beaumont Granville looked as urbane as ever and quite unruffled.

"I can explain," he began.

"No need to," retorted my father. "Everything is clear to me."

"My intentions were entirely honorable. I proposed marriage and was accepted."

I cried out: "You were to wait awhile. That was the agreement."

"You treat me as though I am in the nursery," protested Carlotta.

"You behave as though you are still there," growled my father. "Come, get up on my horse. We'll turn in at the next inn and get you something to ride."

"It is the young lady's wish..." began Beaumont Granville.

"My dear sir, you know the penalties for abducting children."

"I am no child," cried Carlotta.

"You are not of age and therefore under your parents' control. I'll have no nonsense. I could have you before the courts, sir. I have some influence in those quarters. Escapades of this kind are out of date and frowned on."

Beaumont Granville seemed resigned.

"I'll stay with you, Beau," said Carlotta.

"You will return to Eversleigh," contradicted my father. "And sharp about it."

Beaumont Granville looked ruefully at the carriage.

"It was our bad luck," he said to Carlotta. "If this had not happened we should have been married by now, and then they could have done nothing."

Carlotta was near to tears, but I could see she was overwhelmed by my father. Gregory had said very little. His gentleness would have done little good on an occasion like this.

Beaumont Granville shrugged his shoulders and addressed himself to my father.

"I am sorry, sir, to have caused you this inconvenience, but you know how it is when one is in love."

He turned to Carlotta and she went to him and stood close. I felt nauseated, fighting back hideous memories. He whispered something to her and she brightened a little.

He held her hand and kissed it. Then she walked over to my father.

323

We rode off, Carlotta with my father on his big black horse.

Beaumont Granville stood in the road looking ruefully at his coachman who was still trying to pull the carriage out of the rut.

~ Murder ~
at Enderby

All the way back Carlotta was silent, brooding. When I spoke to her she answered in monosyllables. I felt she was blaming me for ruining her happiness.

Harriet was waiting for us when we reached Eversleigh. Carlotta ran to her and threw herself into her arms. I felt waves of jealousy sweep over me. Carlotta was telling me that she believed Harriet was her friend. Harriet would never have been so cruel to her.

I longed to tell her how much I loved her, how I wanted above everything to save her from this man who had proved his cruelty to me and had brazenly admitted that it was her fortune he wanted. How could I make her see? Only by telling her of that fearful night which had cast its shadow over my life.

No man of honour would have behaved as he did. Had it not been for her money he would have been content with seduction; but he wanted to get his hands on her inheritance and marriage was necessary for that.

My poor, innocent, deluded Carlotta, who thought she

knew so much and understood so little.

She avoided me. I was heartbroken. I could neither eat nor sleep.

My mother was growing anxious. "My dear Priscilla," she said, "you must not take this to heart. The young will indulge in these escapades. Of course he is not the man for her. But she will be over it in a few weeks. That's how girls are."

My nightmares returned. I could not get him out of my mind.

"I wish Leigh were here," said my mother. "He would be able to comfort you. I have never liked these long absences of his. It's not the way to make a happy marriage."

"He is making plans to leave the army. We have talked a good deal about taking the Dower House and getting some land."

"It's a wonderful idea. I've asked your father to write to him and tell him he must leave the army as soon as it can be arranged."

"He will, I know, as soon as his term comes to an end."

"And now you must stop fretting about this affair. Your father says the man is something of an adventurer and has been involved in one or two scandals."

"I am sure he is right. Certainly he is not the man for Carlotta."

"I understand your feelings. It was so wrong of him to persuade her to elope."

"She is so headstrong. I am afraid for her."

"Well, you brought her back. She'll understand that she will have to wait awhile. Waiting is often so good in this sort of case. When you are young, ardour fades quickly."

I thought, We must keep them separated. If they don't meet she will forget him. Benjie is there. It is a great revelation for them to know that they are not brother and sister.

I liked to go out alone. I found it hard to endure light conversation when my mind was full of one thing. I hardly listened when people talked and Harriet complained that I was getting absentminded.

I would ride down to the sea or through the woods, trying all the time to assure myself that she would forget, that it was a momentary infatuation.

A few mornings later I found myself close to Enderby Hall, which had been empty since the death of Robert Frinton. It was Carlotta's now. It had been shut up since Robert's funeral and there was talk of selling it.

I had never liked the house. There was an atmosphere of gloom about it. Yet in a way I was drawn to it.

It was foolish to say that it was an unlucky house. Houses could surely not be unlucky; and yet there had been death and tragedy there. And Robert had not lived long to enjoy the place.

Some impulse made me ride up the short drive. I noticed that the bushes were already beginning to be overgrown. I would get Jasper to go over one day and clean up the gardens.

I pulled up and looked at the house, and as I stood there I saw a movement at one of the windows. I saw a hand on the curtain as it moved. There was someone there, looking out.

My first impulse was to turn and gallop away. But I did not. I just stood watching. The curtain had fallen back into place.

Someone was in the house.

I did not believe in ghosts, and somehow since I had been so unhappy I was less careful of myself. A thought occurred to me that it might be some desperate man hiding there, some fugitive from justice.

The wise thing would be to ride back to Eversleigh and bring someone with me to go over the house.

I did not do this. Instead I dismounted, tethered my horse and went towards the house.

I pushed open the door, which was strange, for it should have been locked. I walked into the hall. There was the staircase over which a poor, demented woman had attempted to hang herself. The gloom, the horror of that house seemed to close about me like a fog.

Go away. Go away, urged my good sense.

But as I stood there I heard movement from above . . footsteps, a rustle, the quiet opening of a door.

My heartbeats were thundering. I was trembling a little I did not know what I expected to see. I was just standing inside the hall, prepared to run if need be.

A figure had appeared at the head of the stairs.

It was Beaumont Granville.

"You!" I cried.

"Well met," he said. "I guessed you would pay me a visit. I saw you from the window."

"So . . . it is you then."

"Yes. I have a habit of turning up in your life, haven't I?"

"I wish to God you would get out of my life."

"That wouldn't be very easy for God to arrange as I am going to marry your daughter."

"That shall never be. My father made that clear."

"You did not think I would give up as easily as that, did you?"

"You must go away from here."

"I will for a while . . . with Carlotta. I thought we might go to Venice. That would be rather piquant, don't you think?"

"You remember the scars you received in Venice. You should take care that there are not others."

"I would have the law on any who attacked me for marrying my wife."

"She will never be that."

"You are wrong there, Prim Priscilla. The little girl is on fire for me. You should know I have a special way with women. I am irresistible. You couldn't resist me, could you? You had better take care. I have a fondness for you because it was such a pleasant night we had together, but I could be angry with you. Now keep out of my affairs. Carlotta and I are going to marry. There is nothing you can do to stop that."

"What are you doing here . . . in this house?"

"Staying here for a while until we leave. We shall be going soon and then there will be that belated ceremony."

"She knows you are here... in this house?"

"Yes, in her house. It will be *our* house soon."

"As you hope her fortune will be."

"It is customary for a man to take charge of his wife's affairs, you know."

"Please, *please* go away. She is young and you are old... *old*."

"Experienced," he corrected. "That is what she likes. She wants no green boys, that one."

"Have you no shame?"

"No," he answered, "none."

"What are you proposing to do?"

"Ha! You come here trying to probe our secrets. I am mad with love for Carlotta."

"And her fortune."

"It is part of her charm. I am mad with love for all that but otherwise perfectly sane."

I felt limp with helplessness. What could I do? One thing I could not do was bear to stand there any longer and bandy words with him while I looked at his mocking face.

I turned and went out to my horse.

I rode back in a kind of daze. I had to do something. What?

Whichever way I looked I saw only one thing. Nothing could save Carlotta but the death of Beaumont Granville. Whatever else happened he would always be there. He would never give up. And he had bewitched her. He would have to die.

When the idea came to me, oddly enough, I felt better. I went along to the gun room. I used to watch Carl and Benjie at shooting practice and I had now and then joined them.

"Not a bad shot for a girl," Leigh had once said.

It's the only way, I told myself. I took a small pistol. It was one I had used before. It seemed like an old friend.

I took it up to my bedroom and hid it in a drawer.

329

Could I possibly do this? Could I commit murder? I suppose in certain circumstances anyone could, if it was the only way out of an intolerable situation.

It would be over in a few minutes. I would go into the house. I would call him. He would stand on the stairs. All I had to do was raise the gun and fire straight at him.

It would be the end...and it was the only way if Carlotta was not going to be launched into a life of misery.

I owed this to her. I had not owned her when she was born. I had let another woman take her. I must save her from this sadistic brute, for I could clearly imagine what he would do to her.

What he had done to me had scarred me, I believe forever. I had done that for my father and I would do this for Carlotta. I would choose my moment as he stood there on the stairs mocking me.

I felt better now.

There was the day to be lived through. It seemed so long. In the early afternoon I passed my father on the stairs. He looked at me intently.

He said: "You don't look well."

"I'm surprised that you noticed," I answered.

"I noticed. You're fretting about that girl of yours, I suppose?"

I did not answer.

He took me by the arm and drew me into the room which was called his private study because he did his estate work there.

He looked at me quite kindly.

"She's a girl who can look after herself," he said. "She has a will of her own. If she wants to marry this man, she will, you know. There's nothing you can do about it."

"There is something I can do."

"What?"

"I can stop the marriage and I will."

"We can keep them apart for a while but that may not work. She's a determined young woman."

"And he is determined to get her fortune."

"He's got something of a reputation. But it could work. Sometimes a man gives up his old ways and settles down."

I knew he was thinking of himself.

I said: "Not this man."

"How do you know?"

"I do know something of him."

"Reputations get exaggerated."

"You said we had parted them. We haven't. He's at Enderby Hall."

"At Enderby Hall!"

"Yes. I saw him there this morning."

My father laughed. "Her house, of course. Well, I suppose if she says he can be there he has a right to be. You've led a sheltered life. You've heard tales of him and you're upsetting yourself and everyone else because of it. If she's set her mind on him and he on her ... well, let them marry. It's experience for her. It'll be a taste of life."

"You don't know the sort of man he is."

"Look, daughter, all men have certain experiences in their youth. You don't expect them to behave like monks, do you?"

Then suddenly I was shouting at him. "I know this man. Do you remember lying in a filthy prison in Dorchester? Do you remember being taken to a room of your own and the next morning being released?"

He looked at me in surprise. "Of course I remember. It's something I shall never forget. What has it to do with ..."

"Everything!" I cried. "How do you think your freedom was bought? *I* paid for it ... with that man. I ... the daughter you have always despised."

"What *are* you saying ...?"

"I am saying this: I went to plead for you. He was there ... a great friend of Jeffreys. He would release you at a price ..." I covered my face with my hands. "You have no conception what it was like. That man ... How can I tell you? You see him as a normal, lusty man. I tell you he is capable of the greatest cruelty."

He had taken my hands from my face. He said: "*You*

331

...you submitted to that for *me?* Oh, my God! That was why...I looked for my benefactor and all the time it was my own daughter."

"Yes," I said, "the daughter who was of no account...the daughter who was not a son."

He did not speak. I saw the terrible emotion in his face. It was hatred for that man. It was remorse...yes, remorse for years of neglect.

"Priscilla...." He spoke my name softly.

I did not answer. I felt I had had enough. I was exhausted with emotion and the only thought that sustained me was that of the pistol lying in the drawer in my room.

That was a day of events. During the afternoon Leigh came home.

I was in his arms and he was kissing me, studying me.

"It's been a long time," I said.

"I came as soon as I could. I'm giving it all up now. I've arranged it. I'm going to be home from henceforth."

"That's good, Leigh."

"But, my dearest, you have grown thin...and so pale. You have been ill."

"I think I shall be all right...soon."

My mother was excited. "This is wonderful, Leigh," she cried. "I have been so longing for you to come. Priscilla talks a great deal about your plans for the Dower House."

She was running to the kitchens. A special feast must be prepared. She seemed to think that now Leigh was home everything would be all right.

I felt bemused. I kept thinking of the pistol in the drawer in my room. What could I do now? I had betrayed my secret at last. My father knew. I had not seen him since I had burst out of that room. He had gone out and had not returned.

It was clear that Leigh guessed there was something wrong. I was not listening to what he was saying. I could not think of anything but Beaumont Granville. Talking to my father as I had had brought it all back.

The secret was no longer shut away. It was out in the open.

When I was alone with Leigh, when he took me in his arms, when he was reminding me of how long we had been apart, how he had thought of nothing but me, I was only half listening.

I could not respond. Beaumont Granville had often been between us, but never so much as now.

Leigh said to me: "You must tell me what's wrong, Priscilla. Tell me. Have you met someone? You love someone else? There is someone, is there not?"

"There is someone, Leigh," I answered, and I saw the stricken look on his face.

He cried out: "I always knew. Right from the first. He was there between us."

"Not love, Leigh," I cried, "but hatred . . ."

I knew I had to tell him then. Perhaps I should have told him in the beginning . . . when we were married.

"I must tell you, Leigh," I said. "I must tell you everything. Today I have told my father. All these years I have kept it locked away. It seemed less shameful out of sight."

"Priscilla, my dear, I love you. Whatever it is makes no difference to that. Tell me . . . and we'll forget it. It will be gone then . . . no longer between us."

So I told him as I had told my father.

I saw his face grow dark with fury.

"That man! That man in Venice!"

"He never forgot . . . he never forgave. He bears the scars you gave him. Oh, Leigh, if you had known."

"You were so brave," he said, "so brave, my darling."

"I saved my father's life. They freed him the next day."

"It was a noble thing to do. You sacrificed yourself for him."

"It didn't end on that night. It has been with me ever since. It has been between us. . . . And now, Carlotta. Oh, Leigh, I feel as if it has been slowly killing me."

"He'll not marry Carlotta. We'll stop that."

"How? How?"

"We'll tell her this."

"I couldn't bear to. She would never understand."

He kissed me tenderly.

"My darling," he said, "you are overwrought. This has been a terrible ordeal."

"How can we stop it? He is here now...here at Enderby...her house. Oh, don't you see? He will induce her to run away with him. Once they are married..."

"It shall not be. I am looking after you now...just the two of us are together as we were meant to be right from the beginning. You won't bear this alone anymore."

"I'm glad you know. It has been a terrible burden. It has been there all the time. I could never forget it when we were together."

"I know."

"I was afraid you would realize there was something...I was afraid it would turn you away from me."

"Nothing on earth would do that. You were meant for me always."

I allowed myself to be comforted, but I was still thinking of the pistol in the drawer.

I wanted to tell him, but I knew he would take it away if he knew it was there.

He was all tenderness now, but he was planning something. I was always afraid of what he would do if he knew.

He must not suffer for this.

I said: "I am so tired, Leigh. I feel exhausted."

"My dearest," he answered tenderly, "you have suffered too much but today is going to be the end of it. The secret is out. Your father and I will know what to do."

I did not ask what.

"Lie down now," he said. "You need to rest. Shut your eyes. We will talk later."

I obeyed him. I felt a desperate need to be alone.

"Where are you going, Leigh?" I asked him.

"To see your father. I want to talk to him."

I nodded and he kissed me.

334

"You are so tired. Try and sleep a little. Rest, my dearest. You will feel better then."

I let him go and I lay for a while as the shadows crept into the room.

It seemed very quiet. The quietness before the débâcle, I thought.

I roused myself. What was I doing lying there? My father and Leigh were both violent men. They would want to make Beaumont Granville pay for what he had done to me.

They would go to him with whips. They would thrash him within an inch of his life as Leigh had done before. And Carlotta would hate them and refuse to believe what we said of him.

Carlotta was doomed if Beaumont Granville lived.

I had made up my mind. The fact that my father and Leigh now shared the secret made no difference to what I must do.

I rose and put on my cloak. I took the pistol and put it into my pocket. I went down to the stables, saddled my horse and rode over to Enderby Hall.

I reached the house. I saw a light in one of the rooms. I exulted because he was there.

I felt as though I were in a dream and unknown forces were propelling me forward. There was only one thing that mattered and that was that I should kill Beaumont Granville.

A voice within me seemed to be repeating over and over again: It is the only way.

I pushed open the door and walked into the house. The hall looked ghostly in the dimness. I felt a great impulse to run away.

I seemed to hear the voice of common sense. Tell her the truth. Show her what sort of man he is, and if she will not heed your warning it is for her to reap what she will have sown.

"Go back," said common sense. "Go back."

But I could not go back.

I do not know to this day whether I should have fired that shot when it came to the point, whether I had it in me to commit murder. I shall never be sure.

There was not a sound in the house—only an unearthly quietness. I started up the stairs. I must find the room where the light was burning.

I came to the balcony and there he was. He was lying on the floor. Blood was staining his embroidered waistcoat. He was quite still. I took one look at his face and I knew.

I had come too late. Someone had done the deed before me.

I ran out of the house. I took my horse and rode home as fast as I could. It was dark now. The weather had changed sharply and there was a touch of frost in the air. Overhead the stars were brilliant and there was a slim slice of a moon to add to the brightness.

I kept saying to myself: It's not real. You imagined it. This has preyed on your mind. You are not yourself.

I had taken one look and fled. Perhaps he had not been dead. Perhaps I had not really seen him there. I had had the pistol in my hand ready to shoot.

My mind was in such a turmoil that I was not sure what had really happened. I could not remember untethering my horse and riding away.

In my room I sat down and looked at my reflection. I scarcely recognized myself in the wild-eyed, white-faced woman who looked back at me. I was like a stranger out of a dream—not quite real. I began to wonder whether I had really seen him lying there.

Then the impulse came to me to go back and look again, to assure myself that I had not imagined the whole thing. I had worked myself up into a state of intense emotion. I had planned to murder. Had I really seen him lying there? I kept asking myself, or had it been an illusion, a horrible hallucination conjured up by a tortured mind?

I must go back. I must look again on that dead face. I must make sure that I had really seen what I thought I had.

My need was to act. I could not stay in this room alone. I

must be sure. So I went back to the stables, took my horse and rode once more to Enderby Hall.

I tethered my horse at the entrance to the drive and started forward. The house loomed before me. It seemed to take on a life of its own—leering, sinister.

Come inside, it seemed to be saying. Come inside and face your doom.

I pushed open the door. It was still ajar. I stepped into the hall. How eerie it was with the faint moonlight shining through the windows. There was a terrible silence everywhere. It was as though everything in this house were watching me . . . waiting.

Horror crawled over me. I had known as soon as I had first entered this house that evil was lurking in it.

Run! Run while there is a chance, a voice within me was saying. Don't look on that sight again.

But I had to see. I had to assure myself. It had not been a dream. I had seen him lying there. I had seen his elaborate waistcoat stained with blood.

I went to the foot of the stairs and started up. What a silence there was in that house! The silence of death. My footsteps seemed to make a great deal of noise on the wooden stairs.

I had reached the balcony. I stared.

There was nothing there.

But I had seen him! How long ago? How long had it taken me to get home and back? He had been lying there. I had seen him.

I would not believe I had imagined him. I had looked on his distorted features. I had seen the blood on his clothes.

This was getting more and more like a wild nightmare.

I looked closer. There was a stain on the wooden boards. Blood!

No, I had not been mistaken. I *had* seen him lying there and someone had taken him away.

I turned and fled down the stairs. I came out into the cold night air. I went to my horse and mounted.

And then I saw it . . . the flickering light among the trees. Someone was there.

Who? And what was that person doing?

I dismounted. I had to know. I tied up my horse again and I went back through the gate. I did not go into the house but towards the shrubbery, and there, hidden by the bushes, I watched that flickering light.

Someone was there . . . digging. And I knew that it was a grave which was being dug.

Whoever it was who had killed Beaumont Granville was burying his body in a grave.

I was filled with a terrible fear. I leaned against a bush. I must not be seen. I said to myself: Don't look. You know.

I stood there and covered my face with my hands.

I had betrayed my secret. I had kept it for so long because I had always feared what might happen if the events of that terrible night were known. I had feared just this.

I should never have told.

I recognized the digger. Of course I recognized him. Did I not know him as well as I knew anyone?

I saw Leigh's face clearly in the moonlight and felt an impulse to go to him.

But something stopped me. No, if the body were carefully buried, if all trace of the murder were removed, it might be that no one would discover that Beaumont Granville had been murdered at Enderby Hall.

I went back to the house. I mounted and rode away.

When I reached Eversleigh Court I was in a state of exhaustion. I went to my room and fell onto my bed.

After a while my mother came in.

"My dear Priscilla, you look ill," she said. "What is the matter?"

"I have a dreadful headache," I told her. "I just want to be quiet and lie in the dark."

"What a pity. It was going to be such a happy homecoming for Leigh. Where is he? I thought you and he were together. I shall have to put dinner back."

"I shan't come down tonight," I told her. "I feel too ill."

"We shall have to have the feasting tomorrow, and if you are not better I shall call the doctor in to see you."

"Oh, dear Mother," I said, "I am so sorry."

She kissed me. "It's nothing, dear child. There is tomorrow. It will be all right then. I'll leave you now to rest."

I lay in the darkness. Then I got up and undressed. I must pretend to be asleep because I could not speak to anybody yet.

It was nearly two hours later when Leigh came in.

He came quietly and I pretended to be asleep. He came to the bed, holding a lighted candle and looking down at me. I kept my eyes shut and when he turned away I opened them. I saw his muddied clothes and I felt sick with fear.

He was a long time washing the mud from himself.

That night we lay side by side. I had not spoken to him since his return, pretending to be in a deep sleep. He did not seem to want to speak either. We lay side by side through the night, feigning sleep, but I was aware of his wakefulness.

∾ The Revelation ∾

Looking back, I cannot think how I lived through the next few weeks. The memory of Beaumont Granville was always with us.

The next day I had gone out to that spot where I had seen Leigh among the trees. It was clear that the earth had been disturbed and I knew that the body of Beaumont Granville was lying underneath it.

I was almost beside myself with grief and anxiety. Somehow I had always known that that night which I had spent with him had not been the end. It was only the opening of a hideous tragedy. It was like a macabre masque and this was the inevitable ending.

The affair at Venice had been the prelude. The attempted abduction and the thrashing had set the stage for what was to come.

Leigh was a murderer because of what I had done. I had always known that he would kill Beaumont Granville if he learned what had happened. His nature was one of

341

impulsive passion. When he had heard what had happened, he had planned to kill him and he had done so without delay. Then he had dug his grave and buried him.

Murder is a fearsome thing. I suppose anyone who has committed it can never forget it. I had come near to committing it myself. But should I have fired the fatal shot when I had come face to face with my tormentor? I began to wonder. Instinct told me that I would never have done it. I could never have killed another human being whatever the provocation. But I could almost wish that I had done it myself rather than that Leigh should.

It had been my tragedy. I had made the decision to save my father's life. I should have been the one who took that last action.

But I could never have done it. I realized that now.

And now what was next? I was sure it was not finished.

For a whole week nothing happened. Leigh and I were like strangers. We could not even make an attempt at leading a normal married life.

He seemed as though he did not want to come near me, and yet I was aware that he was yearning for me. I took refuge in illness. It was not difficult.

My mother sent for the doctor, who said I needed to eat more. I was exhausted. I must rest and eat nourishing food, or I might go into a decline.

Carlotta came to see me. I believe she had to be persuaded to do so. She was aloof and sullen.

Harriet came. "What on earth has happened to you?" she demanded. "You are so wan. You haven't been yourself for a long time. What is it?"

I repeated what the doctor had said.

"Carlotta is disturbed," she said. "She hasn't heard from our romantic hero for some time."

"Oh?" I said faintly.

"No. Apparently he had been at Enderby and he has just disappeared."

"At Enderby!" I said blankly.

"Yes. The empty house. It's hers, of course, and it seems he went there so that he would be near and she could go and see him. Then one day...he's gone. She thought he had to go to London and didn't have time to tell her. She's anxious now to go to London."

I said nothing.

"She's determined to marry him," went on Harriet. "I expect she will. Once she's made up her mind she doesn't rest until she gets what she wants. You'll have to get reconciled, Priscilla."

I turned my head away listlessly.

"Well," said Harriet, "it's life. If he's a bit of a rogue she'll get used to it. The young have to live for themselves, you know. No use trying to set them on the straight and narrow path before they have explored the byways."

I wanted to shout at her: Go away. I can't bear any more.

Christabel came to see me. She soothed me because she did not talk about Beaumont Granville but herself. She wanted another child. She thought she ought to have one. She knew it was what Thomas wanted more than anything.

"I thought you were supposed not to," I said.

"It would be dangerous, they said. But I think young Thomas needs a brother or sister."

"Don't be silly," I admonished, "he needs you more."

"I suppose so," she answered. "It was a miracle, wasn't it, the way I became so important to my two Thomases?...I who had never been important to anyone before and only a nuisance to some."

"You always did talk a lot of nonsense about that, Christabel."

A few weeks later she came to me and told me she was pregnant.

"It will all work out for the best," she said. "I know I am doing the right thing."

My mother said it was foolish in view of what had happened at the time of young Thomas's birth. Thomas Willerby was very worried; but there was an air of serenity about Christabel, and she kept insisting that this would make everything right.

343

We all began to believe her.

And I was glad to listen to talk about the coming baby rather than to let my thoughts dwell perpetually on the terrible thing which had happened.

There was a strangeness in the house. My father had changed towards me. I often found his gaze fixed on me, and when he saw that I noticed he would smile in an embarrassed way. When he spoke to me his voice was almost tender. He was noticing me at last.

I wanted to say: It is too late now. Everything is too late. Carlotta is saved ... but by what means!

Leigh and I had fallen into a strange relationship. There had been restraint between us from the first and that had come from me. Now it was stronger. He was uneasy as well as I was.

My husband was a murderer. It might have been a righteous murder, but it was murder all the same. He had killed Beaumont Granville and had buried him under the ground. We never knew from one day to another when some clue might lead to the discovery of his body. The suspense was unbearable.

Harriet was our informant.

"It's very strange," she said. "Our Beau seems to have disappeared completely. No one has heard of him in London for months."

"Are they trying to find him?" I asked.

"They think he's gone abroad. He owed a good deal of money. His creditors are gnashing their teeth. He apparently borrowed a good deal on the strength of his coming marriage."

"I daresay," I replied.

"Then ... he just disappears. People are getting more and more certain that he has gone abroad. He always travelled quite a lot. They are saying that the heiress must have jilted him and he had to get away, as he couldn't face his creditors."

"It seems a possible explanation."

344

"But of course, the heiress didn't jilt him, as we know full well."

"There might have been another reason."

"There must have been. Carlotta is heartbroken. She cannot understand it. They were going to London together and there were not going to be any carriage mishaps that time."

"And yet he has gone."

"I have a theory."

"What?" I asked, trying to keep the note of fear out of my voice.

"He scented an even greater heiress...someone in another country."

"That seems a likely explanation."

"I put it to Carlotta. It made her furious at first, but I think she is beginning to suspect it might be true."

"She rarely comes to see me," I said sadly.

"Oh, she blames you for spoiling the romance. I have come to the conclusion that you acted wisely."

"Thank you."

"He was a little too blatant. Just going off like that without a word! He ought to have stayed and honoured his obligations. At least he should have presented her with a good excuse. I am sure he could have thought of something moderately plausible. But to go like that..."

"Do you think she is getting over it?"

"Yes. She is not brooding so much. Benjie is a great help." She smiled secretly. "They were always such friends...and still are."

I closed my eyes.

"At least she has been saved from disaster," I said.

And I thought once more: And at what bitter cost!

I sometimes went to that spot where on the day after that fearful night I had noticed the disturbed earth. The grass had now grown over it. It was not easy to find.

No one would think of looking for Beaumont Granville there.

They had ceased to talk of him now. I wondered if they still did in London. They would shrug their shoulders. He had no close family. They would presume he had gone abroad as he often did. Perhaps years later they would presume him dead and some distant cousin would take over his estates.

Now the months were passing. Summer had come. I wondered how long Leigh and I could go on in this way.

I sometimes asked myself whether it would have been easier if I had told him that I knew what had happened, that I had seen the bloodstained body of Beaumont Granville, that I had watched him as he dug his grave. Would it have been better if we had been entirely frank?

I could not know, but it seemed to me that whatever happened Beaumont Granville would lie between us for the rest of our lives.

Our marriage should have brought such happiness to us both. We loved each other. There was no doubt of that. I knew I would never love anyone as I loved Leigh and he had committed murder out of his love for me. Yet we were like two people struggling in a mist, wanting to find each other and yet unable to because of the great burden of guilt which lay between us.

Leigh was my beloved husband, but he was a murderer; and I shared his guilt because that murder had been done because of me. Moreover, how could I be sure that if Leigh had not arrived at Enderby Hall before me, I might have been the one who was guilty of taking a life?

And so we went on through those hot summer days. There was no peace for either of us. For me the future seemed completely bleak. There was only one matter which made me rejoice.

Carlotta had been saved.

We had taken the Dower House. We had acquired the land. On that land was Beaumont Granville's grave. Leigh had been adamant that we must have that area.

I thought: We are safe now. No one will ever discover the body. But I would never forget. I wondered whether his ghost would return to haunt us. It was there already. There was no need for strange sounds or weird sights. I believed that he would be there to torment me for as long as I lived. Could we ever be happy again? Oh, yes, he was dead; he was lying there murdered in his grave, but he was still with us.

November had come—the season of mists and darkness.

Christabel's child was born. It was a healthy girl and we were all delighted. Alas, it was as it had been with the other child. She became ill immediately after the birth.

The doctors shook their heads and said they had warned her. She should never have risked having another child.

I went to see her. She looked almost radiant. She was very proud of the baby.

"Thomas has his daughter," she said. "It is what I wanted for him. He has two lovely children and I have given them to him."

I thought: She will get well. She must. She was so contented.

The day after I had visited her, Thomas came over to the Dower House.

"Christabel wants to see you urgently," he said. "She wants you and Leigh, and she says you must come together. You two alone . . . and now."

I said: "She is feeling better. She must be."

Thomas said: "She seems very happy. Very much better, yes. I am sure she is going to be well soon. But she did say she wanted to see you two as soon as possible. Will you come back with me?"

I said we would and went off to find Leigh.

We went over to Grassland without delay and straight to her room.

She was lying propped up on pillows and there was a strangeness about her. She looked almost ethereal.

"Priscilla!" she cried. "Leigh! I am glad you have come. I was afraid you would not get here in time."

"Of course we came," I answered. "But what's the

urgency, Christabel? You are looking better. You look . . ."

"Yes, how do I look?"

"Radiant in a way. . . . You look happy."

"I am . . . in a way . . . now you're here. There is something I have to tell you . . . something important. It's not easy, but I can't rest until I tell you. It's very important. I must begin at the beginning. Then you'll understand. You know my nature, Priscilla. Envy has ruled my life."

"It was because of your birth, Christabel. I understand. But you changed when you married."

She nodded. "I was so jealous of you . . . particularly you . . . because you were born in the right place."

"I know. But there is no need to worry about it anymore."

"People should think before they bring children into the world. A short-lived pleasure . . . and there is a life . . . someone else's life. When I thought Edwin might love me I was very happy. Not that I loved him exactly, but I yearned for what marriage with him would have meant. And then we went to Venice and I was in your confidence and I was pleased about that. Priscilla, I was pleased about your trouble . . . and because of everything that had to be done. I was fond of you. That's why it is so hard to understand. Yet because of your difficulty I couldn't help being pleased in a strange way."

"It's of no importance now," I said. "Please don't distress yourself, Christabel."

"But it *is* of importance. Listen. In Venice when Carlotta was about to be born, Beaumont Granville was there. He sought me out . . ." She lowered her voice and for a few moments seemed unable to go on. "He could be so charming. He knew just how to handle a woman like me. He quickly understood how starved of affection I had always been and how I longed for it. You can guess what happened."

"Oh, Christabel, no!" I cried. "Not you!"

"Yes, I am afraid so. He did what he would with me. There was a picture. He made me pose for him."

I lowered my eyes. I could not look at Leigh.

"And he made me tell him all about you . . . and Jocelyn . . . Carlotta. He knew that it was your baby . . . not Harriet's."

"I begin to understand a great deal," I said.

"He came back. He came back here. He needed money. He knew that I had married a rich man. Priscilla, I gave him money . . . to keep quiet and not tell Thomas. I could not have borne Thomas to know. He had this picture of me. He threatened. Oh, but you understand. I could not let it happen . . . I couldn't. I was so happy. I had all that I had wanted all my life and now he had come to threaten it."

"Oh, Christabel," I murmured. "I understand. He was a wicked man."

"I didn't care what I did as long as I could stop him. He told me about that night with you. He was so proud of his cleverness in ruling our lives, making us, as he said, dance to his tune. We were his slaves. I had to do something. I had to try and hold what I had won at last. And there was only one way. I took a gun and I shot him. Yes, Priscilla, I killed him."

Leigh was looking at me in a wondering bewilderment. We were both beginning to understand so much. It struck me suddenly that he had believed it was I who had killed Beaumont Granville, and I knew that he had taken the body away and buried it in order to save me.

"I came out of the house in a sort of daze. I was a murderess. I couldn't believe that ordinary people such as I could really commit murder. The enormity of what I had done suddenly burst on me. I was afraid to go home. I waited there. I saw Leigh come out with the body. I saw him digging and I knew that he was going to bury it. I saw you, too, Priscilla, and I realized how deeply we were all involved in this. Knowing what I did made everything clear to me. Leigh was burying the body because he thought you had killed him. My great feeling then was a tremendous relief. I had done it. No one need know. Thomas would never hear of what I had been to Beaumont Granville. But it wasn't quite like that. Nothing we do is so neatly cut off and finished. I have been so aware of you always, Priscilla. We are sisters . . . true sisters. I knew that you and Leigh were growing further and further apart and I understand why. This thing was between you. You had never talked of it, never told each other what really happened. He thought you had murdered that man and you thought he had. That was clear to me. It would always be there between you."

"Oh, poor Christabel," I said, "my sister. I know how you must have suffered."

"I realized that there could be no happiness for me if I did not tell and yet I could not bear Thomas to know. He loved me so much. He had put me on a pedestal. I was so happy with him. That was why I had to kill this evil man. And when I had done it, there was some recompense I could make. I could give Thomas a child and I would die doing it."

"You are not going to die," I said.

"How can I live in peace with murder on my soul?"

"He is dead now," said Leigh. "He deserved to die. Why should anyone ever know? He lies there on our land. No one will mourn him."

"Murder is murder," she said. "'Thou shalt not kill.' I am going to die. I know I am. I know I should. My child will live, though, and my love for Thomas will live. He will visit my grave and lay flowers on it and he will say, 'She was a good wife to me.' And my children will comfort him and you two must comfort each other."

She was smiling, and although there was death in her face there was radiance too. It was as though she had been lost for a long time and had suddenly found her way to peace.

Before the week was out she was dead.

Leigh and I came back to the Dower House. We did not speak. There was a great understanding between us. We knew that we were at the beginning of a new life together and that it would be good.

14

TAF-2

Sherwood Preston
535-9800